The dawn light revealed the outline of a bedraggled group of granite buildings. The house was big; far bigger than Maddie had remembered. The roof stretched, and more worryingly dipped, across a vast expanse. Had it been that way in the spring? She closed her eyes and searched her memory. Bluebells had huddled under trees and filled what had once been flower-beds. Blue, grey and green mixed with the scent of wild garlic. She could remember nothing of the state of the roof. With eyes open again Maddie searched the mass of shapes.

There were so many windows and she counted four chimneys, but she hadn't counted on … an old manor house. How had she forgotten it was so big? When the letter had arrived and stated she'd inherited a house in Cornwall, she'd pictured something small, a cottage or bungalow, but Trevenen was not small. She swallowed. What had she taken on?

Growing up in Boston, Liz discovered early on that her best friends could be books. While waiting on a place for Harvard, she moved to London to see if life looked different from the other side of the Atlantic. It did and she soon fell in love with an Englishman. Now happily married with three children, she spends as much time as possible at her home in Cornwall. *The Cornish House* is her first novel. To find out more visit her website at www.lizfenwick.com

The
Cornish
House

LIZ FENWICK

An Orion paperback

First published in Great Britain in 2012
by Orion
This paperback edition published in 2013
by Orion Books
an imprint of The Orion Publishing Group Ltd,
Orion House, 5 Upper Saint Martin's Lane
London WC2H 9EA

An Hachette UK company

11

A CIP catalogue record for this book
is available from the British Library.

ISBN 978-1-4091-3748-1

Typeset by Deltatype Ltd, Birkenhead, Merseyside

Printed and bound in Great Britain by
Clays Ltd, Elcograf S.p.A.

The Orion Publishing Group's policy is to use papers that
are natural, renewable and recyclable products and
made from wood grown in sustainable forests. The logging
and manufacturing processes are expected to conform to
the environmental regulations of the country of origin.

www.orionbooks.co.uk

To my parents for their belief

To my children, Dom, Andrew and Sasha,
for their understanding

To my husband, Chris, for his love

Acknowledgements

This could be very long indeed, but so many wonderful people have aided me on this path to publication which began very early in my life. First thanks to people from the very distant past – Patsy MacDonald who believed I could do it, Sr Mary Assumpta who inspired me and my alma mater, Mt Holyoke College, for teaching me to learn, to reach and to believe I too was an uncommon woman.

I wouldn't be at this point now without the Romantic Novelists' Association. I have benefited not only from the friendship of so many writers, but also the wisdom of those who reviewed my work in the New Writer's Scheme. A few members of the association have quietly held my hand, propped me up, poured me tea or wine and most of all believed I could make this journey. In particular I want to say thanks to Jan Jones, Jenny Haddon, Penny Jordan, Katie Fforde, Anita Burgh, and all of FAW.

Where would we be these days without the Internet? Kate Harrison began the Novel Racers' Blog and during that first year I completed the first draft of this book. The encouragement and friendship of all the Novel Racers helped me along the way. A special thanks to Kate!

I want to thank all my writing friends who understand the highs, the lows and those damn circling crows of doubts. But two in particular need a special mention. Julie Cohen, who when I was in despair with this book reminded me that every story has been told already, but what you bring to it hasn't yet. And without Brigid Coady's support I wouldn't have made it thus far although I may have consumed a lot less wine!

My life is crazy and much of it spent in the air between the UK and Dubai. I want to thank the understanding Emirates Airlines flight crews who have looked after me and worked around me as I beavered away during my commute.

Thanks to Jan for her insights into psychology. Julia Hayward has patiently read all my early work and copy edited with such care. She is a saint. Also Georgie who has been my cheerleader, cajoling me through diets and doldrums.

Thanks to my agent, Carole Blake, for loving *The Cornish House* and for her courage in taking on a debut author. Huge thanks to my editor, Kate Mills, for seeing what the book could be and helping me dig deep to make it shine.

I want to thank my family and especially my children, Dominic, Andrew and Sasha, for their patience and understanding on those many occasions in their minds when I have been unable to afford them my full attention. Also on this list is my best friend, Doz. They have all supported me, loved me, reminded me, and rejoiced with me.

The final thanks go to my husband, Chris. He has been tolerant, supportive and believing. This book never would have happened without him for he introduced me to Cornwall.

❖ One ❖

It was nearly eleven and Maddie had been behind the wheel of the car for over eight hours. She yawned and forced her eyes open wider. Slowing, she approached yet another blind bend. Moonlight silhouetted the twisted trees against the sky. Their tortured shapes rose from the hedges, forming a tunnel. It seemed to be closing in around them. A shiver went down her spine. The engine stuttered.

'Come on, old girl. It can't be much further to Trevenen, and once there, both you and I can have a much deserved rest.' Maddie stroked the dashboard. Smoke seeped from the edges of the bonnet.

She glanced at her stepdaughter asleep in the passenger seat. Hannah looked sweet with her blonde hair in spiky disarray. She changed position and a tattoo appeared on the teen's arm. Maddie took a deep breath. Hannah had disobeyed her. She'd had to call on all her patience reserves when Hannah had displayed it last night. Maddie had just let it go. She too had been a teenager. However, she'd obeyed her parents.

Turning her attention back to the road, Maddie knew if the map was accurate that they must be near their new home, Trevenen. This, of course, assumed she'd followed it correctly and she'd no idea whether she had or not. The last thing she needed was to be stranded on a remote country lane.

When she'd visited the house back in April, the solicitor had driven her there. It hadn't seemed confusing then, but maybe she hadn't been paying attention as well as she should have. That was no surprise. She hadn't done anything as well as she should have since her husband, John, had died.

In an effort to cool the engine, she turned the fan on full, but it did nothing. The car slowed despite Maddie pressing the accelerator to the floor. The engine coughed twice then died. She thumped the steering wheel. The trailer's momentum nudged them further along the lane until all movement stopped. The headlights went dim, then went out. 'Shit.'

Hannah woke. 'What?'

Maddie tried the ignition again but nothing happened.

'Are we at this godforsaken place?' Hannah stretched.

'Err, no. The car has broken down.'

'What?'

'The car …' Maddie's fingers worried the key.

'I heard *that*, but where are we?' Hannah sat up.

'Don't know precisely.'

'Christ.'

'Mind your language.' Maddie shut her eyes. The day had begun at five in the morning when they'd carefully packed the last of their things, but they'd only left London at two after the removers had finished loading the van. Maddie wasn't sure what form of madness had made her agree to move house on the Friday of a bank holiday weekend.

'Hah, fine thing to say. I just heard you swearing.'

Maddie sighed.

'What's wrong with Christ, anyway? Besides, you haven't *done* God since Dad died.'

Silently Maddie counted to ten before she replied. 'We've been down this road before.'

Hannah crossed her arms against her chest. 'No we haven't. I've never been to Cornwall.'

'Don't be pedantic.' Maddie massaged the rigid tendons in her neck. 'Arguing isn't going to help.'

'So?'

Maddie yanked the bonnet release and stepped out of the car. Things could be worse she told herself. It could be raining. Instead it was a perfect late summer night. The fresh breeze scented with honeysuckle caught her hair as she stood in the darkness and struggled with the catch.

'What are you doing?' asked Hannah.

'Looking at the engine.'

'Since when do you know anything about cars?'

Maddie laughed. Hannah was right; she hadn't a clue so she pulled the phone from her pocket to call roadside assistance. The screen lit up with a picture of John. She blinked. He'd been gone eight months.

'Are you just going to stare at it?' Hannah asked.

Maddie dialled the number. No signal. Brilliant.

Hannah leaned out of the window. 'Well, what's happening?'

'Nothing.'

'Nothing? Even better. So we're in the middle of nowhere with no reception and a broken car.'

'That sums it up quite well.' Maddie turned to the heavens for strength, but all she found was the Milky Way. Although not what she needed, it was beautiful and she couldn't remember the last time she'd seen a sky so devoid of light pollution. A shooting star sped across the black canopy and Maddie wondered if she dared to make a wish. At this moment, what would it be? Would it be the same one she'd always wished for, the whole white picket fence fantasy, or had her experience of life this past year destroyed her ability to believe in dreams, or anything for that matter?

Hannah waved her hand in the air. '*Hel-lo?*'

'Yes.'

'What are you going to do?' Hannah fiddled with the zip on her jacket.

'Walk down the road and find help.' Maddie turned to the deserted lane then swallowed.

'Good luck. No sign of life. You've driven us to the end of the earth.'

Refusing to rise to the bait, Maddie held out her hand. 'The torch, please. It's in the glove compartment.'

Hannah tossed it on the driver's seat.

Maddie waited in silence but finally asked, 'Are you coming?'

'No.' Hannah thrust the torch out of the window.

'Fine.' Taking it, Maddie strode from the car alone. She

couldn't force Hannah to come. John was dead and Maddie's relationship with his daughter deteriorated every day.

Slowing her pace, Maddie squinted, seeing only the road ahead fading into the darkness. She resumed her walk at speed and finally a light appeared. She ran until she could make out a cluster of buildings, but only one showed signs of life. Where was everyone?

Hannah's words, 'end of the earth', echoed in Maddie's mind while she pressed the doorbell. There was no response. Maddie jabbed the button again and listened, but all she heard was her own breathing. She rapped on the door.

'Who the hell—' a deep voice grumbled.

Maddie looked up into brown eyes.

'Sorry to disturb you but my car's broken down and I can't get a signal.' She checked her mobile once more. 'Is there any chance I can use your phone?' Silence filled the air and then Maddie heard a woman's throaty voice in the distance ask who was at the door. Her eyes opened wide. His hair was a mess, he wore no shirt and his trousers weren't on quite right. She looked at the ground.

'Of course.' The man stood back from the door.

Despite being the twenty-fifth of August, the rustle of leaves spoke to Maddie of the approaching autumn. This transitional time of year had always been her favourite, when the change in the angle of the sun's rays intensified the colours of the season. Not that she could see much of anything at the moment. Her torch's beam barely pierced the darkness.

A badger braved the dim light and dashed across the lane into a hedge in the distance. There was just enough room for Maddie and the man to walk abreast. He'd had to give the rescue service directions and, as a precaution, had offered to accompany her back to the car. They'd left the woman sipping a glass of wine. Maddie hoped that they could resume their evening, but she doubted it.

'Bloody hell, Maddie, you've taken your time.' Hannah stepped out of the shadows.

Maddie's heart stopped.

'Is this the rescue man?'

Maddie bristled. 'Has anyone come?'

'Are you joking? Someone come down this excuse for a road? Nothing but bats here.' Hannah waved her hand above her head.

'Excellent. They're protected. You're lucky to see them; numbers have been declining.' The man spoke quietly.

'Thanks for the endangered species update, but this place gives me the creeps. And who the hell are you by the way?' Hannah asked.

'Hannah ...' Maddie began but stopped.

He extended a hand to Hannah. 'I'm Mark Triggs.'

Hannah ignored him and turned back to Maddie. 'Have you done anything useful like found out where this Trevenen is?'

'Trevenen?' the man said. 'So you're related to Daphne Penventon.'

'Yes.' Maddie wrinkled her nose for, despite what the solicitor had said, she wasn't sure who or what Daphne Penventon was to her birth mother.

'Have you been to Trevenen before?' he asked.

'Once, a few months ago.' It was all so fuzzy now, just like everything lately. In the dim torchlight, she looked to see if he was horrified by this information, but she saw only the play of shadows across the planes of his face.

'You're planning to sleep there tonight?'

'God, this is worse than I ever nightmared. Trevenen will be a wreck with no roof and no hot or cold running anything,' Hannah muttered. 'I saw the papers that said it was a dwelling – *a dwelling* – and not a house.'

Mark laughed.

Something in Hannah's tone set Maddie on edge. Trevenen was habitable. Even though she'd been in a fog, she'd seen it with her own eyes. 'Dwelling is a legal term.'

Hannah shrugged. 'Hey, when's the car man coming?'

Maddie looked at her watch. 'Within the next two hours.'

'Rush job, huh? Two lone women stuck in a dark country

lane with a strange man and they're going to take their time about it. Good. I can see the headlines next week when the bodies are discovered by a passing farmer.'

'Enough, Hannah.'

'Enough what?' Hannah asked.

'Melodramatics.'

'Is that what that was? Good. Thanks for the vocabulary lesson.'

Maddie's hands balled into fists. 'Hannah.' She took a breath. Obviously Hannah had been scared waiting alone. Maybe the next time she wouldn't be so mulish and she would come along.

'Back off, Maddie.' Hannah paused and turned from them. 'You're nothing to me but Dad's widow. Nothing more.'

'I'm your legal guardian,' Maddie said but she shouldn't have responded. She accepted that Hannah would need more than being left alone on a country lane before a conversion could take place. It might just take a thunderbolt from above, but then miracles never happen.

'Bloody courts.' Hannah climbed into the car and slammed the door. The noise rang in Maddie's ears, almost drowning out the cry of an owl.

The dawn light revealed the outline of a bedraggled group of granite buildings. The house was big; far bigger than Maddie had remembered. The roof stretched, and more worryingly dipped, across a vast expanse. Had it been that way in the spring? She closed her eyes and searched her memory. Bluebells had huddled under trees and filled what had once been flower-beds. Blue, grey and green mixed with the scent of wild garlic. She could remember nothing of the state of the roof. With eyes open again Maddie searched the mass of shapes.

There were so many windows and she counted four chimneys, but she hadn't counted on ... an old manor house. How had she forgotten it was so big? When the letter had arrived and stated she'd inherited a house in Cornwall, she'd pictured something small, a cottage or bungalow, but Trevenen was not small. She swallowed. What had she taken on? No simple white picket fence here, but mullioned windows and responsibility. She was insane to have done this but what options had she had? None, really. The house in London had been worth more than an old house in a remote part of Cornwall. So she sold up in London and paid the bills.

Suppressing a yawn, she climbed out of the car and took a deep breath. The scent of damp earth soothed her. Quietly she closed the car door. Hannah lay sleeping on the back seat where she'd retreated when it had become apparent that the car could be fixed, but that it would take a while. The mechanic had been a master of understatement.

Their new neighbour stepped out of his car. She couldn't believe how kind Mark had been, considering the circumstances. Rather than have them get lost again he'd led them the short distance through the confusing lanes to their new home.

'Morning,' he said.

Noting with envy that he showed no evidence of the night spent awake and outdoors, Maddie searched his face for tell-tale shadows, but found only high cheekbones and a full mouth. His features were not classical but the combination of the components, she imagined, could be quite devastating.

'It's been morning for a while,' she said.

'True, but the dawn chorus hadn't been singing then.'

She raised an eyebrow. 'That's how you define morning?'

'Yes, that and a good cup of coffee.'

'Don't mention something that's nigh on impossible right now.' Just the thought of a double espresso from her local café in Fulham was enough to make her weep, but her exhaustion was so deep that no dose of caffeine could reach it.

'You could come back to my place.'

Maddie looked at him and considered his offer genuine, but then she turned to the house. 'I'm eager to see Trevenen.'

'It awaits you.' He held out his hand towards the old building and grinned as he made a slight bow.

Her body ached but she focused on her new home. Carved stone surrounded some of the windows and others were simple wooden sashes painted white. They all reflected the early morning but revealed nothing of the interior. Trevenen appeared sound, if cold and empty.

To her left, if her memory was correct, was the piggery, which was missing its roof, and behind her on the far side of the yard were the stables. The buildings formed three sides of a large rectangle with the house on the eastern side.

Fortified by a deep breath, she put one foot in front of the other up the overgrown path to the door. She pulled a large key from her pocket and tried it. With a bit of force the lock tumbled over and she turned the handle, but the door didn't budge. She tried again and pushed with her other hand on the flaking paint. Something gnawed at the pit of her stomach while she waited for it to give way. She had to be brave. This should be exciting: she was the owner of Trevenen.

A crack sounded and a blast of musty air greeted Maddie as she stumbled forward across the threshold. The disturbance caused dust to swirl and a sigh seemed to emerge from the walls. Shadows and dead flies covered the floor. Maddie wrapped her arms around herself.

'Do you think there's electricity?' She turned and gave Mark a weary smile.

'Should be.'

The heavy curtains were pulled tight, trapping the smell of damp and adding to the feeling of neglect. Flicking the light switch on, she stood tall. It would be all right – eventually. She and Hannah had a roof over their heads and they could rebuild their lives. Now she needed to look forward and leave the painful memories behind.

Mark moved to her side and she felt his breath caress her cheek. Maddie stepped away. She could not have drawn a man more different in appearance to her husband. When well, John had been lanky and fair. Closing her eyes she could see him bent over his computer madly typing to finish some article before its deadline, with his boyish locks fallen across his brow. By the end, all his silky hair had gone. She twisted a loose curl that lay on her neck.

'Shall I go and have a quick check through the house for you?'

'Thanks.' Maddie paused and scanned the hall again noting the dust and cobwebs. She suppressed a shiver. The house was almost icy cold. 'There aren't any ghosts, are there?'

'Trevenen isn't haunted,' he said.

She took a breath and peered at the closed doors covered in white gloss paint that had become buttermilk with age. Maddie knew the colour couldn't be achieved by just mixing it. That shade only arrived after years of exposure.

'No ghosts, promise. There are several other houses nearby with them, but not Trevenen.'

'You sound like an expert.'

'Absolutely not.' He grinned and disappeared up the large staircase. The wood on the banister wasn't painted but the grain was barely visible. Maddie moved closer to it. The sweat and oil from many hands had stained the oak dark and worn it smooth. The colour of the balusters was three shades lighter. The tread of each stair dipped in the middle. Maddie glanced up again when something caught her eye but there was nothing there. She rubbed her arms.

Leaning against the wall, she willed the tightness around her heart to retreat. The single bulb suspended from the ceiling cast a dull glow on the floral wallpaper. The array of blooms almost obscured the pictures that hung on the walls, but a faded photograph of three women stood out from the rest. Who were they, she wondered, and was Daphne Penventon one of them?

Her hand trailed along the walls of the hall, rising and falling over the undulating surface as she wandered, lost in thought. Thanks to Daphne Penventon, she and Hannah had a new start. Maddie now had Trevenen, although it didn't yet seem real.

Having some security should provide her with the space to find inspiration again. While John was ill she had longed to paint – to paint her pain, her hope and her love, but time didn't permit and now that she had time she was empty. She didn't know what she was going to do. She needed a plan but didn't know where to begin. How could life once have been so clear and now be so opaque?

As she entered the kitchen, her glance fell on the massive

window that dominated one end. Each of its hand-blown panes framed an alternative vision of the scenery beyond. She shook her head and turned away. Great black beams crossed the ceiling and faded gloss paint was in abundance, but the uneven yellowing of the walls put the woodwork to shame. Maddie tried to guess when the room had last been decorated. Judging by the fittings, it might have been the fifties or even earlier. Set in the fireplace was a range that had seen much use and hadn't been cleaned in a long while. Nothing had. It wasn't just the dust that covered every surface, but the smell of decay that hung in the air.

Maddie leaned over the large white sink and fiddled with the latch to open the window and let in the morning air. Piles of dead insects filled the corners of the ledge and a spider's web clung to the frame. There was no sign of the spider. It was as if all residents of Trevenen had departed in a rush, leaving everything behind. There was even a teapot with the mouldy remains of what must have been Daphne's last brew. Had Maddie noticed this when she'd viewed the property?

Mark's footsteps heralded his arrival in the kitchen. Fighting the overwhelming urge to cry, she turned to him. 'You've been incredibly kind. You didn't have to stay.'

He rolled his eyes and smiled. 'Leave two damsels in distress? My reputation would be destroyed for ever.'

Maddie laughed. With his good looks and smile she didn't doubt he had a reputation but it was of no concern to her.

Mark had departed and Maddie checked on Hannah in the car. She was still asleep. It was good that one of them would be rested. The sun beat down on Maddie as she gazed around. The lawn looked like a meadow and there were more weeds than flowers in the garden, but the house appeared cheerful in its surroundings.

Making a mental list of things to do, she began to walk around the house. A climbing rose sprawled over the arch that led to the front. Wild tendrils crawled from the arch to the neighbouring little building. The plant had grown through a broken window pane. So much to do. Adding broken window to the list, she moved on.

Here, at the front, Trevenen seemed to have had a facelift. It was trying to be formal, almost Georgian, unlike the rear which reflected the medieval beginnings of the building and a bit of a few other centuries thrown in. Maddie stepped away from it and studied the shape of her house. She had to say it again: *her house.* This ancient building was hers and its wonky façade made her smile, but it must have annoyed whoever had tried to impose rigid balance on it. It didn't work but the result was delightful with tall Georgian windows capturing the morning light.

The same light picked out the seam in the building where it had been added to. The stones changed in size and were more regular in the newer half. She walked towards the join and ran her hand along it. Her fingers stilled and goose pimples travelled up her arm. A faint crying sound whispered around her. She turned her head looking for the source, but all she saw was the overgrown garden basking in the late August sun. A sleepy wasp hovered around her knees.

She blinked and broke contact with the house. The sound stopped. She shrugged and strolled through the garden towards the large Monterey Pine tree that towered over the far side. Its boughs reached out to the sky in asymmetrical disorder. Chunks of blue were visible between branches, triggering that creative pull. She pushed it aside. Today was not a day for painting. She had a house to discover and clean before their worldly goods arrived next week.

She wandered further through a gap in the hedge to what must have been the kitchen garden. Stakes stood bare and grass ran riot. She bent over one bed and found some spinach that must have self-seeded. It wouldn't take too much effort to make this garden operational again. Maybe she could persuade Hannah to take an interest in this. Cleaning it up would be hard work, but the results would be worth it.

Standing again, Maddie scanned the horizon. The trees that sheltered the buildings thinned and the vista opened up as she came to the far side of the garden. She surveyed the fields that dropped down into a deep crease where the tree cover was dense. Maddie suspected there might be a stream at the bottom, but couldn't see. Fields rose up the other side. With eyes half closed against the sun, the irregular shapes outlined by hedges formed a haphazard pattern of furrowed, planted and pasture.

She turned and walked through the orchard back to the house. All the trees were heavy with fruit. She gave an apple a twist but it resisted. It would be another month she guessed before they would be ripe. What surprised her was the variety of apples and pears she saw. Greens, reds, ochres, yellows made her fingers itch. Soon she would paint.

Moving back to the house, she began to acquaint herself with it. The solicitor had provided her with a brief history. Trevenen had begun as two rooms up and one room down then had grown to a manor house, albeit a small one. The house was built roughly in the shape of an L, with the large kitchen being the bottom of the L and projecting into the yard at the back. The rest of the house followed in a long line. All the reception rooms on the ground floor ran off the main corridor with a hall dividing the old from the new.

Maddie opened every door and flung windows wide open along the way. Each room was unique and clearly had served a purpose in the past, but in most cases that had been long since lost. From all of Daphne's belongings that remained as she'd left them, Maddie could begin to ascertain how her benefactor had used the spaces. It was a big house for an old woman to have maintained alone.

Beside the door to the yard hung an old waxed jacket on a peg. Below it stood a pair of very tired boots. Gloves caked in mud sat on the windowsill with a pair of secateurs beside them. How had Daphne died? Had she been out working in the garden and come in for a cup of tea and keeled over? It all had that feel about it. Maddie touched the gloves, wondering about the woman who had worn them.

Leaving the back entrance, Maddie went to the dining room with its beautiful long table and mismatched chairs. She counted three of a Chippendale style; the others were probably Victorian. Opening a cupboard on the side of the fireplace, a wisp of air spun the dead moths sitting on the china. Maddie sneezed and waved her hand to clear the dust but it had no effect.

She walked out of the dining room and stood in the main hall. Sunlight fell through the tall window on the landing, picking out the large slate slabs on the floor. Most were rectangles of varying sizes. Their veins and scars were visible on the dull surface. Maddie gave into the urge to play hopscotch and jumped on one foot until she was at the base of the stairs. Laughter bubbled up and she felt a lightness that she hadn't felt in years. She took the stairs two at a time.

Something was digging into Hannah's back and she kicked out. Light blasted through her eyelids while the smell of cows assaulted her nostrils. She'd died and was waking up in hell. No, she was in the back seat of the car. Why? Oh yes, Maddie's grand plan to live in a hut in Cornwall. That's why.

Sitting up, she looked around. To the left there was a thing that resembled a stable and directly in front was a wreck with two walls, no roof and certainly no hot and cold running anything. Brill. The wicked stepmum rode again, tearing her from London to this hell-hole. Was that the house? If so, it was a nightmare, complete with bats filling the night air and that drooling eco geek, Mark, who hadn't left them, or more correctly Maddie, alone last night.

How long had Hannah slept? She rubbed her eyes. The sun was high in the sky. Where was Maddie? Hannah turned to the right and saw a huge building with a roof. It was massive and it was ancient, really ancient. She'd always loved old buildings; it was a passion she and Dad had shared. They'd always done the National Trust thing. Now she'd be living in one and she wasn't so sure it would be as cool as she'd thought back then. She could thank Maddie for fulfilling one of her fantasies, but then again maybe not. Reality sucked.

Abandoning the car, she lost herself in granite, windows and slates. The stones making up the walls seemed to have order in some places. Big ones on the bottom slowly getting smaller until the top but that wasn't always the case. Hannah stepped back and wondered if the house had been added to. A seam-like line moved down one part of the house. It wasn't straight. It was like the mason had been pissed when he was building it or maybe the house had shifted over time.

The windows on one side were all shapes and sizes, including a bay over the back door that made her think of a woman sitting there and spinning. Weird time-warp feeling. She set off around the outside of the building until she reached the front of the house where a majestic tree ruled. It made the house look small in a way.

A breeze scented with pine wrapped itself around her and she turned back to the tree. It had been a while since she'd climbed one, but she reckoned she was up to the task. Swinging from the bottom branch, she remembered climbing her first in Windsor Great Park. Dad had taught her how to study the tree before beginning. He'd love this one. It was made for climbing, but of course he'd never see it because he'd died, bloody leaving her alone.

Her phone pinged. A message from her best friend, Abi, appeared.

How bad is it? Hows the witch? x

Hannah paused and looked at the stones that made up the building. It wasn't bad at all.

Cool house. Witch as usual. x

Hannah jumped to the ground and thought maybe she'd been a bit tough on Maddie about this move, but then she heard Maddie's voice and thought again. Who was she talking to? Was that guy still here? Why did men find Maddie so attractive? Hannah had never understood why her father had fallen for her. It must have been the sex. Why else would he marry a tall, gangly woman with wild, curly brown hair and a posh accent? No other possible reason.

Her stomach growled. Food. She continued her journey around the building hoping she'd come back to where she started and find something to eat, maybe in the car. Walking slowly, she arrived in the yard in front of the stables. She'd come full circle. No sign of the witch. Hannah pulled her bag out of the car and rummaged for a chocolate bar while she went into the house.

Dark walls covered in flowered wallpaper. Welcome to the forties. Maybe if Hannah tried to think of this as one of those television experiments that lasted for just a few weeks, she'd survive and then magically life would return to normal. Or as normal as it could be without Dad.

Maddie opened the first door at the top of the stairs and entered a sparsely furnished room. A crocheted bedspread covered the double bed. Small roses adorned the wallpaper and the curtains. She walked to the window and looked down to the courtyard and to the fields beyond. They were filled with cows. The solicitor had said Daphne had farmed up until she was eighty, but now the fields were let to another farmer. This provided a small income and every bit helped. She frowned. She didn't want to think about all of that right now.

The floorboards creaked as she made her way to the next room. Here was the one with the bay window which stood above the rear entrance. It must have been used as a library. Shelves lined two walls and a large desk sat in the bay alcove. A small sofa was pushed up against the bare wall. Needlework cushions covered its surface and a very fine watercolour of a beach hung above it. Tempted though she was, Maddie resisted the urge to pull a book off the shelves; she had more to explore.

Back in the hallway, Maddie counted the doorways and realised that the room she remembered from her visit must be in the 'new' part of the house. It was much larger and airier than any of these, although the one above the kitchen was a big room if a bit narrow. She opened a few windows and then went downstairs to the sitting room.

She didn't linger but wondered if the original floor was still under the horrible wall-to-wall carpet. The seventies had a lot to answer for in terms of decoration and shag pile carpeting was one of the biggest, only surpassed by avocado green bathroom suites. The furniture was lovely and she could visualise the few pieces of her parents' furniture that she hadn't sold fitting in well with what was already there. She closed her eyes. She musn't dwell on what she'd given up; that wouldn't achieve anything. Turning from the room she went into the smaller one beyond and found what must have been Daphne's office. It too had a lovely big window but the furniture was sparse, nothing more than a few filing cabinets, a table and a chair. Maddie glanced at the documents that lay on the desk, but it was just old bills and she didn't need to see those. New ones would arrive soon enough.

Maddie peered into the small loo tucked under the stairs then she made her way up, pausing to look out of a circular window. Once in the room she saw how it echoed the sitting room below, but felt cosier because of the lower ceiling height. Light flooded in. Maddie walked the length of it and explored the sizeable bathroom that sat above the office. There was no evidence that this room had been used by Daphne, or anyone for that matter. The wardrobe was empty and there were no towels or toiletries to be seen. Maybe this side of the house was too much for the old woman to look after. However, it was perfect for Maddie with both the morning and the evening light.

A large four-poster bed dominated the room. It seemed to call to Maddie and she was too tired to resist. Dust rose from the old eiderdown covering it, as the mattress sank with her weight. The light caught the dust motes in their flight and Maddie fought the urge to close her eyes. She knew even as tired as she was that the nightmares would arrive as soon as sleep did. She forced herself into a sitting position then out of bed.

'Hannah?' The precise tones invaded her head. Maddie was looking for her.

'Hannah?'

Did Hannah hear a touch of panic? She smiled. Finally the calm was disturbed. Usually Maddie was oblivious to everything, lost in her world of colours and shapes. Hell, she hadn't even shouted about the tattoo. She'd just closed her mouth and then commented on the lovely use of blue. She wasn't even clued up enough to know it was a fake; so much for getting under her skin. Maddie didn't shout. She didn't rage. She kept on packing for this wretched move to Cornwall and whimpering on about what a godsend it was she'd inherited this house.

Hannah strolled up to her stepmother standing in the hall.

'There you are.' Maddie smiled. 'Having a look around? What do you think?'

Hannah shrugged.

'I've chosen the bedroom over the sitting room. You can have any other room you want. There are certainly enough to choose from.' Maddie paused. 'You may need to take furniture from other rooms too. I'm sure you'll find what you need.'

Hannah rolled her eyes and climbed the stairs. Maddie always had to try and put a positive spin on everything. When was the woman going to realise that life sucked?

Walking back and forth between rooms, Hannah couldn't decide, but she wanted to be as far away from Maddie as she could. The room Hannah stood in now spanned the full width of the building. It sat directly above the kitchen and had a sweet fireplace. Not a big open job like the one downstairs, but a dainty ladylike one with a white wooden mantel around a small black grate.

Most rooms had bits of odd furniture. Maddie had said she could take what she wanted so that didn't need to come into her decision. Maybe she should just opt for the place furthest from Maddie's and be done with it.

Leaning on the mantel, she wondered if the fireplace worked. It might need to because Maddie didn't know if the central heating did. The woman was going to test it later. Any normal person would've had someone check the place out before they came to live in it, but no, Maddie had just rushed ahead and sold the house in London. She claimed she had to, to pay Dad's bills but that was crap. She could've sold this place. It must be worth something to someone.

A bird perched on the windowsill.

'Good morning, Mr Magpie.' Hannah bit her lip. Hadn't she grown out of stupid childish superstitions yet? No, not when they were one of the things her father had taught her long ago before her stepmother had come into the picture. Hannah walked to the window to look more closely at the brilliant black feathers. The bird cocked its head at her before it flew away.

A neat vanity table stood in front of the window. It was dusty as hell, but the wood under it looked nice. Hannah sat down at it. From here she had a wonderful view of the huge tree on the lawn through the open window. Through its branches she could see into the field across the lane where cows munched peacefully in the sun. A waft of cow shit came through the window. Something had to spoil everything.

She turned away from the view. This room was going to be hers. All she needed was the big wardrobe from the other room and it'd be perfect. Not that she was excited about it, but it just wasn't as bad as she'd thought.

⊹ Two ⊹

The long weekend was over and Maddie had worked non-stop to clean and air the house. Light rain softened the outline of the big tree as she stood staring out of the window. Her fingers were raw and there was a lingering scent of vinegar in the air. The roses she'd cut from the garden and put in a vase on the kitchen table had done something to hide the smell, but not quite enough. She sighed and sank into a chair. The tea was brewed but she couldn't be bothered to pour it. It would be wonderful if someone would come and do it for her. She held her breath. She was alone. There was no one any more to help her do anything, from making tea to raising Hannah.

Hannah sulked into the kitchen, her hair only partly concealing the scowl on her face. Things weren't that bad here. It wasn't London but Trevenen was beautiful. Maddie bit back the comment about to escape from her lips. What was happening to her? Was she mad? Was it grief? Or had the continuous battles with Hannah buried her better emotions? Was anger now her normal mental state? Or was it something else? She didn't know, but she had a hard time controlling the maelstrom within. Maybe at thirty-eight she was going into early menopause? There had to be some reason.

Hannah sat down with a thud. Dust and guilt settled on Maddie's shoulders. She frowned. The child looked too thin. The lead up to this move had taken its toll on them both. Maddie stood and poured her a glass of water. Handing it to Hannah, she watched the sullen figure look around the room. It was dire, but Maddie knew she could do something with it.

Trevenen seemed almost to speak to Maddie. Maybe it was

all the little things she kept discovering. Like the beautiful wood panels in the sitting room that reminded her of a ship, or the way her staircase curved up to her room.

She looked around the kitchen. Trevenen appeared sound except for the roof, which needed some patching. She and Hannah could live in it as it stood. The house, although badly decorated, had an appeal. Something stirred inside her when she thought about it. It was hers. It would take time, but she would help it out of the past and into the current century. She stood and ran her hand along the lintel, seeing initials carved into it. TP 1595. A house of this age must have stories to tell. Who was TP? Was he or she a Penventon?

Hannah rocked back in her chair which made a complaining noise. Maddie turned to her and smiled. This morning optimism had filled Maddie and she nearly hadn't recognised the feeling. Once the glass had always been half full, but lately it had been more than empty. She pulled her shoulders back. She could make this work and she would fix things with Hannah, beginning now.

'Have you heard from Abi?'

Hannah rolled her eyes.

'I take that as a yes.'

Hannah put her hands up in her 'whatever' gesture. Maddie stepped back, but then decided to try again. 'She'll want to come and visit I'm sure. Cornwall is an *in* spot and ...' Maddie watched Hannah squirm, so before the girl could open her mouth she continued, 'It's also a new start for us.'

Hannah crossed her arms against her chest and stared out the window. Maddie had to keep trying. If she didn't she couldn't help feeling that Hannah's walls would only get higher. Maddie pulled out a chair and sat opposite. She took a breath. 'I know this has been hard on you.'

'You what? You're joking, right?'

The teenager glared at her across the table. Maddie straightened her back and willed herself to continue.

'No, I'm not.'

'You're more mental than I thought.' Hannah stood and began to leave the kitchen.

Maddie exhaled and decided maybe now wasn't the best time to try and mend their relationship. They were both too tired.

'Hello,' a man's voice called.

'Oh, bloody hell, that man's here again.' Hannah stopped in the doorway.

Maddie stood. 'Hi, Mark.'

'The house is looking better already.' He spoke over the top of Hannah's head as she blocked his entrance into the room.

Maddie smiled, pleased someone had noticed.

'I was sent over with some sausages and mash.' He grinned and manoeuvred past Hannah.

Hannah flicked her hair out of her eyes. 'What? Are you Nigella Lawson in drag?'

'No, but it will be a few days before someone will be able to service the range so a little warm food might not be amiss.'

Hannah grunted.

Maddie tensed.

He coughed and walked to the door. 'I'll leave you two to continue to discover the delights of Trevenen. If you need help with anything, call. I work from home most days.'

'What do you do from home: save bats?' Hannah asked.

'I'm an architect, but not of bat caves.'

'I'll come out with you.' Maddie glanced at Hannah. She knew she was just running away from the problem. Nonetheless, her feet took her out of the kitchen while she tried to think of something other than her stepdaughter. The photo in the hall, which had intrigued her on arrival, came into view.

'Mark?' Maddie paused in front of it. 'Is Daphne Penventon in this?'

He moved to her side. 'I think she's the one in the middle.' He gave her a searching look then studied the photo. 'You really know nothing about her?'

'Nothing.'

'You can see she was a beautiful woman. I hear she broke many hearts.'

Maddie nodded. 'Was she married?'

'No.'

'I wonder why?' she asked.

He looked at her. 'I think she lost her fiancé in the war.'

The women were not smiling, but somehow Maddie sensed their welcome. Her finger traced Daphne's outline while she tried to guess her age in the photo. Was Daphne's heart still whole at that point? To be young again and to still have those decisions in front of you. Would Daphne have chosen to fall for the same man if she'd known it would mean she'd spend her days as a spinster? Did one have a choice in such things? Spinster? Widow? Maddie closed her eyes. Would she do things differently? She knew the answer, but unfortunately there was no going back.

Once out in the sun things looked less daunting. Flecks of mica in the granite walls of the piggery dazzled her. It would have perfect light for a studio, but with no roof it was an impossible dream. Things in the house must take a higher priority. When they reached Mark's 4x4, she tore her thoughts away from musty smells and damp patches.

'Thank you for all you've done. I'm not sure where we'd be without you.'

'Blocking my lane, I expect.'

Maddie couldn't help but laugh as she leaned against the vehicle and absorbed the heat of the metal. Why was she so cold? The day was warm.

'Thanks again.' She held out her hand and watched his strong fingers embrace hers. Something connected and she stepped back, letting go. She looked up and caught a flash of mischief in his eyes.

'No problem. I specialise in rescuing beautiful women.' He climbed into his Land Rover.

'So you mentioned.' Maddie swallowed a lump in her throat. It had been a lifetime – John's to be precise – since someone referred to her as beautiful.

Watching the car until it disappeared round the bend, she noted the clouds appearing to the east. The pain of John's death emerged. She'd done all she could to keep him alive. She'd given everything, but it hadn't been enough. Tears ran down her cheeks. She stopped by a rose, its blood red petals caught in a ray of sun. Maddie felt her heart shatter into a thousand pieces once more.

'Hannah, we need to go.' Poised at the top of the stairs, Maddie waited. 'Hannah?' she called again as she walked down the hall towards Hannah's room.

'Yeah, yeah. Just coming.' Hannah closed the door with a bang.

'Good. We've an appointment so I don't want to be late.'

'Yeah, I know. You never want to be late.'

Maddie cast a sidelong glance but didn't say anything and went out ahead of Hannah to the car.

'Seat belt on?' Maddie asked.

'Duh.'

Maddie reversed the car, dreading the drive and feeling like an old lady the way she was clasping the wheel for dear life. The rear-view mirror revealed the glimmer of a new grey hair, a phenomenon that had first appeared on the day of John's funeral. She'd gone to bed without and woke with ten, which she'd plucked immediately. Despite her vigilance, they'd returned with alarming regularity.

When Maddie felt she could allow her eyes to leave the road, she saw Hannah inspecting the hedges at close range. She was sure that Hannah was terrified of this new start. It couldn't have really come at a worse time: her GCSE year.

'So what's the school we're going to?'

'First, Mullion. Not a top choice as you'd only have a year there before changing schools. The other one is Helston.'

Hannah peered at Maddie. 'Why am I looking at a school for only a year? Are we going back to London then?'

'No, it's just that it's a smaller school and I thought it would be easier to integrate.'

Hannah rolled her eyes.

'I know it's not what you wanted but we didn't have any

23

choice.' She knew they were lucky to have an option as obtaining a place could be difficult. Again, Maddie checked her mirrors and wondered if she'd ever get used to driving in these lanes.

'We could've stayed in London.'

'No we couldn't.'

'Why?' Hannah asked.

'I've told you before. We were on the verge of bankruptcy.'

'You have money.'

'No, I don't.' Maddie paused. 'In case you didn't notice, I didn't work the last year your father was alive.'

'Your parents left you tons.'

Maddie frowned. 'It wasn't tons and that too is gone. All of it was used.' They'd bled money. She swallowed, thinking of the thousands.

'So blame it all on Dad now that he's not here.' Hannah pressed her lips together.

'I'm not blaming anything on him. They were decisions we made. I nursed him. I didn't work. If I don't paint there's nothing to sell. Simple.'

'You're blaming him.'

Maddie ran a hand through her hair. 'No, it was my decision too. Shit. I just missed the turn. Having this discussion when I'm driving is not a good idea.'

'It never is with you. You always find a way not to talk.' Hannah glared out the window again.

The school prospectuses lay on her desk. Hannah didn't want to think about them right now. Term started soon and she needed to make a choice quickly, but it was still August. Summer. No school thoughts allowed.

The bucket at her feet contained the dirtiest water she'd ever seen. She shuddered when she remembered she'd been sleeping in this filth. However, last night she'd slept well, the best she had since Dad died. Must be all the cow shit in the air knocking her out. In fact, today she couldn't smell it. Did that mean they'd stopped shitting or she'd become used to it? She didn't want to go there.

The room was finally clean and now she needed to paint the walls. Why hadn't they bought some when they were out? It would mean another drive with Maddie clutching the wheel as if her life depended on it. Really, she was just too much. During the schools trip she'd played the trendy artist who shows in London galleries. Yeah, right. The last show was three years ago.

Hannah sank down onto the bed. That was just before Dad got really sick. He was still working then too and Maddie hadn't been around too much because she was painting all the time. Life was good. Dad had worked from home and Maddie in her studio.

The large cabbage roses that adorned the walls became swirls of colour. Nothing distinct, just blobs. With a tight fist Hannah wiped her tears away. Dad was gone. End of story. Now she had to live in the wilds of Cornwall with a wicked stepmum. What was it about the woman? Dad had fallen for her immediately. He'd met her when he was writing an article on galleries in London. Her paintings had been in one and he'd interviewed her. That was the beginning of the end, but he'd been happy, happier than he'd been in a long time. When Mum had walked out on them, he'd shut the door on his life. Maddie had opened it, but she should have left after she had.

Bags sat still unpacked in the corner of the room. Hannah grabbed her backpack and with shaky fingers pulled out the picture of Dad. She'd taken it on a day out in Brighton. He had a huge smile on his face and a large ice cream in his hands, but it hadn't been his ice cream, it had been hers.

A few minutes after she'd taken the picture, the gloppy chocolate ice cream splashed onto the pavement. How they both had laughed and when they'd recovered he'd bought her another. He was so good that way. He made everything right even when the world was wrong.

She shoved the picture back in the bag because looking at it wasn't going to bring him back; nothing would. Now she needed to do something like finish the room and drag a wardrobe in here. She just wasn't sure how she was going to do this without Maddie's help because it stood a good six inches taller than Hannah. In fact, she doubted if she and Maddie could do it. They'd need help. Shit.

'Hannah. I'm going to have a bath. Shout if you need me.' Maddie called from downstairs.

Why would I do that? Hannah wondered, as she fled downstairs. This house could be OK. If she was careful she could almost avoid Maddie totally. That wouldn't be a bad thing. In London the house had been smaller and there was no escape, especially when Dad was ill. When she woke up, Maddie had been there. When she'd come home from school, Maddie had been there. When she'd gone to sleep, Maddie had been there. It was like the woman didn't trust her and wouldn't give her any space. Now at last she had space, just no friends, no London and nothing to do. Not such a good trade-off.

'No!' Maddie's own scream woke her from a nightmare again. Her heart raced. Tears ran down her face. Grief was supposed to lessen with time. That was what they'd all told her, but instead of fading, each night she was haunted more than the night before. No matter how many times she told herself to let go, she couldn't.

She didn't know what she'd done to deserve John's death. Logic told her that she had nothing to do with it, but then her actions after his funeral would seep into her thoughts. She'd only done what he'd asked and this had gone against everything in her. Maybe that was why she still wrestled with it every night. Some things were ingrained so deeply that they'd take a long time to leave, if ever. She pushed these thoughts aside.

It was not yet dawn but there was enough light for her to make out the shape of the fir tree as she peered out the window. She must have forgotten to pull the curtains last night. Grabbing her dressing gown, she put it on and walked carefully down the stairs. A noise caught her off guard. She paused on the last step. Her breathing stopped. There was no one in the house except her and Hannah yet she heard a cry. She shook her head and the sound disappeared.

A flash of movement caught her eye and she convinced herself it was just a mouse travelling across the sitting-room floor. If they had mice, a trap would solve it, but if it was a ghost? She blinked. She didn't believe in them. Nonetheless, she went carefully through the house.

She turned on the lights in the kitchen and put the kettle on the camper stove that they were using until the range was repaired. Tea would make her night-time imaginings go away. Ghosts. Mark had said Trevenen had no ghosts. She wasn't sure why she should believe him, but her own common sense agreed.

A thump sounded from upstairs. Maddie's hand jumped, nearly spilling her tea down her dressing gown. No, of course, she wasn't at all superstitious. She laughed and knew that it must be the sound of a book or something else falling off Hannah's bed. Hannah was no apparition. She was real with a broken heart and Maddie didn't know how to fix it. Why she thought she should be able to when she couldn't do a damn thing with her own, she didn't know.

Taking her tea, she walked back to the sitting room and checked that there were no more rodents. She curled up on one of the window seats, pulling her feet under her to watch the growing light colour the morning. Each second more rays emerged and the sky held the pink spectrum close to the earth while lavender climbed to the heavens.

Closing her eyes for a moment, she hoped to ease the dry burning feeling in them, but she knew from experience that only several solid nights of sleep would truly take it away. Her eyes flew open again when a small scraping sound came from beside the fireplace. The wall was covered in painted wood panelling that was flaked and worn in places. Her morning mouse must have slipped into the gap between the wall and the wood.

Now with the sun coming into the room fully, Maddie decided to investigate. She walked to where she thought the noise was coming from and put her ear to the wall. She knew she'd heard something but sound carried in strange ways. Tapping on the various panels, she could tell that the surface was uneven beneath. It even sounded hollow in places. At one point in time, this would have been the end wall of the house and it could be constructed of stone or maybe even cob. Possibly Mark could tell her, if and when she saw him again. Yesterday when shopping, she'd caught a glimpse of him in Helston. He was engrossed with a pretty blonde and not the one Maddie had met the night she arrived in Cornwall. He was obviously a player but he appeared to know a great deal about the houses in the area.

Running her hand along the top of one of the panels, she felt something move and she pulled her hand back. Her fingers were black with dust. She tapped on the wall and the scratching stopped. Overwhelmed with tiredness, she leaned against it and looked out to the garden. Something inside told her it would all work in the end, but she just needed the patience to get there. She stood and resolved to help Hannah. There had to be a way to reach her and Maddie wanted with her whole heart to do just that. She'd promised John and she always fulfilled her promises.

While the electrician hung from the rafters, Maddie held her breath and wondered why he couldn't use a ladder like a normal soul. She knew she should just be grateful that he was here rewiring the stables and not questioning his methods. But she wasn't sure her nerves could handle it.

Scattered around her were easels and canvases: all the requirements of her life. Well, they had been once and they must be again. She bent and opened a box. Her nose twitched. The smell of turpentine permeated the air. Something must have leaked. She dug down and found a pile of letters and cards then dropped them quickly, groping for anything else as the tears welled up. Her hand came to rest on a cool finish. This wasn't good. Who'd packed this box? Who'd put his cards, and the bronze bust she'd made of him, in with the turpentine?

Taking deep breaths, she walked out into the sunlight. John was gone yet touching those few things brought all the sorrow to the fore. When would it stop, or even ease?

'Could you bring the ladder over here?' the electrician shouted.

He was dangling from the other side of the stables. Maddie ran and hauled it over to him. Once he was safely on the ground, she went back to the task. She was a big girl, she could handle this. John's bust came out first. The summer they met she'd made it. She touched his cheeks and could almost feel the warmth of the sun on his skin. Heady memories of days filled with laughter and love swirled around her. Were they real? She didn't know any more. The end was twisting the beginning and trying to rewrite their history in her mind. Too much pain.

She deposited it on the ground. Where would she put it? Did she want it in the house? But then did she want to look at his face all the time as a reminder of what she had lost? She didn't want to go there again. This led nowhere except to a box of tissues.

Blinded by electric illumination that filled every crevice, her eyes adjusted slowly and she accepted that she could work with it. It was strange; she needed light desperately, but too much artificial light could kill her feel for colour.

'Ah, that's better now, isn't it?' The electrician held something that looked like a fried animal.

Maddie nodded and peered at the object in his hand. 'What's that?'

'The transformer. A rat ate through a wire or two. They like them and that caused this to explode,' he said as he wandered off. Maddie made a mental note: put renewing the electrics high on her list of things to do. The question was, how far would the little money she had stretch? At moments like this she wondered if opting for the experimental cancer drugs had been worth the cost. Without them she and Hannah wouldn't be so strapped for cash, but how could she think that when they might have bought them a bit more time with John? Yet maybe with the money she could have ... Maddie stopped and raked her hand through her hair. No, she wasn't going to follow this route of thinking. It was done. No going back.

John's face stared at her from the ground. What was she

going to do with the damned thing? Maybe Hannah would like it for her room. She had spent days in there, coming out only for food and drink. She hadn't even let the movers in. Maddie frowned. She'd spoken to many people, including counsellors, about Hannah's behaviour. They said to be tolerant; Hannah was dealing with a lot. Maddie knew that and she was tolerant. She knew it must be awful to have your mother abandon you then to lose your father.

Closing her eyes, she wondered if her own mother would have kept her had she not died giving birth to her. She'd never know the answer, but her adoptive mother had always been there for her until she passed away eight years ago. Maddie opened her eyes and looked at the bronze again. John had never said much about Hannah's mother, Susan. He would close up at the mention of her name.

Hannah walked in. 'Hey, Maddie, where's the paint?'

'In the corner.' She pointed to the tins. 'You're ready to paint?'

Hannah nodded. 'When did the lights appear?'

'A short time ago.' Before venturing to ask a crucial question, she studied Hannah's face and checked on her mood. It appeared positive. 'Have you chosen a school yet? We need to tell them.'

'Thanks for reminding me that school starts soon.' Hannah spun around.

'Well, it does and we need to sort it out.' Maddie braced herself.

'Mullion.'

'OK.' Maddie sank onto one of the nearby boxes. 'I'll call them today.'

Hannah pushed some paint pots aside, chose one and then left.

Maddie smiled. Well, at least one thing was right. She might never know why Hannah had selected Mullion but she was pleased she had because the smaller school might be easier on a newcomer.

'Hello?' a woman called from outside.

'In here.' Maddie stood and opened the door.

'I'd heard you might need a hand.' A beaming smile radiated from the woman's face as she took a quick look around. 'I'm Tamsin.'

'Hi.' Maddie glanced at the mess around her. 'I do. How did you know?'

'There's no such thing as a secret around here and I'm here to help.'

Maddie laughed. 'Today's my lucky day then.'

'Maddie, you said this should go to the kitchen?' a woman's voice asked.

Hannah dashed to the window. Who else was here? Maddie didn't know anyone but that weirdo, Mark. Below in the courtyard a small woman struggled with a large box. A dark head could be seen, but not much else.

Hannah closed the door behind her as she ran for the stairs. She bounced off each tread, enjoying the *crack-crunch* sound. The house had great noises and the upstairs floors almost sang as you walked across them. Downstairs she liked the solid flap sound her feet made when they hit the stone flags. The only thing that sucked was the mouldy shag carpet in the sitting room. Where did that antique come from? Static electricity with every step and every shade of brown you could never want.

'Hello?' Hannah peered around the kitchen door.

'You must be Hannah. I'm Tamsin.' The woman was pulling things out of the box.

'Hi.'

'Have you finished your unpacking?' Tamsin's voice had a smile in it.

'No.'

'Boring?' Tamsin asked.

'Yes.'

'Not like Christmas come early?'

'Definitely not.'

'Shame.' Tamsin continued to unload.

Empty eyes stared at Hannah from the table. She stopped

31

breathing. She'd always hated that bronze. It was so cold and not like Dad at all. Not that it didn't sort of look like him, but it was metal and not flesh.

'This is good. Did Maddie do this?' Tamsin stroked the top of the bust.

'Yeah, she did.' Hannah grabbed some bread and began savagely buttering it.

'It's brilliant.'

'If you think so.'

'Who is it?' asked Tamsin.

'My dad.'

'Oh.'

Hannah looked up. Tamsin was silent as she studied the face.

'He was a good-looking man.'

'Yeah, he was.' Hannah took her food and left. Tamsin had nice eyes. They didn't accuse you of anything.

✤ Three ✤

Hands full, Maddie leapt for the phone when she reached the kitchen. She couldn't believe it was connected and she prayed that the bag she'd flung on the table wasn't the one with the eggs; otherwise it was omelette for dinner.

'Maddie Hollis.' She turned to see Hannah walk in empty handed despite the car full of shopping. Maddie wondered when the teenage selfish gene mutated and if she'd survive that long.

'Hi.' Tamsin's voice was a friendly balm to the glare she'd received from Hannah. 'How about a drink at the pub tonight? It's time you met the natives.'

Maddie bit her lip. She would love to go, but Hannah … 'Well.' She paused.

'No "wells", just say yes. I'll collect you at six-thirty.'

'Do I have a choice?' Maddie asked.

'No.'

'Had that impression. I don't know about Hannah.'

'Bring her. If she wants to come she will, otherwise she can sit at home.'

Maddie chuckled. 'Can we make it tomorrow? I think we might both be too shattered tonight.'

'Sure, tomorrow would work, but no postponing.'

'I promise.' Maddie hung up and then nearly fell over as Hannah came in with her arms full. Could the gene change that quickly?

'Who was that? When did the phone start working?' Hannah slammed everything on the table. 'Where's the juice I wanted?'

'Shall we try one question at a time?' asked Maddie.

33

'No.'

Maddie opened her mouth then shut it; arguing wouldn't help. 'It was Tamsin. It's in a bag.'

Hannah shrugged and went round the table. 'Oh. What did she want?'

'Asking us out for a drink at the pub.' Maddie emptied the contents of one bag onto the table wondering why all their conversations felt so confrontational. Hannah found the juice and poured a glass before she left.

'That went well,' Maddie muttered as she put the juice into the fridge. How was she ever going to get through to her? It never used to be so bad. In fact it had been quite good once. She longed for those days when she would brush Hannah's long blonde hair and they would chat. Now they hardly spoke and even the long hair was gone. Hannah had it all cut off after John's funeral. The new look suited her petite features, but Maddie missed the old Hannah. But then she missed so many things.

In a moment she would go and help Hannah with her room. Maybe now Hannah had some space for herself she might look more kindly on the move. When they'd met, she had been a sweet child of nine and Maddie had been a welcome addition in their lives. Now, nearly seven years later, Hannah treated her like the plague. Maybe this was normal, but that didn't mean it was a lot of fun.

On her way upstairs she passed a gilt framed mirror and she paused to feel the intricate carving. Her fingers stopped when she saw the smudges of purple under her eyes that matched the hues in the cabbage roses covering the walls. In the past year she'd become as antique as this house.

'Well, you're past your prime anyway so it doesn't matter that the deterioration is accelerating.'

Wonderful. Now she was talking to herself. What had she just said about acceleration? No doubt she'd end up like Daphne, living alone well into her nineties. Maddie frowned, glancing once more in the mirror before she continued down the hall and knocked on Hannah's door.

'Hannah, I thought I could give you a hand with your room.'

Hannah popped her head around the door. 'No.'

'No?'

'Yeah, no.' She drew a big circle in the air around Maddie's face and then made a big slashing motion. 'This is a "Maddie-free zone".' Hannah shut the door.

Maddie stood staring at the closed door. 'That tells me.' She looked at her hands. Maybe she should work on her own bedroom.

The rays of the setting sun filtered through the uneven surface of the glass in the tall window on the landing. It cast a diffused glow on the wall of the downstairs hall, warming up Daphne's serious face peering out from the photograph. Maddie paused on the bottom step. She'd been about to utter a prayer of thanks, but stopped herself. Once she would have thought her prayers had been answered with this inheritance, but she didn't pray any more. She ended that type of communication months ago yet old habits die hard. Her hand fell to her abdomen then she cursed herself for thinking. It was history and the only history that mattered now was that of Trevenen and the Penventons who had left it to her.

In the kitchen she stood wondering if it had always been the kitchen. Or maybe it had been the sitting room? The layout of the house fascinated her, as did the features, like the beautiful mullioned window which hinted of Tudor times. Other evidence of the past was dotted about with no doubt more to be discovered piece by piece, but the biggest puzzle in her life at this moment was why she'd been left this place. Surely there must have been closer relatives, but maybe not. The solicitor had been unable to shed any light on the subject. He said that Miss Penventon had been tight-lipped but specific that the house would go to Maddie upon Miss Penventon's death.

What intrigued Maddie was the length of time the solicitor had said Maddie had been the intended recipient of the will. He implied that Daphne had altered her will twenty-five years ago when Daphne's brother had died and she had become the sole owner of the estate. But if Daphne had known about her for at least that long, why hadn't she contacted her sooner? She wasn't complaining. She needed this house.

She wrote *House History Search* on her 'to do' list. Beside the paper lay her business card as a reminder to call the gallery. *Artist* stood out. She laughed. 'Artist? Well, that won't be true any more unless you start painting again.'

That worried her. Inspiration. She could no longer wait for its arrival. London had provided none. It held only pain and she'd leapt at the opportunity to flee. Looking back hurt too much. The only way now was forward.

Lost in thought while looking out of the big kitchen window, Hannah jumped when the phone rang. 'Hello, Maddie's Mad House.'

'Hi, Hannah,' said Tamsin.

'Hi.' Hannah smiled.

'Are you coming to the pub with us tonight?'

Hannah picked up an apple and polished it on her shirt. Did she want to? Not really. 'Not sure.'

'You should.'

'Maybe.'

'No pressure. How's your room coming on?' Tamsin asked.

'Great, except I don't have anywhere to hang my clothes.'

'No wardrobes in the house? That's a surprise.' Tamsin laughed.

'There's plenty but none in my room and I can't shift them.'

'True.' Tamsin paused. 'I have a solution but you'll have to come to the pub.'

'What's the solution?'

'Not telling but it will be with you about six-thirty.'

'OK, I guess.'

'See you later and don't forget to tell Maddie I rang.'

Hannah put the phone down wondering why she felt like she'd been conned. One good thing would happen though, she'd be able to hang her clothes. She just didn't know how it would happen.

*

At six-thirty on the dot Hannah heard a car pull into the yard. She went to the back door and saw three big blokes following behind Tamsin like ducklings. They all towered over her. Hannah ran a hand through her hair and wished she'd spent a bit more time on her appearance. One of them was quite cute and the other two weren't bad either.

'Here's your help. These two,' Tamsin waved a hand, 'Fred and Matt, are mine and the other one, Will, feels like mine half of the time.'

'Hi.' Hannah stuck her hands in her pockets.

'Now if you ask nicely and bat your lashes, I'm sure these three can shift your wardrobe.'

Hannah swallowed. Nothing like being put on the spot. 'Would you mind? My bedroom's this way.' God she felt like a fool. That was not what she meant to say. She turned as she ran to the stairs and called, 'And the wardrobe's next door.' She heard the footfalls behind her. They sounded like a stampeding herd.

'In here.' She let them pass her into the room. The wardrobe looked impossible to move.

'Where's it going?' asked the oldest one, who Hannah thought might be Fred.

'My room, which is here.' Hannah walked out into the hallway and into her room. She liked what she'd done to it already. The walls were painted terracotta and she had enough room for two old armchairs she'd found. They were covered in a retro dark green chenille and it worked well with the pinky brown walls.

'OK, I think we can do it.' Fred walked back to the others and Hannah heard him give them instructions. She hoped this would work and was almost afraid to look when she heard one say, 'Oh, shit.'

A cracking sound followed and Hannah ran to them, but all she could see was a sweaty back and the top of the wardrobe.

'Back in and angle it to the right.' Tamsin's voice was clear.

Hannah held her breath while she watched them do it. They followed Tamsin's precise instructions. Hannah walked backwards towards her room, trying not to notice the muscles on the boy holding the top of it, but they were distracting. It wasn't Fred and she thought it might be the cute one, Will.

'How's it going?' Maddie asked.

Hannah couldn't see her and just wished she'd go away.

'Fine. They may take out a wall or two. Relatively painless and it should be done in minutes.' Tamsin laughed. 'They make a good wrecking crew.'

Hannah bit her lip. She didn't want them to hurt the house. She kind of liked it despite the fact it was in the middle of bloody nowhere. The nearest shop only sold biscuits and milk and even that was two miles away.

'Where do you want it in here?' Fred asked. The three of them stood it in the middle of the room.

'Just there on that wall.' Hannah pointed, trying not to look at the chipped paint on the door frame and the corresponding white mark on the wardrobe.

'Are you sure?' Will asked. 'We won't be moving it again.'

Hannah nodded.

'Such a gracious lot, aren't they?' Tamsin linked her arm through Maddie's and ushered her out.

Will held open the car door open for Maddie. 'Trevenen's cool. I always wondered what it was like on the inside.'

Maddie nodded. She liked the look of him and she knew without being told that he had to be related to Mark Triggs. The resemblance was strong except for the eyes. They weren't brown but a green made up of a mess of blues and yellows in a haphazard fashion. Aside from a few spots, he was a very handsome boy and she'd watched Hannah clock him from his longish wavy hair to the cut of his low slung jeans.

'Is the house listed?' Will asked from the back seat.

'I don't think so.' Maddie thought of all the paperwork she'd read through.

'It's pretty old.'

'Yes and it's such a hotchpotch of styles,' Maddie said.

'Do you plan to do anything with it?' he asked.

'Not much, just bring it gently into this century.' Maddie mentally ticked through the list of Trevenen's best features, seeing the elegant windows, multiple fireplaces, slate and oak floors. The house had so much promise if she could look past the woodworm, draughts and roof.

As she'd lain in the bath earlier, she had felt a wave of warm contentment spreading over her, and it was not the hot water because there wasn't much. All of her other dreams may have slipped away, but this beautiful house was hers. There was so much work, but she was not afraid of that. However, she was worried about her real work. She'd set the stables up but she was already struggling with the lighting.

'You know my Uncle Mark. Is he going to help you with that?' Will studied her.

'I hadn't thought about it.' Maddie turned and smiled at him.

'He's really good with old houses.'

'He is and of course you could use my Anthony as your builder.' Tamsin grinned.

Maddie caught Hannah's eye in the far back of the people carrier. She was looking determinedly out the window. 'Well, you have me all sorted then, but I think it'll be a while before I can do any more than refresh the interior.'

'You've been busy this week,' Tamsin said.

'Yes, a bit. So much to do. I'm desperate to paint,' Maddie said.

'What do you paint?' Tamsin glanced at her as she drove.

'Not that type of painting, but the walls,' Maddie said.

Tamsin laughed. 'Fine, but what do you paint? The other day I saw the bronze you'd made and all the canvases in the stables but they were blank.'

'Everything. Currently I have a commission for a large abstract landscape, but I love portraiture and still life too.'

'Any of your work here?' Tamsin asked.

'Yes.' Maddie sighed. 'But it will be a while before I've put any up.'

'No rush as you're here to stay.' Tamsin smiled at her and turned her attention back to the road.

Tamsin parked and turned to Hannah. 'So what do you think of our bit of Cornwall so far?'

Hannah looked around her and thought she was going to be sick. This place was just too cute. Chocolate box didn't cover it. Thatched roofs here, gothic windows there. A creek with swans floating by. Really, where did they find this place, a BBC film set? 'It sucks.'

Hannah heard Maddie's sharp intake of breath.

Tamsin laughed. 'Well, it can only get better then.'

'Where are we?' Maddie asked with a smile before throwing Hannah a warning look.

'Helford.' Will waved to a group of people, but didn't stop to talk.

Hannah stayed hidden by the car until they passed. She didn't feel like meeting the locals; in fact, she wasn't quite sure why she came. Oh, yeah, Will, Matt and Fred were OK and Tamsin hadn't given her any choice.

'You coming, Hannah?' Will called. 'The others have gone ahead. Girlfriends are waiting.'

'Yeah. Just looking at the view.' Even she had to admit it was amazing. The water was blue. Maddie would know what special type of blue but intense was a pretty good description. The fields on the other side of the river were bathed in evening light. Pretty cool.

They arrived at a thatched building on the waterfront. Strings of coloured lights swung across the terraces. Quaint. Hannah tried not to gag.

'They've gone inside. Do you want to sit in or out?' he asked.

'Anywhere away from her.'

'What? Is she a bitch or something?' Will tipped his head to one side, waiting for her to answer, and she forced her thoughts away from how cute he was.

'Yes.'

'If you say so.' He shrugged. 'What do you want to drink?'

'I'd better go and deal with this.'

'No, I'll get them.' He stood his ground but he was almost laughing.

'I owe you one.' Hannah turned away from the crowded tables and Will.

'Don't worry about that.'

She smiled. They clearly made them sweet here. 'Well, she's in there so I won't get anything interesting.'

'What do you want?' he asked.

'Better make it an OJ. Don't want to get you in trouble.'

'Sure?'

'Yeah.' Hannah watched him walk away. He was OK, well possibly more than OK. At least there was some talent here.

Laughing like the world was good, happy families eating steak and chips crowded the terraces. Were they fooled or what? It could all turn upside down really quickly. She sat on the edge of the lower terrace with her feet dangling above the water. It seemed black now that the sun had disappeared.

Will returned and handed her the drink.

'What's that over there?' she asked.

'The north side of the river.'

She rolled her eyes at him. 'When we were walking here I could see some lights and houses and stuff.'

'It's Helford Passage and the lights were at the Ferryboat.'

Hannah squinted but from this angle she couldn't see it. 'Yeah, so what's that?'

'A pub.'

She took a sip of her juice. 'How do you get there?'

'By ferryboat.'

'Huh?'

'If you continue walking to the point.' Will waved his hand. 'They run a ferry across the river. It's the only way to go unless you want a long drive or have your own boat.'

'Do you?'

He opened his eyes wide. 'Do I what?'

'Have your own boat?' Hannah noticed all the boats rocking on the incoming tide.

41

'Yes.' He smiled and she wondered why he made it sound so natural that, of course, he had one.

'Cool. Would you take me?'

'Now?' He stared at her like she had three heads.

'No, not now.' She liked the idea of just him and her in a boat away from here. The corners of her mouth twitched a bit.

'Sure. When?'

She shrugged, wondering when she could escape with him.

Everyone seemed to know Tamsin and she seemed determined that Maddie should meet everyone in the pub. Thankfully it was too crowded for much movement and Maddie was relieved to catch a moment's respite while Tamsin went to the loo. So with a fixed smile on her face, Maddie sipped her wine.

'Lovely old house, Trevenen.' An old man leaned across the bar.

Maddie blinked. How did he know about her and her house? 'Yes, it is.'

'Are you pleased Daphne left it to you?'

Maddie's mouth opened but nothing came out for a moment. 'Yes.'

'So what are your plans for it?' he asked.

She smiled at him. 'Besides cleaning it, you mean?'

'Yes.' He laughed.

'Nothing too drastic. I need to live in it a bit and get a sense of it first.'

'Sensible girl. There's no rush, is there?' His face had seen many years of weather.

'You don't know how old it is, by any chance?'

'Much older than me, ancient though I am.' He winked.

She took a sip and realised she had a great deal to learn about Trevenen.

'So are you a Penventon, then?'

Maddie nodded. Her birth mother had been a Penventon so she was one even though she didn't think of herself that way. Smith had been her legal name before she married John. 'Have the Penventons always owned Trevenen?'

'As far as I know. Speak to the local history society or the museum people in Helston. They might be able to tell you.' His eyes disappeared with his broad grin.

'Ben, you old flirt. Trying to steal Maddie's heart already?' Mark moved towards them at the bar. Maddie smiled. Finally there was a familiar face in the crowd.

'No chance of getting in there before you. No, sir. No one's quicker than him.' Ben pointed his thumb in Mark's direction.

'So the truth's out. It's not just me that he's so kind to.' Maddie watched Ben's face crease up.

Ben chuckled. 'You sure have her fooled.'

'Don't go telling tales.' Mark smiled but his voice was flat.

Ben leaned nearer while Mark spoke to a woman whom Maddie recognised as the one who'd been at Mark's the night her car had broken down. Maddie's eyes widened as the woman moved very close to Mark and placed a hand on his bottom. Maddie looked away.

'Has Ben been giving you a hard time?' Tamsin was at her side again.

'Not at all.' Maddie gave the old man a big grin.

'Glad to hear it. Now come with me. There's someone I want you to meet.' Tamsin grabbed Maddie's hand and pulled her through the crush at the bar. Between the crowd, an empty stomach and the wine, her head was beginning to swim.

'Judith, this is Maddie Hollis, another newcomer to our part of the world.'

'Hi,' said Judith as she extended a very elegant hand.

Maddie's eyes opened wide. She hadn't expected to hear an American accent.

'Judith's an expert in historic gardens and you have one,' Tamsin said.

'It may be historic but it doesn't resemble a garden beyond the odd flower blooming,' said Maddie.

'Ah, you're the new owner of Trevenen.'

'I am. Not sure how everyone knows.'

Judith laughed. 'You'll soon learn that everyone knows everything, but they just may not talk about it unless it suits them.'

'I see.'

'Tristan, this is Maddie, the new owner of Trevenen.' Judith waved the handsome man closer.

'Hello.' He smiled and shook Maddie's hand.

'When you've had a chance to settle in, I'd love to see Trevenen's garden,' Judith said.

'I don't think there's much to see.'

'You'd be surprised.' Judith laughed. 'The old bones of the garden will still be there, I bet.'

'If you say so.' Maddie saw Mark moving towards them and noticed Tristan tensed.

'Hello, Mark.' Judith leaned forward and gave Mark a hug and a kiss on his cheek. The two men nodded at each other. Tristan turned from Mark and he whispered in Judith's ear.

'If you'll excuse me, I have to speak to someone.' He walked out of the pub.

'Sorry about that, Mark. I'll keep working on him.' Judith touched Mark's arm.

Maddie looked at Tamsin and raised an eyebrow.

Tamsin leaned to her and whispered, 'Tell you later.'

'Have you seen Hannah and Will?' Maddie asked.

'Outside,' Tamsin said.

'Hey, Mark, you can't keep all the pretty women to yourself.' A man came up and stood beside them.

'Not trying to. Come meet your new neighbour, Maddie Hollis.' Mark stepped aside.

'With pleasure.' The man grinned. 'I'm Nate Barton. Are you the new resident of Trevenen?'

'That would be me.' She smiled, wondering how she was supposed to remember all these people.

'Will you be living here full-time?' he asked.

'Yes.' Did people only stay a short time? From what little she'd seen and experienced, it was beautiful and everyone was welcoming.

He leaned closer. 'Great news. Are you single?'

'Nate, that's a bit forward, even for you.' Mark laughed.

'Well, a man needs to know these things. Don't want to lose

my heart to the unattainable, do I?' Nate opened his eyes wide and batted his lashes at her.

'I'd hope not.' She grinned.

'You still haven't enlightened my waiting heart.'

'I'm a widow.' As she said the words, Maddie knew they sounded harsh. No one expected to hear them from a woman of her age. She wasn't used to the term herself. *Widow*. That meant a Victorian woman dressed in black, not her, but yet it was her. She was here in a pub in Cornwall and John was in the ground in London.

Mark placed a hand on her arm.

'So sorry.' Nate spoke quietly.

Maddie forced a smile but knew he could never be as sorry as she was.

'Can I get you a drink?' he asked.

'Thanks, but no. I haven't eaten in hours and I won't be responsible for what I do.'

'Sounds great; another glass it is, then.'

She looked him directly in the eyes. 'Seriously, no thanks.'

'If you insist.' He still looked hopeful.

'I do.' Maddie tried to keep things in focus while she politely extricated herself from Nate's outrageous flirting.

'Had enough for tonight?' Tamsin asked.

Maddie nodded.

'Shall I round up Hannah and the boys?'

'No, I'll get them. The fresh air will do me some good.' She began to move through the crowd. The air was thick with the scent of grilling meat, which tormented her stomach. Hannah was nowhere to be seen among the people on the lower terrace, where the water came right up to the edge. Lights swayed in the growing breeze, drawing bright shapes on the reflective canvas below. Maddie started when Will, quickly followed by Hannah, came through a gap in the fence. 'Are you looking for us?'

Hannah hung behind Will as he looked beyond Maddie and waved to someone in the distance.

'We're heading back. Are you ready?' Maddie asked.

'Some of my mates have just arrived.' Will turned to Hannah. 'Do you want to stay for a bit longer?'

Hannah eyed Maddie. 'Yeah. That'd be good.'

'Maddie, do you mind if we stay?' Will's direct stare caught her off-guard. Maddie didn't like the idea of leaving Hannah. However, Will seemed quite responsible and Hannah needed to make friends here.

'How will you get home?' she asked.

'Easy. We'll walk or catch a lift. It's not a problem. She'll be back by ten.' He smiled.

'OK.' Maddie paused and took a deep breath. 'See you both later. Call me if you need me.'

'Yeah,' Hannah said as she turned away.

The darkness was overwhelming once they'd left the village behind and the road was covered by overhanging trees. Hannah's eyes had taken ages to be able to see anything at all, let alone the road in front of them, which didn't have the decency to be flat or straight.

'Did you mean what you said to Tamsin earlier?' Will matched his stride to hers.

She turned to him. 'What did I say?'

'That it sucks.'

Hannah looked around and thought about it. Despite the lack of light, she could almost make out shapes, but she couldn't shake the feeling that she was navigating her way along the road almost blind. It should feel spooky, but it didn't, though she wouldn't want to be walking alone. Will was good company and he was cute. 'Sort of.'

'That's OK then.'

'Why?'

'Well, it doesn't suck and it's my home. Just wish I could be here all the time.'

'You're not?' she asked.

'No, which really sucks.' He laughed.

'I guess so. Leaving London was the same.' Hannah paused. 'Why aren't you here all the time?'

'School.'

'School?'

'I go to school in Devon,' he said.

'Like it?' She stopped walking so she could catch her breath. It was a steep climb.

'Most of the time. I just hate leaving here.'

The silence around them was weird, almost as weird as Will liking this wild place filled with bats. 'I sort of get it. Wish I could go away to school.'

'Why?' Will stopped.

She set off again. 'Get away from the wicked stepmother.'

'She looks all right to me.'

'She would; you're a guy,' Hannah muttered and walked faster. The buzz from the beers had disappeared. A two-mile walk did that for you. Bloody marvellous.

Finally, the looming shape of the house appeared. 'That's Mark's car. Why's he here?'

'Maybe gave Maddie a lift, I guess.'

'Great.' She stopped and kicked a large granite bowl by the path.

'What's the problem with that?' he asked.

'Nothing.' *Everything*, Hannah added silently.

Stumbling, she found her way up to her room and slammed the door. She groped for the light switch, turned it on and then the bulb popped. Shit. Fumbling a bit more, she found her backpack, which she knew had a torch.

Her hands stilled at the sound of feet hitting the stairs. She wiped her eyes with the back of her fist. She wouldn't let them in.

'Is everything all right?' Maddie asked.

'Go away.' Hannah found the torch.

'Are you OK? You ran off so suddenly. Can I come in?'

Hannah heard a hand on the door handle. 'No!'

'What's wrong?' Maddie asked

'Nothing, just go away.' Hannah turned on the torch but

nothing happened. Coming here had ruined everything, including her sodding torch.

'What do I say to Will? He's concerned.'

'Oh, just fuck off. He's fine.' Hannah slammed the torch into the pillow and finally light emerged from it. She grabbed a tissue and blew her nose. Maddie had no right. She'd obviously never loved Dad. If she had, she wouldn't be making up to Mark.

Hannah repeatedly hit the pillow until it spat feathers. They were luminous in the torch's beam as they floated down. She got up, kicked the bed and then limped over to the hammer lying on the vanity table. She'd used it earlier when she'd hung a mirror. Her fingers stroked the hammer, enjoying the feel of the wooden handle.

Maddie didn't care. Never had. How could she think of another man? 'She's betraying us, Dad,' Hannah muttered as she swung the hammer round. It picked up speed as her arm moved with the weight of it. In the small ray of light, it blurred like a pin wheel – like the red and blue one her father had bought for her when she was five.

She wiped her eyes with her sleeve, still mesmerised by her spinning arm. Sweat from her palm eased her grip on the hammer. Slowly it slid from her grasp, through the air and bashed into the bottom of the wardrobe. Shit.

Maddie must have heard the noise because she rapidly reached Hannah's room again. 'Hannah, what was that? Are you all right?'

'Yeah.'

'Mark and Will have left. May I come in?'

Hannah's throat went dry. Her eyes darted from one end of the room to the other. 'No. What do you want?'

'To talk.'

'Forget it.'

'What set you off like that?' Hannah could hear Maddie's breathing through the door.

'Like what?'

'You just ran off.'

'So.' Maddie was a tart and she'd leave any day now with the first man to have her. Hannah wondered if that was how her mother had behaved. Even now, nearly thirteen years later, Hannah was still so angry that her mother had done that to her and to Dad. He'd rarely spoken about it except to say she'd left. Hannah had always wanted to know why and now she never would. Was there some way to find the deserter? Did she really want to find the woman who didn't want her?

'Hannah, I don't like talking to the door.'

'So don't.' Hannah heard Maddie sigh. Now she was stuck with moaning Maddie. Foster care would have been better.

'Hannah, I'm here for you, whenever you want.'

Hannah decided that silence was the best option. She didn't want Maddie and never had.

✦ Four ✦

Hannah studied the wooden box. Pulling the hammer out of it had caused more damage than when it had gone in. Its beautiful surface was marred by a big gash in one corner. The central part of the top was carved but the remainder was smooth. As she lifted it to examine it closer, she smelled a faint hint of beeswax. The grain of wood was mostly straight and fine. She couldn't be sure but she thought it was oak. Old worm holes marred the bottom and sides but there were very few on the top.

She chewed her lower lip. She hadn't seen the box tucked in the back of the wardrobe when she cleared out the old clothes. The colour of the wood had blended into the dark interior and the box had been wedged between two supporting struts that stabilised the big beast. It looked sad. Splinters of broken wood stood up at awkward angles. Fortunately the contents were unscathed. It was just the box that was damaged. She didn't know what she could do to fix it but she wanted to.

She flipped through the stuff. There were papers, some of which seemed really old. Hannah couldn't really make out the writing but one appeared to be a list, then there was a cup and saucer with a crest on it and a grotty old exercise book. The poor box, or maybe chest was a better description, was now useless. She touched the fractured wood. It looked angry.

There was nothing she could do at this moment as she was supposed to be going to a party. She grabbed a hoodie and went downstairs and bumped into Fred coming in. 'What are you doing here?'

'Nice greeting.' He smiled and held up a bag. 'Dropping off something for Maddie from Mum on my way to work.'

'At the pub?' Hannah asked.

He nodded.

'Is that near Padga-something?'

'Padgagarrack. As near as you're going to get if you're asking for a lift.'

'I am.'

'Going to the barbecue?'

Hannah nodded. 'I guess so.'

'You met Emma, Matt's girlfriend, the other night. She'll be there.'

'Yeah.'

'Tough being new, huh?'

Hannah cocked her head to the side and then followed him to the car. For a bloke, Fred was pretty perceptive. As they drove he didn't say a lot, which was good because her stomach kept turning over. Looking out the window didn't help. Fred stopped the car.

'Thanks for the lift.' Hannah hopped out.

'Say hi for me.'

'Will do.' Hannah paused before she closed the car door. 'Down this road and onto a path. You say it's about a ten minute walk.'

'Yup. Keep right and follow the path along the coast. You'll hear the noise and know you've hit the right beach.'

'Thanks.'

Fred sped off and Hannah looked down the road in front of her. She still wasn't sure why she was doing this. Maddie wanted her to get out and meet people so that was a good reason not to go. But she did need to make some friends because if not then she would be stuck with no one but Maddie to talk to and that was a fate worse than death.

Hannah just wished that at least one of Tamsin's boys were going but none were. Fred was off to work, Matt was helping his dad, and Will wasn't here because he was at school. So she was off to a party with people she hardly knew. However, it was a Saturday and she could go or she could be bored out of her mind sitting in her room avoiding Maddie. This seemed the better option.

The day was warm for late September. Hannah took her hoodie off and tied it around her waist. Her backpack held the bottle of wine she'd pinched from Maddie's meagre collection. She had to bring something and didn't know what else to bring. The invitation had been vague.

As the road turned to the left, Hannah took what looked like a drive to the right. Between tree branches, she could see glimpses of the river where a sailing boat was making its way out to the bay. But that was all. It seemed strangely deserted. Each week she'd noticed the numbers of boats on the river declining yet the weather had remained good. Today, aside from that one lone boat, the river was empty, but it wasn't actually a river. It was a drowned valley, a ria. Weird.

She came to a house and followed the footpath behind it. Although she could see the river, the path was enclosed in trees and high above the water. She had to watch her feet so she didn't trip up on their roots while she tried to remember who was going to this party. Aside from Matt's girlfriend, she really couldn't think who. She looked at her watch. She'd been walking for fifteen minutes and there was no sign of a beach. To her left were coves below the path but nothing she'd call a beach. She peered over the edge and saw a small bit of sand appearing between the rocks that led to a cave. That was not a beach in her opinion but it was pretty.

After another five minutes of walking there was still no sign of people, let alone a party. Had they been pulling her leg, inviting her to something that wasn't happening? Winding up the city girl? Had they changed the location and forgotten to tell her? Should she turn back? She really didn't want to go and party with people she didn't know. She stopped and looked at her watch again. Twenty-five minutes of walking and nothing but trees and the river. Maybe she'd turned the wrong way.

The sounds of shouting reached her. She squinted and

noticed a cove in the distance. The path trailed down and over a stream.

'Hey, Hannah, you found us.' Emma, came up.

'Yeah, it took a while.'

'Really?' Emma's eyebrows pulled together. 'It's only a twenty-minute walk from the road.'

'It took me half an hour and Fred said ten minutes.'

'Maybe for him with the long legs.' Emma smiled. 'Come and meet some people.'

Hannah wrinkled her nose.

'They don't bite.' Emma placed a hand on Hannah's arm. 'Well, most of them.'

Hannah looked around but wasn't too sure. The tide was way out, exposing the rocks that projected into the river. A demented version of cricket was under way on the sloping beach.

'I'm going to go collect some mussels. Do you want to come?' Emma picked up a pail and a knife.

'No thanks.'

'Why don't you see if you can give them a hand with the fire?' Emma walked off and Hannah turned to the group of boys playing with matches. At the rate they were going, the whole beach would be alight pretty soon. They had no need of her help.

'Hey, Hannah?' a bloke called.

She turned.

He smiled. 'Don't suppose you'd go and get some more kindling from the woods along the path?'

Hannah shrugged. 'Sure.'

'Great.' He went back to setting the beach on fire.

Hannah crossed the stream and walked up the footpath, collecting small twigs as she went. She pulled out her phone to text Abi.

This place is the pits. Stuck here collecting twigs so the locals can set the world alight. x

The text wouldn't send until she reached the top of the next hill. Bloody place. She walked further still, picking up bits of branches until her arms were full. Her phone pinged but she couldn't look until she'd delivered the wood. Abi was probably shopping on Oxford Street or hanging out at a friend's house.

A few more people had arrived and she dumped the kindling. Someone offered her a beer and she took it. A few faces were familiar from school but most were not. She downed the beer and crushed the can. No sign of Emma on the beach.

Her eyes stung. She tried to put it down to the smoke from the fire but she didn't need to lie to herself. The smell of the crackling branches brought her father to mind. Would she ever stop missing him? Stupid question. Had she ever stopped missing her mum even though she couldn't remember her? She closed her eyes, trying to pull something about her mother from her memory, but she only saw her father's anger.

Bloody hell, Dad, what have you left me with? Anger and Maddie.

Hannah wandered away from the others. She was too different from them. The damp sand beneath her feet was littered with small pebbles and seaweed. It was so compact, her feet barely dented the surface. She looked up to see Emma still on the rocks. Emma waved and beckoned her out but Hannah didn't want to forage for her food. She was a city girl.

Hannah stopped walking to look at the river. Pretty but nothing worthwhile in sight. No shops, no buildings bar the odd hut visible on the other side. She smiled. The owners of the multi-million pound houses would be pissed off to have them called huts.

She perched on a dry rock. The water was still going out. The party plan was based on the tide. How weird.

'What time's the party? Oh, at low tide ...' They were mad, all mad, and she didn't fit in.

She stood and scrambled over to the next cove. It looked so peaceful compared to all the activity on the one she'd just left. The sun was catching what looked like a small cave and something blue glinted on the sand. She continued until she reached the piece of sea glass. Held to the light, the blue almost pulsed. She put it in her pocket and bent to pick up a green piece. The sand was covered in small bits of it. Like jewels, they glinted in the damp sand.

Soon her pockets were full, but she'd only found one piece of blue. It was rare. Hannah wondered if she could find some on the next cove. Walking along, she enjoyed the popping sound the seaweed made as she stepped on it. That type wasn't too slippery but the neon green one was worse than walking on ice. She stopped and listened. Small tapping sounds came from the sand. She bent to the ground. Was it water running to the river or was it stuff that was living in the sand? She couldn't see any movement so she stood and continued her search.

She clambered up the rocks and looked over. The light wasn't reaching the sand so she couldn't tell if it held any treasure. She found none so she went further on to the next cove. She scaled up and down over the slippery terrain encrusted with limpets and barnacles, which Hannah hadn't noticed on the last rocks she'd crossed. Looking up, she could finally see shells and bits of glass. She wasn't sure what she was going to do with all she'd collected, but she wanted more. Placing her foot down on a rock she slipped. 'Shit.'

Her ankle was twisted at an awkward angle and her hands had crashed down onto the jagged edges of the barnacles. Blood trickled from a thousand small cuts in her palms.

Maddie picked up her sketch pad and put it into her backpack. Stretching, she admired the view again, but this time with no plan for painting it. The river split below and a densely covered woodland lay in between. A wet nose came and nudged her hands. Startled, Maddie looked down to find a springer spaniel. It was Tamsin's dog and Tamsin appeared on the path.

'I'm so pleased I bumped into you,' Maddie said.

Tamsin grinned.

'Did you know Daphne?' Maddie picked up her bag and fell into step beside Tamsin.

'Not really. Why?'

'I'd like to find out a bit more about her.'

'Makes sense. I guess you should start with Helen Williams. She has her finger on the pulse of most things and if she doesn't know, then she normally knows someone who does.'

'Excellent. Where do I find her?'

'At Pengarrock. She's the housekeeper there.'

'Pengarrock?'

'Yes, the big house further up the river. You remember meeting Tristan the other night?'

Maddie nodded.

'Well, it's his place.'

'Which reminds me, you never did tell me what was going on.'

'Nothing wrong with your memory,' said Tamsin.

Maddie smiled. 'Nothing at all. So what was up between Mark and Tristan?'

'Oh, just some old stuff.'

'That tells me absolutely nothing.'

Tamsin smiled.

Maddie fell behind as the path narrowed and dipped close to the water's edge. 'So Judith and Tristan are a couple.'

'I believe so.'

'Then let me guess: Mark made a play for Judith and stepped on Tristan's toes.'

Tamsin stopped and turned. 'No, Mark got there first.'

'Why does this not surprise me? Does he make a move on every available woman?' Maddie rolled her eyes. He was incorrigible.

Tamsin nodded.

'So they dated. Tristan didn't strike me as the insanely jealous type.' The dog raced ahead of them and Maddie looked out onto the smooth water of Frenchman's Creek. Tree branches reached down to the surface and broke up the reflection of the sky above.

'Don't remember. He's only just moved back.'

'So, tell.' Maddie wasn't sure why she was so keen to know what was going on. Maybe thinking about other people's lives was easier than examining her own.

'It happened a long time ago.'

'What did?' Maddie stopped.

'They fell out over Claire.' Tamsin walked out onto a tree trunk that had fallen into the water. She sat down.

Maddie followed. 'Claire who?'

'Mark's wife.'

'He's married? Now I've heard everything.' Mark was the last man Maddie could picture being married. Every time she'd seen him lately he was with a different woman.

'A widower.'

Maddie's eyes widened. 'When?' She looked down at the fish swimming along the bank. The water was so clear she could see the bottom.

'Years ago.'

'If it's so long ago why is Tristan so awkward with Mark?' Maddie asked.

'It was all a long time ago.' Tamsin stared down the creek towards the river.

'You said that.' The wind picked up and ripples altered the surface reflections. The clarity of the water in the creek below her feet disappeared almost instantly.

'I did.' Tamsin stood up.

'Come on, you can't just leave me hanging.' Maddie remained seated, blocking Tamsin's exit.

'Just after he married Claire he went to the States on an architectural programme and Claire stayed behind.' Tamsin crossed her arms.

Maddie raised an eyebrow. When married to John, she'd hated to leave his side. 'Why?'

'She was finishing her physio training.'

Maddie pursed her mouth. 'This still doesn't make any sense. Why would Tristan be upset about that? Surely it was none of his business.'

'True. Claire was ill but Mark didn't know.'

Maddie frowned. 'Why?'

'Don't know but I do know she didn't want him to know.'

'I don't understand.'

'Nor do I but I don't think he's ever forgiven himself or her.'

'Ouch.' Maddie stood. How could Mark forgive himself? She'd nursed John and she still couldn't let go. It must be far worse if you hadn't done anything.

'He didn't come home for a long time.'

'How long?' Maddie asked.

'Fifteen years.'

'A long time in purgatory.' Maddie frowned. 'What's Tristan's part?'

'He loved her too.'

'OK, now it makes some sense.'

Tamsin called the dog. 'Must dash home and prepare dinner for the troops.' She set off at a brisk pace and Maddie couldn't help feeling that she hadn't heard the whole story.

Hannah tried to put weight on her ankle but pain raced up her leg. She dragged herself further up the beach, away from the encroaching tide. Sand, or more likely salt, stung in the cuts covering her palms. What was she going to do?

'Hello!' she shouted. No reply so she tried again and again but there was still no response. Tears filled her eyes but she refused to cry. That would be stupid and totally useless. Her phone. No signal. Fuck and double fuck. Her bum was wet from the sand, her phone didn't work and she was trapped on a disappearing beach. How had she never noticed that the tide moved so swiftly? It had taken ages to go out, but now with each second more of the cove disappeared.

Forcing herself onto her knees and using her knuckles, she crawled further up the beach and found a rock she could pull herself onto. It sat below the steep embankment of stone and earth. Roots of trees, almost like fingers, crawled out of it. Hannah shivered. Untying her hoodie, she put it on. The jagged rocks around her were covered with smooth, dark jelly-like things. Her foot throbbed. She bent down and loosened the laces but it pulsed even more.

'Help!' Her voice carried even less here. She looked out to the river but it was empty. She was alone. Tears slipped down her face. The rocks she had climbed over were now submerged.

She swallowed. Was she supposed to die here? Would anyone even notice?

'Be calm and don't panic,' she whispered as she tried her phone again. The signal bar flicked then disappeared. She raised her hand to throw it but then saw it flash again.

She pushed herself onto one foot and balanced. The signal seemed to stay. Who should she call? Maddie? She'd just lecture her about the dangers of wandering off on your own. She'd already given her the talk about tides and Cornish beaches. Hannah laughed. She'd actually listened to that one. Yet here she was, cut off with no place to go. She dialled. Hannah held her breath, not daring to move while it connected.

'Hannah, I'm driving, I can't talk right now. Have just seen a police car. Will ring you when I get home.' The phone went dead.

'Help.' Hannah cried but it was too late. She tried the number again, but Maddie must have switched the phone off. Hannah closed her eyes. She didn't know what to do. 'Think, damn it, think.' She banged her phone against her head.

Stupid. 999. That was who to call, not Maddie. She dialled but her phone beeped then went dead. The battery was flat.

What was she going to do? She looked up. It was too steep to climb. The water had eroded the earth, creating an overhang. In fact, it looked like the bit above could crash down at any time.

Sunlight gleamed on the water but she was in the shadows. She couldn't swim well to begin with, but with a busted ankle she had no hope. Her mouth went dry.

'Hannah?' Maddie called as she brought the shopping into the house. There was no response. She picked up the phone and dialled. She'd hated cutting Hannah off but Maddie had forgotten to attach her hands-free earlier. The phone went straight to voicemail. Whatever Hannah had wanted, it couldn't have been too urgent. Maddie put the groceries away and then spread her research on the table. Daphne was born to Edward and Agnes Penventon on 24 March, 1921. She'd been born at Trevenen and it was here she'd died.

Much to Maddie's surprise, there had also been information on the house itself on the internet and in the library. Will had been correct in his assumption that the house was listed. How had she missed that fact? She could have done without the complication. On the upside, she might be able to receive some financial help with the repair of the roof.

There had been a dwelling on this site since the late 1100s. The current house had begun in 1500 with a large downstairs room and two small rooms above the eastern half. Where the dining room and hall now sat, a single storey extension was added around 1540, according to the listing. Maddie looked at the kitchen, trying to imagine what it would have been like when half the room was open to the roof.

In the late 1700s, the final major changes came when a second storey was added above the dining room and hall, plus a double height extension, which was now the living room and Maddie's bedroom. The internet sources had described Trevenen as one of the finest examples of domestic Cornish architecture. Maddie swallowed and walked to the hall to look at the picture of Daphne. Maddie could see that one of the women in the picture must be Daphne's mother, Agnes. The other woman shared their height and Maddie assumed she must be Agnes's sister. 'Ladies, what have you left me? How am I supposed to take care of this house? Daphne, how did you run it on your own?'

Maddie turned and went up the main stairs to the room Daphne must have used as a bedroom. The woman hadn't chosen any of the larger ones, but the plainest in the house. At least that's what Maddie had guessed by the clothes and papers she'd found when she'd cleaned it. In the bedside table drawer was a worn prayer book with an inscription to Daphne. She'd received the book on her confirmation in May 1936. The pages were yellowed not just with age but with use. From it fell a faded black-and-white photograph of a young man in uniform. She turned it over and on the back in faint pencil was the name Arthur Tripconey. Had this been the love of Daphne's life?

Slipping the picture back into the book, Maddie touched

the clothes she'd sorted on the bed. They were all old. Maddie wouldn't even call them vintage because that implied style. Daphne's taste had leaned more to work clothes. There were only two dresses. Who was this woman?

She walked downstairs and went through the sitting room. The carpet made her nauseous to look at it. Scanning the edges of the room, she sought out a place where she could lift it and see what the floor beneath looked like. Near the fireplace she could see a bump where she might be able to pull it up. The urge was too strong to resist.

Bending over, she gave a tug and then another. Suddenly she fell backwards onto her bottom and was looking down at a beautiful wood floor, but one in dire need of attention. She got to her knees and pushed the carpet back into place. Maybe in the spring she could get someone to help her pull it up and then she could think about what to do. A cold draught ran over her fingers as she pushed the old tack back down. She looked up to where she had seen the mouse. There must be some gap in the chimney where the air and the mouse were getting in. She pursed her lips. Just another thing to worry about.

Back on her feet, she forced her thoughts back to Daphne. There had to be more information on her life somewhere in the house. Maybe she kept her personal papers in the office. Maddie passed the room several times a day but never went in. Standing in the middle of it, she took a closer look at what exactly was here. All as before but this time she noticed an old, large Bible sitting on the desk.

Maddie pulled it to her. The leather was cracked and flaking. The pages were thick and slightly warped but in good condition. She opened it and her heart stilled. This was the Penventon family Bible. The family tree covered the pages at the front. Her hand shook as she scanned the ornate writing.

She didn't want to know the early history. She only wanted to know about this century. Halfway down the back page, Maddie found what she was looking for: Daphne's name. It was the second to last one. Daphne had a brother, Diggory, and that was all.

Hannah pulled out a tissue and tried to stem the tide of her tears. They weren't going to save her and there was enough water surrounding her already. She was stranded on a rock. The sand had long since disappeared. She was going to drown on a beach in Cornwall. No one would care, not even Maddie. Maddie would be angry. Angry that she'd hung up the phone the one time Hannah called for help. *I'm here whenever you need me.* What bullshit. The one time Hannah really needed help was now.

Shit. She was going to die. Tears returned in force. She closed her eyes and thought of her father. He'd just stopped breathing. And now she was going to drown under the icy water. Maybe she wouldn't fight it? Maybe she was supposed to die now? What about her real mother? Hannah swallowed. She wouldn't care either. She'd ditched Hannah years ago.

'Stop it.' She pulled the bottle of wine out of the backpack. If she was going to die, she might as well do it drunk, then she might not notice. She shook her head. She couldn't get that pissed on a bottle of cheap white wine. She twisted off the screw top and took a big swig. She gagged but took another. Maybe she could knock it back in one and just pass out? The stuff tasted vile and it was warm, unlike the water below her, which was now halfway up the rock. The light was beginning to fade but it was still hitting the hills across the river. Why was there no one on the water?

The wind had changed direction and a cold easterly came straight into the mouth of the river, stirring up the water. It was no longer blissfully smooth. Waves even made it into her cove, her cove of death.

Another drink of wine and the bottle was half gone. A humming filled her ears. She looked at the bottle. It was only 13.5 per cent alcohol but it sure packed a punch. The noise was getting louder and then she saw a small boat next to a buoy.

She tried to stand but fell in to the river. 'Shit!' She took in a mouthful of water. Her body went rigid. 'No.' She grabbed the rock and pulled herself up, her hands stinging like mad. The person on the boat looked up, and then went back to pulling in a line.

Finally out of the water, Hannah shook from head to toe. 'Help!' Her voice didn't carry. What could she do? The person pulled a cage into the boat. 'Help!'

Hannah watched as he bent to the engine.

Her heart raced. 'Oi, you!'

The figure remained with his back to her. 'Fuck.' She clasped her hands together and took a deep breath. 'Oi, over here!'

The figure turned around and scanned the water.

She waved her hands wildly. 'Here! Here!'

He turned away and Hannah slumped. Water was nearly to the top of her rock. This was it.

✤ Five ✤

Maddie looked at the clock. It was dark and Hannah wasn't home yet. She chewed her lip then picked up the phone and tried Hannah's mobile. She knew she needed to give her space but she had no idea where she could be. There had been no note on the table.

It didn't ring but went to answerphone. Maddie closed her eyes and wished for the umpteenth time that John was here. He'd know what to do. He'd known how to handle her. She rubbed her forehead. It wasn't fair but there was nothing she could do about it. She had to remember that things were worse for Hannah.

The phone rang and Maddie jumped. 'Hannah, where are you?'

'It's Tamsin.'

'Hi.' Maddie collapsed into a chair.

'So Hannah's not with you?'

'No.'

'Do you know where she is?' Tamsin asked.

'No and why are you asking?'

'Emma's here and she couldn't find Hannah when they left the beach so she asked me to ring you to see if Hannah was home.'

'What beach?' Maddie stood up.

'They were at a party on a beach by the river.'

'When?' Maddie didn't like the thoughts that were going through her head. Surely Hannah hadn't been foolish enough to wander off on her own.

'This afternoon. I'm sure it's all fine and Hannah hitched up with some new kids. We'll make a few calls. Don't panic.'

'Right.'

'I'll call you again when we've spoken to some of the others.'

'Thanks.' Maddie put down the phone. Something couldn't have happened to Hannah. She must be OK. But what if she wasn't? Maddie put her head in her hands. She'd promised John she would take care of Hannah. What if she'd failed?

Hannah fell into the boat. She couldn't speak, her voice was so raw from screaming, but it had worked. Mark had heard her. Her limbs shook. She was wet from head to toe. Mark wrapped her in his sweater and then put the boat into gear. He said nothing as he peered over her to find their way in the darkness. Lights flickered on both shores and the little boat rocked violently in the swell. Her hands hurt too much for her to hold onto the side of the boat. Hannah's stomach fought with the wine in it but she was shaking too much to throw up.

A large lobster stared at her from a cage. Its beady eyes never left her and its large claw snapped. Hannah pulled away. These things were living in the water that she had been in. She shook even more.

'We're almost there!' Mark shouted. She didn't dare look at him. God only knew what he was thinking. She was a fool but at least she was alive. Glancing up she saw a pontoon. They were safe. Mark tied up the boat. Hannah tried to stand when he held a hand out but her legs wouldn't hold her. He scooped her up and placed her on the decking.

Before she could say a word, he was carrying her up to the sailing club where he stopped just outside the ladies' room.

'Hello?' he called. No one answered, so he walked straight in and through another door before he placed Hannah on a bench.

'I'm going to put the shower on and then place you under the warm water where I want you to stay until I come back.'

Hannah nodded or thought she did. Her whole body was

65

moving of its own accord. She had no control over it. She now knew what shock and hypothermia felt like.

Maddie put the phone down and paced the kitchen. Tamsin was on her way over. What was Maddie going to do? What could she do? Nothing. She stopped and leaned her head against the window.

Headlights pierced the darkness in the courtyard and Maddie wondered how Tamsin had managed to drive here so quickly. She frowned when she saw Mark climb out of his vehicle and lift something out of the back seat.

Her heart stopped. A blonde head rested against his chest. Hannah was wrapped in a blanket and there was a bandage around her right foot and ankle. What had happened? Maddie raced to the door and opened it.

'Hi. Hannah's fine.' Mark carried Hannah straight upstairs. 'Which one is hers?'

'At the end of the corridor.' Maddie was right behind him. 'Let me get the door for you.'

He paused and she dashed past him and into the room. She pulled the duvet back on the bed and watched Mark place Hannah gently down.

'What on earth happened?'

'A little misadventure,' Mark said and he gave Maddie a look. 'Hannah, get some rest.'

Maddie tucked Hannah in. The girl's eyes were wide and her hands were bandaged.

'Thanks.' Hannah's voice was barely audible.

Mark gave Hannah a salute and took Maddie's arm, pulling her out of the room and down to the hall.

'Mark?' Maddie stopped at the base of the stairs.

'She's OK.'

'Yes but what happened?'

'I was out checking my lobster pots and heard her scream.'

'Where was she?' What if he hadn't heard her? Maddie's stomach turned.

'On a rock in the river.'

'What?'

'She'd been caught by the tide,' he said.

'Oh my God. She called but I hung up on her.'

Mark raised an eyebrow.

'Driving.' Maddie hung her head.

'Unfortunate but understandable.' He put an arm across her shoulders and led her into the kitchen. 'Do you have anything to drink? I could use one.'

'Of course. It's the least I can do to thank you.'

'I can think of a few other ways.' He grinned.

'I bet you can.' Maddie smiled weakly and went in search of the whisky.

Maddie placed a tray with tea and toast on the table beside Hannah's bed. Hannah was still sound asleep and her face was far too pale. The girl had nearly drowned. She must have been terrified. Maddie didn't want to dwell on what could have happened. She had failed once again.

It was nine-thirty and she was supposed to take Hannah to the surgery. Mark told her the doctor wanted another look at Hannah's ankle once the swelling had receded a bit to be sure it was a bad sprain and not a break. Thankfully the doctor had been having a meal at the sailing club last night and had checked Hannah.

Sitting on the edge of the bed, Maddie longed to stroke Hannah's hair, which was so like her father's; instead she clasped her hands together. She had no idea of how to deal with a teenager. In fact, she had no idea of how to 'deal' at all. How would John handle this? Part of Maddie wanted to throttle Hannah for being so foolish and the other part just wanted to hold her close. She didn't know what was the right thing to do.

She placed a hand on Hannah's forehead and Hannah's eyes opened. They narrowed and Maddie braced herself. She now knew that Hannah must have been calling her for help and what had she done? Hung up on her.

'Sorry.' Maddie stroked Hannah's forehead again and Hannah pushed her hand away.

Maddie stood. 'I need to take you to see the doctor. Do you want me to help you dress?'

Hannah rolled her eyes.

'If you change your mind then give me a shout.' Maddie walked out of the bedroom. What was she going to do? How was she going to make this right?

The basket was full of apples. Maddie wasn't sure what she was going to do with all this fruit. She adjusted her shoulders while she surveyed the laden orchard that stretched down to a fold in the land. Judith had popped by and had a look at the garden and the fruit trees. She suspected that some of them were rare early varieties and local ones too. Judith had taken pictures. She said she'd come back to Maddie with the answers when she found them.

The apple tree branches were all covered in lichen, changing the colour from mottled grey to soft green. The pear trees were bent almost double with the weight of the still unripe fruit. Maddie wondered if the weather would stay warm enough for them to ripen. It would be such a waste not to use the fruit but how much preserve, apple butter, chutney and so on could she make? The past few days she'd felt as though she were back in school cookery class, but at least it took her mind off Hannah. She wasn't talking; well, she wasn't speaking to Maddie and Maddie couldn't blame her. Every question was met with silence. If Maddie hadn't heard her chatting to Abi on the phone, she would've thought Hannah had lost the ability to speak.

With her arms full, she made her way towards the house. She liked the way it sat on a level stretch of land, almost a plateau, with the fields falling away steeply below and rising gently above. The lines and planes of the group of buildings triggered thoughts for a new painting, but she knew by the time she'd reached the house, the idea would be gone. She didn't seem to be able to hold onto anything at present. Glimmers of inspiration would flicker as she moved through her day but before she could capture them, they'd disappear. It was like some connection inside her had been cut. She could see the world, she could transfer the image to her unique view of it, but it stopped there. The link to the output had been severed or lost completely.

Possibly she was thinking too much. She just needed to paint, paint, paint. But before she could begin that, she must figure out what the hell to do with all this fruit. She placed the latest addition on the kitchen table.

Aromas of cinnamon and cloves floated over her worries. Small jars littered every surface. It looked very domestic. Maddie laughed. She'd never seen herself as that. A bit arty and bohemian, definitely, but never a domestic goddess. Yet she was enjoying it.

Leaving the kitchen, she admired the work she'd done so far on the house. The air of neglect had disappeared with a coat of paint and heavy use of a duster. She had re-hung a few of the old photographs, including the one of the Penventon women, and had put up some of her own work, which, although modern, went beautifully with the ancient lines of the house. It was like walking through a gallery showing a retrospective of her work. It reminded her that all creativity seemed to have died with John.

Pain crowded around her again, taking her air away and blocking the light. How could she still be in mourning? What was she grieving: him or what she had lost? She honestly didn't know and didn't want to prod it too deeply because it hurt too much. She'd become a wimp. The man she'd sworn to love for ever was now the source of an open wound that showed no signs of healing.

She marched through to the dining room and sat on the window seat. Despite the chaos of the paperwork she'd dumped on the beautiful table, she found this spot a place of peace. Pulling her long legs up, Maddie hugged them to her and looked out at the tree. At eye level, a graceful branch was framed in a pane of glass that distorted the line and blurred the edges. The blend of greens set Maddie onto her feet and out to the stables. She needed to paint. Forget the apples, forget the house, forget everything and paint.

*

Hannah watched Maddie fuss about the kitchen. If she hovered over her any more, Hannah was going to hit her. Ever since the beach incident, Maddie had been unbearable, always asking how she was. Right now the woman looked exhausted, almost worse than when Dad had died.

'Can I get you anything else?' Maddie asked.

Hannah shook her head. Maddie paused and stood near her, towering over her. Hannah ground her teeth. This was too much; she was just going to have to say something.

'What's wrong with you?'

'I'm fine, thank you.'

'Good.' Hannah thought she looked like a rabbit caught in the headlights. 'Then go out or something. I'm not going to wander off to some beach.'

It would be a long time before Hannah would even want to go near the river again. A chill went down her back.

'Hannah.'

'Don't "Hannah" me. You've not left me alone in ages. Go out.'

'I'm fine.'

'You're not. Maybe you need a trip to London or something. Maybe even the pub would do. Get out of here and get a life!' Hannah bit into an apple. 'I'm going to call Tamsin to come and take you out tonight.'

'That's not necessary. I don't need to go to the pub.'

'Yes, you do. You're cracking up.'

'Nonsense. I'm just down. It happens.'

'If that's all then go get your chakras done or something, but I think the pub would be a better bet. Have a glass of wine or two or three. Live.'

Hannah left the kitchen and went to her room. She had started trying to transcribe one of the documents from the box. It was bloody slow work, but with a bum ankle the past few weeks, there hadn't been much else to do except school work.

She sat on her bed and pulled her pad of paper out, then opened up the parchment. She loved the way the letters swirled and blended, but it made it difficult to read. So far she had deciphered about ten words and one of them was Penventon. She should really show this stuff to Maddie but she didn't want to, or at least not yet. It was her find.

'So are you going to tell me why Hannah wanted you out of the house?' Tamsin asked as they walked from the car to the pub.

Maddie rolled her eyes. 'Don't know.'

'She mentioned that you were unbalanced and needed to drink heavily.' Tamsin opened the door to the New Inn.

'Did she?'

'Yes, she said maybe you might need some sex to rebalance your chakras.'

Maddie laughed. 'Is that how it's done? I've always wondered.'

'I haven't a clue. No wonder they do a booming business if that's the case.' Tamsin chuckled and walked up to the bar. 'Red wine?'

Maddie nodded and went to stand next to the blazing coal fire. 'How's Mark?'

Tamsin turned. 'On usual form. Why?'

'Haven't seen him and was just wondering.'

'Were you, now?' Tamsin smiled.

'Oh, don't go like that. Can't I ask about someone without getting the third degree?'

'No.'

That tells me, thought Maddie. In future, she would keep her mouth shut.

Tamsin turned and handed Maddie a glass. 'Now get that wine down your gob and tell me what's up.'

Maddie spluttered. 'I don't know.'

'Well, that's honest.' Tamsin waved at a man across the room before she sat at the table. She patted on the bench beside her and Maddie sat.

'I'm low, but I don't know if the move took the stuffing out of me or what.' Maddie looked down at her hands. She used to be so in control and now things felt like they were falling apart.

'Hannah's right. You do need a drink, a bonk and something else like a slap across the face.' Tamsin raised her hand.

Maddie laughed. 'Well, the first is easy. I'll duck for the last and no candidates for the middle.'

'I'm sure I could find a willing partner for you.'

Maddie watched Tamsin review the possible contenders standing at the bar. None of them were what she was looking for, but then did she know what she wanted? She missed the closeness, the holding each other, the unspoken communication, but that would never come from a date. She had no idea how to let a man back into her life. In fact, she didn't know if she even wanted to. Then, of course, there was Hannah.

'Oh, I don't doubt that, but I don't need someone put up to the task, either. I'm not the type to bonk and run. I just don't work that way.' Maddie's fingers played with the stem of her wine glass.

'That's the problem with us women. We need the love bit too, don't we? Damned foolish creatures we are.'

Maddie smiled. Tamsin made it all seem so simple.

'What if I set you up on a blind date?' Tamsin asked.

Maddie shuddered. 'No.'

'Come on. A date couldn't hurt; just a quiet dinner in Truro or somewhere.'

'Just where would you dig up this poor soul?' Maddie had horrific visions of all the available men of the county being lined up as if in a firing squad and her indomitable friend would vet them for their suitability. Knowing Tamsin, none of them would be appropriate for what Maddie really required, but would be fine for a good time. But possibly that was what she needed.

'Trust me.'

'That's the problem, I don't.' Maddie laughed.

'Well, you'll have to. Now drink up.'

'Let's get off the subject of me.' Maddie took a sip.

'Fine. Take a look at what just walked into the pub.'

Maddie studied the tall blond man. Viking was the word that came to mind; a very tasty one.

'Yes, I agree completely,' said Tamsin.

'With what?' asked Maddie.

'What's written across your face.' Tamsin laughed.

'What are you talking about?'

'L-U-S-T. He's lust in a tall package.' Tamsin whistled softly.

'Quiet or he'll hear you,' Maddie whispered.

'Hmmm. Why don't you get us another glass of wine?' Tamsin pushed her off the seat and practically into the Viking's arms.

'Sorry, I tripped.' Maddie turned and frowned at Tamsin, who smiled innocently back at her.

'No problem.' His voice was deep and hinted at Nordic influences.

Maddie stood waiting for him to finish at the bar while she looked for the rest of his party in the pub, but he appeared to be alone.

'May I buy you a drink?' he asked.

'Sorry?' Maddie snapped to attention under the gaze of his icy blue eyes.

'May I get you a drink?' he asked.

'Thanks but my friend and I are fine.' Maddie smiled and looked away.

'Then why are you standing at the bar?' he asked.

Maddie sought a polite reply. She could see that Tamsin was killing herself laughing. This was no good.

'I'm buying drinks.' Maddie looked at her feet.

'Then allow me.' He bowed slightly.

What was she going to do? If she refused, she would sound like an ungracious git and if she accepted, she'd feel worse. Damn.

'Thank you.'

'What were you drinking?'

'The Cabernet.' Maddie sensed Tamsin come up behind her.

'Hello. Thank you for the drink. I'm Tamsin.' She extended her hand.

'You're welcome. My name is Gunnar.'

'Hello, Gunnar. What brings you to this part of Cornwall?' asked Tamsin.

Maddie kicked Tamsin's shin discreetly and took a sip of wine while she studied the man. With chiselled jaw and white-blond hair against a tanned face, he looked like he should be on the front of a longboat.

'I'm filming a documentary on the effects of global warming on the fishing industry.'

'How interesting,' said Tamsin.

Maddie was going to gag if Tamsin played up any more.

'Yes, it is affecting fishing around the world, but here in Cornwall it is personal; not just the big factory boats but small ones. It makes the story more meaningful.'

'How long do you plan to be here?' Tamsin asked.

'Through the summer. Now, it's mostly research and a little filming, but as the weather improves, we will be filming more.'

Great, thought Maddie, the next question out of Tamsin's mouth would be 'where are you staying?'

'How long ago did you arrive?' Tamsin continued the interview.

'A week ago,' he replied.

'That's all? Where are you staying?' Tamsin asked.

Maddie held her breath, in awe of her friend's audacity.

'I've rented a cottage here in Manaccan.' He smiled.

'Welcome to our little world, Gunnar.' Tamsin beamed.

'Thank you.' He raised his glass and stared directly into Maddie's eyes as he drank. She had to admit that the Viking was rather attractive with his white teeth gleaming in the low light.

❖ Six ❖

'When did you last have sex?'

Tamsin's words seemed to echo. Everything had a fuzzy edge in the kitchen, including Tamsin's wicked smile that appeared over the rim of her glass. Maddie leaned back in her chair and took another sip of wine. It was well past midnight and they were beginning their third bottle. She knew she'd regret it, but right now it felt good.

'What did you just ask?'

'You heard me,' Tamsin said.

'Not a fair question.'

'Why not?' asked Tamsin.

'I don't know. When did you last have sex?'

'Last night, as it happens.' Tamsin grinned.

'With your husband, I hope.'

'Not telling.'

Maddie leaned forward. 'Nor am I.'

'Been so long you can't remember?' asked Tamsin.

'No, unfortunately it's not that. I can remember. We knew it would be the last time. It was all terribly poignant.' Tears threatened but she blinked them away and gave Tamsin a wobbly smile.

'Sorry.' Tamsin reached out and touched Maddie's hand. 'Not since then?'

'Oh, God, definitely not. Who'd want an old hag like me?' Maddie forced a laugh.

'You're no hag, and Gunnar asked for your number tonight, and then there's Mark. He's been hovering around since you arrived.'

'Well, he didn't have a choice. I sort of landed on him.'

'He certainly wasn't complaining.'

Maddie smiled. Mark was attractive, but he flirted with everyone. That wasn't her type of man, however tempting the package might be. Maybe she could ask him to pose for a nude study, though. His beautiful build hadn't escaped her notice. Her cheeks flushed.

'See, you like him. I can tell.'

'Seriously, Tamsin, who wouldn't like Mark?'

'Hello, you two.' The object of their discussion came through the kitchen door with Tamsin's husband, Anthony, who was here to give Tamsin a lift home. Maddie slid lower in her chair. Had Mark heard any of the conversation?

'Hello, boys.' Tamsin stood up and grabbed a couple more glasses, then splashed a bit of red wine on the table as she filled them.

Anthony's eyes strayed to the empties by the bin. 'Good evening, I see.'

'Yup.' Tamsin's smile was lopsided as she looked at him.

Mark pulled out the chair next to Maddie. He smelled of the sea.

'Where've you two been?' Maddie took a large sip of wine.

'Oh, at the sailing club for Race Night. You missed a good time.' Mark stretched his long legs out under the table.

'No, we didn't. It's been great. Maddie cooked a lovely meal after our visit to the pub.'

'Hence all the dead soldiers.' Anthony swept a hand towards the bin.

Tamsin whacked his arm. Maddie laughed at the affronted look on his face. They were so easy with each other. Had she and John ever been like that? Had they ever had the chance? They had only just stepped beyond the newly-wed passion when the cancer put the brakes on everything.

'Well, let's hear what you two were talking about,' Anthony said.

'Not on your life!' Tamsin slapped her hand on the table.

'Oh, sex then.' He laughed and avoided his wife's stare.

Mark looked at Maddie. 'Where's Hannah? Out?'

'She's just above us so she can probably hear everything.' Maddie gave a wry smile.

'How's her ankle?' Mark asked.

'Seems to be OK. The young heal quickly.' Maddie said.

'She's a pretty girl. Very different colouring to you,' said Anthony.

'She's my stepdaughter.' Maddie thought of the petite blonde above and frowned. What would her own child have looked like? Blonde like John or dark like her?

'What happened to her mother?' Anthony asked.

Maddie ran a hand through her hair. 'She left when Hannah was three.'

'Just left? Went missing?' he asked.

'Left. Told John she was going and never wanted to see him or Hannah again. John said if that was the way she felt, could he have it in writing.'

'Wow,' said Tamsin.

'I know,' said Maddie.

'Don't know how any woman could leave her child.' Tamsin spoke quietly.

Her words brought a lump to Maddie's throat. She wouldn't leave Hannah, no matter how far Hannah pushed, but she would never blame Hannah's mother for leaving. What had forced Susan to such an act? Was it post-natal depression? Was it John? Maddie stopped there. She wasn't being fair to John. Yet she wondered if he had asked as much of Hannah's mother as he had of her.

Anthony turned to his wife. 'But you could clearly understand her leaving her man, then?'

'Why, of course, I was just thinking about it the other day when I was eyeing up that new lad you have helping. What's his name, Michael?'

'You'd wear him out. He's too young.' Anthony laughed. 'So Hannah's yours now?'

'Yes. The courts made it official a few months ago. Hannah wasn't too pleased.' Maddie sighed.

'Terrible thing to live with, your mother not wanting you,' said Tamsin.

Maddie nodded. They only had each other now and Maddie must make it work. She had promised.

Hannah paced her room. It took her exactly thirteen strides to go from one end to the other. She knew this because she'd checked it twenty times. Boredom sucked. She pulled the book out of her backpack. The yellowed pages didn't look appealing but her teacher said it was a good place to start to learn about Cornwall during the 1500s. Strangely, he never asked why she wanted to know, which meant she must look like some sort of history geek. This was worrying.

Currently she was trying to read one document that had been written in 1570. It had taken her ages to work out the date because she had totally forgotten her roman numerals. The handwriting was exquisite and the paper crumbling.

Hannah picked up the pigeon feather she'd found in the garden and held it in her fingers, trying to imagine the elaborate movements required to make the writing so beautiful. She looked at her prep on the floor with the chicken scratch that served for her handwriting. It was pathetic. It was fast, furious and dismissive of the person who would read it. How true that was. It was for her English teacher. Before coming to this hell hole, she'd mildly enjoyed English as a subject, but the idiot here was a cow through and through. Nothing was good enough, so Hannah decided she'd try even less. Her last paper had been totally obliterated by red ink. The bitch hadn't seen anything yet.

Hannah placed the feather down. It was so frustrating not being able to read this stuff. She looked at the letter again and the pile of other papers. It was all gobbledygook, but beautiful.

Silence had finally descended on the kitchen so she crept out towards the stairs. As she passed the room she'd thought of as the spinning room, moonlight made eerie patterns on the floor. Instead of turning down the stairs, she went to investigate.

Maddie hadn't done anything in here. History oozed from the walls and hung from the cobwebs in the corners.

While she was staring out at the courtyard in the ghostly light, Hannah sat at the desk in the alcove. A cracked leather top sat above intricate handles on the drawers; they felt cool in her fingers. She pulled out the central one and found a dusty photograph album. Placing it on top, she opened the cover as a draught swept through the cracks in the windows. She shivered.

Hannah began to leaf through the grey pages. The house looked different in black and white. The piggery had had a roof when these were taken. The women in the photos were tall, much like Maddie in a way, which made sense as Maddie was related to them somehow.

Her breathing stopped and Hannah's hand stilled. In front of her eyes, in black and white, Maddie posed at the base of the big tree in the front garden. Hannah pulled the album closer. It was definitely a teenage Maddie. The nose was the same, the hair, everything she could see from the image. The only thing that looked odd was the shirt she was wearing. It was all retro seventies style.

This was too weird. Maddie had said she'd only been to Trevenen this April, but her blatant lie was staring Hannah in the face and now she had evidence. Slamming the book shut, she wondered what Maddie would have to say when confronted with this tomorrow.

It had to be at least noon. Hannah's head hurt. First things first, she needed a cup of tea and something for the headache. She wouldn't be the only one. Maddie had been totally pissed last night. Tamsin was quite funny and she'd winked at Hannah as she filled Maddie's glass again. Maddie was going to suffer today, especially when Hannah asked why she'd lied. Hannah smiled. Today was going to be excellent. She hopped out of bed.

Once in the kitchen, Hannah retuned the radio. Life could be good sometimes. She unbolted the window and waved at the sun. Food would help her head. Her favourite song played while she cracked some eggs into a bowl. She began to sing and dance around.

'Good morning, Hannah. You're in fine voice.' Mark leaned against the door jamb with his hair all messed and a five o'clock shadow that was more like a sprouting lawn.

Hannah jumped. 'What the hell are you doing here?'

He walked into the room. 'Just woke up.'

'So, like, you come here for breakfast?'

'No.'

Hannah slapped the pan on the table. Her best day was rapidly becoming her worst. Mark slept here. He'd slept with Maddie.

He stretched. 'What happened to the chest?'

'You were in my room?' Hannah stopped beating the eggs.

'Yes, I was still sleepy and thought it was the loo.'

'You took a leak in my room?' Hannah didn't like the images forming in her head.

'No. I did admire the paint though,' he said.

He'd trespassed onto her ground. It was bad enough that he'd slept with Maddie. Not that she would've been in any state for anything. There were three empties and one half full bottle left on the table. Wait, why was he looking for the loo in her room? Maddie's was en suite. He must've been in the room next to Hannah's and turned the wrong way.

'Are you going to tell me?' he asked.

'Oh, an accident.'

Mark grabbed the coffee. 'With a hammer?'

Hannah looked up.

'Care to tell me?'

She bit her lip and then said, 'Wait here.' She ran upstairs, grabbed the box and then ran back to the kitchen. She placed it on the table.

Mark studied it. 'Have you told Maddie?'

'No.'

'Figured that.'

'Why?' she asked.

'You don't tell her much.'

80

'Why should I?' Hannah looked at her feet.

'Why indeed.' He smiled.

'Now you're going all pompous on me.' Hannah wrinkled her nose.

Mark laughed.

'What's so funny?' she asked.

'I've never been called pompous. Many, many other things, but never that.'

'About time,' she said.

'Maybe it is.'

'Yeah. Do you think it can be fixed?' She really hoped it could be. It was too beautiful with its rich dark wood.

'Don't know. Much of the wood on this end is damaged. It's old.'

'Yeah, from the fifteen hundreds, I think.'

Mark looked up. 'How do you know that?'

'From some of the paperwork that was in it.'

'Paperwork?' he asked.

'Stuff.' She shrugged. He didn't need to know.

'Have you showed anyone these things?' He moved to sit in a chair.

'No.'

'Keeping them a secret?' he asked.

'Yeah. It's my discovery. All I want to know is can it be fixed?' She tapped her foot.

'Possibly. The man who could tell you lives about a mile from here. Old Tom Martin. He's many things but furniture restoration is probably what he loves most.'

'Right. Do I call him?' she asked.

'Yes, or you could just walk. He's getting on a bit and never leaves his workshop much so I expect he'll be there now if you wanted to go.'

'How do I get there?'

'Turn right out of the drive and follow the road until you see a sign on the left for Martin's Field. That's his place. Go around to the workshop at the back. Tell him I sent you.'

'You said he was old. How old? Like you?'

'Older.' Mark chuckled. Hannah shook her head. She just didn't get him.

The thatched roof appeared before she could see the rest of the cottage. The intricate pattern on the bottom of the thatch surprised Hannah and reminded her of a gingerbread house. Classical music floated out from the shed. Big doors were flung wide open and a fluorescent light hung from the rafters where a tall skinny man bent over a bench, stroking a piece of wood.

'Hello?' Hannah walked cautiously among the bits of wood and parts of furniture scattered on the floor. Eyes as blue as she had ever seen looked at her. Creepy.

'Are you Tom Martin?' Hannah stared at the leather-like skin on his face. He was way older than Mark; in fact, he looked like he might have walked out of the grave.

'Yes.' He put down the chisel and extended a hand. 'You are?'

'Oh, yeah, I'm Hannah Hollis.'

'Of Trevenen?'

'Yeah. How do you know?' she asked.

'Small place, the Meneage.'

'Too right there.' Hannah rolled her eyes, thinking of how Tamsin and everyone else seemed to know everything.

'What can I do for you?' His eyes dropped to the object in her hands.

'Mark said you may be able to restore this.'

'Mark Triggs?' he asked.

Hannah nodded.

'Let's have a look.' His fingers stroked the grain of the wood until it came to the shattered corner.

'Care to tell me what happened?' Those piercing eyes searched her face. Hannah felt as if she was at school. She pulled her shoulders back and returned his stare.

'It broke.'

'I can see that. How?' His eyes never left hers while he spoke. She shifted from foot to foot. 'Do you need to know?'

'Yes, in a way. It helps me to know how the wood was damaged so I can think about how best to repair it.'

'Don't see how it could make any difference.' She took a deep breath. 'A hammer slipped from my fingers.'

'With a fair bit of force?' he asked.

'Yes. I didn't know what it would hit, did I?' She shrugged.

'Clearly not. Well, young lady, I think I can help.' He smiled.

Hannah sank against the table. 'Great.'

'Hand me the pliers from behind you, please.'

'Oh, what's it going to cost me?' she asked.

'Does this chest belong to someone else?' He took them from her and carefully removed the most broken splinters of wood from the box before laying them down on the worktop.

'No, it's sort of a finder's keeper's thing.' She glanced at the rafters.

'I see. So it's yours?'

'Yes.' Hannah looked down. She knew it must be Maddie's, but somehow Hannah felt everything in her room was hers.

'I don't expect that you have a great deal of spare money.'

Hannah nodded.

'Fine, then, you can help around here.'

'OK.' Hannah noticed the sawdust and wood chippings everywhere.

'There's a broom in the corner.' Old Tom turned to the chest. Hannah hated cleaning. She hadn't minded doing her room at Trevenen because that was her space, but this was someone else's shit. Slowly she walked to the broom. Hanging on the walls were bits of metal that looked like ancient torture devices. Was this old guy into torture? Should she be here alone with him?

'Could you turn the kettle on while you're over there? I don't know about you, but I'm parched.' His voice reminded her of one of those posh men in black-and-white films. He didn't sound or look Cornish at all. He must've been fair when he'd had hair.

The kettle made a terrible racket when she switched it on. The broom was right in front of her and taunted her until she began to push the piles of sawdust around. Wind swept through, creating little tornadoes which knocked her dust mountains flat. It was hopeless. She'd better make small piles and then quickly put them in the bin.

The click of the kettle brought her head up into the worktop.

'Fuck.' She ran her hands over the bump.

'What was that? I didn't quite catch it.'

Hannah glanced at him. He had a straight face, but she could swear that he was laughing. Old sod.

'Tea is in the canister behind the kettle. There's some milk in the pitcher, but if it's not enough then you'll need to pop into the kitchen.'

Hannah made her way to the kettle, still rubbing her head with one hand while holding the dustpan in the other. She could feel the lump coming up and all the blood around it throbbing.

She took two cups off the shelf. Her glance caught a flowery teapot that matched the cups. There were saucers too, but she wasn't going to use them because she knew that she would be assigned to the washing up. She could just tell. It had already grown from two cups to two cups and a teapot. Damn the saucers; she couldn't be arsed to wash them too.

In the canister, she found an intricately carved silver spoon with a looped handle. She liked the feel of the bumps and ridges. She sniffed.

'What's this shit?'

Tom raised his head. 'Did you ask the type of tea?'

'Yeah, sort of.'

'It's lapsang souchong.'

'Yeah, lapsang is so shit in my opinion,' Hannah muttered under her breath.

'It's a refreshing smoked Chinese tea.'

'Yippee. Whatever happened to builder's brew?' she asked.

'Are you a builder?'

Hannah threw in a teaspoon of leaves and then poured the water into the pot. She wasn't going to be able to drink this stuff. She watched the leaves spiral in the hot water.

'There are some biscuits.' The old man considered the sunlight streaming in through the doorway. 'Do you think it's too cold to sit outside?'

Hannah peered out. The sun was still shining so it should be OK if he had a sheltered spot. 'Yeah, it should be fine.'

'There's a tray on the floor behind the bin.'

Hannah pulled it out and smiled at the seventies happy face that adorned it. It didn't fit with the bone china cups and teapot but what the hell – it wasn't hers. She put the milk, teapot, cups and biscuit packet on it. Before she could lift it, he reached over her and brought down the saucers, a strainer and a plate. He then took the biscuits from their wrapping and placed them on the plate.

The cheek. Hannah closed her mouth and followed him out to the garden. They walked through a gap in the hedge to a lovely sunny spot filled with laden fruit trees.

'So, Miss Hollis, would you pour?'

Hannah looked away from the apple tree she was studying and swung round. 'You must be joking?'

'Why would I jest?' Tom was seated on a bench with his skinny legs crossed. He seemed far too comfortable.

'Why? How do you know I can pour?' Hannah stared into those blue eyes.

'I was under the impression that it was a basic skill that everyone had learnt by a certain age. Am I wrong?'

Hannah bit her lip as she picked up the delicate china. Her hands felt clumsy but she managed not to miss or overfill the little strainer. She held out the cup but he didn't take it.

'Hel-lo. Your tea,' she said.

'No, not my tea.'

'Not your tea? What are you on about?' she asked.

'My tea will be complete. Cup, saucer and spoon.'

'You're mad. We don't even have sugar. Why do you need a spoon?'

'To stir the tea,' he said.

Hannah blinked. She was stuck here holding out a cup like an idiot. Just do it his way then she could have hers simple. She took the saucer and placed the cup on it. There were no spoons so she trotted into the workshop to find them. They were just like the one in the tea canister: silver and intricately worked. Neat.

Back outside, she ran to the garden. No, orchard, it would be orchard if she was thinking like Old Tom. There were no flowers, just fruit trees, so it wouldn't be a garden. A tree root caught her foot and she hit the ground.

'There's no rush, Miss Hollis.'

'Hannah.' She brushed the grass off her jeans and then walked sedately to the table. The tea she'd poured initially would've gone cold. Would he take offence if she chucked it out and started again? Well, she hated cold tea, so she tipped it onto the grass, holding her breath. No complaint, so she began again.

'Milk?' Hannah studied him from under her hair.

'Yes, please, just a small amount. Lapsang is a very delicate tea and too much milk kills the flavour.'

'I'll need lots of milk then.' Balancing the cup, saucer and spoon carefully, she offered it.

'Thank you, Miss Hollis.'

'Hannah.' She poured her own tea, wondering if it would taste like the ashtray it smelled like. With cup only in hand, she leaned against the back of the wooden chair then threw a leg over the side arm.

'So, Miss Hollis, what brings you to Cornwall?'

'Call me Hannah. Miss Hollis makes me sound like some old school marm.'

'Is that a problem? Most old school marms, as you call them, of my acquaintance are delightful people.'

'Sure, but boring I bet.'

'Not at all.'

'Right. Not to you, maybe.' Hannah braved a sip and winced.

'Back to the question: what has brought you to Cornwall?'

'Bloody bad luck,' she said, frowning at her tea.

'No need to swear,' he said.

'I didn't swear.'

86

'You did,' he said.

'What? Are you talking about bloody?' she asked.

'Yes. It is a curse.'

'No,' she said.

'Yes.'

'Well, maybe in the dark ages it was, but it isn't now.' She began to wonder if she'd walked through a time machine when she'd come through the gate earlier. It was a nice one, though. The orchard was beautifully laid out and the table and chairs were a lovely weathered blue.

'Who advised you of this?' he asked.

Hannah sat up and put her empty cup on the table, not quite sure when she had drunk it. 'Look, it's a word that's used every day.'

'Yes, but does that change its meaning?' he asked.

'No, but no one takes it like that any more.'

'Who is no one?' he asked.

'I mean no one who hasn't lived in the dark ages.' She looked at his wrinkled skin and tried to guess his age.

'You mean anyone over the age of, say, sixty?' he suggested.

'Yeah, sort of.'

'Well, as I fit that category, could you refrain from using it?'

'Yeah, I guess. If it bothers you that much.'

'Thank you. Would you be kind enough to pour more tea?' Old Tom leaned back into his chair.

The sun wasn't coming through the east window when Maddie opened her eyes for the second time that day; instead, she found Mark standing at the end of the bed with a tray. She blinked.

When she last peered at the bedside clock, it had been eight a.m. and she'd thought that if she slept for another hour, she would begin to feel human. What a wasted day. What had Hannah been up to? Had she come into the room and seen her like this? Well, it was a lesson in what not to do in life.

The end of last night, no, this morning, was more than fuzzy; in fact, she didn't remember coming up to her room. The last clear memory was saying goodbye to Tamsin and Anthony. She and Mark had gone back into the kitchen and had another glass of wine or two.

'Good evening,' he said.

'It's not that late?'

'Almost time for a drink.' He smiled.

She winced. 'Oh, don't.'

'Would a bit of tea and toast help?'

'It might.' Maddie eased herself onto her elbows and then slipped back down again. She was only wearing knickers. Mark's eyes widened.

'Could you hand me that shirt on the end of the bed?' she asked.

'Certainly.'

She wrestled with it under the duvet.

'Sorry. I couldn't find your pyjamas last night.'

'What?' Maddie sat upright. 'You helped me to bed last night?'

He grinned. She felt the blood rush from repairing her hung-over brain to her face.

'Oh, God, what did I do?'

The grin became wider.

'No, what did I say?' Maddie rubbed her head. Things were going downhill rapidly.

Mark sat on the end of her bed and handed her the tray.

'You're enjoying this,' she told him. 'If I behaved with wild abandon and danced naked in the garden, please put me out of my misery and tell me, then allow me to wallow in self-loathing.'

His laughter started as a rumble in his chest and then burst forth. Maddie couldn't help but join him.

'That bad, was it?' she managed to say.

'Worse.'

'Dear God, did I proposition you?' She took a tentative sip of tea.

He coughed.

'Oh no. We didn't. I didn't. No, I couldn't have.' Maddie looked at Mark's smiling face. 'Did we?'

'No.'

'Phew.'

'Is the idea of sleeping with me that frightening?' he asked.

'Uh, I really hadn't thought of it.' She cast him a sideways glance. She was struggling with the idea of going on a date, let alone the thought of sleeping with someone. Closing her eyes, she thought back to the pub. Had she really agreed to have dinner with Gunnar?

'I'm really sorry for my behaviour, whatever I did.'

'Do you want to know?' he asked.

'To be honest, I'm not sure if I do.' Maddie swallowed. She was far too old to behave like this.

'As you wish. Just so you know, I slept in one of the spare rooms in the other half of the house.'

She rubbed her temples. 'Ran from my proposition?'

'Well ... I think I won't comment as whatever I say will be taken the wrong way.'

Maddie peered into her teacup. 'Hmmm.'

'Don't go all quiet on me now.'

'Did Hannah see any of this?' she asked.

'No.'

'That's a relief.' Maddie let her hair fall over her face so that she could try and read his expression from its protection. She looked around her room. There was no sign of her clothes. Panic began to grow. 'Mark, I guess I do need to know what happened.'

He raised an eyebrow. 'If you insist.'

'Yes.'

Hannah's voice erupted from the staircase. 'Hey, Mark. Your mobile's ringing.'

'Just coming.' He turned and looked Maddie in the eyes. 'I'll be back.' His hand stroked her ankle through the duvet and a tingling sensation raced up her legs.

The world had stopped spinning now that Maddie was seated at the kitchen table. Never again would she drink so much, she promised herself. She glanced up at Mark.

'How's Hannah been today?'

'On excellent form.'

'Good. I still feel awful about what happened to her.' Hannah's continued silence added to Maddie's guilt over hanging up on her. It grew every day.

'It wasn't your fault.'

'But if I'd listened to her instead of worrying about the police—'

'It's over and she's fine.'

'I hope so.' Maddie crossed her fingers and then hid them when she heard Hannah come into the room.

'So you made it out of bed?' Hannah asked.

Maddie eyed her over the rim of her cup.

'Earlier there was a call from that gallery.' Hannah looked at the ceiling.

Maddie's head shot up. 'Yes?'

'Yeah, well, I told them you couldn't come to the phone because you had your head down the loo.'

'You what?' Maddie stood quickly, nearly spilling her drink. Mark backed to the sink.

'Well, that's where you were from the sound of it at the time.'

Maddie collapsed in a heap on the chair and placed her head in her hands. 'Thanks. I can't fault your honesty but you may have lost me a sale.'

'I didn't say you were there because you stupidly drank three gallons of red wine last night.'

Maddie looked up. 'Thank God.'

'I said it was because you drank four.' Hannah stood up and waltzed out of the room.

Maddie's mind was reeling. How could she repair the damage that Hannah had done? Hopefully they would think it was a joke.

Hannah returned and slapped an old photograph album down on the table.

'You lied to me.'

'What?' Maddie rubbed between her eyes. Things with the gallery could be on the rocks and now Hannah was having one of her tantrums. This was her punishment for enjoying herself last night.

'You said you'd come to Trevenen for the first time this April.'

'That's right.' Maddie frowned.

'Bullshit. Here.' Hannah opened the album and pointed to a picture.

Maddie gulped. There she was in front of the big tree. But it couldn't be her.

'Here's the proof.' Hannah jabbed her finger at it.

All the blood rushed from Maddie's brain and the room began to sway.

'What the hell's wrong with you? Caught out in your lie and you go all faint?'

Maddie pulled the album onto her lap. Tears began to stream down her cheeks and Hannah backed away. Mark walked towards her. She tried to pull herself together.

'That's not me.'

'What the hell are you on about? Turn the pages and you'll see it's you. You as a teen. Geeky choice of clothes, though.'

Maddie blew her nose. 'Where did you find this?'

'In the desk in the room with the books. So you remember being here now?'

'I wasn't here. My mother was.' Maddie tried to comprehend what this meant, for there was no doubt that the girl in the photo was her mother.

'That's not your mother. She was short and fat.'

'That was my adoptive mother. This is Nancy Penventon, my birth mother.'

Hannah sank onto the table. 'You were adopted. You never told me.'

'I thought I had.'

'No, I'd remember that.'

Maddie vaguely registered that Hannah sounded disappointed. 'I'm sorry.'

Hannah shrugged her shoulders. 'Didn't you want to know about your mother?'

'I did, but I didn't know I was adopted until I was in sixth form.' Maddie could hear longing in Hannah's voice. She understood this. Hannah's mother's desertion must haunt her. Because of Maddie's own wonderful adoptive mother, she hadn't been left with anything but questions about her birth mother. There had been no shortage of love in Maddie's life. Hannah, she was sure, had been left with more than questions. Maddie wondered if Hannah blamed herself.

'Did you look for her? Meet her? Where is she?'

'In a graveyard in north Cornwall. She died giving birth to me when she was sixteen.'

'Whoa, just a bit older than me.'

Maddie nodded.

'Had you seen photos of her before?'

'No.' Maddie looked up at Hannah and watched her swallow a lump. Then, to Maddie's surprise, Hannah reached out and put a hand on her arm. Hannah hadn't voluntarily touched her since John had died. Great sobs racked Maddie's body.

Hannah backed away. 'I'm outta here.'

'Do you want me to stay?' Mark's voice seemed very far away as he handed her a box of tissues. She shook her head. She needed to be alone.

The room was in darkness and Maddie wasn't sure how long she'd been staring at the same picture. The window rattled behind her and Maddie turned to the first page again. Daphne, her lanky body clothed in dungarees, stood with a shovel in the garden. Her face seemed very familiar although much older than the creaseless one that followed Maddie around the hall daily. Daphne must be somewhere between forty-five and fifty in the photo. It was undated.

Maddie moved on with her hand shaking. Her mother had been here. She wasn't sure why this surprised her. Plymouth was listed as Maddie's place of birth on the certificate and she'd simply assumed that her mother had lived nearby. She'd thought her link with Trevenen was distant yet these pictures told a different story.

Before Maddie's eyes, Nancy looked awkward but beautiful, posed on the beach. Even in black and white, Maddie could see evidence of sunburn across her mother's shoulders. She carefully lifted the photo and turned it over. The year was 1970. Maddie tried to do the maths. Was her mother pregnant with her then? Nancy's body showed no signs, but then her own body hadn't either.

Who was her father? Had he loved her mother? Maybe it hadn't been love? Maddie caressed each picture of her mother as she went slowly through the album. Nancy's smile radiated more in every photo. No dark shadows clouded the clear eyes. Nancy looked to be in love, but with whom?

When Maddie had learned of her adoption and her mother's death, she'd wondered about her father but it was a dead-end. The birth certificate had stated: 'father unknown'. That was all her adoptive parents had had. Yet if she was honest, questions had lingered, but her life had been good and art school had beckoned, so Maddie had let go. She'd told herself that she had no need to know about the past; the future was what mattered.

Future? What did she have to look forward to now? Widowhood and a resentful teen? Maddie carefully placed the album on the table. Stretching, she touched the beams crossing the ceiling. She could see the old worm holes and scars from their rough-hewn origins. Everything around her spoke of the past. Somehow, she had to make this work. She needed something to look forward to. Life needn't end because she was alone. Maybe learning about her mother was a good thing and by finding the past, she'd be able to move forward.

Before Trevenen, her past had been simple. Was she destroying that? Was she betraying her adoptive parents by wanting to know more about her birth parents? Maddie rubbed her temples. Charles and Grace Smith loved her. All they'd asked of her was to be true to her faith. Maddie laughed. She'd failed them there, so discovering more about her birth parents couldn't hurt more deeply than what she'd already done.

'Trevenen, what other secrets do you have in store for me?' A shiver ran through her. She gazed out of a window to the tree. Her mother had stood just there, laughing for a photographer. Nancy had spent at least one summer here with Daphne. Who was she to Daphne? And who would have these answers?

❧ Seven ❧

Maddie kept glancing at the photo of her mother. She couldn't get enough. For someone who had let go so easily all those years ago, she now felt obsessed by it. She'd even taken a photo out of the album and put it in her sketch pad. Now, on this glorious day when she should be inspired by the beauty of her surroundings, questions about her conception filled her thoughts. What had happened? Who was her father? Where was he?

Although it was late October, it could have been August. The heat of the sun was strong as she leaned back against her pack and watched the sheep feed on the long yellow grass that covered Nare Head. There was no wind to cool her skin and the gentle sound of waves hitting the rocks below was enough to lull her to a sleep-like state.

'Hello, what have we here?'

Maddie smiled with eyes still closed, enjoying the sound of Mark's voice.

His shadow fell across her. 'Will a kiss wake the sleeping beauty, I wonder?'

Panic and excitement fought to pull her out of her sun-induced lethargy. She opened her eyes and his face was so near that she could see the length of his lashes. A smile hovered on his lips. A small movement from her would bring their mouths together. What did she want? Mark's flirtation was just his mode of operating, but she wasn't naturally that way so she couldn't quite account for her own behaviour.

'Hi.' Maddie fought for sanity. The heat of the day had seduced her even before Mark had arrived.

Mark pulled back. 'She wakes.'

Maddie blinked and forced a smile. 'I must remember to be careful. One never knows who will be wandering across the headland threatening to disturb my beauty sleep with a kiss.'

'Yes, instead of me waking you it could have been Nelly the sheep over there.'

Maddie laughed. 'What brings you out here?'

'The coastal watch station.'

Maddie cocked her head to one side.

'Their telephone's down thanks to new pole installation on the road and I was entrusted with a forgotten lunch.'

'Rescuing someone again?'

'You know me.'

'Yes.' Yet Maddie couldn't figure him out at all.

'I'll be back in a moment. Just being delivery boy.' He set off with long strides.

Watching him go to the hut, Maddie was surprised to feel a twinge of desire. She shouldn't beat herself up over that but recently she did berate herself for everything. She compared the sketch of Falmouth Bay on her lap to the view. At the moment, a red-hulled tanker was anchored and the contrast in colour was almost eye-watering. Her first attempt was pathetic.

She pulled out her oil crayons and a fresh sheet. Her fingers flew and, for a few minutes, no thoughts other than those relating to shape or colour invaded. Bliss. Total release.

Mark stood, studying her work. 'That was quick.'

Maddie glanced up. She hadn't noticed that he'd returned. These moments of escape were far too infrequent these days.

'It can be, sometimes.'

She dropped the paper and picked up the pad. With charcoal in hand, she roughed the outline of Mark's features. Her movements slowed when she came to his mouth. Using her thumb, she smudged the shadow below his lip and lingered. She stopped and looked up. His stare was intense. She swallowed.

This time, sketching hadn't transported her from the world, but had forced her back into it. She brought her hand to her mouth. His eyes followed her actions and then a smile appeared on his face.

'The charcoal looks far better on the paper but I must say you wear it well.'

Maddie laughed. Her fingers were covered in black dust and she knew her mouth must be the same.

He picked up the photo. 'She was very beautiful. Very like you.'

Maddie laughed and shifted her legs to a more comfortable position. 'Thank you.'

'Is it good to finally have a picture of her?'

Maddie began to say yes and then stopped. 'I don't know.' She stared out to sea. A sailing boat made slow progress in the light wind, no doubt frustrating the sailors, but at least it wasn't becalmed. 'The pictures are wonderful but ...' Maddie struggled. 'I can't help wondering if maybe I was better off not knowing anything.' She gave a dry laugh. 'That sounds terrible, doesn't it?'

'Not really. I do understand. Some things are best left alone because knowing the answers doesn't change anything.'

'True.' Maddie stood. 'Did you drive?'

He nodded.

'Can I catch a lift back with you?'

'Of course.' He smiled.

'You look happy.' Tamsin smiled at Hannah.

'Hmmm.' Hannah played with the heart on her necklace.

'Life here's not so bad, huh?'

'No comment.'

'Might this happiness have something to do with a certain someone coming home soon?'

Hannah looked at her hands. 'Wouldn't know what you're talking about.'

'Of course. How foolish of me. You look ecstatic because you're studying for a maths exam.' Tamsin kept a straight face and Hannah burst out laughing.

'Absolutely.' Hannah picked up her books and walked out of

Tamsin's back door. She didn't know why she was so excited to see Will again. It wasn't like they were friends or anything, but she did have to admit to herself that she was counting the hours. He was due back on Friday and there was a thing on at the sailing club on Saturday night. Not that he'd asked her directly, but through Tamsin's boys. She'd been thinking about going anyway. Otherwise there was bugger all to do.

She couldn't even distract herself with the internet. Maddie hadn't sorted it out and blamed it on the house, or more particularly on the house's wiring. So Hannah was stuck using the computers at school to communicate with the rest of the world. She was living in the bloody dark ages here.

Resting her backpack on the hedge, she pulled out her phone and read Abi's message again.

Snogged Andrew last nite. Brilliant. Know you fancied him but you're not here. Hope you don't hate me. x

Hannah chewed her lower lip. How did she feel? She punched in a reply.

Don't hate you. Feel left out not that I'm into 3some things. When are you going to visit? x

Before pressing send, she paused to look at the view. At this point, she was high enough to see the fold in the land. It was scattered with fields and a startling glimpse of the sea. Every time she saw it, it made something in her go *ping*. She guessed it was the unexpected beauty. The odd combination of nature and man – neat-rimmed fields, clumps of trees and the sea. Today it was so clear that she felt she could almost touch the water despite the distance.

It felt odd to admit that she'd never seen anything nearly as beautiful as this when she wandered around Fulham. The Thames was nice but it didn't take your breath away – that was down to the pollution. She laughed at her own thoughts and though she missed London, this place did beat it for beauty. But that was the only thing.

She hit the send button, picked up her bag and began to walk home, then stopped. Home. Was Trevenen home? No. It wasn't home, but then she didn't have one any more. Trevenen was where she lived for the moment. It was the thing that kept the rain off – just. No, that wasn't fair on it. Trevenen was interesting; she mustn't be too hard on the house. That pleasure she'd reserve for Maddie who had dragged her there. Yes, Maddie was responsible for everything, including Abi snogging Andrew.

Maddie threw a couple of skirts onto her bed. She didn't know what she was going to wear and she certainly didn't know why she'd said yes to Gunnar's invitation to dinner. Well, that wasn't true. He was gorgeous and surely that was reason enough, but she hadn't been on a date in so long. She mustn't wind herself up. It was just going out to dinner. Dinner was simple. She knew how to eat and how to make small talk. That was all that was required.

Maddie ran the water and poured the last of the bath oil that John had given her into it. Somehow she felt he'd approve. He'd asked only three things of her. The first was to look after Hannah – and she wasn't doing too well on that one at present. The second was that she continued to embrace life. Well, she hadn't done too well on that, either. She was quite the failure, except for the last request. That, she had done.

Once in the water, she enjoyed the scent of gardenias floating around her. Tears rolled down her cheeks unchecked. Caressing her arm, she remembered the last time they'd made love. It would've been almost comical if it hadn't been so sad. John was weak, too frail, yet they had anyway. They'd laughed and cried. He'd stroked her skin, as if trying to imprint love through each pore. He'd deteriorated so swiftly afterwards. That was just over a year ago.

She still didn't understand how he could love her so much yet leave her. How could he have asked what he had? It was all so jumbled in her head. He knew how and what she believed and yet he'd asked her to do the one thing she swore she'd never do. Now forgiveness was impossible.

The loofah scratched at her skin, getting rid of the old. She wished she could remove the painful memories as easily.

The soufflé melted in her mouth. Maddie would love to know how the chef had blended the crab, lemon and cheese in such a divine way.

'The starter pleases you?' Gunnar smiled.

'Very much so. It's so light yet so rich. Would you like a taste?'

'That would be kind.' He handed her his fork.

She filled it and wondered how she could have been worried about tonight. Gunnar's almost old-fashioned manner had made the start of the evening very easy. He took the fork from her and smiled. His eyes lit up. She wasn't sure how such a cold blue could express so much warmth. Maddie's stomach contracted in a very pleasant way.

Looking up from the table, Maddie saw Mark walk into the restaurant with yet another woman in tow. She grinned. Did he know how to be with just one woman? Somehow she doubted it and she wondered if this saddened him.

The touch of Gunnar's fingers on her hand brought her back to their conversation. They were smooth and they stroked her pale skin. She enjoyed the sensation and glanced up.

'Tell me about your painting?' he asked.

'That I haven't been doing anything but sketching?' She laughed.

'When did you know that was what you wanted to do?'

'That's easy.' She smiled. 'Always. My mother said I was forever drawing, painting and so on.'

'Never thought of being anything else?'

'No.'

The waiter arrived with the main course. Both of them had opted for the sea bass filleted and served on a celeriac mash.

'I love the food here.' Gunnar paused. 'They use local in-gredients so that you taste the area around you.'

Maddie blinked. She thought she understood what he meant. 'Yes.'

'This fish was probably caught just off the coast by the Manacles.'

'Manacles?'

'A treacherous reef just off the coast. It has caused many a shipwreck.'

Maddie's eyes widened.

'Yes, if you visit St Keverne Church you can see many of them listed. It is sad, but the reef is good for fishing. I was out there several weeks ago.'

She nodded. Shipwrecks made her think of Hannah being stranded.

'Is something troubling you?'

She blinked. She didn't want more guilt to ruin her evening. 'Nothing more than: do I have room for pudding?'

'We could share.'

'True.' Maddie studied her date as he spoke a bit more about his fishing trip on the Manacles, but she couldn't shake off the images of drowning people.

'I think you must be tired,' he said.

'Oh, that doesn't sound too good.'

'Not at all. Shall we go?'

She nodded.

Gunnar paid the bill and wouldn't hear of her wanting to share it. He could be a knight in shining armour except she liked the image of him as a Viking. He held her coat for her and Mark caught her eye. She turned to Gunnar. 'Thanks.' She led the way to the exit and waved at Mark.

Mark stood. 'Maddie, how lovely to see you here.'

'We've just had a wonderful meal. I hope you enjoy yours.' Maddie nodded her head towards the table.

'Have you met Natalie?' Mark asked.

'No.' Maddie smiled and extended a hand to the petite blonde.

'Hi,' Natalie said.

'Mark, have you met Gunnar yet? He's living in Manaccan.'

'Hello, Mark.'

She watched Mark size Gunnar up and noted that the Viking was taller, but not as broad in the shoulders.

'How's Hannah?' Mark asked.

'Fine.' She half smiled. She moved away as she saw the waiter approaching. 'Here comes your meal. Enjoy.' Maddie smiled vaguely at both Mark and Natalie before guiding Gunnar out of the restaurant with her hand on his lower back. She'd forgotten what a man felt like. How their flesh was solid. Just touching Gunnar, even so impersonally, brought memories back. Cold air hit her heated cheeks as they walked to the car.

'Thank you for dinner.'

'A pleasure.' He held open the car door. No one had done that for Maddie since her father had died. It was a small, gentlemanly action that he had always done. She was thankful it was dark and Gunnar couldn't see her. She swallowed a lump in her throat. Her father had been gone a long time. Why was it making her so emotional now? Big drops of rain began to hit the windscreen. Gunnar focused on the road and she gained control of her emotions. She'd had a lovely evening and that was what she needed to think about.

'Maddie, can you direct me to your house, please?'

'Of course.' His accented English was sweet.

Trevenen seemed to appear without warning. She was home. It was cloaked in darkness except for the light above the door. Hannah had barely spoken earlier other than to say she was going out with Tamsin's crew. She looked at her watch: ten. Still early.

The car had stopped and now what should she do? Should she ask him in? Was that too forward?

She turned to him as he held the car door open. 'Would you like a coffee?'

'I would love one but I am meeting some fishermen in the morning, which means five a.m.'

'Oh.' Maddie turned to leave.

'Maddie, believe me, I would love a coffee, but that hour of the morning seems to come too early.'

'True.'

Maddie turned when she came to the door. The rain had softened but she still felt drops running down her face.

'Thank you again for this evening.' She stood on tiptoes to kiss his cheek. Her lips tingled from the brief contact with his invisible five o'clock shadow. She paused, still close to him, enjoying his nearness, when she felt his head turn and his lips touch hers. Maddie didn't move; she couldn't.

'Have dinner with me next week when I don't have fishermen on the agenda first thing in the morning.' He spoke close to her ear.

'Yes, that'd be good.'

'Tuesday?' he asked.

'I think so.'

'If there is a problem, call me.'

She stood in the doorway and watched him climb back into the car. Once he was out of the drive, she traced her fingers over her lips. How could one innocent kiss send her all aquiver? She was too old for this nonsense. Nonetheless, she closed the door and leaned against it, wondering what it would be like to be properly kissed by the Viking. Maybe on Tuesday she'd find out.

'Hello?' Maddie saw a head peering around the stable door.

'Hi.' Maddie put her brush down and the stout woman came in.

'That's a lovely sky you've painted there.' The woman pointed to the canvas.

Maddie wrinkled her nose. She'd spent the morning trying to transfer the sketch from the day she'd spent on Nare Head into something, anything, but everything was flat to her.

'I'm Helen Williams and I got your message about Daphne.'

Maddie could barely push the word out. 'Yes.'

'You know, you've the look of her and of her niece.' Helen looked her up and down.

Maddie's eyes opened wide. 'Her niece?'

'Nancy,' Helen said.

'Did you know her?' Maddie asked.

'Yes, a bit. We were of an age. She used to spend the summers with Daphne.'

Maddie couldn't believe it: first the photos and now someone who had known her mother. Helen looked about the studio, taking in the details. Maddie wondered if she was remembering it from times past.

'Did you know Nancy's parents?' Maddie asked.

'Diggory, her father, was Daphne's brother and grew up here, but left to seek his fortune. Married some London woman. They never visited much. However, he'd send his daughter every year.' Helen sighed. 'Such a sadness for Daphne.'

'What was?' Maddie tried to follow.

'Losing Nancy, and then contact with her brother.'

Maddie shook her head. 'I don't understand.'

'Diggory blamed Daphne for the downfall of his beloved daughter. I suppose it was understandable that he and Daphne never spoke again.'

'Her downfall?'

'You're the product of Nancy's summer of love, are you not?'

Maddie nodded, her heart racing.

'Well, it became known that Nancy was in disgrace. Somehow, news like that travels quickly.' Helen gave a small laugh.

'Do you know who my father was?' Maddie asked.

'I wish I could say. Nancy was such a beauty, like you.' She smiled. 'All the boys were after her, but I can't remember her returning any of their affection particularly.' She paused and took a long breath. 'Except, of course, she spent a lot of time with Petroc.'

'Petroc?' Maddie's mouth went dry.

'Petroc Trevillion.'

'Do you know him?' Maddie forced herself to breathe slowly.

'Oh, I knew him very well. I was his housekeeper.'

'Was?'

'He died this summer.'

'I'm sorry.'

Helen nodded.

'Could he be my father?'

Helen looked hard at Maddie. 'I suppose it's possible.'

Maddie sighed. 'It doesn't matter anyway. It's too late to find out.'

'I knew Petroc all my life.' Helen walked closer to the painting on the easel. 'I wonder, I wonder.'

'He never said anything?'

'No, but it wasn't the sort of thing he'd have spoken about.' Helen smiled at Maddie. 'It would make you Tristan's sister.'

'Tristan?' Maddie thought about the man she'd met at the pub. He was tall and dark like her.

'Petroc's son. I suppose you could ask him for his DNA. That might answer your question.'

Maddie chewed her lip. 'Was there anyone else?' Maddie paused. 'It's just that before I approach a man I've met once to ask for a DNA sample, I'd like to know how likely it is that Petroc could be my father.'

'I'll keep thinking about it and ring a few people to see what they remember.'

'Thanks, Helen.' Maddie watched the woman walk around the studio looking at the paintings and sketches thrown about. Maddie really must do something to make the place more inviting.

'How did Daphne take all of this?' Maddie asked.

'Badly. She loved Nancy like she was her own. I think it broke her heart when your mother died.' Helen placed a hand on Maddie's arm. 'You knew none of this?'

'No,' Maddie said.

'It's good seeing the old house being lived in by a family again. It's just what it needs. Such a lovely home. Mind you, the Penventons have had their ups and downs over the years. But I think it's wonderful that you're here now.' Helen stopped in front of one of Maddie's older paintings of the Northumbrian coast. It had always been a favourite but from the look on Helen's face, it wasn't to her taste. Maddie knew better than to ask that question after all these years. No matter how tough-skinned she had become, it still stung when someone expressed distaste or disappointment.

'Is this your work?' Helen asked.

Maddie nodded. 'Do you know much about the Penventons?'

'Me, no, just that they've been around these parts for a long time and, like all families, have had their share of trouble. If you want to know about Daphne, Keziah Bates knew her well. She lives in St Martin. Now, I must be on my way. I'll let you know if I think of anything else.'

'Thanks.' Maddie waved and then picked up her brush. She knew without a doubt that she was well and truly part of the Penventon family's troubles. What she hadn't known was that coming here would reveal her mother's short life. Then there was poor Daphne taking the blame for Nancy's mistake. It all seemed so wrong.

✦ Eight ✦

The *pling, plink* of rain hitting the buckets distracted Maddie from her work. Her hands and feet were frozen. October shouldn't be this cold but the forecast said it would last another three days before normal weather patterns returned. Bring it on.

The stables as a studio seemed a good idea in the dying days of August, but with a north wind howling, she was going to have to find money fast to refurbish the piggery. First, though, the house's heating and wiring needed attention. Money. Focus. Get the damn painting finished.

The initial work had gone well yet she had lost the vision with just one week before it was promised. Those bright days painting on the Nare felt so distant with their clear air and colours so concentrated she could almost taste them. The resulting studies were vibrant yet the painting looked like mud. Where was her passion? How had she lost it in the translation from sketch to canvas?

Placing the brush in the turpentine pot, she wondered if she was using the wrong medium. Maybe acrylics would work better than oils. She rubbed the back of her neck as she flipped through her sketches, searching for something. Things had become so desperate, she was willing to contemplate just about anything so that inspiration would return; anything except prayer. She'd never seek solace in God again.

'Maddie?' Tamsin stood and shook her umbrella in the doorway.

'What brings you here on this filthy day?'

'Need of coffee and conversation.'

Maddie watched her examine the painting.

'Interesting.'

'Translation: dire mud pit.' Maddie didn't need Tamsin's expression to confirm what she herself knew. What was in her head was coming out in the painting.

'Well, I wasn't going to say it …' Tamsin smiled.

'Great. You make the coffee, I'll clear up a bit.'

'Sure.' Tamsin fled.

Maddie unscrewed a tube of crimson and squirted the entire contents onto the canvas. She stood back, wiped her hands and walked out the door. Once outside, the horizontal rain hit her in the face and she accepted that days of sideways rain could seep into your brain and bring you down.

'Time to spill,' said Tamsin when Maddie came in.

'When I defrost.' Maddie rubbed her hands together.

'It's not that cold.'

'It's damp and the stables are like working in a colander with wind and rain blasting through.' Maddie's knuckles were raw and she was sure her nose was red. The heat of the range didn't seem to make an impact on her.

'The house is big. Couldn't you work in here until spring?'

'No. First of all, it's not much better and second, there isn't a place big enough for the large canvases.'

'Fine. What about renting a space from someone?'

'Maybe, but I just want to work here.' She couldn't explain it, but she didn't want to leave Trevenen. It had wrapped itself around her. Maddie fell into a chair. What was she going to do? She couldn't paint. It was a disaster. Thirty-eight was a bit late to retrain to do something else.

'OK, I get the distinct impression that nothing is going to be a good idea today.' Tamsin placed a steaming mug in front of her. Maddie smiled and wrapped her hands around it.

'Are you going to tell me what's up? Is there a problem with Hannah?'

'There's always a problem with her.'

'True, but more than normal?' Tamsin asked.

'No.'

'That's a blessing, then.'

Maddie nodded, watching the steam twist up until it disappeared. 'How are your boys?'

'Diverting the subject from you? Hmmm. They're fine and filthy as usual. So what's wrong? Something more is troubling you than how cold it is in the stables. I've seen some of your other paintings and none are as dark as the one you've been working on. Spill.'

'I wish I could. I'm not sure what's bothering me.' But Maddie knew. She just couldn't vocalise what was chasing around in her head. Every night she lay awake, tormented, and then when sleep finally arrived, her dreams were warped with visions of John's shrivelled body. Each night it changed subtly. Each night it was worse. She would rise every morning exhausted, having been woken by the possibility of what could have been had she not acted.

'Maddie, are you with me?'

She tore herself away from the images etched into her brain.

'Maybe we need another boozy night,' suggested Tamsin.

'Good God, no. I've only just recovered from the last one.'

Tamsin chuckled as she pulled up a chair. 'Is it money? That can bring you low faster than anything.'

Maddie nodded. There were those worries too. This month's bank statement was a thundering reminder that there could be no more honeymoons from work. If she didn't find inspiration soon then she had better find a job – any job.

'Didn't Daphne leave any money with this place?'

'There was none once the taxes were paid.'

Tamsin nodded. 'You've become too locked in here. You need to get out more.'

'I've work to do.'

Tamsin blinked and Maddie could almost see the smoke coming from Tamsin's brain. She braced herself.

'I'm not sure whether that thing on the easel is something you are pleased with, but your time might be better spent finding out a bit more about who you are.' Tamsin took a sip of coffee but her eyes never left Maddie.

'I'm trying to but it's a balancing act.'

So many questions troubled Maddie. Had Nancy been alone when she gave birth? Had her parents disowned her? Why had she chosen to have her baby?

Tamsin reached out and put her hand on Maddie's. 'What were your adoptive parents like?'

Maddie sensed Tamsin was gearing up into full cross-examination mode.

'They were old, sweet, deeply religious and thought I was the answer to their prayers as they could never have any children of their own.'

'Religious? What type of religious? Bible bashing?'

'No, devout Catholics.' In the spare room sat three boxes of her parents' books, crucifixes and other paraphernalia that she couldn't bring herself to bin. She had so few items of theirs left that she had held onto these relics.

'You?'

'Not any more.' Maddie gave a dry laugh and felt her throat constrict. Leaving her faith shouldn't hurt but it did. She turned and looked out of the window.

'Did art school take it out of you?'

Maddie swallowed. What did one little lie matter now? 'Yes.'

Tamsin chuckled.

Hannah sauntered into the kitchen and slung her bag onto the table. 'Shit awful weather. I thought Cornwall was supposed to be warm.'

'Hello.' Tamsin smiled.

'Hey, Tamsin.'

'Cornwall's positively balmy. Haven't you seen the palm trees?' Tamsin asked.

'Bloody palm trees look great covered in sodding rain.'

'Good day at school?' Tamsin asked.

'What do you think?' Hannah grabbed a biscuit and left the room.

'She makes your life a joy. No wonder you're tired. I must be off as my lot will be home destroying it by now.' Tamsin threw Maddie a beaming smile and left.

Maddie closed her eyes. John's death had come so quickly in the end and even though she'd willed him to live, he'd just let go. He'd left her to fulfil her promises and he'd left her to grieve all alone.

It was half term and Hannah was bored. Maddie had mentioned a trip to London but for no obvious reason that was axed. Hannah had looked in the stables at the painting Maddie was working on and saw that it was very different from her previous work. The only good thing about it was a gash of bright red in the centre. Like someone's heart had been ripped open, but the blood hadn't started to flow. Neat in a way, but very dark.

Why had she woken so bloody early? It was six-thirty in the morning and the house was silent. Hannah tried again to avoid that damn squeaky plank on the landing but still managed to hit it. In the kitchen she grabbed an apple and then ran out the door. The peace of the early morning was almost spooky. The wind caressed only the highest branches as it whistled its way down the hill to where the stream trickled under the road. One of these days she was going to follow it to the creek, but not today.

Old Tom would already have been in the workshop for an hour. So if Hannah wanted to spend any time there, she needed to become an early bird too. It sucked, really, but she loved the feel of the wood and seeing the grain come to life. The broken box was looking much better and they were just waiting for a piece of oak to come from another restorer. Then they'd cut the tongue and groove fittings for the broken corner. The key, Old Tom said, wasn't to make it look like new, but to let the sympathetic repair be visible. It was weird. He showed her a good restoration and then one he was trying to fix. Before the visual demonstration she had argued with him, but with the evidence in front of her, she shut up.

Light glowed from the workshop but she didn't go there first. In the kitchen, she smiled and reached for the coffee. While waiting for the kettle, she took down the French bistro-style cups with their gold rims. From a drawer she took out the silver spoons with the coffee beans on the end. Next came the silver sugar bowl with brown sugar. From the fridge she took the milk and tipped a small amount into the silver jug. Pouring the boiling water over the grounds, she enjoyed the smell. It was something she'd never noticed before. For the last few mornings, she'd taken over this ritual from Old Tom. The first day he'd tut-tutted his way round; the one after that she pushed him back to the workshop so she could enjoy the freedom of exploring his kitchen.

Balancing the tray on one hand she walked across the garden.

'Good morning, Miss Hollis.'

'Morning.' Hannah placed the tray on the worktop. 'Are you ready for coffee?'

'Yes. Thank you.'

'Here or the summer house?' she asked.

'Here this morning, if you don't mind.'

'Sure.' Hannah pushed the tray securely onto the worktop and plunged the cafetière. Old Tom wandered to the sink and methodically washed his hands. Nothing was ever rushed. She could see why he'd remained a bachelor. She'd only spent a few days with him, yet at times his ways had nearly sent her over the edge.

'How is your mother today?' he asked.

'She's not my mother. She's my stepmother and she's fine.'

Hannah poured. Tom took the cup and she watched the bit with the sugar. First the spoon took a whole scoop, then it was tapped on the side of the bowl until it was exactly half. Why the hell couldn't he have taken half in the first place?

'How was your dinner out last night?' she asked.

'Excellent, thank you. What did you do?'

'I began the book you lent me on Tudor Cornwall. It's better than the one from school.' Hannah paused. 'When did you quit teaching?'

'Twenty years ago.'

'Why?' she asked.

'Academic life changed,' he said.

'Yeah, free sex and drugs. Sounds as if it would've been better.'

'It depends on your viewpoint and besides, that particular change was earlier.'

'Must you be exact in everything?' she asked.

'Why not be, if one can?' asked Tom.

'I don't know. Gets boring, I guess.'

'Never.'

'If you say so.'

Hannah watched Old Tom glance at the clock. He was a mystery. If he'd retired twenty years ago, did that mean he was eighty-five? He looked pretty good, but surely he had to be younger or he wouldn't have the strength to do some of the woodworking? She watched him step up to a piece of wood and start sawing it. Old Tom's movements through the wood were slow. He stepped back for Hannah to take over. The first day he'd done this, she'd rushed and ruined a piece of wood by splitting it. Now she knew that haste was fine for rough wood that didn't need finesse but delicate wood needed a gentler touch.

The handle felt warm and smooth in her hands. She didn't feel clumsy as she pushed and pulled the saw to a slow rhythm in her head. Old Tom stood and watched before he turned to another piece of work. Once he was sure of her, he'd never corrected her again and let her move at her pace and that of the wood.

'Maddie?' Hannah walked down the stairs holding an old book and bumped into Maddie coming out of the sitting room looking wild-eyed.

'*Hello*, you have a weird look on your face.' Hannah stopped right in front of her. 'What have you been doing?'

'Nothing. What on earth are you reading?'

'A book on smugglers in Cornwall. You know this house is sorta at the start of Frenchman's Creek.' Hannah waved the book about.

'Is it?'

'Where've you been this last month?' Hannah paused. 'No, don't answer that. Anyway, it is and I was looking through this book on smuggling and wondering if we had any secret rooms?' Hannah was sure there must be some concealed room or passages in a house this old, this big and this close to a known smugglers' route.

'Since when are you interested in smugglers?'

Hannah almost snorted. 'Nothing bloody else to do here, is there?' She watched the corners of Maddie's mouth twitch. 'You must lack all natural curiosity. You didn't do much research on your mother or your father and now you have this great old house ...' Hannah's voice trailed away.

'That's not quite fair. I did research my mother and I've no idea who my father is.'

'But the fact that you looked nothing like your mother, the one I met.'

'Oh, well, I actually looked like my father.' Maddie smiled. 'He was tall and dark like me. Nothing to be curious about.'

Hannah frowned. 'I still don't get it. How could you not be suspicious?'

'I had no reason to question it.' Maddie paused. 'Maybe you're right. Maybe I lack curiosity or possibly I just become absorbed in other things. Do you wonder about your mother?'

'Whoa, enough of the self-revelation stuff.' Hannah put her hand up. She didn't want to talk to Maddie about her mother. 'I just want to know if you'd found anything suspicious.'

'No.' Maddie shook her head, then a funny expression appeared on her face. 'Wait. A while ago I heard a scratching sound in the sitting room.'

'So, we have mice.'

'Yes, we have mice.' Maddie smiled but turned and walked back to the sitting room. Hannah followed and watched with an open mouth as Maddie went straight to a panel by the fireplace. She tapped a few times and then ran her finger around the edge of the panel. A door opened.

⋆ Nine ⋆

Dust clouded the air and Maddie coughed. The door was small, consisting of two panels which came only as high as Maddie's chest.

'Cool.' Hannah stood by Maddie's shoulder.

'Yes, it is.' Cold air circled Maddie's ankles. 'But I wouldn't get too excited just yet; we can't see anything except cobwebs.' Maddie pulled one off her hand.

'I'll go and get a torch.' The excitement in Hannah's voice was contagious. Maddie stepped back and pulled the door wide. The light in the sitting room didn't go very far into the recess. A few woodlice moved about the edge of the slate fire surround.

About to turn on the lamp, Maddie spotted a candle. She took the matches from the fireplace and lit it while she waited for Hannah to return. Holding it in front of her, she bent to go through the door.

The flame flickered in the draught and the hairs on the back of her neck rose as a crying sound filled the small space. The candle blew out. Something dropped onto her. She jumped and knocked her head as she backed out of the door.

'Hey, wait for me.' Hannah stood with hands on hips.

'Sorry, you were taking so long.'

'Yeah, right.'

Maddie rubbed the back of her head. 'Not much that I could see.'

'You look very white.'

'Must be the dust.'

'No, like you've seen a ghost.'

Maddie shrugged. 'No ghost, but …' She paused and put

the candle down. 'I do feel as though someone has walked over my grave.'

'Weird. You died and I didn't notice. Let me have a look.' Hannah pushed past. Maddie waited while she heard Hannah whistle.

'Cool.'

'What is?' Maddie hoped she wouldn't have to go in and look at whatever it was.

'This.' Hannah came out with a small round ball in her hands.

'What is it?' Maddie asked and Hannah handed it to her. The weight of it nearly caused Maddie to drop it.

'Not sure but I'd guess it's a cannonball.'

'Really?'

Hannah nodded.

'Why would there be one in there?'

'Beats me,' said Hannah.

'Anything else?' Maddie asked, turning the metal ball over in her hands and enjoying the feel of the uneven surface.

'Yeah, something that looks like a gravestone.'

'A what?'

'Are you too spooked to come and see?' Hannah laughed.

Maddie swallowed. 'No, lead the way.'

'Can't as the space is too narrow for two of us.'

'Fine.' Maddie held out her hand for the torch. She knew that other than insects, the odd cannonball and maybe a mouse, there could be nothing in there. The sound she'd heard must be the sound of the wind.

She bent through the doorway and slowly stood. With the light from Hannah's torch she could make out the large stones that made up what had once been the back wall of the house and the chimney. No outside light penetrated, which Maddie took as a good sign. The air smelt of earth mixed with damp and something she couldn't put her finger on. It might be a hint of flowers but she wasn't sure. The walls were cold to the touch. It felt like a tomb. The space, although two foot wide and ten foot long running around the chimney, seemed to close in around her.

Air disappeared. Maddie gasped for breath.

'All OK in there?' Hannah called.

'Yes, just coming out.' Maddie rubbed the goose pimples on her arms.

Maddie twisted her hair up yet again and pushed a paintbrush through the knot. She hoped it would hold. It distracted her every time she began to feel she was heading in the right direction. In the past, she wouldn't have noticed a herd of elephants in her studio, but now every creak of the roof, let alone her wild hair, was enough to pull her out of her work.

She smiled. John used to come in at the end of the day and say he could stand in front of her stark naked and she wouldn't notice unless he was what she was actually painting. He'd been right. One day he'd stood close, nibbling her neck and caressing her, yet she had been completely oblivious until she finally came out of her trance, as he called it.

Maddie swallowed. They'd made love then and there on the cement floor of the studio. Crazy. Wonderful. Gone. She blew her nose on her paint rag, which, the moment she'd done it, she knew had been a mistake. Without looking in a mirror, she could tell her face was covered in various shades of green.

'Greetings, oh Martian woman.' Mark leaned against the stable door and held up his hand in a Spock-like fashion.

Maddie laughed. 'Live long and prosper. Green paint's the key, didn't you know?'

'Damn, that's what I've been doing wrong all these years.' He stood straight as she came closer. 'Joking aside, how are you?'

'You mean other than a face covered in paint and a canvas not?'

He nodded.

'Fine. Why don't you put the kettle on while I go and remove the damage and then you can tell me why I have been honoured with your presence.'

Maddie watched him turn to the kitchen while she escaped with the turpentine. Green paint wasn't too bad for the complexion but turps was another thing. It was all she could do not to scream when she saw her reflection, red-rimmed eyes complete with a green nose and mouth. It was a wonder Mark hadn't run from the stables at the sight of her.

Why had she suddenly remembered one of the good times with John? It had made a pleasant change but, good or bad, she didn't want to think about him or the past. She dabbed her face, revealing blotchy skin beneath. The green was more attractive. She splashed her face in cold water and pulled the paintbrush from her hair, hoping her mane's chaos would disguise a bit of the disaster it surrounded.

Mark handed her a mug. 'Successfully de-Martianed?'

Maddie nodded, noticing that he didn't have blotchy skin or look like he'd fallen off the back of a lorry. Despite the cloudier weather of the past week, he still had a glowing tan. She needed to get out more.

She smiled. 'As you're here, would you have a look at a secret room we've discovered?'

'A secret room?' he asked.

'Well, hardly a room, more a dark space behind the chimney in the sitting room.'

'Lead on.' He fell into step behind her.

Maddie swallowed as she released the catch on the door.

'Torch?' he asked.

Maddie handed him the one she'd left on the mantelpiece. She stood back and watched him disappear. She looked out of the window at the tree. Its branches remained perfectly still. Mark emerged from the door, looking dusty but undisturbed.

'Standard smuggler's stash, I'd say. The chimney needs re-pointing in the near future.'

'Because of the noise it makes?'

He frowned. 'No, because of the fire hazard.'

'Oh.'

'Been making noises, has it?'

She nodded. 'Is it safe for the moment?'

'As long as you're not using it, I should think so.'

'That's a relief then.' Maddie sank on to the sofa. 'What brings you to Trevenen?'

'I need an excuse?' He affected a hurt puppy look.

'Yes.' She smiled.

'Well, then, just chasing your application for the sailing club.'

'Oh.' Maddie paused. 'It's in the kitchen. I was holding off until I knew there would be enough money in the account.'

'Things that tight?'

'Yes. I'm waiting for some funds to be released that are locked in a fixed term, which should make things easier.'

'Self-employment has its benefits, but the downside can be cash flow.'

'Too true.' Maddie laughed. 'I imagine that work for architects is a bit steadier.'

'Compared to artists, definitely. Well, even if you haven't got the funds at the moment, get the app in with a note as the committee meets on Friday. You don't want to have to wait for the next one for approval.'

'OK.'

He looked at her closely. 'You aren't yourself.'

Maddie smiled, hoping to distract him. 'You're right. Just struggling to find a routine.' She looked around. 'Especially when I haven't had one for so long and, well, I guess in new surroundings ...'

'Don't be so hard on yourself.'

She took a deep breath. 'Easier said than done but I'll try.'

'Promise.'

'I don't make promises any more but I will try.'

'Yes.' He smiled. 'I have to be off. Next stop: a redo for a bungalow in St Keverne.'

'Enjoy.'

'Will do. See you around.'

Maddie watched him leave and couldn't shake the feeling she'd let Mark down in some way. She couldn't make any more promises because she always kept them and the ones she'd made most recently had cost her far too dearly.

Maddie smiled as she heard Hannah singing at the top of her lungs in the kitchen. Maybe for once their moods matched.

'You've a good voice.'

'Crap,' Hannah said.

'No, seriously. Do they have a choir at school?'

Hannah looked hard at Maddie. 'You've totally lost it now.'

'Have I? Just because I mention that you can sing?'

'Yeah. Go and have your ears tested.'

'Fine. I'll remember not to compliment you in future.' Maddie turned to the fridge and pulled out a head of lettuce. She ripped the leaves off it.

'It'll be better that way. If we don't talk, then we can't argue.'

'If that's what you want.' Maddie ground her teeth.

'Yeah, it's what I want.' Hannah walked out of the kitchen and then turned. 'By the way, I'm out tonight.'

'With whom?' Maddie took two paces closer to Hannah.

'None of your business.'

Maddie took a deep breath. 'It is my business. You're in my care, like it or not.'

'Just get lost. You really don't care, anyway.' Hannah thrust her shoulders back.

'Now, just a minute—' Maddie put the piece of scrunched lettuce down.

'No.' Hannah turned and walked to the door.

'Hannah, get back in here.' Maddie held both hands down by her sides.

Hannah spun around. 'Fuck you.'

'That's enough. I've had enough of your attitude!' Maddie shouted.

'Tough shit. I don't give a toss,' Hannah said, opening the front door.

Maddie raced to her.

'What do you want?' Hannah swung around to face her.

Maddie's hand flew up to strike, then she turned and walked back into the kitchen. Grabbing a saucepan, she threw it against the wall.

'Why do you hate me?' Hannah asked.

Maddie stared at the wall. She couldn't speak or even move. She heard Hannah leave. Maddie shook all over. She didn't know what to do and she sure as hell didn't know what had come over her. Anything could ignite her at the moment with her emotions flying in every direction. Glancing at the phone, she knew she needed to talk to someone and Tamsin was the only person who might possibly understand.

'I nearly hit her. I was shaking with rage.' Maddie's voice wobbled.

'It's OK. You didn't.' Tamsin spoke softly.

'No, I bashed the wall and broke the handle off my favourite saucepan.' The wreckage lay in front of her. How could she lose control like that? What was she thinking?

'All repairable. That wouldn't have been the case if you'd struck her.'

'I know, I know. I was in such a good mood, too.' She had a date tonight with Gunnar and she'd been looking forward to it.

'What happened?' Tamsin asked.

'I came in and said she sang well.' Maddie sniffled.

'There you go, then. You were nice.'

Maddie laughed and then blew her nose. 'Sorry.'

'No problem. Come over for a cup of tea.'

'Can't. What if she comes back?' Maddie asked.

'Don't you mean when?'

'Well, yes, I suppose so. Where do you think she went? What if she runs away?' Maddie felt a sense of panic set in.

'Slow down. You had a row. You didn't cast her out.'

'No, all I wanted to know was who she was going out with. Was that unreasonable?' Maddie asked.

'Of course it was. You should've asked me. It's with Matt, Will and Emma. They're going to Helston to the cinema.'

'Why couldn't she just have told me?' Maddie rubbed her temple.

'Because that would be telling.' Tamsin laughed.

'I don't understand.' Maddie had done everything for Hannah and yet most of it Hannah would never know. Maybe she should just tell her how she'd used all of her inheritance and sold her mother's jewellery for the last drug for John. Would Hannah understand then?

'She'll cool off. She wants to go out and I doubt she's dressed for it so she'll come home to change.'

'Oh.' Maddie played with the edges of the newspaper.

'Don't panic. Fighting is normal. I used to fight with Mum all the time.'

'I never did; mine was too old and frail.'

'Poor you. It's one of the key rites of growing up.'

Maddie walked over to the window. No sign of anyone. She stopped in her tracks when she realised that she was relieved not to see Hannah. How could she feel this way? Why was she so angry with her?

'Thanks for listening. I still don't know what to say when she comes back.'

'Simply repeat the question. That's all.'

'What if she starts the slanging match again?' Maddie asked.

'Ignore it and then tell her you know who she's going out with anyway. It's a small world here.'

Maddie laughed. 'I'll have a bath and hopefully she'll return.'

'Yes, you've a hot date tonight.'

'Nonsense. Gunnar and I are going out for dinner. Hardly a hot date.' Maddie twisted a loose strand of hair around her finger. This was their third date.

'Time will tell.'

'You're incorrigible.'

'Exactly.' Tamsin hung up.

Maddie didn't know what she'd do without Tamsin. Everything she'd said made sense. The woman was such a good mother, but then she'd had the chance of learning the skills from day one, not inheriting a child with issues. Was that the problem? John had doted on Hannah and he'd done everything with Hannah in mind. Would he have done the same for their child? Maddie wanted to believe that he would have, but she couldn't shake the doubt chasing around in her brain after what he'd asked of her.

The temperature outside had dropped like crazy and despite the warmth of the pub, Hannah still couldn't shake the chill. Fred was at the bar, Will was playing pool with Matt while Emma had disappeared to the loo. Hannah knew that Matt and Emma had been an item for a while and she wondered what it would be like to have a steady boyfriend. Her past history told her nothing, but since her dad had died she'd been looking for something more.

Will would be a bad choice. He was away too much and he was Mark's nephew; two strikes, as the Americans say. Now she just needed to find a third and then she wouldn't even have to think about him. She had better find it quick because every time he smiled at her, she went weak at the knees. Had she been this stupid before? Or was it just a Christmas thing? All the mistletoe and stuff tended to make people think of kissing. And she wanted to kiss Will – a lot.

'Hey, do you want the next game?' Matt called to her.

'Yeah, all right.' Hannah walked to the table where Matt was leaning on his cue while Will lined up a shot. Unfortunately it gave Hannah a good view of Will's butt, which was great even in the baggy jeans he was wearing.

He sank the last three and Matt handed her the cue.

'Good luck. Don't let him win too much money,' he said.

'Thanks.' Hannah called to Will, 'what are the stakes?' She put chalk on her cue.

'Let me think. I just won a couple of quid from Matt so I don't need money. How about a kiss?' Will smiled.

'That's if I lose. What if I win?' Hannah told herself to be cool. Had he been reading her mind?

He walked slowly to the other side of the table, never taking his eyes off her. 'What do you want?'

What did she want? She wanted to lose. 'How about the money you won off of Matt.'

'Deal. You break.' He set up.

Shit, even though she wanted to lose, she didn't want to make a fool of herself. Her palms began to sweat. The cue kept sticking as she pulled it back and forth. Double shit, this was a nightmare, but she looked up at Will and smiled as she took her shot. She held her breath until all the balls stopped and then stood back from the table.

'Well done.'

'Thanks.' Hannah watched him move around the table, assessing it. He seemed so calm and she was all nerves. The clunk of his shot brought her attention back to the current problem of how not to lose face. He lined up the next one and Hannah began to feel she might not even have another go. Was this what he was studying at school?

'Your turn.' Will grinned.

The table looked a mess. She had no idea which one to go for, but it didn't matter. She planned her shot and closed her eyes until the dull thud caused her to open them wide. Jumping up and down, she did a happy dance around the table. A big smile swept across Will's face.

'Well played,' he said.

'Yeah, I bet you thought I'd be a walkover.'

'No, but I'd like to see you play with your eyes open.' He coughed.

Caught. Bugger. He'd been watching. She pulled her shoulders back and went to the other side in search of inspiration. It was as clear as mud. Anything she hit would just make it easier for him. Head held high, Hannah picked one and hoped for the best.

'Your go.' She stepped away. He nodded in her direction and bent to his task. Maybe if she coughed he'd mess up and she'd win, but she didn't want to. She wanted to kiss Will more than she'd wanted to kiss any other boy she had ever met. This was not good. He managed another four before it was her turn. Why was she bothering to try? She didn't know, but she was damned if she was going to give up completely.

Taking the cue, she said a little prayer. She had success with two before she missed. There weren't many left and he made short work of them. Her stomach flipped.

'You win,' she said.

A slow smile spread across his mouth.

'You knew you were going to.' Hannah swallowed.

'Yes.' His eyes were wicked.

'Crap.'

Will laughed and went to join the others. Hannah put the cues back and thought about this. He wanted to kiss her. That was good. She wanted to kiss him. That was bad. When would it happen? She schooled her face into a smile and joined the others.

'That game took some time.' Matt's arm was draped over Emma's shoulders.

'Yeah. You know what he's like.' Hannah cast a glance towards Will.

'Sure do.' Matt laughed. 'Hate to be the party wrecker but Emma has to be home in five minutes. Drink up.'

Hannah looked at her Coke. She needed something stronger. Payment of her debt was coming, or at least she thought it might be. The others began to go and she followed. By the time she reached the car, her heart was racing. It was only a kiss, she reminded herself while she was wedged into the back seat next to Will. Every one of her nerves was alert.

When Emma left, Hannah slid across the car seat. She looked up and gasped. Will's eyes were intent on hers. His hand reached for hers. She swallowed, trying to think straight. He was cute. He was here for Christmas, then not until his next break. What did she have to lose?

'Hey, Fred, you can drop me off at Hannah's and I'll walk from there.' Will smiled at her.

'You sure? It's bloody brass monkeys, mate,' said Fred.

'I'm sure.'

'OK. See you tomorrow then. Bye, Hannah.' Fred looked in the rear-view mirror.

Hannah could swear she saw Matt wink at Will.

'God, it's cold out here.' Will stepped closer.

Hannah fumbled for the key in her pocket while light poured out of the kitchen window. 'Do you want to come in for a bit?' Her throat felt dry and the words didn't sound right.

'That would be good.'

'Yeah.' Hannah pushed the door, shed her coat and saw no signs of Maddie. 'Come into the kitchen. Would you like something to drink?'

'Sure.'

'Beer, tea, cocoa?' Hannah's teeth were chattering a bit.

'Cocoa sounds good. You're frozen.'

'Yeah, it'll pass. Can you hand me the milk?' She pulled out a saucepan and stretched to reach the drinking chocolate in the cupboard. A sudden sensation of warmth indicated that Will stood behind her. She felt his breath on her neck. His hand found the bare skin at her waist. She almost dropped the stuff. She turned. His fingers trailed across her back until she faced him. Strange things were happening.

'Hi,' he whispered.

Hannah saw the flecks of yellow in his eyes as words deserted her. He was going to kiss her. His mouth came closer. It teased hers. She put her hands out to steady herself and found his shoulders. He moved nearer still and the heat of his body met her shivering form. Finally he kissed her. She moved her fingers up his neck to his hair. His hands caressed her skin and she felt little shivers rippling everywhere. Kissing had never been like this before.

❧ Ten ❧

Intricate ice patterns covered the inside of the kitchen windows while Maddie's breath made little clouds in the morning light. Still wrapped in her duvet, she surveyed the debris strewn across the kitchen table. There were two cups. She wondered who'd been here with Hannah. In the sink Maddie found a frying pan that was still warm. Was Hannah up and out already? Well, it was nine-thirty so it wasn't that early.

She searched for her slippers, with the passing thought that if Gunnar had spent the night then keeping warm wouldn't have been a problem. What was she thinking? She'd never slept with a man she barely knew. But maybe now was the time to try.

Shivering, she knew she must do something about the heating or she'd be reported for child abuse, or she and Hannah would die of frostbite before the winter was over. Her feet were still frozen even with slippers on so she dug into the laundry basket to find her woolly socks. Her strappy nightdress wasn't designed for a draughty old house.

She hummed 'The First Noel' and tried to find the seasonal spirit while she pulled on her socks. Looking up, she found Mark standing in the doorway. Maddie stood too quickly, then tripped and promptly fell into a heap on the floor. Mark extended a hand to help her up.

'Thanks.' She wondered why he always looked so bright-eyed and satisfied with himself and then remembered the probable reason. Her smile disappeared. 'What brings you to the frozen wasteland?'

'The cold, actually.'

'Really.' The steam from the kettle rose into her hair, making it even more unruly.

'Yes. Knowing your heating situation, I remembered I'd some spare space heaters and thought you might need them.'

'What would give you that idea?' She let her teeth chatter.

He looked her up and down. 'The latest in duvet fashion.'

She pulled it tighter around her shoulders.

'You like it?' Maddie attempted a twirl but a corner caught one of the kitchen chairs and Mark had to save it from hitting the floor.

'Yes, but only on a bed.'

His look and the tone of his voice as he said those words stopped her breathing. She blinked and the look was gone.

'My room's so cold I couldn't bear to dress in there.'

'I'll put one in your room and one in Hannah's and then I'll take you up on the coffee you're about to offer me.'

He disappeared and Maddie set about making the coffee. It wasn't long before Mark walked back into the kitchen.

'Hopefully the room will defrost in the next couple of hours. I took the liberty of picking up some clothes for you.'

'Thanks.' She looked at the jeans and the thick sweater. She'd need that and more if the day continued as cold as the morning promised.

'I'll go for a walk in the garden if you want to throw them on.'

Maddie gave him a wry smile. 'Thanks. It should only take a second. Why don't you admire the frosty view?'

Mark chuckled. She loved the sound and its effect on her spirits. Once he'd stepped out of the kitchen, Maddie reluctantly shed the duvet and put on the icy clothes.

'Coast's clear,' she called.

'Have you looked outside yet?'

She shook her head.

'Come.'

Pulling the duvet back over her shoulders, she joined him on the doorstep. The sun sat above the horizon, catching the frost on the leaves in a silver glow. The hydrangea heads by the back door were crystallised.

'Breathtaking,' Maddie murmured.

'Yes.' Mark wasn't looking at the flowers when he said it, but at her. Her heart stopped.

'You're shaking.'

'Yeeeesss.'

'Inside.'

She nodded. Steering her to the range, he rearranged the duvet. He took her hands in his, surrounding them, then he brought them to his mouth. His breath teased her icy fingers. His lips were so close. She longed to touch them. Her eyes met his. The heat in them began to spread all over her. In fact, her backside felt particularly hot, unnaturally so.

'Mark, I think my bottom's on fire.' Maddie leaned away from the range and into Mark as she tried to see.

'Let's have a look.' He pulled her closer still so that the whole length of him was against her. Her eyes opened wide as she felt his arousal. She placed her hands on his waist to steady both of them but the action did nothing for her equilibrium.

'I've done many things in my life, but to date I've never set a woman's bottom on fire, or at least not in the literal sense.' He laughed and she joined in.

'I bet.' She dropped the duvet and saw the scorch marks across it. A slightly acrid smell filled the space between them.

'That was close. I'm feeling warmer though.' Maddie threw the duvet over the far end of the table.

'In all seriousness, when are you going to do something about the heating in the house?' he asked.

'I don't know when I can.' She gave a derisive laugh.

'It won't be as bad as you think. To renovate the whole house would cost in the region of forty thousand pounds, excluding the roof. You could get a mortgage.'

'Get a mortgage on this place? You have to be joking.' She looked around the kitchen, loving the way nothing was straight or even.

'The house is worth well over half a million. You've land, too.'

Looking at him now, the heat had left his eyes and it was all business. She missed the warmth. 'Banks don't like people with erratic incomes.'

'True. You could sell the land.' He sat in one of the armchairs by the range.

'I doubt that a few acres of agricultural land could be worth forty thousand.'

'You've an old shed on one of them. You may be able to get planning permission to convert it into a house and then it would be worth much more than that.'

Her shoulders sank. 'I wouldn't know where to start.'

'I do.'

Maddie walked to the other armchair. 'Really?'

'Of course. I'd be happy to help.'

'Thanks.' Maddie took a sip of the coffee and then made a face.

'What's that for?' he asked.

'Sorry. This is terrible.'

'Yes.' He smiled.

She frowned. 'Why didn't you say something?'

'Too polite.'

Maddie burst out laughing. 'Well, actually, I suppose that's true.'

'Your view of me is outstanding, I see.'

'Oh, Mark. Don't take me too seriously. Life's all upside down and I don't know what to think any more.'

'Really.' He leaned forward and stared at her.

She fiddled with a piece of hair. 'Yes.'

'How?'

'Well, I'd thought that things between Hannah and me would get easier as time passed, but I was wrong. When I married her father, I bought into the whole family thing and I thought it was working, but since he's been gone, she's taken every opportunity to pull further away.'

'You've tried talking?' he asked.

'Yes, to the wall. Yesterday I complimented her then asked

130

where she was going out and with whom. You'd think I'd asked her deepest thoughts. She flew off the handle and then I behaved even worse.' Maddie dropped her head.

'She confides in Old Tom Martin.'

'Who's he?'

'He's a retired professor who lives a mile down the road.'

'So, how and why?' she asked.

Mark paused. 'I sent her there with something that needed to be repaired and it seems they hit it off.'

'What needed repairing by a professor?' she asked.

'Oh, just an old wooden box. He plays with restoration now.'

'And Hannah's been going there every day?' She just couldn't make this information match up in her mind.

'Yes.'

Maddie frowned. 'Does he do drugs or something?'

'Ye of little faith. He's an old-school sort who drinks two whiskies a night. I think that's as bad as it gets,' he said.

'Really?'

'Don't look so stunned. Tom's great company and Hannah's bored.'

'That's an understatement.'

'You're hard on her.' Mark smiled.

'Am I?' Maddie shrugged.

'Yes. She's had it rough.'

'Ah, so bad: she has a home, someone who loves her, and food on the table.'

'That's not what I meant.'

'Well, it's true. Many kids have a lot less than she does.' Maddie's hands formed fists.

'Don't get so fired up. You'll wear yourself out.'

'I just get tired of "poor little me". She has had it tough. Yes, her mother walked out on her. Yes, her father died. But hell, she still has me. I guess therein lies the problem.'

'Don't know about that. All I'm saying is cut the kid some slack. She's not all bad. Just mouthy.'

'You don't have to live with it.' Maddie sighed. She shouldn't have said anything.

'No, I don't, but at least she's confiding in someone.'

She looked up. 'Is she?'

'Yes. They may seem an odd couple but Tom and Hannah work together peacefully.'

'I'm glad. She needs someone. I'm just sorry it's not me.' A dry laugh escaped from her.

Mark leaned over and placed a hand on her knee. It was a friendly gesture but Maddie still remembered the passion in his eyes only a few minutes ago.

The house seemed so empty once Mark had left. To fill the void, Maddie began cleaning the one room she hadn't touched at all. It looked sad now that she'd painted so many of the other rooms, yet with its book-lined walls it had appeared in the best condition when she had arrived a few months ago. It was funny how perceptions changed.

Maddie set about dusting. She pulled a copy of *Pride and Prejudice* off the shelf. The leather was cracked on the binding. She opened it to the title page and found that the book had been awarded to Daphne for a poetry competition in 1937. She would've been about Hannah's age. Maddie wondered if Hannah had read it and decided that she'd put it by her bed so that they wouldn't have to discuss it. It would just be there. Maybe they both just needed more time. After all, John was not yet dead a year and no one could say how long grief lasted or how it would affect people. She'd have to keep trying to talk to Hannah.

Maddie was already in Hannah's room before she considered the possibility that doing so wouldn't be a good idea. She hadn't been in it since they'd moved the wardrobe. Walking quickly to the bed, she stopped in her tracks. There was a pile of old documents on the floor. Maddie could see they were fragile and fading in places.

Where had Hannah found these things? Why hadn't she mentioned it? Maddie sifted through the pile and then picked up an old exercise book. She flipped through the pages and gasped when she read the date: 2nd July, 1970. The first page stated that this was the private property of Nancy Penventon. Maddie turned to the next.

2nd July, 1970
Trevenen

It's so good to be back at Trevenen and to have celebrated my birthday here. Aunty Daphne had made the most delicious cake and somehow found sixteen candles to put on it. She looks well and is as brown as a nut from working in the garden. P came round after dinner and we joined up with everyone on the beach. He's grown about a foot and is so handsome.

Who was P? Petroc? Maddie closed her eyes and then opened them to begin reading again.

The big change at Trevenen is that there's a lodger in the stables. He's a painter from America and Aunty said she could use the extra money. I caught a brief glimpse of him and his accent is divine. Haven't met him properly yet, though.

Maddie stopped. Did she want to read this? What would this diary reveal? Would she be better off not knowing? Then the thought struck her: had Hannah read it and not told her? She gripped the book until her fingers went white. How could Hannah be so selfish? She clutched the book.

'What are you doing in my room?' Hannah stood in the doorway.

Maddie spun round. 'Just when were you going to tell me you had my mother's diary?'

'Answer my question first. This is my space. You've no right to come in here.'

'Oh yes I do. This is my house and you're in my care. I have a right. I've every right.' Maddie's heart beat hard against her chest.

'Just because of the bloody courts. I should've gone to a foster home. Maybe I should've tried to find my mother.'

'Maybe you should have.' Maddie bit her tongue. She hadn't meant that, had she? Where the hell was this going? Why did Hannah always make it her fault when she was the one who'd been hiding Nancy's journal?

'Too bloody right. Get out of my room.' Hannah pointed at the door.

'Not until you explain why you haven't told me about my mother's diary.' Maddie glared at Hannah, feeling hatred build up inside. She didn't want to feel this but nothing she could think of could stop the bile turning inside her.

Hannah's face went red. Maddie didn't know what to do. She couldn't back down.

'I—'

'Yes?' Maddie waited, holding her breath.

'I never looked in that book.'

'What?' Maddie sank into a chair. Could this be true?

'It was boring compared to the other stuff in there so I never read it. You can have your mother's damn diary. I don't give a fuck. Now just get the hell out of my room.'

Maddie stood, began to walk and then stopped. She turned to Hannah, who was looking out of the window. Maddie wanted to reach out to her but couldn't. She dropped her head and left the room.

In her hands she held her mother's thoughts and in her heart she knew the cold fact that Hannah really hated her. Hannah must if she wanted to find the mother who had deserted her. God, Maddie had messed things up. It wasn't supposed to be like this. She'd married the man she'd loved and he'd loved her. Where had it gone so wrong?

Hannah needed to get away from the witch. How was she supposed to know the grotty old book was Maddie's mother's diary? If she had, she'd have given it to Maddie. What did Maddie think she was? Hannah slammed her door shut and stomped downstairs. There was no sign of Maddie as Hannah left the house.

Her stepmother wasn't happy. She'd become a bitch supreme. Hannah just wasn't sure where Maddie was getting off going into her room and then flying off the handle about the diary. She hadn't been the same since they'd moved here. This place was doing strange things to her.

The road was lightly covered in frost and the sun was breaking through the tangle of branches above. As she thought about Will and seeing him tonight, Hannah couldn't remember when she'd been this happy. Her step would've been light but with the road this icy, she'd just fall on her arse.

Last night had been wonderful. Someone had taught Will to kiss really well and that thought made Hannah pretty pissed off. Yet the kissing had been wicked. She would gladly lose at pool any day to be kissed like that again. If she was lucky, that could be tonight.

The gate to OT's drive was a bit stuck with the frost. It took a good whack with her hip to get the damn thing to budge. Smoke rose from the chimney on the house but no light came from the workshop. Hannah's steps quickened. The kitchen door was unlocked as usual but there was no sign of OT.

'Hellooooooooo.' She turned on the kettle. 'Hellooooo.' She walked through to the sitting room. Lights were on.

'Mr Martin, are you here?' Hannah looked at an open book beside a chair. He couldn't be far.

'Yes. I've had a bit of a fall.' He sounded breathless. She raced up the stairs. OT was sprawled on the landing.

'Are you OK?'

'Not on top form, I'd say. Quite a lot of pain in the hip area that worries me.' Each word came with a wince.

'Don't move while I call for help.' Hannah ran down the stairs, punched in 999 and waited. It took ages for the voice to come through. She didn't know what she'd rambled on about but she was told to stay with OT and to keep him warm.

Hannah hung up and then called Maddie. She'd know what to do.

'Maddie, I need you here now. OT's had a fall and we're waiting for help to arrive.'

'OT? Speak slowly, Hannah.'

'Old Tom Martin. I need you here now.' This was not a time for Maddie to be thick on her.

'On my way.'

Hannah took the throw off the sofa and raced to OT. He looked paler but still alert. 'Hi. They're on their way. I'm going to put this on you.'

'Did they say how long?' he asked.

'No. The roads aren't great at the moment. So I'm to keep you warm and to keep you talking.' She prayed it really wouldn't be long because he didn't look good at all.

'Fine.'

'How did it happen?' she asked.

'I spilt some tea and then slipped on it.'

Hannah saw the effort it was taking him to speak. Maybe he could just listen. He could stay alert that way, couldn't he?

'While I have your full attention, I think we have a smuggler's hiding place at Trevenen.'

'Possible, considering the age of the house.' OT grimaced and she knew the pain had to be bad. There must be something she could do. Why wasn't Maddie here yet?

'Good. It's quite cool the way you have to know where the catch is to open the panels.'

'Panels?' He tried to smile.

'Yeah, panels, and it's quite a big space and it has a strange slate floor.' She paused as OT grimaced. 'Maybe it'd better wait. I think I hear a car.' Hannah tried to listen but OT's breathing was a bit loud. That ambulance had better come quickly.

'Hello?' Mark called up the stairs.

Hannah looked up from OT. Why was Mark here?

'Maddie's just coming.' Mark took the stairs two at a time. 'Hello, Tom. Doesn't look good.'

'No. I think the hip's gone.' OT's voice was faint.

'Well, let's hope it's just a bad knock and not broken. Here's Maddie.'

Maddie walked upstairs and Hannah watched her survey the whole scene. The landing wasn't big, especially now that Mark was here.

'Hello, Mr Martin. I'm Maddie Hollis.' Her long arm stretched out to OT's. He squeezed her hand.

'A pleasure.' OT's breathing was more laboured.

'Aside from the hip, is there any other pain?' Maddie asked.

'My shoulder, which took the second hit,' OT said.

'Nothing else? Head?'

'No.'

'Good.' Maddie gave Mark a look. 'If I may, I'll go and find another blanket to put on you. Shock will be setting in and we don't need you shaking too much.'

OT smiled weakly. Hannah knew that Maddie would know how to handle this. She'd been brilliant with Dad. Had she just thought that? Maddie – good at something? This shock thing must be getting to her as well. Shit, she couldn't go soft on Maddie.

Mark's face looked dark and serious. Did he know that she was out with Will last night? Suddenly that seemed a long time ago.

Maddie returned with an old eiderdown in her hands. She laid it carefully over OT. He looked so frail, like he was ageing in front of her eyes.

The phone rang. Mark went to answer it. Maddie sat close to OT, holding his hand in hers. She took his pulse.

'Hannah, would you see if you can find some cushions? I think I might be able to make Mr Martin a bit more comfortable.'

'Sure.' Hannah's legs were stiff from sitting in an odd position. Mark was still on the phone as she passed. It sounded like he was giving directions. She wondered why they didn't have GPS. An ambulance should, shouldn't it? Thank God he was here. She couldn't have done it by herself.

Maddie shifted in the plastic seat. She felt Hannah's fear at being in the hospital. This had been one of the reasons they'd chosen to care for John at home.

Hannah looked up, eyes wide. 'How long did they say they'd be?'

'It shouldn't be much longer. I doubt we'll be able to see him.' Maddie glanced at the clock on the wall. She wasn't too keen on hospitals either. The clinical smells brought back memories she didn't want to dwell on.

Hannah played with her hands. 'He looked so awful when they took him away.'

'He was in tremendous pain.' Maddie turned to Mark. 'Does he have any family?'

'No. Well, not anyone close,' Mark said.

'Who will look after him?' Maddie asked.

'I expect they'll keep in him in for a while and then bring help in.' He sat down opposite.

'How awful. People you don't know, in your home looking after you.' Hannah stood and paced about the room.

'It's better than not being in your own home.' Maddie watched her circle until she sat down.

'True. At least Dad was with us.'

Maddie reached over and touched Hannah's hand. Hannah started to pull back but stopped.

'Are you the next of kin for Mr Martin?' a young man in hospital greens asked.

'Yes.' Mark stood.

'He's fine. The break was clean and we've reset it. He's very lucky, considering—'

'Yes,' Mark interrupted the surgeon. 'No other damage?'

'Just heavy bruising along his left side.'

Maddie studied Mark, trying to assess why he'd cut the surgeon off.

'He's in the recovery ward now if you wish to see him. He's groggy but awake. Don't stay long; he'll need his rest.'

'Thank you.' Maddie touched Hannah's shoulder. Hannah's eyes were filled with unshed tears.

'Shall we go and see the old codger?' Mark asked.

'Don't be so rude, Mark,' Hannah snapped.

He laughed out loud as they walked along the corridor to the ward where they found tubes coming out of every part of Old Tom, but he did look better.

'Hello, old man.' Mark walked up to the bed.

'Hello.' Tom's voice was barely audible.

'How are you?' Mark asked.

'Been better.'

'I'll bet.' Mark smiled.

Hannah pushed Mark out of the way. She wasn't holding back the tears now. In her young hand she cradled his old one with the intravenous drip hanging out of it.

'Get better,' she said.

'I will.' Tom's eyes closed.

'Get some rest.' Hannah kissed his wrinkled cheek. 'Love you.'

Maddie held back her own tears as she listened to Hannah's quiet words.

Hannah had crawled into bed and Mark had just left. It'd been one hell of a day, thought Maddie as she poured herself a whisky and sank into a chair in the kitchen. She picked up her mother's diary and wondered if she'd the strength to read it. Yet she knew that these pages could shed light on what she'd never dared to hope to know.

> Played spin the bottle on the beach last night and I got to kiss P. That was the first time. At first it was strange kissing such a good friend but we tried it again as he walked me home. It got better.
>
> The lodger's from California and he's really handsome. He's very polite and spends most of his days out by the river painting. I stole into the stables to see his work. It has vast swirls of colour yet I could feel the sea.

Maddie wondered if Helen Williams had discovered anything. This old notebook could hold the answer but it might not.

Seeing the pictures of Nancy had certainly explained who she looked like. Pieces were falling into place yet she felt like she was coming apart. She took a sip of the burning liquid. Part of her wanted to rush through the pages and another wanted to hold onto each word. She closed her eyes and pictured her mother in Penarvon Cove. She needed to know more.

> Spent hours on the river sailing with P. I can talk to him so easily. He loves Cornwall as much if not more than I do. Maybe we should marry in a few years and then we'd never have to leave.

The next page was water-damaged and Maddie couldn't read the top half.

> I spent the day on Denis Head with him. He was so absorbed in what he was doing, I don't think he knew I was there half the time. However, at lunch he talked and asked me all sorts of questions about my life and what I wanted to do. No one aside from Aunty Daphne has ever listened to me before. His hazel eyes danced when he laughed, which he did when I said I wanted to be an actress. He said I'd need to move to California then and become a film star. I told him I didn't want to do film, but stage. He went quiet for a bit and looked at me differently, like he was just seeing me for the first time.

Maddie stood and walked around the kitchen. Her mother wanted to be on the stage. Well, Maddie hadn't inherited that from her. She was terrified when she had to speak in front of too many people. She sat and found the next legible passage.

> The day was very hot and the cove totally deserted. I was desperate for a swim, but hadn't brought my costume. He'd already taken off his shirt and rolled up his jeans. I kept looking at the water over my book. He finally said he wouldn't look if I wanted to skinny dip. All I could think of

was that I wanted him to join me. I didn't care if he looked. I wanted him to look at me.

Maddie wasn't sure she should be reading this. It was too private. She closed her eyes. She couldn't read any more tonight.

❧ Eleven ❧

The curator at the museum had been most helpful when Maddie had presented the cannonball. He hadn't been able to say without a doubt, but it looked to him like one that may have been used in the Civil War. He mentioned that it wasn't unusual to find them in houses around the Helford. When Maddie had looked blankly at him, he'd pointed her in the direction of books on the war. He'd continued to oblige her by telling her where she could begin to find out more about Trevenen and the Penventons.

She placed the pile of books from the library on the window seat and then searched out the latch for the hidden door beside the fireplace. A book on the history of the Helford River had mentioned smuggling and she'd immediately thought of the concealed room. This extension had been added sometime in the late 1700s and it might not have been used by smugglers. There was the possibility they just used the space to store wood. Maybe she should do the same. Winter was approaching and they would need all the help they could get to keep the house warm.

A small click and the door slipped open about an inch. A spider hung down in the thin, dark opening. His legs moved swiftly to recover his web and stash of dead insects. Maddie moved into the space but the torch wouldn't turn on. She stopped. She couldn't move. Her skin went clammy. Something seemed to grab her but nothing was there.

Stepping backwards, she blinked and hoped that sanity would take hold of her again as she shut the door. She was imagining things. She sank onto the window seat, knocking off the books. The sound echoed in the silence which filled the room now that the door was closed. Maddie's heart attempted to beat itself out of her chest.

Trevenen had no ghosts. The house had a good feel to it. Her fingers worried the worn velvet of the cushion, trying to smooth out the ripples on the surface. She was just jumpy because she was tired and had been reading old tales. That was all. The sounds were nothing more than the wind pushing through the dodgy pointing on the chimney.

Collecting the books, she placed them carefully back on the seat and took one last look at the fireplace with the panels surrounding it. If it hadn't been for the mouse, she'd never have known about the hidden space. She turned away and decided that fresh air was needed.

Once standing in the garden, a cold breeze cooled her cheeks. Her imagination was running away with itself and her nightmares were entering her days. She would go for a walk right now and hopefully the exercise would help her to sleep tonight.

Coming back in, she announced, 'There are no ghosts.' But she still didn't feel convinced. Looking at the picture of the Penventon women on the walls, she continued, 'No spirits to haunt me either, just goodwill.'

Standing outside the restaurant in Manaccan, Maddie rubbed her sweaty palms on her skirt. She pulled open the door. Surely she'd nothing to be nervous about. She scanned the room. Gunnar wasn't there yet. 'Hello, there's a reservation in the name of Gunnar Karlsson.'

'Yes. Would you like to have a drink at the bar or go to the table?' the young woman asked.

'Table.' Maddie twisted the fringe on her scarf as she followed the waitress across the busy room. She sank into the chair, realising she was tired. For the past few days she had thought of nothing but men; in particular Gunnar, Mark and Old Tom. She'd been to the hospital with Hannah daily. Tom was improving and if they were lucky, he'd be home for Christmas.

Christmas. She glanced at the decorations. This time last year

John was clinging onto life. Everything about Christmas would now be a constant reminder to Hannah. She must be suffering. How should Maddie handle this? How could they mark the holiday and remember John yet move on with their lives?

Lost in thought, she looked up and saw Gunnar standing head and shoulders above a group at the bar. The flickering lights caught the sheen of his hair. He was so handsome, and he was looking for her. Maddie pinched herself.

'It's good to see you.' Gunnar bent to kiss her.

'Thanks.' Maddie was finding it hard to breathe.

'It's been a crazy few days. How were yours?' he asked.

'The same. Spent a good deal of the past few days visiting a friend at the hospital.'

'That doesn't sound good.'

'No, but not as bad as it could've been. How was the filming last week?'

Maddie watched his eyes as the candlelight played off the darker blue flecks in them and she didn't hear a word of what he was saying. Somewhere in the middle of the story they ordered. Maddie slipped her scarf off and leaned forward. She could see that with his storytelling techniques, he was a natural for his chosen profession.

'Have you been painting at all?'

Maddie nearly choked. 'No, I would die of cold in the stables at the moment. It's bad enough in the house, but there is no real protection out there. So I've done nothing more than a few small watercolour sketches in the kitchen.'

'In your only warm room.'

'Well, yes. Mark's loaned us some heaters so Hannah and I aren't freezing at night.'

'Mark? Is he the man we met? He is a good friend, yes?'

'Yes.' Maddie sat up. The Christmas lights came back into focus.

'That is kind of him.'

'Yes, it is.' Maddie smiled, acknowledging Mark's ability to reach out to everyone, yet no one in particular.

'So your bedroom is not too cold now?'

Maddie blushed as she caught the intonation. Was he going to come and check the temperature? They might have to turn the heater off if the promise in his eyes was anything to go by. Was she ready for this?

'It's bearable.'

He smiled.

'Would you like to see the dessert menu?' The waitress had appeared out of nowhere. Maddie's mind was still tangled with thoughts of Gunnar in her bedroom.

'After all that wonderful food?' Maddie patted her stomach. 'Definitely not. Do you have room?'

'Would you join me with some chocolate fondant?' he asked.

If he smiled at her again she might do anything he wanted. 'I'll have a spoonful.'

'I hoped I could tempt you.' He grinned.

'Just a bit.' Maddie sipped her wine.

Was he talking about the pudding or something else? Gunnar took a spoonful of the dessert and held it in front of Maddie's mouth. His eyes were saying something entirely different from the simple offering of food. She savoured the rich flavour seducing her taste buds. Colour rushed to her face.

'Have you had enough?' he asked.

Enough what? Fondant or him? Maddie collected her thoughts.

'Yes.' She caught the last bit of chocolate off the corner of her mouth with her tongue and smiled.

'Did you drive?' he asked.

'No, I had a lift. Do you mind taking me home?'

'A pleasure.'

As they stepped into the dark, rain soaked Maddie to the core before she reached the car. The windows were fogged, making the Christmas lights outside look like huge glowing balls. She didn't know how to interpret the chaos in her mind and body. She was out of practice with seduction.

'Is your stepdaughter home?' He drove carefully through the lanes.

'Not yet, I should think. She's been out every night this

week. The holiday spirit has set in. Are you heading home for Christmas?'

'Yes. My mother is alone and my brothers can't make it so I will leave on Friday. Weather permitting, that is.'

'Yes, they say it could turn nasty.' Maddie surveyed Trevenen for evidence of Hannah. None. It would be safe to invite him in.

'Coffee?'

'Yes, I would like that.' He turned to her and smiled.

Maddie dashed to the door through the downpour before Gunnar could assist her.

'It's terrible out there. A bit colder and I bet it would snow.' She shook off her coat and hung it to dry on the back of the kitchen door.

'I can't imagine this landscape in snow.' His head just cleared the beams.

'No? Very different from Norway, I guess.' She moved to the warmth of the range. 'Coffee, tea, a brandy?'

'Brandy sounds good.'

'Yes, it does.' She slid past him to the sitting room where she kept the liqueurs on an old butler's tray. The windows were fogged with frost and a draught blew down the chimney. She glanced at the panelling and shivered.

Slightly breathless on her return, Maddie knew she must look drenched and wild. There was nothing she could do at this point so she should relax. Gunnar, lounging in the chair by the range reading a country living magazine, was the picture of ease.

After pouring the drinks, she turned and he rose as she walked to him. She knew he had to be a good six foot five because near him she felt petite. John had only been an inch taller than her. She frowned. Why did she have to think of John just now?

'Thank you.' Gunnar's fingers lingered on hers as he took the glass. 'Cheers.' His eyes looked into hers and then he raised the glass again in a little salute. Her heart missed a beat.

The brandy tasted like fire warming her yet she was already feeling the heat. Gunnar stood near and she wished she had

146

a sofa in the kitchen; it would be much more comfortable. A gust hit the house with a thud and a piece of paper blew off the counter. Maddie leapt to collect it and collided with Gunnar.

'Sorry.'

'No problem.' His hands didn't let go once he had steadied her.

She was caught. Her breathing became shallow. She tried to bend to pick up the paper. It only brought her closer to him. The smallest fraction of space kept them apart. She considered pulling away. This was too soon. John's face appeared. He haunted her dreams and now her dates. Yet as her head advised caution, her body moved closer.

He lowered his head. Her eyes closed. The touch of his mouth was a whisper against hers. It was making promises. She began to respond. Gunnar's hands travelled from her arms to her back. She leaned against the table. His fingers moved along her spine while his mouth trailed kisses to her cheek.

'What the fuck's going on in here?' Hannah's shrill voice pierced the haze filling Maddie's brain.

'Hannah!' Maddie tried to gain a little distance from Gunnar but she had the table behind her and couldn't go anywhere. 'This is Gunnar Karlsson.'

Gunnar stood to his full height, making Hannah look like a seven year old. He held out his hand to her.

'You've got to be joking.' Hannah laughed.

'Hannah!' Maddie snapped.

'Hello, Hannah. I am your mother's friend.' Gunnar spoke slowly.

Hannah crossed her arms against her chest. 'She's not my mother.'

Gunnar turned to Maddie

'You're splitting hairs, Hannah.' Maddie tried to keep cool.

'I'm not. You're not my mother.'

'Well, let's thank God for some things,' Maddie muttered.

Hannah glared at Gunnar. 'She's my stepmother.'

'Ah, I see, but still your parent.' Gunnar walked closer to Hannah.

'You see nothing.' Hannah spun around and disappeared.

Maddie sank against the table.

'She's a handful,' he said.

Maddie nodded, feeling all her energy drain away. 'That's an understatement.'

'It's probably best that I leave now. I will call before I fly.'

'That would be nice.' She looked at her hands, wondering how the atmosphere in here could have changed so quickly. The warm fug of passion had been replaced by polite distance. Gunnar walked over to her and kissed the top of her head. She fought back tears and smiled at him.

'I'll walk you to the car,' she said.

'In this weather?' He stroked her cheek. 'No. Go and get some rest, Madeline.'

'Yes.' She nodded. 'Happy Christmas.'

He was gone and Maddie stared at the empty kitchen.

'Bah humbug.'

She picked up her mother's journal and walked upstairs. Once in bed, she opened it. The corners of the paper were yellowed and smelt musty. She pulled the duvet tighter around her and angled the pillow before settling into her mother's world. Whatever had damaged the previous pages had bled through and Maddie couldn't read much of the entry.

I stripped off my clothes and ran to the sea. I could feel his eyes watching me. Never before had I felt so alive. I dived straight into the cold water and every nerve sang. It wasn't long before I felt him beside me. His strong strokes took him out to where I was near the rocks. He thought the water was too cold, but I thought it was perfect. He's perfect.

Maddie blinked. Things had moved on from spin the bottle. There were no more entries for almost a week.

The school bus dropped her at the top of the lane where Will stood waiting. Hannah smiled and he took her backpack.

'Free at last,' Hannah said.

'Not for long.' He laughed.

'Don't rub it in that you've got longer holidays.' She tapped his arm.

'It makes sense. My parents pay a fortune so I can go to school less.'

Hannah felt her legs go weak as he took her hand. Once they were in the cover of the lane, she knew he would drop the bag and kiss her. It was almost worth going to school to come home to this.

'You and Maddie speaking yet?' he asked.

'No.' The magic bubble disappeared with the mention of her name.

'I think you're being hard on her.'

'What do you know? She's a tart. She was practically having sex on the kitchen table with some blond bloke last night.' Hannah grimaced.

His eyes lit up. 'Really?'

'Well, I don't know, but it looked that way.' She pulled away, but his hand held on tighter.

'Should we try?' he asked.

'Yeah, right, you wish.' She jabbed him in the ribs.

'Yeah, I do.'

'In your dreams, mate.' She laughed.

'That's right.' Will pulled her into his arms and began kissing her neck. She melted against the wall. His hard-on was pressed against her and she squirmed, enjoying the sensation of power. Hannah brought his mouth back to hers. His tongue chased hers and she thought the world was spinning.

'Get your tongue out of her throat, mate, and I'll give you guys a lift.' Fred leaned out the window.

Cold air blasted Hannah's heated body when Will stood straight. She pulled her top down from where his hand had been. He picked up her bag and Hannah climbed slowly into the car.

'Mum told me to get you because Maddie's gone into Truro to collect Old Tom. You had your mobile switched off.' Fred pulled out into the lane.

'What's up?' Hannah leaned as far forward as the seatbelt would allow.

'We're off to Old Tom's house to give Mum a hand re-arranging things.'

'Great.' Hannah idly stroked the hair on the back of Will's neck as she watched the scenery pass. It was no longer frosty, which was a shame. It didn't really feel like Christmas when it wasn't cold.

The sky was dark when they drove up to the cottage. Tamsin shouted to them as they walked through the kitchen door.

'What did you say, Mum?' Fred immediately began foraging in the fridge.

'Out of there, Fred. I need help in here, please.' Tamsin's voice squeaked.

Hannah dashed into the sitting room to see Tamsin struggling with a tree. Hannah pushed it back upright.

'Thanks. It was in danger of collapse. Did I hear Will too?' asked Tamsin.

'Yes.' Hannah smiled.

'What are those two great lumps doing?'

'Hunting and gathering,' Hannah said.

'Typical.' Tamsin sat back. 'That should stay up now. Must have the place looking a bit Christmassy for Tom.'

Hannah glanced around. 'You've worked wonders. Have you been cleaning all day?'

'Nearly. Now I need those two buffoons to move a bed down into the dining room and the table into the workshop. Preferably without damaging anything.'

'Good luck.' Hannah didn't think they could be persuaded.

'That's what I thought, too. However, I have a secret weapon. I've a chocolate cake hiding in the car. Fred was tearing the house down trying to find it.'

Hannah followed Tamsin into the kitchen. The kettle was on, the biscuits were out and the two boys were sprawled at the table.

'Up, you two. Did you think you came here for tea?' Tamsin raised an eyebrow.

'Muuuum,' Fred drawled out in protest.

'I need help. We have work to do,' she said.

'I'll make the tea.' Hannah watched Fred drag his feet. Will stayed behind and placed a kiss on the back of Hannah's neck as he left. A shiver ran up her spine. She was going to miss him when he went back to school.

The teapot was in its usual place. Hannah stroked the surface then pulled down the tea and started humming 'The Twelve Days of Christmas'. She couldn't shake the image of Will every time she got to 'my true love gave to me'. She wasn't in love. She was in lust. Love was precious and not to be tampered with. You could play with lust, and boy was it fun.

'Hey, Hannah, can you come for a minute?' Fred's voice interrupted her thoughts.

'Yeah.' The dining table with its gleaming surface was now in the sitting room, perilously close to the tree which Tamsin was pulling to one side.

'Can you pull the sofa back and then we can leave this in here,' said Fred.

'Sure. But I think it'll be too crowded.' Hannah moved it.

'Yes, but we damn near scratched the thing taking it out of the dining room. We don't want to move it further than we have to.'

'Why don't you take the base off and it shouldn't be a problem?' She smiled sweetly at Fred.

'OK, smart arse, you have a look under there so we can put the fucking thing down,' Fred grunted.

'Fred, language.' Tamsin's stern tones emerged from the tree.

'Sorry, Mum.'

Hannah slid under the table to look at the fixings. It would take two seconds to separate the top from the bottom. Men! Totally useless.

Will joined her under the table. 'Thought you might need a hand.'

'Yeah?'

He slid over and kissed her. Maybe they weren't useless after all.

'When you two have stopped snogging under there, could you tell me what we need to do?' Fred's feet were visible at the side of the table.

Hannah laughed and Will slipped out.

'She needs a screwdriver.'

'Really?' asked Fred.

'Kids, enough.' Tamsin came out from behind the tree.

Heat rushed to Hannah's face. It was quiet and safe where she was, but she would have to go to the workshop.

'I'll just go and get it.' She crawled out.

'Need help?' Will was right behind her.

'Yeah, pour the tea,' Hannah called over her shoulder as she marched into the cold air.

Mark's car had just pulled up. He waved while he grabbed bags of groceries out of the boot. Hannah wondered if Will was going to be as tall as him. You could tell they were related, despite the eyes. Will's were blue/green like his dad's. His dad wasn't from Cornwall but an import. Hannah knew she didn't look like she belonged in Cornwall at all. Her blonde hair and blue eyes looked more Anglo than Celtic. She looked like her dad. Well, she thought she did. She had no photos of her mother to go on. When her mother had left, her dad had destroyed them all. She could understand why he'd done it, but she wished that he hadn't.

On entering the workshop, Hannah was greeted by a damp smell and a fine layer of dust that had settled on the worktop. Tomorrow she must come in here and clean. OT would be disappointed to see this place looking so unloved.

Dashing back out, she bumped into Fred carrying bags.

'You got the easy job,' he said.

'Yeah, I did. It's what happens when you've brains and no brawn.' She smiled and walked past him.

'Cow,' he called out to her.

Hannah laughed as she went into the kitchen.

'Has one of Malcolm's cows broken through into the garden again?' Tamsin asked as she filled the fridge.

'No.' Hannah smiled and hit Fred in the ribs with her elbow.

'Just a passing comment, Mum.' Fred grinned.

'That wouldn't be you being rude again?' his mother asked.

'Aw, Mum, you know me so well. Just two more bags and I'm done. Did Mark buy enough to feed an army or what?'

'If you guys stick around, it'll only just be enough,' Tamsin said.

Fred left Hannah and Tamsin alone in the kitchen. The door banged behind him.

'How do you think Old Tom will feel about the rota of people streaming through his house?' Hannah took one of the cups of tea.

'Better than having a stranger in the house, as you said yourself to Maddie.'

Dunking a biscuit, Hannah studied Tamsin. She looked like a mother should except for the short hair, which made her seem a little too trendy.

'How serious are you and Will getting?' Tamsin asked.

'That's a bit direct.' Hannah's eyes opened wide.

'That's me.' Tamsin shrugged.

'It's just fun, that's all.'

'Holiday romance?' Tamsin asked.

'If that's what you want to call it.' Hannah had wondered herself what it was.

'Just checking.'

Hannah put her hands on her hips. 'Was Maddie asking?'

'As a matter of fact, no. She hasn't even mentioned it. I just hear things from the boys.'

'So what are they saying?' Hannah sank against the counter.

'Just that you're an item and that you're spending a lot of time together.'

'That's bad, is it?' Hannah asked.

'Not at all. It's just me being nosey.'

'That's OK then.' Hannah smiled.

'They're just helping him to dress. It won't be long, Mrs Hollis. Take a seat and I'll call you.' The nurse waved at the empty chairs in the waiting area. Maddie sat and remembered she had her mother's notebook with her. She looked at it and then she pulled her phone out. She dialled Helen's number.

'Hi, Helen, it's Maddie Hollis here.'

'I hear you've been helping with Old Tom Martin.'

Maddie smiled. 'Yes, I have. But I was wondering if you had luck with finding out about Nancy and Petroc?'

'Not really, my lover. It was long ago and memories fade.'

'True.'

'However, Tristan's here at the moment; why don't you have a word with him now?'

Maddie swallowed. 'It can wait.'

'What can wait?' asked a deep male voice.

'Sorry, Tristan, this is a bit awkward.'

'What is?'

'There's a possibility that your father Petroc ...' Maddie paused.

'My father what?' he asked.

'This is a long shot, but my mother died in childbirth, you see, and, well, your father and my mother ...' Maddie couldn't say the words.

'Are you implying that Petroc's your father?'

Maddie tensed. 'I honestly don't know. I'm grasping at straws but after all this time, this is the closest I've come to knowing who my father might be.'

There was silence on the end of the line. Maddie held her breath. She'd done her research. Getting a DNA test was expensive and not guaranteed for siblings.

'I don't see what this has to do with me.'

'Not much, in a way.' Maddie chewed her lower lip. 'It's just that after all these years, it would be nice to know who I am.'

There was a dry laugh. 'Isn't that what we all want to know?'

❧ Twelve ❧

Lights reflected off the baubles in the pub, which was packed with people enjoying the holiday season. Maddie collapsed onto the bench by the fire, thinking of the long day she'd had and how tomorrow was Christmas Eve. It had crept up on her despite the piped holiday music everywhere. With everything going on, she was too tired to feel cheery. Even the amazing transformation of Tom's house by Tamsin and the kids hadn't put her in a holiday mood.

'Here's your wine, ladies. I think you've earned it.' Anthony placed a bottle on the table.

'That's an understatement.' Tamsin pulled it closer.

Maddie's eyes sought out Mark, who was leaning on the bar. Almost without thought she followed the line beginning at his boots, lingered on his backside before she stopped at his shoulders. He'd made light work of helping Tom into the house. Now those hands that were so gentle with an old man were wrapped around a pint. They were strong. Not like the long fingers of the Viking. She turned away when a woman walked up to him.

'Penny for them?' Tamsin asked.

Maddie coloured. 'Oh, nothing important.'

'Well, you were looking at Mark's arse, so I didn't assume it was.'

'Tamsin, you're incorrigible.' Maddie glanced at the bar again. The woman had disappeared into the crowd, leaving Mark alone with his pint.

'Just stating the facts. He has a great bum,' said Tamsin.

155

'Does Anthony object to you looking at other men's backsides?'

'Well, I don't object when he looks at other women, so we're quits.'

Maddie laughed and took a sip of wine. The last time she'd been here, she'd met Gunnar. He'd stood out. Mark belonged here. The landscape suited him and had shaped him. And what a great shape it had stamped on him.

'You're staring again,' said Tamsin.

'No, I was trying to see the menu board.'

'Nonsense.' Tamsin chuckled.

Anthony stood in front of them, blocking Maddie's view. 'Ladies, have you decided?'

'Maddie knows what she wants.' Tamsin managed to keep a straight face.

'Why do I think I'm missing something here?' he asked.

'My order perhaps.' Tamsin smiled.

Anthony cocked his head to one side and waited with pen and pad in hand. 'Yes, of course. What are you having, my love?'

'Aside from you, I'll have the steak.' Tamsin stroked Anthony's leg.

'Right, and you, Maddie?' he asked.

'I'll have the monkfish, thanks.' Maddie smiled.

'No takers for the turkey?' He waited.

'We'll have enough of that in two days, you great oaf,' Tamsin said.

He faced his wife. 'Can one ever have enough turkey?'

'By the fifth day of Christmas you won't be asking that question, I promise.' Tamsin looked at his retreating back. 'Men, they never learn, do they?'

Maddie studied her friend. 'You're in a wicked mood.'

'I am, aren't I?'

'Yes.'

'It must be the season. Something to do with lights and mistletoe.' Tamsin glanced around.

'Red wine?' Maddie stroked her glass.

'Possibly. But what's your excuse? Get any nooky with the Viking?' Tamsin asked.

'Tamsin!'

'That means no.'

'Hannah came home too early.' Maddie watched as Mark turned and smiled in their direction. She loved the way his eyes crinkled up.

'Foiled by the young.' Tamsin laughed.

'That and then some. She flew off the handle. We were only kissing.'

'Only kissing? You intended to do more?' Tamsin's eyes widened.

Maddie thought about it. Would she?

'Forget me. Seriously, I'm worried about her. I could be wrong, but I think she thinks I'm being unfaithful to her father.'

'His ghost, you mean.' Tamsin sipped her wine.

'Don't joke about that. I saw his face clearly before the Viking kissed me.' Maddie looked to the door, half expecting to see Gunnar walk in.

'Was he smiling or frowning?' Tamsin asked.

'Smiling.'

Tamsin leaned back into the cushions. 'There you go, then; the Ghost of Husband Past approves.'

'What?' Maddie frowned. She didn't like this talk of ghosts. It reminded her of that creepy feeling when she first entered Trevenen. She shivered.

'He wants you to be kissed. You could try Mark, too. He's supposed to be very good. He's had enough practice.'

'Do you know this personally or is it just general knowledge?' Maddie asked, glad to think of something other than ghosts.

'No, never me. Just the old peck on the cheek routine.' Tamsin rolled her eyes.

'Don't sound so sad.' Maddie smiled.

'Ah, missed experiences. Found Anthony too young.'

'Leave you two alone and all you talk about is sex.' Anthony slid next to his wife.

'Hardly. It was mud wrestling, actually,' said Tamsin.

'Excellent idea. Why don't you two get down to some serious mud wrestling,' he suggested.

Maddie gagged on her wine. 'I didn't know it could be serious.'

'Oh, we would take it very seriously,' agreed Mark as he sat on a stool.

'You'd expect us to be in skimpy bikinis.' Maddie glanced at Mark.

'Of course.' There was a wicked light in his eyes as he smiled at her. He was flirting again, but then so was she.

'The skimpier the better,' Anthony added.

'You dirty old man.' Tamsin hit Anthony lightly on the arm. 'Here comes the food. I'm starved.'

'Me too.' Mark's eyes didn't leave Maddie's. She wasn't sure she wanted food any more.

OT's snoring reached Hannah in the kitchen as she put the pizza in the oven and thought about a salad. Could she be bothered? Would Will want it? He was sitting with a beer watching some stupid end of year programme. She hated them. Who wants to remember the year gone past? It was well crap. The only good bits were Will and OT.

Will's laughter almost drowned out OT's snores. Maybe that's why OT had never married. Who could live with the noise? She was glad she wasn't doing the night shift. She'd never get any sleep with that racket. Mark was staying here every night over Christmas. Maddie had suggested that she and Hannah move in, but Hannah suspected that maybe this was just because of the heating situation in Trevenen.

'Need any help?' Will called.

'No. Do you want a salad or anything?' she asked.

'Just you and the pizza.'

Hannah smiled. This was the way life should be. She settled onto the sofa and snuggled under Will's arm. 'What time will Mark be back?'

'Hopefully not for ages so that I can have my wicked way with you.' Will nibbled her ear. Hannah's toes wiggled.

'Sounds good, but don't forget we have company.'

'Old Tom's out for the count by the sound of it and won't notice if I chase you around the house.' His hand stroked her shoulder and started working its way lower.

'True but it might be awkward if they came back while you were chasing me.'

'Do you think so?'

'Yeah. Embarrassing, too. Have you ever caught your parents at it?'

'No. Close once, but thank God no. You?'

'Yeah. Dad and Maddie were banging away hammer and tongs and never even noticed I'd slipped into the room.' She grimaced.

'Poor you.'

'It was gross.'

'I bet. Caught Maddie at it since?' he asked.

Hannah paused. Mark and Maddie were spending a lot of time together because of OT. Maybe she needed to stir things a bit.

'Yeah, I told you about that guy. He's called Gunnar.'

'Mark's not going to like that.' Will sipped his beer.

'Why should he care?' Hannah shrugged as it all went to plan.

'He fancies her.'

'Really?' Hannah played with the beer bottle in her hand.

'Yeah.'

'Shame. I was just beginning to like him,' she said.

He turned and looked at her 'Why would it bother you that he wants to date her?'

'She's still in mourning; like, it hasn't even been a year.' Her hand tightened on the bottle's neck as she thought about her father and then Maddie having it off with two men.

'Huh?' Will frowned.

'It hasn't been long enough or maybe she just never loved Dad. She shouldn't be involved with anyone. Mark should stay well clear because she's a man magnet.' Hannah released her fingers.

Will played with a strand of Hannah's hair. 'Looks like he'll have to if she's shagging this guy. Don't think he likes sharing. Anyway, he's not known for getting too close to anyone, so I wouldn't worry.'

'Interesting. Any idea why?'

'Well.' He took a gulp of beer. 'I shouldn't say.'

'Why ever not?' She kissed his hand.

'Because I've only heard bits.'

'So fess up.' She ran her hand along his thigh.

'Well, Mark was married ages ago.'

'So?' Her fingers caressed a little higher.

'That's not the problem. It's what happened after.'

'Come on, tell me, don't tease me.' Her hand stopped just short of his crotch.

Will swallowed. 'Well, he went to the States on some top architectural programme and Claire stayed behind.'

'So?'

'Well, she had some disease and died while he was away and he didn't come home.'

'Whoa. Not too good with commitment then, is he?'

Will shrugged. 'I guess.'

'Not good with illness?'

'I don't know.' Will picked at the label on his bottle.

'So?'

'Well, that's all I know. He's never gone out with anyone for long. He didn't come back to Cornwall for ages.' Will sank back against the cushions.

'I'm not surprised. Why did they let him return at all? Was she a local?' Hannah's hand caressed his thigh again.

'Yes.'

'Shit, he blotted his copybook.' She laughed.

'You could say that.' He looked closely at her.

Hannah smiled.

'Why are you smiling?' He put his beer down.

She moved her hand ever so slightly forward and then kissed him.

*

'Hush little baby, don't you cry, Mama's gonna buy you …'
Maddie woke to the sound of her own voice. Her arms were
cradling a pillow. She sat up. The clock read 2.30. Shaking her
head, she tried to clear the disturbing images, but they remained
like the lingering effects of looking at the sun. She closed her
eyes, hoping the burning would stop. And then she heard a
baby's cry. Not just a baby but a new-born.

Throwing on her dressing gown, Maddie moved to the window, thick with ice on the inside. A moonlit landscape didn't
reveal a cat, which Maddie had hoped might be the cause of the
sound. She stood still, barely breathing. The noise continued.
She wanted to dismiss it but it wouldn't stop. Where was it
coming from? Could it be the wind? No, the night was still.
She swallowed.

The desire to crawl back into her bed and pull the duvet over
her head was strong, but she knew that she wouldn't be able
to sleep. The sound would reach her because she knew it was
there. There in the smugglers' keep.

Cold penetrated the fabric of her dressing gown as she
clutched a torch and walked down her stairs to the sitting room.
The dark shape of the Christmas tree looked like a large person
loitering in the shadows. She turned on the light switch.

The tinsel did little to calm the weird thoughts going through
her head. Maddie turned the fairy lights on as well to try and
relieve the tension enveloping her body. She ran her finger over
her mother's favourite ornament depicting the nativity. Staring
at the face of Mary, Maddie heard the crying. There was no
mistaking it. It was the sound of a new-born and not a feral cat.

What should she do? Was she still sleeping? Her breath created little clouds in the frigid air. But this was too real, unlike
the dreams that plagued her nights. In them the details swirled
and changed and she was left trying to say no, but no words
came out.

This was not a dream, nor a nightmare. She was awake in
the early hours of Christmas Eve and a baby was crying. It was
either real or she had slipped into severe mental illness. Maybe
she shouldn't discount that. She knew she was mad to do what

she was about to do. With her hand trembling, she turned on the torch and walked to the fireplace.

Everything in her yearned to soothe the baby. Each step closer and the cries became more urgent. She stood shaking with fear, but Maddie knew there couldn't be a child in there so what was she afraid of? Her own thoughts? Spiders? A trapped cat? What did she think she would find? A ghost? Her baby?

Before she could talk herself out of it, she found the release and the door came forward. The cries pierced her heart. Maddie made the sign of the cross as instinct took over.

Every hair on her body stood on end when she pushed her torch through the opening. Her throat tightened. It became harder to breathe. The air was colder than in the sitting room. She walked through the door and frost seemed to cover her skin yet she broke out in a sweat.

Hovering on the threshold, she forced her feet to move and her hand to point the beam of light into the dark corners. Nothing. But the space seemed to grow around the chimney itself. The cries were almost as if the baby was gasping for air. Maddie's hand went to her throat.

Bits of straw protruded from the walls and she could make out the beams above. The floor was made up of large slabs, not like the ones used in the hallway and kitchen but, as Hannah had said, more like old gravestones. Maddie's heart stopped. She turned and began to run.

And then she fell forward screaming.

⚘ Thirteen ⚘

'You had better put something on your face.' Hannah peered at her.

'I will.' Maddie gently prodded the bump that was forming above her left eye.

'And while you're at it, book yourself into a loony bin. I mean, you say you heard a baby crying and that's why you tripped.' Hannah rolled her eyes and went into the freezer. She pulled out a bag of frozen peas and handed them to Maddie. Maddie could tell she hadn't been pleased to have been woken by her scream at three in the morning. In fact, the girl looked shaken. 'Thanks, Hannah.'

Hannah turned with a haunted look on her face. 'Yeah.' She shivered and then disappeared.

Maddie wandered round the kitchen, the cold from the peas adding to the chill in the room. She looked at the kettle. Coffee? She was wide awake so caffeine wouldn't hurt and she could continue reading her mother's diary.

Aunty Daphne found me posing naked on an old chair in the stables. She frowned and I could tell she didn't like what she saw, however she didn't say anything. He suggested we stop for the day, but I didn't want to. I loved the feel of his eyes on me even if he wasn't looking at me as me, but as a model. His sketches caressed me.

Maddie tried to figure out what was going on here. Was Nancy in love with the artist? Several pages had been ripped out of the book. Judging by the yellowing, it wasn't a recent action.

She had to assume that her mother posed for the artist and not Petroc. Nancy would've been a perfect model with her long limbs and defined features.

I want him. He's so beautiful. His hair curls almost in ringlets and his arms are so brown from the sun. I want to feel the strong muscles I glimpsed in the sea. How am I going to break his barriers down? I love him and I want him to look at me that way too.

Is Nancy talking about Petroc here? Maddie rubbed her forehead. Tristan didn't have curls but she'd only seen photos of Petroc in his later years. Her research on the man had led her to his books on garden history and the back sleeve picture had showed a distinguished grey-haired gentleman. She had no idea what he'd looked like in his passionate youth. At the start of the summer, Nancy was clearly thinking about Petroc but now Maddie wasn't too sure.

I took a bottle of wine from the cupboard and went out to meet him by the river's edge. The light was fading on the hillside. I wanted everything to be perfect. I knew what I needed to do. I'd heard a girl in upper sixth telling all in detail. He's perfect and I love him. He's not like those spotty boys in London.

Maddie swallowed. Was she conceived on a bottle of wine by the river? She looked around her then picked up the package of peas again and put it back over her eye.

I didn't expect it to hurt, but it did, but it wasn't so bad the second time. His body's so beautiful. I so want to tell him how much I love him. I just don't know how to yet. Maybe tonight when Aunty Daphne goes to sleep I can sneak away to him.

Maddie closed her eyes. The entry finished there and only blank pages followed.

Maddie shouldn't have listened to Tamsin. Going to a church service was not what she needed to do on Christmas Eve. She slipped out of the door and took a large gulp of air. The coldness made her chest contract more. Her hands gripped and released of their own accord, trying to shed some of the anger and pain. She hadn't been inside a church since they'd buried John. The service that had just finished couldn't have been more different from the funeral. The notes of the organ carried on the clear air but they couldn't lift her spirits.

Visions of the small knitted sheep from the Nativity Parade swam before her eyes and she grabbed hold of a gravestone for support. Why was she standing here almost a year after John's death and feeling her heart break again? The squeals of the children in the church stabbed through her.

'Are you all right?' Mark was beside her. She wondered how long he'd been there.

'Yes, thank you.' She swallowed and turned away.

'Sure? You look pale and that's quite the black eye.'

Her hand flew to her face. Her fall this morning had developed beautifully into a mix of purple and yellow around her eye and cheek. 'Yes, I'm fine. Have you seen Hannah?' Maddie struggled to keep her voice even.

'Yes, she's chatting to my sister.'

Maddie raised an eyebrow.

'Will's mother.' Mark took her by the elbow and moved her away from the throng of people leaving the church. He studied her face and then stroked her cheek lightly. She trembled. She didn't need kindness at this moment, just space.

'Do you need a lift to Tamsin's?' he asked.

'I have my car.' She turned away from him. 'I need to check on Hannah. I don't know what her plans are.'

'Do you ever?' He placed a hand on her sleeve and warmth spread up her arm.

'No.' Maddie sighed and then scanned the crowd. 'She's there collecting hymn sheets. Who would have thought?'

His hand fell away and Maddie walked against the crowd

into the church. Her chest tightened and she forced breath back into her lungs while reminding herself that Manaccan Church looked nothing like the stark modern church in London. She was being ridiculous. God wasn't going to come down and strike her dead. Although it might be a relief if He did.

'Hannah.'

Hannah stopped sorting the sheets and looked up.

'You OK?' Maddie paused. She wondered if it all had hit Hannah like it had her, but Hannah looked at her like she was insane. Maybe she was. 'Do you need a lift?'

'No.' Hannah turned away and spoke to a grey-haired woman.

Maddie rushed out of the church with her head down to hide the flow of tears. The sound of the happy voices filled the air as she fumbled with her keys, trying to get into her car. Damn. Damn you, Hannah Hollis.

Safe inside, Maddie let them flow. No one needed to witness how Hannah got to her. It was Hannah's and John's fault. It was for them that she had done the one thing she swore she would never do. Her own mother, Nancy, could have and probably should have done it, but hadn't. Because of them, she was going mad and Hannah had stood laughing at her.

Her phone beeped. She'd missed a call from Gunnar while she'd been in church. She couldn't talk to him right now. She sent him a quick text.

Wishing you a Happy Christmas and looking forward to seeing you when you return.

A group of children walked past singing 'We Wish You a Merry Christmas'. Maddie's sobs shook her as she tried to push the pain away. When she'd married John, she had thought she'd have her own children. Yet all she had was a hateful stepdaughter. What had she done wrong? She couldn't fight the overwhelming feeling of resentment towards the teen any more. Had Hannah sensed this even though Maddie hadn't realised it herself until now? It was all so bloody stupid. Maddie thumped the wheel. Pain shot through her hand. She had to let go. This was her life now.

Steamed windows surrounded by glittering lights revealed glimpses of the crowd that filled Tamsin's house. Maddie squared her shoulders and entered. With luck, she would be able to lose herself in a dark corner. Christmas carols belted out of speakers and she had a glass thrust in her hand before her coat was even off. She forced herself to relax. It was too crazy in here for anyone to notice anything. She sipped her drink and pulled an arm out of her coat. Mark caught it and smiled at her.

'Not what you expected?' he asked.

'Not quite. How many people?' Maddie scanned the crowd.

'Lots. People filter in and out on the way to other things. It's a bit of a tradition.'

'I can see that. There are as many young here as old.'

'Yes, without a doubt. I see Hannah's beaten us here.' Mark took her coat. 'I'll put this upstairs.'

'Thanks.' Maddie moved into the crowd looking for Tamsin and wondering how long she needed to stay before she could slip away. This was a big event for her friend and she didn't want to hurt her feelings, but she wasn't in a party mood. Why couldn't she have drawn the short straw to sit with Tom? That would've been exactly what she wanted to do.

Smiling vaguely as she went, Maddie made it through to the kitchen where millions of nibbles littered every surface. Tamsin pulled her head out of the oven.

'Can you grab a tray and find a spot for it?' Tamsin asked.

'Sure. Happy Christmas, by the way.' Maddie kissed Tamsin's cheek.

'What happened to your eye?'

'Tell you later.' Maddie fled with hands full. Tamsin had that searching look about her. The light must not be low enough in the house after all. Maddie wove her way through people, distributing some food as she passed. Finally, spotting a bare table, she placed the tray down and went to stand in a quiet doorway. From here she could survey the room but stay clear. It was dark and unless someone needed the loo, she was out of the way.

Maddie spotted Mark across the room talking to a pretty woman. He caught her eye and smiled. She smiled back and then turned away to give her full attention to the painting beside her. It was a nineteenth century watercolour of Trelowarren House and was exquisite in its detail.

'Hiding?' Mark asked.

Maddie's head shot up. He stood very close.

'Sorry?' She pushed a stray piece of hair behind her ears.

'You don't seem yourself.'

'No?' Maddie looked at the painting again. She was sure her eyes would say more than she wanted them to.

'No. Do you want to talk about it?' he asked.

Maddie gave him a wry smile.

'No problem. I'm here if you need me.'

'Thanks.' She looked into those eyes and wished she could say all the things in her head, but she wasn't sure what would come out.

'Come on, man, get on with it or I'll do it for you. That beauty's standing under it.' A large man stood behind Mark. Maddie looked at him and then Mark.

'No need to trouble yourself.'

Slowly, Mark bent his head. Maddie's mouth opened in surprise. There was a wicked glint in his eyes. Before she could speak, his mouth touched hers. Her words died.

'Now could the two of you get a bit more intimate so I can get to the loo?'

Mark's body was thrust next to hers. Her breasts pressed against his chest. He deepened the kiss. She could taste cinnamon and mulled wine. All thoughts of where they were disappeared.

'Hey, way to go. Glad to see the old folk know what to do.' Fred's voice reached Maddie. 'But can you two move it elsewhere? There are a few spare bedrooms upstairs but only one bit of mistletoe and I've someone waiting for a kiss.'

Mark pulled away from her but continued to shield her. She could hear the laughter and she wanted the floor to swallow her.

'Up to your old tricks again, Mark?' a woman asked.

Maddie didn't recognise her.

'Absolutely. Never one to miss an opportunity.'

Maddie felt each movement of Mark's chest even though they were no longer touching. She was trying to breathe properly but all she managed were shallow gasps. Her knees were weak and she felt like a fool. Mark had kissed her under the mistletoe and she was behaving as if the earth had moved. She glanced at him. He appeared as cool as anything.

The large man who had pushed them together came back their way. Maddie darted quickly into the crowd. She needed to get out of here. She knew it was all in good fun but she didn't feel that way right now. She walked straight into Hannah.

'Bet you enjoyed that, cow.'

'Hannah!'

'What's your problem?' Hannah swayed.

'You're drunk, for a start.' Maddie stood back from her, trying to assess how badly inebriated Hannah was.

'So?' Hannah slurred. 'At least I'm not hearing things.'

Maddie bit her tongue and walked into the kitchen. Now was not the time or the place to have a row with Hannah. It was Christmas Eve, the time of peace on earth and goodwill to all men. Tears threatened again; she'd better get out of here fast. Tamsin wasn't in the kitchen but Anthony was propping up the back door with a large glass of wine in his hands.

'Happy Christmas. Where's your beautiful wife?' Maddie asked, trying not to look at him.

'Outside with Margaret who wanted a fag.'

Maddie forced a smile and headed to the door.

'That eye looks nasty. Where's my Christmas kiss?' Anthony blocked the door.

'Oh, she's all kissed out. She just snogged the hell out of Mark in the sitting room.' Anthony's youngest son, Hugo, grabbed a plateful of sausage rolls.

'Have you now?' He smiled kindly.

'Mistletoe has a strange effect on people,' Maddie mumbled.

Anthony placed a hand gently on her arm. 'That it does. Are you all right, love?'

Maddie nodded and fled into the garden, only to be grabbed by Helen Williams. 'Maddie, I'm so glad I found you.'

'Happy Christmas.' Maddie smiled, pleased it was dark outside.

'I've found something that I think you should see.'

Maddie frowned.

'We've been clearing out some unused rooms up at Pengarrock and I found a painting I haven't seen in years.'

Maddie's mouth went dry.

'You see, when I was visiting you at Trevenen, your painting reminded me of something, but for the life of me I couldn't remember.'

'Yes?'

'I found this painting that looks a lot like yours does, but the date on the back says 1970.'

⚜ Fourteen ⚜

The cold stone dug into Hannah's ribs as she hung over the stile. Will's hand held back her hair. The acrid taste of bile mixed with the scent of cloves was making her retch again. Waiting for the last set of tremors to stop, Hannah stood up.

'Thanks.' Hannah took Will's handkerchief and cleaned her mouth. It picked up black streaks of her mascara. She must look bloody wonderful. In fact, she probably looked better than she felt, which didn't say much.

'Can you walk now?' Will stood back and looked at her.

'I think so.'

'We could call Maddie and ask her to come.'

'Are you out of your mind? I would rather die than have her come and get me.'

Will shrugged and pulled his jacket closer. 'Your choice.'

'Yeah.' Hannah put one foot in front of the other and tried to stay upright. He came to her side and put his arm through hers. That felt better.

The sky was clear and there would be a frost. Lights flickered in a farmhouse in the distance. It should be so fucking romantic, but she felt so sick. She might need to retch again. What a great Christmas.

'Can we try and walk a little faster? I need to get home.'

Hannah tried to pull away. 'Sorry.'

'No, it's not that I don't want to be with you, but it's after midnight and Mum will want me home. That's all. I'll be in the shit if I'm too late.'

'Oh, yeah, right.' Hannah looked down at the ground.

'Come on, Hannah. You were dead set on getting as pissed

171

as you could tonight.' He kept on walking, pulling her along with him.

'Thanks for reminding me.'

'Look, just a bit further. I can see Trevenen now.'

'Great.' Hannah saw the dark outline of the house. There was a light on in Maddie's room and one in the kitchen. She could see the Christmas tree lights in the sitting room window. It looked bloody perfect but it was all a lie. Dad was dead, Maddie hated her and Will didn't like her any more because she was a stupid git. Merry Christmas one and all.

'You're shivering.' Will put his arms around her.

'Yeah. No problem.' Hannah's teeth chattered in her head. They reached Trevenen.

'Merry Christmas, Hannah.' Will planted a kiss on the top of her head and pushed her in the door. He waved as he ran up the drive.

Hannah walked into the kitchen and poured a glass of water. She sat in the chair by the range, waiting for the warmth to reach her. She was starved but she thought it was best not to eat until morning. Her stomach would need time to recover. She stood and went into the sitting room to turn off the tree lights. It was as cold as outside. Hannah rubbed her arms and laughed as she saw the presents under the tree. Who was Maddie trying to fool?

She pulled the plug and then she saw the stocking hanging from the fireplace. It was full. Santa had come and she had been a very bad girl indeed. She brushed the tears away from her eyes and ran to her bed.

Hannah's head thumped. She needed water and painkillers. Last night was a bit of a blur. How could Maddie have kissed Mark in front of all those people? It was mortifying and just plain gross. Maddie was showing her true colours. Two different men in the same week. She had no loyalty.

Hannah needed to pee badly, so she might as well venture downstairs. It was Christmas morning, after all, and she had those presents under the tree plus the stocking. They all must be for her as she'd bought nothing for Maddie. A small twinge of guilt hit but she let it pass.

When Hannah padded into the kitchen, Maddie was sitting beside the range drinking tea and reading a book. Hannah went for the teapot.

'Happy Christmas.' Maddie looked well-rested and had colour in her cheeks for the first time in ages.

'Yeah, whatever.'

Maddie looked up from her book. 'Do you want to have breakfast first or to open your presents?'

'Don't care. Don't feel much up to breakfast. Toast will do.'

'Fine.' Maddie closed her book with a precise movement and then rose from the chair. She towered over Hannah and probably always would. Hannah had stopped growing and this pissed her off no end. Her dad had been sort of tall but her mum must have been short. Damn, there she was thinking about her mum again. She wondered if she should ask Maddie about finding her but didn't think now would be the best time.

In her hungover state she began to wonder what would've happened if Maddie and Dad had had kids. Would they have been giants like Maddie? Well, she could be thankful that that never happened.

Hannah poured more water into the tea. It was too strong. She was just waiting for Maddie to say something about the fact that she'd been drunk last night but Maddie was busy popping bread into the toaster. She seemed way too calm. Christmas carols were playing on the radio and the peaceful atmosphere was enough to make Hannah scream.

Maddie placed the toast in front of her and all Hannah wanted was to throw it at her. Wouldn't she stop smiling? Didn't she know that Christmas sucked? That Dad wasn't here any more? It was the anniversary of his death on New Year's Eve. The holidays were crap and here was Maddie humming softly to 'God Rest Ye Merry Gentlemen'.

'I'm heading to Old Tom's in half an hour if you want to come.' Maddie smiled. The black eye looked worse.

Hannah still didn't understand what Maddie had been going

on about the other night. She thought that Maddie may have been concussed because she hadn't been talking sense. A baby crying? Really weird. Hannah had been in the passage several times but had found and heard nothing. Yet thinking harder, Hannah remembered one night when Maddie had crashed early and Hannah had heard something odd, but she was sure it'd been a cat. She focused on Maddie again.

'Are you on duty?'

'No, but I thought it would be nice.' Maddie went back to humming.

'I could just spend the day with him.' Hannah longed to pass it quietly with just OT and avoid Maddie's pathetic attempt at festive cheer.

'You could, but I think that Tamsin would be disappointed.'

'How can she be having us to lunch after the thousands she had in the house last night?' Hannah nibbled her toast.

Maddie wiped the counter down before hanging up the cloth. 'She's a witch, I think.'

'You may be right on that.' Hannah laughed. 'She seems to know everything the boys do.'

'Yes. She does.' Maddie paused and looked at Hannah. 'So are you coming with me this morning?'

'Might do.'

'Fine. I'm going to change. See you in ten minutes if you're coming.'

'What about the presents?' Hannah asked.

'You could bring them to Old Tom's.' Maddie left the kitchen.

Hannah threw the napkin at the door. She wouldn't bring the presents to Old Tom's because that would show her up for not buying anything for Maddie. She stood and chucked the toast into the bin then walked through to the sitting room. Maddie had Christmas music playing in here too. The lights twinkled on the tree, which was decorated with old ornaments, some of which had been Maddie's parents' and some silly ones Hannah had made with Maddie the first Christmas they'd spent together. Bending over, Hannah looked at the packages. There were five presents for her and not a single one for Maddie. Hannah took them and her stocking upstairs with her.

Walking through OT's back door, Maddie knew that Hannah must be hungover yet she was hiding it well.

'Is that Mrs Bates?' called Mark from the sitting room.

'No,' Maddie replied, placing her things on the counter.

Hannah came in and slammed the door behind her and rushed past Maddie through to Tom while Maddie followed at a more ladylike pace.

'Happy Christmas to you too, Hannah,' said Mark as she nearly knocked him over in her rush to OT.

'I'm pleased it's not just me she gives the cold shoulder to.' Maddie placed a light kiss on Mark's cheek and then took a deep breath. Their kiss last night was still far too vivid in her mind. Mistletoe had a lot to answer for. 'Happy Christmas.' She held out a large brightly coloured parcel.

'For me?' Mark asked.

'Yes. Nothing special.'

'Now you have me curious.' He smiled.

'I bet.' Maddie laughed and moved towards Tom. 'Happy Christmas.' Maddie kissed him while slipping off her coat. 'Are you drinking tea? Because I've brought some champagne. Thought a little Buck's Fizz might brighten a grey morning.' *And provide a bit of hair of the dog for Hannah*, she added silently. She caught Mark's knowing look.

'Sounds a wonderful idea. Hannah, would you be so kind as to bring some glasses for us all?' Old Tom beamed as Hannah sloped off to the kitchen.

'Have you had breakfast?' Maddie looked at Mark. There was something in his eyes. She couldn't read it.

'No, not yet,' Mark said.

'Good. How does scrambled egg and smoked salmon sound?' she asked.

'Wonderful.' Old Tom clapped his hands.

Mark placed his gift in front of the tree. Maddie hoped he liked it. She'd gone out on a limb and given him the watercolour that she'd done the day he interrupted her on Nare Head. But she just wanted to say thank you somehow for all he had done for Hannah and herself. Without his and Tamsin's help, things would have been a lot harder.

'That looks interesting.' Tom leaned forward.

'Yes, it does, doesn't it? Shall I open it after breakfast?' Mark asked.

'I wouldn't get all excited about it. It's just one of Maddie's paintings.' Hannah placed the glasses on the coffee table.

'Hannah, you're a spoilsport,' Old Tom scolded her. Hannah blushed. Maddie watched the interplay between these two. Tom could say what everyone else was thinking and not have his head bitten off. It was a miracle.

Mark followed Maddie into the kitchen. As much as she was embarrassed about last night, it had been an amazing kiss. She had definitely overreacted; too much emotion and not enough space or time to deal with it.

'Sorry about Hannah. Although she hasn't admitted it, she has a stinking hangover and feels like death, I should think.' Maddie wasn't really sure why she was apologising for her stepdaughter. Mark knew her well enough.

'That's no excuse.'

'I know.' Maddie paused. 'But it's a tough time of year for us both as it's a bit too close to the anniversary of John's death.'

Mark stepped nearer and placed a hand on her shoulder. She leaned back against him for a moment, enjoying the feel of him.

'When are you going to tell me about your eye?'

Maddie stepped away and laughed. 'Another day. Would you hand me the eggs? Let's make this a good Christmas morning, shall we?' Maddie smiled brightly.

'What are we doing here? I thought we were going to Tamsin's?' Hannah opened her eyes. She'd fallen asleep as soon as she got into the car.

'Helen Williams asked me to pop by to see something.'

'Helen who and what's so important that you come to a

bloody great palace on Christmas Day?' Hannah pinched herself to be sure she hadn't woken up in the middle of a *Dr Who* Christmas special.

'You can stay in the car. I won't be long.'

Hannah sat up. 'No, I'm coming. Where exactly are we, anyway?'

'Pengarrock.' Maddie left the car and walked to the massive door. This place made Trevenen look petite, which took a bit of doing. In the distance, Hannah could see the mouth of the Helford River bathed in bright noonday light.

The door was opened wide by a stout woman with a beaming smile. 'I'm so pleased you could come by today. Hello, Hannah, we haven't met.' The woman held out her hand.

Hannah took it. 'Hi.'

'Come in.'

Seeing the twenty foot Christmas tree, Hannah knew she was definitely in a *Dr Who* special and the Tardis would be lurking around the next passage. This place was amazing.

'I don't want to keep you from your dinner,' Maddie said.

'No, not at all. I know how important this is to you.'

Hannah looked at the two women and wondered why they were speaking in code.

'Thanks.' Maddie smiled.

'I've brought it down to the drawing room. Just through here.'

Maddie followed and Hannah reluctantly left the tree to go with them. But she was glad she did. The room had two walls of French windows which framed the stunning view outside. Awesome.

When she could tear her eyes from it, she saw Maddie and Helen looking at the back of a canvas. So maybe Helen wanted some help with restoration. Hannah didn't think that was Maddie's thing but maybe she was so hard up for cash that she was turning to anything.

She watched them carefully turn the painting around.

'I can't quite make out the last name but I'm sure the first is Peter.' Helen was watching Maddie closely. 'Can you read what it says?'

Maddie nodded. 'I think it's Johnson or something very similar.'

Hannah looked at the work. Who was Peter Johnson? Was this his Christmas present from Maddie? It was a cool painting and just a little different than Maddie's normal style, but then she didn't seem to have a normal at the moment.

✦ Fifteen ✦

The research to locate the painter, Peter Johnson, had proved remarkably simple. He was an artist born in Santa Monica, California, in 1948, with a wife and three sons. He was well established and apparently successful. His paintings were eerily familiar, as Maddie had seen in Pengarrock. What she didn't know was what she should do now.

There was no proof that this man was her father and it was even tenuous that he'd been the artist who had lived in the stables that summer. The only thing she knew for certain was that he'd painted the view from Pengarrock in 1970. That and the fact Peter was twenty-two compared to her mother's sixteen. Petroc had been seventeen in the summer of 1970.

She had the phone number of the gallery that hosted Peter's last exhibition. Should she do this? She knew she couldn't just come out and say why she wanted to contact him, so she'd have to lie. This morning she'd stared at the ceiling for hours trying to decide how to do it. No answer had come until she looked at yesterday's newspaper.

Maddie dialled the number in California and held her breath.

'Hello, Farnsworth Gallery,' a woman answered.

'Hi, my name is Madeline Hollis and I'm a reporter from the *Helston Packet* in Cornwall, England. I was wondering if you could help me.' Maddie heard some noise behind her. She didn't need Hannah around for this.

'I'll try.'

'I'm putting together an article on artists who have visited and been inspired by this area and the name of Peter Johnson has come up. I know you held an exhibition of his works recently.' Maddie paused. 'I was wondering if you could put me in touch with him?'

'Peter in Cornwall, England? I don't think that can be.'

'It was in 1970.'

'Well before I knew him.' The voice almost sounded relieved.

'Do you think it would be possible?' Her throat was dry and Maddie wasn't sure why she was doing this.

'I don't see why not. What's the name of the paper?'

'*Helston Packet*.' Maddie hoped she would be forgiven for the lie and the woman wouldn't check. There was a thump on the table behind. Maddie tried to focus as the woman gave her an email address.

Maddie put the phone down with unsteady hands and turned to see Hannah glaring at her.

'Just what were you on about? You're no reporter for the *Packet*.'

'No.' Maddie didn't know where this was going to go.

'See, I knew you were a liar. Here's all the proof I need.' Hannah paused and pushed back her hair. 'Just who is this Peter Johnson that you're so desperate to get in touch with?'

Maddie frowned. What could she say? She'd just been called a liar. 'My father, I think.'

Hannah went rigid. 'Your what?'

'My father. Helen knew I was trying to discover who my father was and she remembered the painting, the one we saw on Christmas Day. She knew it looked very similar to mine.'

'I thought that was your painting.'

'I know. It shook me when I saw it.'

'Whoa. So are you going to contact him?' asked Hannah.

Maddie knew this would hurt Hannah no matter how she sugar-coated it, so she didn't try. 'To be honest, I don't know.'

'I would.' Hannah stared directly at her. 'I'd like to talk to my mother.'

Maddie felt like a knife had pierced her heart. 'Really?'

'Yes, but I don't know how.' Hannah's shoulders sagged.

'There must be a way.' Maddie touched Hannah's hand. She knew this path would be filled with minefields. John had tried to make sure Hannah would never have contact from Susan.

'Yeah, how?'

'I haven't a clue but I'll work on it.'

'Thanks.' Hannah nodded and left.

One more thing to add to the list: find the mother who abandoned her child. Maddie sighed. How was Maddie going to find Susan? They had no idea what she was doing or what her name was now. She might have married. Maddie closed her eyes and tried not to think of the difficulties and the potential pain.

The address in her hands was the possible key to unlock who she really was. Maddie's father may be alive and she could, if she wanted to, contact him. Was Hannah any different from her?

The smell of extinguished candles hung in the air as Maddie carefully closed the church door. She didn't know why she'd come, but the silence was soothing and its peace began to creep into her as she sat in the last pew and admired the beautiful flower arrangements. Being here didn't hurt as much this time. It was New Year's Eve and a year since John's death. She needed to move on and find a new life, such as it was.

No, she wasn't going to have the brood of children she'd longed for, but she could make a happy life here in Cornwall. She'd made some good friends and she might receive planning permission for the old shed and then be able to sell it. This would give her money to fix Trevenen and build a proper studio out of the piggery. The new year was filled with possibilities to turn things her way.

Unfolding the paper in her pocket, she looked at Peter Johnson's email address. She'd drafted three different emails so far and not sent one. She hadn't expected that she'd be so confused, but she did assume that he didn't know she existed.

She slipped the address back into her pocket. Maddie had had no success so far in her search for Hannah's mother. She had done the obvious things of Googling and Facebook, but nothing appeared. It all weighed heavily on Maddie's mind.

What if Susan still didn't want anything to do with Hannah? Would that be more damaging than not knowing her at all? Hadn't Hannah been too young to feel the full brunt of the rejection the first time? But what if it happened a second time: would it break her? There were no answers and it wasn't really Maddie's choice.

She left the sanctuary without any solutions, but she hadn't expected any. God wasn't part of her life any more, but without Him it was harder than she'd expected. This had been the toughest year of her life and nothing had made sense, when in the past everything had seemed to. She kicked a stone on the path and watched it come to a halt before a fallen twig. Quite a few of them littered the path where the heavy north wind of last night must have brought them down.

The storm had also cleared the clouds that had filled the days between Christmas and New Year. The sky was a bright blue and the air was so clear and cold that it hurt when she took a breath.

She heard the church door open behind her. 'Hello.'

Maddie turned to see the vicar. 'Happy Christmas.'

'Thank you.' He walked to her side. 'Please tell me if I'm speaking out of place, but you seem troubled. I wondered if you might like to talk?' He paused. 'I know this time of year can be trying for many.'

Maddie stifled the hysterical laugh that threatened to escape. 'Thank you. But I'm fine.' That was the biggest lie she'd told in a while. She was still mourning her husband, she was in continuous battles with a stepdaughter who hated her, she was haunted by what she'd done and her house was possessed. She was the exact opposite of fine.

'I'm pleased to hear that. I know that you're new to the area and everything can be overwhelming. I'm here if you need me.'

Maddie smiled, wondering how he knew she was new to the area. She'd only set foot in the church for the first time on Christmas Eve and the second time today. She didn't think she'd had met him anywhere else.

'I will. Thank you.' She began to walk, listening to his

footsteps on the gravel heading in the opposite direction. She turned and dashed to catch up with him.

'Actually, do you have any knowledge or –' Maddie looked away from his keen eyes before continuing – 'experience of ghosts?'

'Trevenen's an old house.' He stopped.

She nodded. What on earth had prompted her to ask a vicar, of all people, about ghosts?

'I personally don't believe in them but I don't discount the idea either and, of course, being Cornish, one has, shall we say, a leaning to all things mystical.'

She smiled as she realised he didn't seem to think she was mad.

'So you think you've one in Trevenen?' He rubbed his hands together.

'Yes, I'm afraid so.' Her toes were now numb. Having this discussion with him in a graveyard on the most frigid day of the year might not have been the most sensible thing she'd ever done. But these days, she had forgotten what sensible was.

'Have you seen it or have others told you about it?'

'I have. Well, heard but not seen.' She swallowed. She sounded foolish. Although an artist, she had never been away with the fairies.

'Heard. Now that's interesting.' He looked out over the roofs of the village towards the fields on the other side of the valley. 'Just you?'

She nodded.

'I'd heard from Hannah that you lost your husband a year ago.'

She nodded, wondering when and why Hannah had talked to the vicar. 'May I ask why this would be important?'

'Well, in times of grief we often see or hear things.' He stopped as a woman walked up to them. 'Hello, Mrs Bates, yes, I'm just on my way.'

The woman smiled and walked down the hill and Maddie wondered if she was the Keziah Bates that she'd need to contact about Daphne.

'I think, Mrs Hollis, we might need a bit of time for this conversation and unfortunately I'm due at the village hall for a coffee morning. Will you ring me?'

The buzz of her mobile jogged her gloved fingers. Maddie nodded and smiled, wondering if he was implying that the ghost was just in her head. The vicar disappeared from her sight.

'Hello?' She stomped her feet, disturbing the frost on the ground.

'Happy New Year.' Gunnar spoke with great enthusiasm.

Maddie put her thoughts aside. 'Did you have a good Christmas?'

'Yes. I have just come back and am looking at the fine weather. I wondered if you were free to go for a walk at Loe Bar?'

Maddie looked around and tried not to be too hesitant. It was bloody cold. 'Yes.'

The long stretch of sand below the car park was deserted. Everyone must be preparing for the evening ahead and sensibly staying warm. Maddie was planning to join Tamsin and Anthony at the sailing club. She didn't know what Hannah's plans were but hopefully they didn't include too much drinking.

'Have you been here before?' She looked up at Gunnar.

'Yes, looking for some scenic shots of the area. You haven't?'

'No. I've stayed on the Lizard so far. There's so much to paint on the doorstep without even going the short distance to Helston. It's a bit naughty of me, really.' She gave him a lopsided grin.

'You, naughty? Hmmm.'

Glancing at him, she caught a gleam in his eye. They were clearly not thinking of naughty in the same way.

'You've covered a lot of ground already in your research,' Maddie said.

'Yes. It has been good. I like Cornwall. It has a, how do you say, magical feel about it.' He waved a hand in the air.

'Yes, it has, hasn't it?' She pushed her hair away and studied the waves pounding the shore. Once out of the car, the wind nearly blew her away. 'Are you sure about this?'

'Yes, it's good, isn't it?' His smile went from ear to ear. He pulled the hamper off the back seat and took her hand.

Maddie wasn't too sure if it was. The power of the sea was awesome and she fought against the wind's force with eyes half shut. Conversation would be a non-starter with the noise but she let him pull her along. They went up and down hills but Maddie didn't take in much.

'Here we are,' Gunnar announced.

A long stretch of sand divided the sea. On one side waves crashed in while the other side looked peaceful. 'Beautiful but very exposed.'

'I think if we walk towards the Pool, we will find a quiet spot for lunch.'

Maddie hoped that the hamper held some hot tea, hot soup and hot anything. A chill was setting in and though it looked lovely and romantic, she was hungry and cold. Gunnar took her hand again and at least one part of her was warm. They walked for another ten minutes before he stopped at an enclosed area bathed in sun and out of the wind.

'You're shivering, Maddie.'

'Yes,' she said through chattering teeth.

'It's because you are so thin.' He looked her up and down.

After Christmas, the last thing Maddie felt was thin. He put his arms around her and the noise of the wind died down. She stopped shaking.

'That's better. Are you hungry?' He loosened his hold so he could look at her.

'Absolutely starving.'

'Excellent.' He opened the hamper, took out a rug and indicated she should sit. Once on the ground, Maddie could feel the sun on her cheeks. He handed her a mug filled with a steaming liquid. The scent of spices wafted on the breeze. It tasted warm and sweet as it rolled across her tongue.

'Now, tell me what you like. I have smoked salmon, ham, beef and cheese.'

'I like all of them. You choose.' She pulled her legs tighter under her while he handed her a piece of bread with salmon. She devoured it before he had his. It wasn't polite but she was too hungry to care.

'You're shaking again,' he said.

'I'm afraid so.' Her words sounded funny coming out between the shivers.

'Come closer.'

Maddie shifted and he placed an arm across her shoulders while offering her more food.

'That's better.' He kissed her lightly on the top of her nose.

She smiled and snuggled nearer.

'Feeling better?' he asked.

'Yes, a bit. Thanks.'

'Look at the clouds over there.' He pointed to the west.

Maddie nodded.

'It means the weather is going to change.'

'Really? How?'

'The sky doesn't tell how. It only speaks of change.' He smiled at her and looked deeply into her eyes.

She laughed and glanced away. 'Well, as long as it doesn't cover the sun right now, that would be fine.'

'Maybe.' He pulled her off the ground onto his lap and enveloped her in a bear hug. The heat of his legs warmed her cold bottom. She felt like a small child, but that sensation was fast disappearing as a very grown-up one took its place.

His lips touched her temple. It was so tender that Maddie turned her head in surprise. His mouth found hers and lingered there. The touch of his lips on hers was nice. She kissed him back and relaxed. There was no toe-tingling feeling like when Mark kissed her on Christmas Eve, but this wasn't bad going either. She felt safe and protected. Gunnar was big enough to keep the world away.

'Better?'

'Definitely.'

'Ready for something sweet?' he asked.

Maddie raised an eyebrow as Gunnar released one arm and pulled out some chocolate. Now what could be better than chocolate and kisses?

⁕ Sixteen ⁕

The flame on the candle flickered in the window while Hannah sat and held the photo of her father. Tears fell. She rubbed her cheeks with the back of her hand before she touched his face.

'Dad, why did you have to leave? I'm so damn lonely. Maddie's not my mother. She'll leave if she has the chance. I don't know what promises she made to you, but she'll break them.' She blew her nose. 'Men trail around after her and she'll go off with one of them and leave me. You left me so why did you think that she'd stay?' She paused. 'Everyone's left me. Maddie won't be any different. It's just a matter of time.'

Abruptly she got up and put out the candle. Her father couldn't hear her. He didn't care. Maddie didn't care and her mother, wherever she was, certainly didn't either. Life sucked. She blew her nose again and looked in the mirror. She had big red blotches under her eyes. A good look for tonight.

Will and the gang were collecting her in an hour. Maddie wasn't home and hadn't been all afternoon. Hannah didn't have a clue as to where she was, but bet she was out with some man; she just knew it.

The water in the shower was reasonably hot and the tears mingled with the intermittent blast. The sooner Maddie put some money into this old wreck, the better. OT had said he'd heard Mark and Maddie setting up a meeting to do the plans for the shed next week, which meant Maddie could sell it and with planning permission, she'd receive a decent amount for it. Yay, they might have constant hot water then. Stepping onto the cold linoleum floor, Hannah accepted that she liked

Trevenen. Her phone beeped and a message from Abi arrived.

Have split with Andrew. It sucks. You still with Will? x

Hugs. Why? Yes x

Hannah replied.

She waited for a response, wondering if she had enough credit to call her. Maddie always got pissed off if Hannah called too many mobile numbers, and she looked at all the numbers too.

He snogged Karen at Tim's party. x

Were you there? The bastard. x

Yeah totally sucks. Miss you. x

Hannah shivered. What if Will was snogging someone at school? How would she know?

Miss you too. Visit soon. x

Will try. x

As she shed her towel, she heard a car in the drive. Peering carefully over the windowsill, she was relieved to see it was Maddie and not the gang. Hannah hadn't a clue what she was going to wear. It was New Year's Eve and you were supposed to make an effort, but she didn't feel like it. A short denim skirt would be effort enough.

'Hannah, are you still here?' Maddie called from the stairs.

Hannah threw on her clothes. 'Yeah.'

'Great. What time are you heading out?'

'In a bit. Why?' Hannah came out of her room.

'I was wondering if I could catch a lift with you to Tamsin's rather than having Mark come by, that's all.'

'Oh, well, Fred's supposed to be here in forty minutes but we aren't going to Tamsin's. We're going to the Prince.' Hannah wasn't sure why she'd just told Maddie that. She didn't need to know anything.

'I meant on the way.' Maddie was smiling.

'Yeah, well, why don't you drive?'

'Because I'll be having a few glasses of wine tonight and it makes sense not to if someone else can.'

'Let Mark come and get you.' This was just Maddie's way of finding out her plans. Hannah kicked a dust bunny on the floor.

'Fine, I just thought it'd be easier all round. Never mind.'

Maddie turned and went downstairs. Hannah smiled. Maddie would have a nasty surprise when she tried to have a bath: she'd used all the hot water.

Midnight approached and everyone gathered to watch the final countdown. Maddie moved to the back. She felt flushed from too much dancing and drink. Overwhelmed by the need to escape, she slipped quietly onto the terrace and then down the steps, hoping that no one would miss her. The joviality was too much. John was dead, her life had changed unalterably, and she'd spent the evening acting for the entire world as if she was fine and that she had no past to drag her down.

The smell of the sea lifted her spirits as she ventured to the water's edge. Moving in the breeze, the lights of the Ferry Boat Inn on the far side looked festive. The sound of footsteps alerted Maddie to the fact she was no longer alone and disappointment replaced the feeling of freedom. Now she would have to put her mask back into place. Rearranging her features into a smile, she turned. 'Hello.'

'The crowd too much?' Mark walked to her side.

She nodded. She hadn't expected him. The warmth from the club had worn off and she shivered. Mark placed an arm around her shoulder and she fitted easily against his body. Something inside told her that she should resist this urge to lean on him but she refused to listen.

Noise erupted from above and fireworks went off across the river.

'Happy New Year.' Mark spoke close to her ear.

'Yes, Happy New Year.'

The raucous sounds of 'Auld Lang Syne' drifted down to them. Mark turned her and pulled her closer in his arms. His lips met hers in the lightest of contacts. Something inside her clicked. She deepened the kiss. A hunger began. She didn't know where it came from but she didn't have the strength to deny it. Why did she have to be sensible? Why couldn't she have what she wanted right now?

Her hands moved up his chest until she reached his neck. At the touch of bare skin they stopped. His heart beat against her breast. She knew this was madness. But she didn't stop. Her fingers wound themselves in his hair. A small sigh escaped her. Mark drew back.

'Don't.' She couldn't get enough of the taste of him. Her lips teased his until he gave in. She pressed against him. His arousal matched hers. She was shocked at her own need but she didn't care.

Mark's lips trailed down her neck, igniting her further. All her nerves were centring and reminding her that she was a woman, one who desperately wanted this man. She drove her hips closer to his. She'd forgotten what desire felt like. It was insanity.

'Maddie?' His hand stole round to caress her waist.

'Yes.' She wanted to be naked and on a bed with this man right now.

'Are you sure about this?'

'Yes and no, but don't stop.'

His fingers hovered just below her breast. It was aching to feel his hands. His mouth claimed hers again and she felt the tension within her rise to the next level.

'Hello, you two. Seeing the New Year in on your own, I see.'

Mark's hand fell to her waist.

'Hi, Ben. Slipping out for a smoke?' Mark asked.

'Yes, told the wife I'd give it up. More fool I. Don't let me stop you, by the way.' He chuckled as he walked past them onto the sand.

Maddie stood back from Mark. He still held her but the cold night air had crept between them. He kissed her on the temple.

'You're shivering. Maybe we should go back inside.'

She nodded, not wanting to leave his arms, but knowing that the moment had passed. There was something in the chemistry between them that, once triggered, sent her up in flames. This wasn't a good thing. He'd no staying power, drifting from one woman to the next. Was this what she wanted or needed? Did she care? Did it matter? Could she afford to lose him as a friend just because she wanted him so badly? He'd been a constant friend since she arrived in this new world where everything seemed to turn upside down. Did she throw that away for the sake of an affair? And if an affair was what she really wanted, wasn't Gunnar a better choice?

Mark held her hand while they walked up the hill to the club. The music throbbed out some eighties number that Maddie vaguely remembered. Entering the club, the first face she saw was Hannah's and it looked like thunder. Mark's hand slipped from hers in the crush of the crowd and Maddie felt naked. The only person looking at her was Hannah, but that was enough.

'Hey, stranger, where have you been?' Tamsin came up and gave her a glass of champagne.

'Just getting a bit of fresh air.' Maddie took a sip. 'When did Hannah turn up?' Maddie looked at her stepdaughter with Will's arm wrapped around her. It all looked so simple on the young.

'Just before midnight.'

Maddie nodded. She needed to leave now but Tamsin was clearly in party mode. 'When were you thinking of going?'

'Oh, we're going to head back to Paul's house. You're invited too.' Tamsin beamed.

'I'm definitely too tired to party into the small hours. How you do it, I don't know.'

'Vitamins.' Tamsin knocked back her champagne and went to dance with Anthony.

'Shall we dance?' Mark asked. Maddie closed her eyes, trying not to think about their encounter on the beach, but the music was slow and she would be in his arms again. Opening her eyes, all she could see was Hannah and Will making a vertical expression of a horizontal desire on the far side of the dance floor.

'Yes, why not?' There was nothing wrong with wanting a man. They were both unattached. It didn't have to be complicated unless she made it that way. She took a last sip of her champagne and slipped into Mark's arms. He held her and she rested her head on his shoulder and closed her eyes, inhaling the scent of him: soap and sea.

'Where's Gunnar tonight?' Hannah asked from close by.

Maddie's head shot up. 'I don't know.'

'Thought you were with him this afternoon,' Hannah spat out.

Maddie blinked. 'I was.'

Mark pulled back a bit.

'You should know where your boyfriend is. Didn't anyone tell you that it's bad manners to shag two men at once?' Hannah's words hung in the air. Will moved her away.

Every muscle in Mark's body was tense. What was going on in his head? His face gave nothing away; it was a polite mask. How could she explain her relationship with Gunnar?

'You could have invited him tonight.' Mark was so civil he might have been talking to a stranger.

'Yes, but I didn't want to.' Maddie paused and thought about what she needed. 'Look, I'd really like to go home. Do you think there's anyone going my way and not on to Paul's?' She moved out of Mark's embrace. Out of the corner of her eye, she could see Hannah smiling.

'I promised that I'd be back at Tom's as soon as things here finished. I'll drive you home.'

'Thanks.' Maddie looked down. She couldn't shake the feeling that she was a scarlet woman and the world could see the big A that Hannah had all but painted on her.

'Ready now?' Mark asked.

'Yes, I'll just say bye to Tamsin and Anthony.'

'Fine. Meet me by the car.' He turned and walked to the door.

❧ Seventeen ❧

Maddie's hands gripped then released the steering wheel, trying to find the nerve to face Mark. Since New Year's Eve, they'd only spoken briefly on the phone. She opened the car door and viewed the mud that edged the drive. Her feelings were as clear as that. She took a deep breath. He believed Hannah. She didn't know what to say, let alone how to begin.

Gunnar. She wasn't doing any better with him either. Just keeping him at arm's length while her head battled with what she wanted. But she knew she might not have a choice of either of them. She paused. She never would have imagined that she'd find herself in this situation.

Recalling the first time she'd done this, she rang the doorbell. She'd had no idea then that she would fall for the man who answered it. She couldn't be in love with Mark, could she? She wasn't an impressionable kid. She knew the real meaning of it. Joy, pain and loss. Applying the reality to the word – was she in love with Mark?

Yes, she was. He made her heart dance with his smile, her legs weak with his kisses, but it was his kindness that was her undoing. He was even good with Hannah, which said a great deal. She'd go through hell and back for him just as she'd done for John. But had she come back from there yet?

'Hello.' Maddie smiled at Mark as he opened the door and then glanced beyond him, endeavouring to keep her thoughts locked away. He had no need to know them. He deserved more than what she had to offer: a broken woman, a grumpy stepdaughter and an old house in dire need of repair.

'Hi.' He stepped back from the door.

194

'I really appreciate this. There's no way I'd be able to do this request for planning permission without you.' She bit her lip to stop the flow of words ready to tumble out. She didn't share her secrets with anyone and this one couldn't be any different.

'Well, you could, but you'd need another architect.'

'True.' She smiled. 'But I don't know any.'

'It will have to be me, then.' He took her coat.

'Yes, it will.' It was definitely him. What was she going to do? He seemed so formal. Bloody Hannah had messed things up and Maddie wasn't sure how to fix it. But maybe Hannah had done her a favour? Or at least Mark one?

'Can I tempt you with a glass of wine?' Mark walked towards the kitchen.

Maddie stopped in her tracks. He could tempt her with anything. 'Certainly.'

'Red?' he asked.

'Great.' She looked around his house, enjoying the views displayed through a large expanse of glass covering one wall.

'Go and have a look on the table in the office and I'll be there in a minute.'

Maddie found his office. The painting she'd given him hung on the wall opposite his desk. He couldn't despise her if he looked at her work every day; or maybe it just filled the wall space. She looked down and scanned the plans. They were simple and utterly right for the site.

He returned with the wine. 'What do you think?'

'Perfect. Someone will have a wonderful house.' She smiled. 'The views are good from there as well.'

'You'll invoice me for this, won't you?' She sounded so business-like and hoped she was setting the right tone to match his. She wished she'd never kissed him as then she'd never have known what she was missing.

'Maybe after the sale, but definitely nothing until then.'

'Are you sure?' she asked.

'Yes.'

She looked over the rim of her glass, trying to imprint the details of his face into her brain. She'd go home and sketch him, then she might be able to release some of this feeling. But who was she trying to fool? She'd do it so that she could look on him whenever she wanted.

He smiled. 'I'll submit them tomorrow. It will be six weeks, give or take.'

'Right.' Maddie wandered out of the office to the kitchen. The air seemed to be thick with unspoken words. She placed her glass on the island in the centre of the room and kept shifting from one foot to the other.

'Mark, I want to say something about New Year's Eve.' She swallowed. His eyes were guarded and their colour had almost turned black.

He leaned against the counter. 'What's there to say?'

'I don't normally behave in that way.'

'What way would that be?' he asked.

She couldn't read anything from his face. 'You know what I'm talking about: what happened on the slipway.' She walked to the other side of the island, away from him, then stopped and rested her hands on the wooden surface.

'Tell me what happened there,' he said.

She glanced down and swallowed. She'd never be able to move forward until this was over. 'Mark, I was a bit wanton and I wanted to apologise for my actions.'

'Nothing to apologise for.' He spoke quietly.

'Right, if that's the way you feel, then fine.' She straightened up, snatching her hands from the counter. This was bloody awful. She'd just realised that she loved him and he was acting as if they'd just met yesterday and had shared nothing.

'It has nothing to do with the way I feel.' He walked over to her, removing the barrier between them. 'I enjoyed every moment. In fact, I regretted that we'd stopped and went back inside.' He stood just an inch away.

Maddie took shallow breaths. She turned towards him. 'Mark?'

'Yes?'

'What are you saying? We have a great friendship.'

He nodded.

'It'd be more than foolish to tamper with it.' Of this she was certain.

'Are you sure?' Mark wasn't touching her but was so close that she felt his breath on her skin.

'Yes.' Her voice was husky.

He ran a finger across her mouth. It settled on her bottom lip. She couldn't breathe.

'Mark.'

'Yes?'

'This is crazy.' Somehow she found words but she couldn't move.

His fingers slipped down to her neck. 'Yes.'

He lowered his head and kissed her. This was exactly what she wanted.

Looking at the darkness outside the kitchen window, Maddie listened to the enthusiasm in Gunnar's voice and wrinkled her nose. Could she or should she push him away yet again? Did she want to go for dinner at his place with all the intimacy that that would entail?

'Not sure of Hannah's plans. Can I let you know?' She knew her words were feeble as she put the phone down and she wasn't sure why she was even considering it.

'That's a funny face.' Tamsin looked up from the plans on the table.

'Is it?'

'Yes. What's up with the Viking?'

Maddie frowned. 'Wants me to come for dinner.'

'Sounds good.'

'Yes.' Maddie fiddled with the edge of the dish cloth.

'You don't sound too sure.'

'No.' Maddie glanced at her friend who appeared so at ease with life. It was all sorted for her. She hadn't been thrust back out into the singles world again. She was married to the man she'd always loved.

'Does this have something to do with Mark?' Tamsin asked.

Maddie's head flew up.

'It's just that when I arrived at his house last night, the two of you had a look about you.' Tamsin paused. 'I'd the distinct impression that I was interrupting something. It might've been the dishevelled hair or the wide-eyed expressions.' She looked closely at Maddie. 'Am I wrong? Was something going on, because I felt like a great big gooseberry.'

Maddie blushed.

'Aha. Something was. So if I hadn't arrived, you two would've been rolling around on the floor?' Tamsin's left eyebrow arched.

'No comment.' Things had heated up very quickly.

'Ha, proves it. 'Bout time, too. You two have been circling each other for a while now. Never seen Mark hold off for so long.'

'Why?' Maddie moved closer to Tamsin.

'Why what?'

'Why has he held off? Is there something wrong with me?' Maddie played with a button on her cardigan.

'What would make you think that?'

'Oh, I don't know. Everyone talks about Mark's womaniser reputation. I was beginning to feel left out.'

Tamsin blasted out a hoot of laughter. 'Seriously, I think he held off because he cares for you. You're a friend and he's all too aware of what people say.'

'Somehow that doesn't make me feel any better.' Everything was upside down in Maddie's head.

'Silly girl. He's liked you for a while. He really must if he's waited this long to make a move.'

'I'm not sure he has.' Maddie looked at the grain of the wood on the table.

'What?' asked Tamsin.

'I think I may have.'

Tamsin laughed. 'All the better.' She looked at her watch. 'It's after six. Pour me a glass of wine.'

Maddie bit her lower lip but did as she was told. 'You think a glass or two of wine will make me spill and tell you more?'

'Yes. By the way, what are you doing about the Viking's dinner?'

'I said I'd call him back.'

'Why don't you want to go?' Tamsin studied Maddie.

'I want to. I think.' She swirled the wine in her glass.

'Can't be shuffling two men?'

'That sounds awful.' Maddie remembered her last encounter with Gunnar, which, aside from the cold, had been wonderful and romantic. He hadn't pushed her too far but had moved things forward from just friendly to getting interesting.

'Sounds pretty good to me.' Tamsin sat in the armchair, which swallowed her. Her legs couldn't quite reach the floor.

'You're terrible.'

'Yes, I know.' Her friend's eyes didn't leave her. 'Now back to you.'

'Me?' Maddie looked out the window.

'Yes, you and two men.'

'Now there's a thought.' Maddie laughed.

'You wicked woman.' Tamsin took a sip of wine. 'Didn't know you had it in you.'

'Neither did I. Till now, of course.' She flung herself into a chair. 'But I don't. Basically, I can't swing two men. My head can't go there.'

'Can't or won't?' Tamsin asked.

'Both.' She couldn't lead Gunnar on, knowing her heart lay elsewhere, could she? No, she couldn't; it wasn't her or at least it wasn't the Maddie she knew of old. Yet in the past year, she'd changed.

'Fair enough. So which one do you choose?'

'Don't know.' She did, but she didn't want to declare herself to Tamsin, or anyone at the moment.

'Who turns you on the most?' Tamsin grinned.

Maddie flushed slightly.

'Come on, fess up. Clearly one of them does.'

Maddie nodded. She remembered just how close she and Mark were to rolling around on the floor, as Tamsin had put it. She could have screamed with frustration when Tamsin arrived with Anthony's costings for the plans.

'Not going to say?' Tamsin waited. 'I think I know who, anyway.'

'Really?'

'Yes. You'd better call the Viking and say you can't make it if you really aren't up to running two men.'

'Tamsin.' Maddie looked at her wide-eyed.

'Maddie, I'm no fool. I've seen the look in your eyes when you see Mark. The Viking is tasty but you want Mark.'

'It's that obvious?' Maddie asked.

'To me. I doubt the rest of the local population has discovered this yet, but maybe.' Tamsin shrugged.

'No, don't tell me that. I'll go and become a nun.' Maddie sipped her wine, contemplating the peace of a cloister.

'Wasn't that what you thought you were doing when you came down here?'

'Well, maybe. It would've been simpler. I had no idea what to expect. I was desperate.'

'Well, life here is good.'

'Yes and I don't want to mess it up.' Maddie paused. 'I was never able to just have an affair. It wasn't me. I don't think it is now, even though I'm a different person lately. And Mark isn't a good bet for a more serious relationship, is he?'

Tamsin opened her mouth but quickly closed it again when they heard a squeal from the drive.

'Who's that?' Tamsin leapt to the window to see a car pull away. 'Well, I'm pleased to say it wasn't one of mine driving. Hannah's home.'

'Great.' Maddie took a big slug of wine. 'Friday night in with my lovely stepdaughter. Maybe I should accept the Viking's invite.'

'You should.' Tamsin walked back to the chair.

'What?'

'I know you fancy Mark more, but the Viking is gorgeous, interested and no strings attached.'

'Are you trying to warn me off Mark?' Maddie asked, feeling her mouth go dry.

'No, I'm just saying he's more complicated.'

'Thanks for the warning.'

'What are friends for?'

Maddie jumped when the phone rang. Tamsin picked it up. 'Hello?'

Maddie didn't think it could be Gunnar but she would have to think up an excuse quick if it was.

'Hi, Mark. How was Penzance?' Tamsin went quiet and Maddie watched the expressions play across her face. 'But you weren't calling to speak to me. It's Maddie you want.' Tamsin grinned.

Maddie cringed. How could she be composed on the phone after that? 'Hi.'

'How are you?' Mark asked.

'Fine thanks.' Maddie swallowed.

Tamsin was giggling in the background. Maddie was sure that Mark could hear her. She tried to signal for Tamsin to be quiet but her friend ignored her.

'I was wondering if you're free for a drink or dinner tonight?'

Maddie knew what she wanted but she wasn't going to say it on the phone. 'Dinner sounds good. Tamsin mentioned they were going to the Shipwrights.' Maddie thought there might be safety in numbers; safety from her own desires.

'Shall I meet you there or pick you up?' he asked.

Meet me here and we don't have to go anywhere was what she thought. Instead she said, 'Why don't we meet there about seven-thirty?'

'See you then.'

Putting the phone down, she turned to face Tamsin.

'Things aren't so bad when you have two offers for a Friday night, are they?' Tamsin giggled.

Maddie smiled. 'Not bad, just complicated.'

Hannah ran to her room, avoiding Maddie and Tamsin in the kitchen. She punched her pillow. Will wasn't coming home for half term. His family was going skiing, which sucked. Why did she have to have a boyfriend who was away at school? Stupid fool.

His email had been so apologetic. But Hannah knew he must have someone else at school. Why wouldn't he? After all, she was here in the back of beyond and he was there.

Picking up her phone, she texted Abi.

Think I'm going to break it off with Will x

She paced her room until her phone got a signal.

Why? Thought you liked him. x

I do but he's not here. Need someone here x

Maybe that's what she needed to do. There were plenty of blokes at school who were OK. Maybe she should hang out with one of them. But what would happen when Will came home? Hah, it would serve him right for not coming back more often!

'Hannah, the phone!' Maddie yelled.

Hannah trotted downstairs, wondering when they were going to have more than one handset. When they fixed the house she supposed, whenever that miracle would occur.

Hannah grabbed the phone from Maddie and smiled at Tamsin. Why couldn't Maddie be more like Tamsin? She was cool. She was how a mum was supposed to be, not some hippy chick artist attracting all the men for miles.

The voice on the other end of the line made her smile. It was Emma. They were going out tonight and did she want to come. YES! A night in with Maddie was the last thing she wanted, but at least it looked like Maddie was in and not out with Gunnar or Mark. Mark hadn't been around since New Year's Eve so her plan had worked. Will had been shocked but she didn't care.

'Was that Emma?' Tamsin asked.

Hannah wondered if Tamsin was clairvoyant sometimes. 'Yeah.'

'Asking you out?'

Hannah glanced at Maddie. She really didn't want her to know her plans. 'Yeah. Cinema.'

'Great. Who gave you the lift today?' Tamsin asked.

'Oh, Ted.' Hannah wondered where this was going.

'Ted Dunne?'

'Yeah. Why?' Hannah frowned.

'Just wondering whose car was being abused.'

'You're too funny.' Hannah took an apple and left them to their wine. She heard a burst of laughter as she climbed the stairs. She'd never understand them, two old women sitting around on a Friday night. Boring.

Should she wear her ballet flats or her Converse with her skinny jeans? Hannah tried them both on and then kicked them off, hitting the wardrobe. It reminded her of the night the hammer slipped. Without that she never would have met OT and that would have been terrible. He was so much better now. She'd spent yesterday evening with him and couldn't believe the progress he'd made. He didn't need someone there during the day any more, just the nights, and that was down to Mark much of the time. Those two seemed to be quite close.

Hannah tried on the flats again and decided they'd do. She wound a bright purple scarf around her neck and was ready. What now? She didn't want to sit with Maddie; if it was just Tamsin, that would be another story. Tamsin was great to talk to because she just listened and didn't try and make a fuss about anything. Maddie was really messed up these days. Hannah wished she knew what had caused it. Maddie had never shown emotion before, but now that was all she was doing. It was like someone had tapped a hole in her dam and she was gushing forth.

Hannah glanced at her books, but she didn't want to do homework. OT was pushing her to do more with her studies and she was, but enough was enough. She wished he could be her teacher. He must have been so cool.

She should deal with the Will issue, so she picked up her phone. It really wasn't going to work with him away. It'd been fun but she should just break it off. She wrote the text and then paused as her phone beeped.

Thought you said he was a great kisser x

He is x

She didn't want to end it. She read Will's email again.

Hannah,

I thought I'd told you about the trip ages ago. We go every year and I really wish you could come with us. I asked if you could. Mum was cool about it but there's no room in the chalet.

So if you want to, you could come with us next year.

I hate that we won't see each other for ages but we'll have a month at Easter.

W

Hannah played with her necklace. Would he invite her to go with them next year if he had someone else? She deleted her text.

She stood and went to the wardrobe where she pulled out the repaired chest. Her damage was now just part of its history, visible but not disastrous. Lifting the lid, out came the cup and saucer with the Penventon crest on it. She'd looked it up on-line. It matched the one carved in the stone above the window in the kitchen. OT had translated the motto from Latin for her. It said 'strength through God', which sounded pretty lame to her, but it wasn't her motto so it didn't matter. What would hers be? She didn't have a clue. OT's would be 'respect before action' or something.

She took the next item out, thinking she should make an inventory of what was in here. With care, she touched the multi-folded document. It looked official because of the heavy red seal on it. On closer inspection it had the same coat of arms as the plate. She felt she should take this straight down to Maddie as she was a Penventon and this could be important somehow. She placed it carefully on her desk as she heard the sound of a car in the drive. It was the guys coming to collect her. She'd deal with history later.

⁂ Eighteen ⁂

Why couldn't someone, like Tamsin, be waiting to hear all about her evening, thought Hannah as she opened the front door and turned on some lights. In the kitchen she switched on the telly and the kettle. How boring to have to make herself a cup of tea. With mug in hand, she settled down to watch a horror film. It was almost midnight and no Maddie. When Hannah had left, Maddie had planned to go out with Tamsin. Nothing unusual in that, but it was late now. Maybe they'd gone back to Tamsin's, but it niggled in Hannah's mind while she watched heads being chopped off victim after victim.

At half past one, the film had finished and there was still no sign of the step-witch. Hannah tried Maddie's mobile but there was no answer. Should she call Tamsin and see if she was there? But that would make her seem like a fool. She grabbed the instant coffee and made a cup of the revolting stuff. She lumped in three spoons of sugar just to make it palatable.

Once in her room she saw the document on her desk. Picking it up, she turned it over in her hands, enjoying the weight of the paper. She ran her finger under the flap until it came to the seal. It hadn't been opened before, which didn't make sense. Even without knowing the exact date, it didn't take a genius to know that this was old. Either it had never been discovered before or people just totally lacked curiosity. Or could it have been resealed?

Should she leave it alone and wait for Maddie? Hannah walked back down to the kitchen and picked up a knife. Who would even know if she opened it? It could have been that way when she found it. She glanced out the window to the drive and then slipped the blade under the seal before she could change her mind.

Her hands shook as she unfolded the document. The handwriting was very ornate but she made out Trevenen, Penventon and the date 1570. The language was awkward; she thought it was maybe a will. The names Catherine, Mary, Philip and Thomas were easy enough, but the rest could be anything that involved 'herewiths' and so on. OT would be able to help her with this.

She switched the telly back on but there was nothing interesting. By two o'clock she couldn't stop yawning and turned it off. Where the hell was Maddie? She paced the floor, trying to think. She tried ringing Maddie's mobile but it went straight to voicemail. Fuck Cornwall. There was no bloody reception when you needed it. She should just go to bed. Clearly they were having some sort of late night fest. She might be out with the blond bloke who looked like he belonged in bad X-rated films. Maybe she was banging away in his house. The tart.

Hannah walked up the stairs, shivering with cold. Maybe she should make a hot water bottle. She turned and went down again to boil the kettle. While she waited, she dialled Maddie's number again. It was now nearly two-thirty. If she was going to spend the night out, Maddie should at least have let Hannah know. It wasn't as if Hannah cared or anything. It was just good manners or something. Again the phone went immediately to message. Where the bloody hell was she? Hannah had a vision of Maddie in hospital at death's door. Picking up the house phone to make sure it was still working, she heard the dial tone loud and clear.

Well, if Maddie was dying or dead, they'd come and find her. Taking the hot water bottle, she went to bed. The wind was picking up outside and the great tree swayed wildly while rain pelted the window. Lovely night to spend on your own. Hannah curled around the hot water bottle and tried to sleep.

As soon as she set foot in the Shipwrights, Maddie had a bad feeling. She saw Tristan and knew that Mark would be on edge.

It would be bad enough that Mark couldn't let go of his past without someone constantly reminding him of his failure. She knew what living with your mistakes was like: hell. Tamsin steered them quickly to their table.

'Shall I see what's on the menu board while Anthony gets the wine?' Tamsin fled, leaving Mark and Maddie at the table.

'You OK?' Maddie asked, glancing in the direction of Tristan and Judith.

'Yes.'

'Good. I'm just going to go and say hello, then.' Maddie noticed the dead look in Mark's eyes.

'Fine.'

She walked slowly through the crowd to the end of the bar.

'Hi.' Maddie smiled at the couple.

'I think you could be Petroc's,' said Judith.

Maddie's eyes opened wide.

'Americans,' Tristan said with a big smile.

'I see. Did Helen tell you about the painting?' Maddie asked.

'Yes, but not what it means,' said Judith.

'I'm not sure I know either, but there was an American artist living in the stables at Trevenen.'

'Yes,' said Judith leaning forward.

'Well, the painting in Trevenen House looks like one of mine. Of course, this could be a fluke, but I found Peter Johnson on the internet and, well, all his work is hauntingly familiar.'

'Cool.' Judith leaned back.

'So we're not related?' Tristan asked.

'Who knows.' Maddie shrugged.

'Why don't you do the DNA test and then you'd have a clearer idea?' Judith sipped her wine.

Maddie bit her lip and thought of the three hundred pounds.

'Have you contacted the artist?' Tristan asked.

'Not yet.' Maddie laughed. 'I'm trying to figure out what to say.'

'Awkward.'

Maddie nodded.

'Hello, all.' Nate Barton walked up to them. Maddie vaguely

remembered meeting him on her first trip to this pub. 'Tristan, sorry to hear planning permission was refused on the barns. Will you try again?'

Tamsin tapped Maddie's arm. 'Hi, everyone. Sorry to pull Maddie away but we need her food order.'

'Let me know if you want to do the test.' Tristan smiled.

'Will do.' Maddie followed Tamsin to the blackboard.

'What test?' Tamsin frowned.

'Long story.' Maddie looked at the board.

'I like those.'

'Yes, I know that.'

'Never mind. Something much more interesting has just walked into the pub.' Tamsin looked at the door and Maddie turned and saw Gunnar walking towards them.

'Hi.' Tamsin beamed. 'We've dragged Maddie out to dinner. Would you like to join us?'

'That would be great.' He smiled at Tamsin but gave Maddie a searching look. Maddie shrugged and hoped that would do.

Bumping into Gunnar had been particularly bad timing. Tamsin hadn't been able to stop smiling. It wasn't fair. Maddie had wanted to keep the two men separate, but there they'd stood beside each other at the bar, one blond and laid-back and the other dark and moody. Maddie had never thought of Mark as moody before, but there was no denying the look on his face. What did it mean? Bloody Tamsin looked like she'd swallowed all the cream and then some.

Maddie stood by the window in Tamsin's kitchen, watching the three men try to start Fred's car, which had cut out as he drove in. She could hear Tamsin humming as she cleared the remains of the pudding she'd whipped up when they'd come back here from the pub. She still wasn't sure how they had all ended up playing charades, but it had been a bit of a laugh. Shame it described her life at the moment though.

Maddie moved from the window when she felt both men watching her. No doubt Mark was thinking of Hannah's lies again. He'd asked her out and now he was spending the evening in the company of his rival for her affections. What the hell was she doing? Was she really ready for all this? No, she most definitely was not.

It was two in the morning and Maddie yawned.

'Your glass is empty.' Tamsin walked over to her. 'Had you worried, having them together, didn't it?'

'You could say that.' Maddie covered her glass with her hand. 'Water. I need to keep some wits about me.'

'Which do you prefer now that you've seen them side by side?'

'Tamsin!'

'What have I said?' Tamsin asked with a gleam in her eye.

'More than enough. They could come back inside at any minute.' Maddie glanced out the window and counted heads.

'So, what's the problem? It's obvious to anyone they both fancy you.'

'I know but I don't like it.' Maddie chewed her bottom lip.

'Why ever not?'

'Look, you know me now, but not so long ago I was very different and I think all this change has me confused.'

'How were you so different?' Tamsin leaned against the kitchen counter.

'Despite living in an artistic world, I didn't sleep around. In fact, apart from John, I had had only one other lover. I was a good Catholic girl – a bit of a freak, I guess.'

'So what are you trying to tell me here?' Tamsin raised an eyebrow.

'Just that I lived a very tame life and this whole thing is really new to me.' How simple life had been then.

'So, you've a new start. Never too late to have a bit of rebellion. Run two men, live a little.' Tamsin hiccupped.

'Easier said than done. Old habits die hard.'

'No pun intended.' Tamsin smiled.

Maddie laughed.

'You're a free and beautiful woman. Let go and, like I said, live a little.'

'I don't feel free.' No, free was the last thing that Maddie felt. A ball and chain was attached and the weight of it was beginning to tell.

'Why?'

'Good question. I realise now that I've been mourning John longer than he's been dead. No matter how many times I told myself the drugs would work, I guessed in my heart that they wouldn't. It might have begun with the diagnosis, in which case it's been years. That should be enough time.'

'Ah, the cause would be Hannah then?' Tamsin suggested.

'Do you think so?' Maddie downed her water.

'Absolutely. She doesn't want you to move on. She's threatened in some way.'

'I doubt that Hannah's threatened by anything.' Maddie pushed her hair back.

'You misread her. She's so insecure.'

Maddie took a step back. 'Maybe, but what about me?' The words slipped out of her mouth.

'Are you insecure?' Tamsin sipped her wine.

'That's not what I meant.' Maddie played with her fingers.

'Well, then tell me.'

'Maybe I do need that glass of wine after all.'

'Sure.' Tamsin poured some for her.

'It's just that Hannah never gives a thought for me. I'm the source of all evil. You'd think from her point of view that I'd murdered her father instead of putting my life on hold to nurse him. Because of those years, I lost most of my career, my money and my soul.' Maddie winced, wishing she hadn't uttered those last words. Wine was making her talk. 'I'm not saying I regret it, but it's not what I'd ever imagined when I married John.'

'Was it the whole white wedding thing?' Tamsin asked.

Maddie shook her head. She didn't want to think of her joy now that all the promise and happiness were dead. 'Not quite, but I thought I'd found my soulmate and I opened my arms to Hannah. I wanted a family, a home, and a life. Instead I got one year of marriage to a wonderful man and then it all disappeared.'

Tamsin put her hand over Maddie's.

211

'I know it's stupid and selfish, but everything was taken away from me with John's diagnosis. In one blow I lost everything, including any affection Hannah had for me. For some reason, her father's illness was my fault. It was my fault that we had to sell up in London and it's my fault that I'm alive.'

'Oh, Maddie.'

'Don't "oh, Maddie" me. I know I'm being maudlin but I've given everything for John and his daughter and what have I received in return? Nothing but grief.' Maddie took another sip of wine. She longed to blurt out her pain over the baby. It was festering and growing bigger inside her. Time had not helped.

'I know what it makes me sound like. I know Hannah has no one, but neither do I. To her, I'm the stepmum from hell and I'm bloody tired of it. I've put a roof over her head and food in her stomach; she could be grateful for something. Anything would do.' Maddie's eyes were rimmed with tears. She was tired of holding it all in.

'It's OK to feel that way.' Tamsin walked closer.

Maddie laughed. 'No, it bloody isn't.'

'No one expects you to be a saint, you know.'

'Just me.' Boy did she fail that one.

'Well, I can't help that.' Tamsin smiled. 'I can just tell you that you are normal.'

'Thanks.' The corner of Maddie's mouth lifted. 'I'm just like the zillions of other women without children of their own who want them and realise that life has slipped by. The only difference is I have a harridan at home who hates the sight of me.'

'You aren't too old to have a family of your own,' Tamsin pointed out.

'Can you see that getting past the monster in my life?'

'How long have you been feeling this way about your relationship with Hannah?' Tamsin topped up Maddie's glass.

'I don't know, but it's become worse since we moved here.' Everything had intensified, as if the clear air had lifted the filter numbing her feelings.

'How?'

'It's hard to put my finger on it except that nothing's right.

The last act of kindness from her was when she found my mother's picture. I know it's stupid to be hurt, but at Christmas she couldn't be bothered to even write me a card let alone give me a present.'

'Ouch, but she's a kid and clearly she's still hurting. Didn't you say her mother abandoned her?'

'Yes, which I could never understand until now.' Maddie blinked; she never should have uttered those words.

'That's not true. You'd never abandon her, even now. I know she's hard going, but think about how she must feel. Her mum left and then her father died.'

Maddie hadn't abandoned Hannah, but she'd done worse. What would Tamsin think of her if she knew?

'Yes, well I'm still here, but I really don't know why at the moment.'

'Because you love her,' suggested Tamsin.

'Do I? I don't know any more. If all I have to look forward to from her is bitterness, I'm not sure it's worth sticking in there for the long haul. I should sell Trevenen and send her away to school and be done with it. In fact, it's what I may do.' Maddie turned the glass in her hands. Spring was coming and that would be the best time to sell Trevenen.

'Have you really reached that point?'

'I think so. The only thing holding me back is some silly loyalty to the damn house. My mother loved it and it has always been in the Penventon family.' Maddie swallowed. 'If I sell, that blows it, but it ends with me anyway. I'm the last of the bloodline so I might as well bite the bullet and rid myself of Hannah and Trevenen, who both clearly need more than I have to give.'

'But you'll have plenty of money once you sell the barn.'

'You mean if.' Maddie shrugged. Everything was so tenuous. She took a sip of wine and watched Mark and Gunnar walk into the kitchen. What did she really want?

✣ Nineteen ✣

Mark stood close as Maddie opened the door to Trevenen. Neither had uttered a word during the walk from Tamsin's except in farewell to Gunnar, who had left them at the crossroads. Tiredness oozed out of every one of Maddie's pores. She wasn't sure if it was the lateness of the hour or her chat with Tamsin, but all she wanted was her bed.

'Thanks for walking me home.'

'No problem,' he said.

'Do you want to crash in the spare room rather than walk back?'

'It's a thought.'

'Yes, it is, but be quick because I can't keep my eyes open.' Maddie leaned against the wall.

'I can see that.' Mark bent down and kissed her. She wanted to respond but her body wouldn't cooperate. Even if he came to bed with her she wouldn't be able to stay awake. He pushed her through the door and closed it behind them. Maddie blinked as the light from the kitchen blinded her.

'Where the hell have you been?' Hannah shouted.

'What?' Maddie's eyes opened wide and saw Hannah flying at her.

'You heard me. Where the hell have you been? It's bloody three-thirty.'

'Yes. It is.' Mark spoke calmly. Maddie could feel the strength of his body as she backed into him.

'Were you worried?' Mark asked.

'No. I wasn't.' Hannah stood with legs apart and arms across her chest.

'Then why are you in the kitchen with a blanket at this hour of the morning?' he asked.

'I couldn't sleep.' She turned away.

'Ever tried hot milk?' Mark eased Maddie and Hannah back into the kitchen.

'Very funny,' Hannah practically spat at him.

Maddie sank into the nearest chair. Her head floated almost free of her body. She watched without focusing as Mark put a pan of milk onto the range. Hannah stood speechless. Maddie would have laughed if she had the energy.

'Now, Hannah, you were about to tell me you were concerned about Maddie. In fact, you were worried enough about her that you couldn't sleep.' He pulled some mugs out of the cupboard.

'You ass. I couldn't sleep, that's all.'

'Then why did you want to know where she'd been?' he asked.

'It's none of your fucking business.'

'Hannah, language.' Maddie tried to sit upright.

'Shut up. Out until all hours with Mark. Think I don't know what you're up to. He just wants to shag you like all the other women he's had and then he'll dump you quick enough.'

Maddie rose to her feet. 'I've had enough of your foul mouth.' She slapped Hannah across the face and was surprised her aim was so accurate. Maddie could see her red handprint clearly on Hannah's cheek.

Hannah stood still yet Maddie could feel tremors running up her own legs. The burst of energy that had captured her quickly drained away with the realisation that she'd actually struck Hannah. For so long she'd held back, but humiliating her in front of Mark and insulting him was a step too far. Much as she hated to admit it, the sense of release was huge. She was repulsed and relieved that she had snapped.

'Christ, Maddie!' Mark spun around. 'Sit down.'

Maddie collapsed into a chair and stared at Hannah, who looked like she was about to stalk out.

'Hannah, stay put. You two need to talk.' He poured the hot

milk into mugs. 'I'm serious. This is getting out of hand.'

'Oh, how very homey, Mark. What a domestic god you are, coming to her rescue yet again. I should call ChildLine.'

'Well, you could, but what good would that do?' Mark measured up a heaping spoon of cocoa.

Hannah swung around, catching the tin and spraying its contents all over the floor as she left the room.

'Shit.' Maddie flew to try and clear the mess.

'Just sit down. I'll take care of it.'

But Maddie had already dived under the sink for the dustpan and brush, thinking that once again Hannah had left a tornado in her wake, yet she had every right to this time. Reality hit Maddie and she sank to her knees.

'Leave it. The mess can wait.' He removed the dustpan, pulled her up and pushed her into the armchair before putting the mug into her hands.

'Mark.' She tried to get up again.

'Just sit. There's been enough damage in here for the moment.'

Maddie winced. She'd struck her stepdaughter. How stupid. She used to have everything in control and now nothing was, including how she felt for Mark. God knows what he thought about her after what he'd just witnessed.

The front door slammed.

'I need to go after her.' Maddie stood.

'Sit down. You're in no fit state to go anywhere.' He placed his hand firmly on her shoulder and pushed her into the chair. 'Stay put. She'll be fine.' He looked out the window then left her and walked into the hall, where she lost sight of him. She had truly gone over the edge. Her stepdaughter had walked out of the house at four in the morning.

He came back into the kitchen. 'She's heading towards Old Tom's.'

'She can't wake him up at this hour.' Maddie yawned.

'He's always up early and I can't think of anyone better for her to talk to. He's balanced and he quite likes you.'

'Thanks.'

'Can you tell me what just happened here?' he asked.

She shook her head. She didn't know.

'Let's start at the beginning, then. Has it always been like this between you or is it only me that brings it out in her?'

Maddie laughed. 'I'm afraid you're nothing to do with it.'

'Really?' He sat down.

'Hannah's relationship with me had its good points but since her father's death, she's pulled away almost completely. Now she hates me.'

'That wasn't hatred she showed, waiting up to see if you were OK.'

'What was it then?' Maddie wanted to believe that but couldn't.

'It was concern. She didn't know where you were and couldn't reach you.'

'How do you know that?' Maddie's adrenalin had crashed. The mug was too heavy so she set it down.

'I just heard your phone beeping in the hall. Tamsin's house is notoriously bad for reception.'

'If she was that worried, why didn't she call Tamsin?' Maddie asked.

'Because that would show weakness.'

'So by hitting her, I've become the complete cow she already thinks I am.'

'No. I didn't say that,' he said.

'Yes, you did.' Maddie wondered if things could get much worse.

'Maddie, you aren't seeing this clearly. She did need to be shaken up. She was way out of line. I'm only saying that she was worried about you.'

'That gave her the right to be so rude?' Maddie frowned.

'No, but she's a kid who doesn't know yet how to handle strong emotions.'

'Clearly neither do I.' She slumped in the chair.

'That's not what I said.'

'No, it's what you implied.' Maddie sighed.

217

'I didn't. That's your interpretation. I would've hit her too. In fact, I'd thought about it.'

'You did?' Maddie leaned forward, resting her head in her hands.

'Yes, but it was more along the lines of a kick up the backside.' He placed a hand on top of hers.

'Well, that would've been more appropriate, but it's done now. She probably will call ChildLine.'

'No, she won't. She's done the best thing by turning to Old Tom. He'll listen to what she has to say and then let her hear her own words and how they sound. He's good for her.'

'I know he is. I'm not.' Every bit of her ached.

'That's not true. You love her.'

Everything was upside down. Hannah had stayed awake waiting for Maddie while Maddie had been out all hours. 'Yes. Yes, I suppose I do, but right now it's easy to lose sight of that.'

'If you didn't love her then her words wouldn't hurt you so much.'

Maddie gave him a small smile.

'Off you go to get some sleep. You'll need all your energy for later.'

Maddie stood. 'Are you still planning to crash in the spare room?'

'Unless you're offering a different accommodation?' Mark raised an eyebrow.

'And give Hannah something to really shout about? I don't think so.'

Mark laughed and kissed her forehead. Maddie walked slowly through the sitting room, wishing she hadn't been so rash and sent him to the spare room. The thought of curling up to him was more than appealing. However, she doubted she even had enough energy to climb the stairs, let alone cope with the temptation of Mark in her bed.

The pillow over her head hadn't blocked out the cries. Tossing and turning, Maddie accepted defeat and sat up. Her head hurt but not too badly. She should feel worse because she deserved to feel rotten. Her loss of control last night was reprehensible. Hannah would never forgive her. It was the second unforgiveable action of her life. Maddie was wracking them up willy-nilly.

The bedside light illuminated just how cold it was in her room. Mark's heater couldn't cope and she understood how not coping felt. Sighing, she knew that snuggling under her duvet looking at her breath wasn't accomplishing anything and it hadn't made the sounds go away.

With her warmest clothes on, she crept downstairs and turned on the sitting room lights. The noises had stopped, she noted with relief. There must be a stray cat or maybe a fox. She hadn't followed up her conversation with the vicar, or anyone else for that matter. But after she'd made herself some tea, she'd come back and be a rational adult and look properly behind the door without fear. She might even ask Mark for help, and she needn't tell him that it was because she heard a baby crying.

Looking at her watch, she realised it was seven and much later than she'd thought. The mornings were still so dark. She threw on all the lights as she made her way through to the kitchen, the scene of the crime. She frowned, knowing her first task would be cleaning up the spilt cocoa powder.

'Good morning.' Mark sat at the table with a pen and paper.

'Morning.' Maddie smiled.

'Sleep well?' he asked.

'No. You?'

'No.'

'What disturbed you?' She put the kettle on and started getting the teapot and two mugs out.

'A cat, I think.'

Maddie stopped. 'You heard it too?'

'Yes, I had a look around but couldn't find it.' He stood and stretched. 'It seemed to be coming from the smuggler's room, but then sound can carry in strange ways.'

Maddie nodded and took a deep breath. 'Did you go into the room?'

'Yes, but found nothing. I did admire the floor, though.

Impressive sized slabs. You just don't find pieces that large these days, or at least not for flooring.'

'They remind me of gravestones.'

He laughed. 'They're about the right size for it. Maybe they are cast-offs.'

Maddie shivered and decided to change the subject. 'What's the pen and paper for?'

'Oh, just my to-do list.' He smiled.

'Can I add something to it?' she asked.

He nodded.

'A list of good estate agents for me to contact.'

'It's come to that, has it?'

'To be truthful, I don't know but …' Maddie trailed off and looked out the window.

'But what?' he asked.

'I guess I need to know what options I have.' *Or if I have any at all*, she added silently.

'Do you want to sell Trevenen?'

'No.' Maddie sighed. 'But sometimes what we want in life has very little to do with what we get.'

Hannah rubbed her eyes when she heard Mark talking with OT in the kitchen. When did he arrive?

'I was wondering when I'd see you.' OT's voice was quiet but clear.

'Is she still here?' Mark asked.

'Yes, sound asleep on the sofa. Poor mite is worn out.'

'I'm not surprised. What has she told you?' Mark asked.

Hannah hated it when other people spoke about her, but she was too tired to move.

'In between the tears, that Maddie slapped her. That you were sleeping with Maddie and that her life was ruined. That Maddie would leave her or, more to the point, you would take Maddie away.'

'Right, then, that's simple. If I pull back, Hannah should calm down.'

Mark had a brain. Hannah rolled over.

220

'No. The next man who takes an interest in the beautiful Maddie will suffer the same fate and Hannah will just push Maddie further away to try and protect herself.'

'What are you saying?' Mark asked.

'Hannah is afraid of being abandoned again.'

Hannah sat up.

'Really?'

'Yes. I surmise, looking beyond her anger, that she thinks that Maddie will leave her just as her own mother did. She feels Maddie will go off with some man and forget her,' OT said.

Hannah swung her feet to the floor.

'So it's my fault,' Mark said.

'Not quite, dear boy.' OT paused. 'The child has been traumatised by the events of her life and has become a bit of a drama queen in the process. All is not yet lost though. Maddie loves Hannah. You are fond of Hannah and you are in love with Maddie.' OT coughed.

'So you have it all worked out?'

'Yes.'

'You think it's that simple?' Mark asked.

'No, it's not simple at all. You note, I never married. I know only too well that while things might appear simple, they are not at all. How's Maddie?'

'Shattered and worried.'

Too right, the cow. Where was that ChildLine number? Hannah stretched.

'Call and tell her Hannah is fine,' OT said.

Fine? Bloody not fine. She rubbed her eyes.

'Yes, sir.' Mark laughed.

Hannah could hear Mark punching in the numbers. 'Maddie. She's here and sleeping. Tom says she's OK.'

Hannah listened to the silence.

'No need. Do you want to talk to Tom?' Mark asked.

No, that is not a good idea. Hannah didn't want OT telling Maddie any of her thoughts. She felt betrayed enough by what he had said to Mark. She could break up Maddie and Mark, she was sure of it. OT had it all wrong.

Hannah left the comfort of the sofa and walked into the kitchen. 'What are you doing here?'

'About to have tea with Tom. You?' Mark smiled.

Liar. Hannah plonked into a chair. 'You bloody well know why I'm here.'

'Language, Hannah.' OT frowned.

'Sorry.' She slumped.

'Hannah, would you be kind enough to make tea for us all? I would be most grateful.' OT rose from the chair and walked towards the sitting room.

'Sure.' Hannah cast Mark a filthy look. Maddie must have sent him. She'd do that, the cow. She wouldn't have the courage to come herself, but sent the male to do her bidding.

Without thinking, Hannah laid the tea equipment onto the tray. OT was so set in his ways yet he was always grateful for her company. She swirled the boiling water in the pot and watched a few old tea leaves slip down the plug hole. They'd drunk three pots this morning when she'd arrived. He'd been reading by the fire when she turned up. The red mark on her face had calmed down in the cold air yet she was sure it had been visible. Even now she could still feel Maddie's hand on her face.

Hannah looked at Mark sitting in the small armchair by the fire as she carried the tray into the room. He seemed all thoughtful, yet last night he'd been calm considering the slanging match he'd witnessed.

'Thank you, Hannah.' OT gave her one of his wonderful smiles that told her she was OK.

'Sure.' She slid onto the sofa, knowing that the next words out of OT's mouth would be 'please pour'. It was always a ritual with him and everything was treated with respect.

'Will you pour please, Hannah?' OT asked.

'Yes.' She slipped into the practice she'd followed since her first few visits. She missed their time in the workshop, but knew that standing for long periods wasn't on the agenda for OT for a while.

She held out a cup for Mark and looked at his big hands, which reminded her of him making the hot milk last night.

He wasn't a bad bloke, but he wasn't going to be with Maddie. Hannah must stop it before it went any further, but she would need to do this carefully because Mark was Will's uncle, after all.

'Thanks, Hannah,' said Mark.

Resisting the urge to give him the finger, she produced some sort of smile. She handed OT a cup. He was so much better. The colour of his skin seemed normal again. He didn't look too well around New Year. No doubt the time in the hospital hadn't helped. Hannah was pleased that her father had spent so little time in one. She could still see him lying on a bed in the sitting room. Her friends couldn't understand why he'd wanted to be there in the centre of things. They just couldn't cope with his illness. But just because he was ill didn't mean that he didn't want to live the life he had left.

Hannah wasn't really sure why she was thinking about her dad. Neither of these two men were anything like him. Mark was the exact opposite in looks. Dad had been shorter, thinner and fairer. And OT was just old style very English.

'Hannah, would you care to see if there is any cake left? I'm sure that Mark might enjoy a piece, as would I.'

Hannah smiled at OT but sent Mark daggers as she fled to the kitchen. How could OT be so considerate of Mark? Yes, Mark had been a star when OT was really in need of help and he'd saved her from drowning, but he loved Maddie. Well, that was what OT had said and Mark hadn't denied it.

She could hear their voices but not the words as she found the cake and slapped it onto a plate. She was almost back when she remembered plates, napkins, knives and forks. All this ceremony got to her sometimes but OT was great, so she put up with his quirks.

'Ah, you found some. Excellent. Thank you. Mark, can we tempt you?' OT's hand waved out over the cake like he was giving some blessing. Why was he keeping Mark here when he knew he was almost the last person she wanted to see? OT never did anything without a reason, so what was his cunning plan? Hannah watched Mark smile and nod. She almost wished she could like him, but that was impossible while he was connected to Maddie.

❖ Twenty ❖

The cursor flashed on the screen. Maddie began to transcribe her jumbled notes onto the computer.

Dear Peter,

My name is Madeline Hollis and I'm the daughter of Nancy Penventon.

She paused. That was straightforward enough but where did she go from here?

I'm writing to you because I have recently inherited a house, Trevenen, in Cornwall and ...

And what? Do you remember sleeping with my mother? No, that wasn't going to work.

... certain things have come to light.

Maddie's fingers hovered over the keys. It was suitably vague.

I was wondering if you could remember the summer of 1970 and your stay here at Trevenen? I'm trying to piece together a bit of a puzzle ...

That was a bit of an understatement, thought Maddie.

... and I'm wondering if you could help. If you don't mind, I would like to call you at your convenience.

Maddie winced. It was ghastly and didn't say what she wanted it to. This was probably because she didn't know what that was, but it was better than the last five attempts. She was tired of thinking about it. She signed off with her contact details and pressed send before she could change her mind.

Maddie pulled the papers out of her bag. She'd spent the afternoon in the Helston library working on the internet. Before her lay the research she'd done for Hannah on her mother. She wasn't having much luck but she supposed it was better than her last attempt. Maddie wondered if any of John's old friends had kept in touch with Susan. Tomorrow, she'd ring a few and they might be able to shed some light on what had happened all those years ago.

She glanced at the clock. It was six-thirty and Hannah wasn't home. Each day this week she'd held her breath until Hannah had come through the door. Now Maddie was dressed for dinner with Gunnar and there was no sign of her. She should have been home an hour ago. Maddie told herself that she shouldn't be worried, but she knew that was useless.

Since last Saturday night, Maddie had been walking on eggshells. They'd barely spoken. She wanted to apologise and the more she thought about it, the more she realised how wrong her actions had been. Yes, Hannah's behaviour had played a part, but that didn't justify what Maddie had done. She was an adult and had long ago learned to keep her anger in check. Maddie didn't know how to stop the gap between them from reaching the point of never being crossed again, but the continued silence didn't help.

She jumped when the phone rang.

'Maddie, Tom here.'

'How are you?' she asked.

'Very well. I was ringing to say that Hannah is here at present, helping me with my books. Didn't want you to worry.'

Maddie let out a sigh. 'Thanks, Tom.'

'The young don't appreciate the worry we have. They don't see the problem.'

'Yes, so I gather.'

'Are you free to come to dinner tomorrow night?' he asked.

'That would be lovely. May I bring something?'

'Pudding. I'm hopeless at them, but I love them so.'

'It would be a pleasure. What time?' she asked.

'Seven-thirtyish,' he said.

'Wonderful. Thanks.'

Maddie put the phone down, wondering if it would have hurt Hannah to call her herself? No, she mustn't think like that. It only built up the anger again. Hannah was a teen and she needed to learn these things. If only Maddie would be allowed to help her, but clearly that wasn't going to happen.

Maddie glanced at her watch. Gunnar was late. At this point, she really needed an uncomplicated relationship. She might possibly want some wild sex to remember that she wasn't the dried up old fart she felt like most of the time. She laughed. Maybe she could combine uncomplicated with wild sex and still keep life simple. So possibly she should cast all caution aside? Somehow, she doubted she could achieve this as some things ran too deep. But she could sure as hell give it a go. Maybe Gunnar was in for a lucky night ...

The phone rang again. Slowly, Maddie rose from the chair. 'Hello.'

'It's Gunnar here.'

'Hi.' Maddie smiled.

'I'm sorry to do this, but I have to cancel. My producer wants the script by tomorrow so I'll be working all night.'

'That's OK.' Maddie tried to keep the disappointment from her voice. If Gunnar only knew what an opportunity he was missing; but maybe this was payback for the other night.

'May I ring in a few days to set up another date?' he said.

'That would be great.' Could she hold onto the wild abandon she'd felt moments ago until then, or would common sense prevail?

'Must get back to work. Bye.' He rang off.

Well, so much for some debauchery and hello to Friday evening telly. She looked at the fridge. No inspiration for dinner emerged while staring at the outside but maybe a peep inside would motivate her to whip something up.

She must remember, as Tamsin had said, that so much had happened in her life recently that she shouldn't be too hard on herself. But sitting alone on a Friday night didn't help.

'Well, Trevenen, it's just me and you tonight, isn't it?' She paused and the only response she could hear was the pelting rain.

'Oh, are you not speaking to me either? What have I done to you?' Again, silence except for the hum of the fridge. 'Nothing, you say. Well, that's not quite true. I want to do so much but can't yet.' She closed her eyes and hoped that Mark was right about the barn.

She turned to the window. Why did she have to think about Mark? He hadn't asked her out tonight. In fact, she hadn't seen him since he left last Saturday. No doubt after he discovered he wasn't needed as a witness in a child abuse case, he'd run for the hills, and she couldn't blame him. But, damn it, she missed him. Was it the way his eyes crinkled up when he smiled or was it the way her body reacted when he was near? Stop it, stop it. She pulled the leftover chicken soup out of the fridge and slammed the door. A bit splashed onto her silk blouse.

'Shit.' Maddie looked at the spot.

She placed the bowl on the table and then walked through the house. Trevenen required lots of love and she'd tried as best she could with what she had available. But the coats of paint she'd slapped on when they first arrived had only touched the tired surface and didn't reach its real needs. She paused in the sitting room.

Her first look, as always, went to the fireplace. Mark had agreed that the slate slabs did look like gravestones. She sighed. The cries filled every night. Maddie continued to tell herself that it was a cat, but her heart said something different. She knew the sound of a new-born's cries. This, of course, was insane.

Forcing her eyes away, she studied the rest of the room, loving its proportions. The ceiling was high, the plaster crumbling around the edges, and damp patches decorated the walls. She had some of the skills required to mend the decorative mouldings, but not when she was trying to earn a living. She hadn't done either and she didn't know why. In the past, she'd managed her time far better than now. Both her career and Trevenen deserved more than she was giving them. Truthfully, she acknowledged that applied to everything in her life.

Once in her bedroom, she flung off the pretty silk top and put on a soft cashmere sweater. It was moth-eaten in a few places, but warm. Next, she found her favourite jeans. Finally, she pulled out thick socks and then padded back to the kitchen, at last feeling comfortable in her own skin.

With the soup on, she hunted for some bread that didn't have a life of its own. No success until she delved deep into the freezer and found a loaf. She stood eyeing a bottle of wine when she heard wheels crunch on the drive. Glancing out of the window, she couldn't make out the car in the gushing rain. It was a filthy night and she wondered briefly how Hannah was going to get home. But Maddie knew she wouldn't take too well to being rescued by her stepmother, so she wouldn't offer this time.

Maddie walked to the door, waiting for the knock, but she still jumped when she heard it. Flinging the door wide, she found a waterlogged Mark.

'Come in quick.' Maddie backed away from his dripping form.

'Hi to you, too.'

'Sorry, I was just being practical.' She gave him a light kiss on the cheek, making sure that her lips were the only part of her to touch him. She was mesmerised by the beads of water rolling off him but moved into action. On the way to the kitchen, she took a towel out of the airing cupboard. Handing it to him, she watched as he rubbed his hair. The resulting hairdo sent her into a fit of giggles.

'That good?' he asked.

'Definitely. What happened?'

'Flat tyre.'

'No roadside assistance?' She raised an eyebrow.

'No signal and I'm capable of changing my own tyre.'

'Of course.' Maddie couldn't keep the smile from her face.

Mark threw the wet towel at her.

'Hey,' she complained.

He walked to her, never taking his eyes from her until he stood inches away. 'I was on my way over to see you. I've been in Tresco on the Scilly Isles all week. With all the bad weather, the phones never seemed to work.'

'Oh.' Maddie grabbed the back of the chair behind her.

'I was worried about you,' he said.

'Thanks.' She licked her lips. He was too close.

'Are you OK?' he asked.

'Yes, drier than you, anyway.' She laughed.

'That wouldn't take much.' The corner of his mouth turned up.

'No, it wouldn't. Why don't you stand by the range and take the wet things off?'

'Because everything is …' He looked down at the puddle by his feet.

'I see,' she said.

'No, you don't, but you would if I did.' He smiled.

She swallowed. He closed the gap between them. A cold wetness permeated her jeans but she still felt warm.

'You'd better take your clothes off, they're completely soaked,' Maddie whispered.

'You sure?' He hadn't moved away. His mouth was an inch from hers.

'Yes. You'll catch a cold.'

'I don't feel cold,' he said.

'Neither do I.' She stepped back and bumped into the table. 'I'll go and get my old dressing gown for you.'

'I'm sure I'll look my best in it.'

'Absolutely.' Maddie raced from the kitchen with visions of Mark covered in a pink and purple flowered dressing gown, which had her tripping on the stairs to her bedroom. Flinging the cupboard doors open, she grabbed the old thing. She wasn't even sure why she still had it. It was ghastly but it had been a present from her mother years ago. The dear woman would be horrified if she knew a naked man would be wearing it. Trying to shake that thought, Maddie walked calmly back to the kitchen.

Her composure disappeared with the sight of Mark only wearing the towel she'd thrown at him earlier.

'Are you just going to stand there or are you planning on painting me?' he asked with a big grin.

'There's a thought. Would you pose nude for me?' she asked.

'I damn near am now, but it's a bit draughty in here.'

'True.' She walked towards him, taking her time. She didn't want him covered in the ratty old dressing gown. She just wanted to look at him and then slowly touch him all over. Holding out the robe, she kept her distance, but couldn't stop her eyes from drinking in every bit of him on display.

'I didn't have you down as a voyeur,' he said.

'Sorry, part of the job description.' She blushed and turned her back to him but she heard his chuckle. Try as she might, she couldn't shake the desire she was feeling from just looking at him.

'It's safe now,' he said.

'It wasn't before?' she asked as she turned.

'That depends.' His eyes had a wicked glint in them.

'Does it?' Maddie bit her lip.

'Yes, your eyes were sending me some very interesting signals.'

'Were they?' She raised an eyebrow.

'Yes.'

'Well, I'm afraid to break this to you, but purple and pink are not your colours.' She reached beyond him and turned the soup off.

'Well, no hope of getting lucky in this get-up, then,' he said.

'Absolutely none.' She smiled. He still looked divine. 'Are you staying for supper?'

'If you're offering. The spare on the car is flat as well. I only just made it here.'

'Oh, do you need to call someone?' Maddie sliced the bread.

'I thought I might borrow your car until tomorrow. No need to bring someone else out in this weather. So where's Hannah?' He looked up to her room above.

'With Old Tom.' Maddie found she could barely speak as the knot in her stomach was so tight. 'I think she's spent a great deal of this week there. He's asked me to dinner tomorrow night.'

'Me too.'

'I bet it's a thank you, which means that Tamsin and Anthony and a few others will be going.'

'Yes, I should think so.'

She took a deep breath. By not looking at him and having an ordinary conversation, she could try and ignore the fact that Mark was stark naked under the flowers.

'Shall I lay?' he asked.

'What?' Maddie swung round.

'The table.' Mark was grinning.

'Yes. Thank you.' Maddie gave her full attention to the toaster. Now she had to remove the image of Mark lying naked across the table from her mind. She was not some sex-starved teenager, but she was beginning to feel that way.

'Just soup?' he asked.

''Fraid so. I wasn't expecting company.' She turned to find him smiling at her. Seizing on anything that would make the fact of Mark wearing a dressing gown at her table seem totally normal, Maddie poured the soup and placed the toast on a plate. She held her breath, trying to stem the tide of desire she was feeling. He, on the other hand, sat relaxed at the table, revealing a large expanse of chest, courtesy of the robe. Her mind swiftly travelled to what must be exposed below the table. She sat down.

'How was Hannah this week?' He took a mouthful of soup.

'Don't really know.'

'In what way?' he asked.

'When she's not at Old Tom's she barely utters a word to me.' She put her spoon down.

'That's bad?'

'Yes.' She frowned and he smiled at her. 'Do you want more soup?'

'That was perfect.'

She laughed. 'Leftover chicken soup, perfect? Now that's a new one.'

'But it is. You don't make chicken soup for one.'

'You're right, I never thought of it that way.' She tipped her head to one side and studied him.

'Did you when you were single?' Mark asked.

'No.' Maddie smiled and then frowned. Why was Mark still single? He was gorgeous, talented and kind. It didn't make sense. 'Mark?'

'This sounds serious.'

Maddie bit her lip. Should she go on or just leave it? 'Why have you never married again?'

'So the grapevine has caught up with you.'

'Not sure what you mean about that, but Tamsin did mention that you'd lost your wife a while ago and I just wondered. No, never mind. It's none of my business.' The light atmosphere had disappeared with her words and she wished she hadn't begun this conversation.

'Let's just say I'm not too good at commitment.'

'Oh.' She had hoped he would say something like, 'I just haven't met the right one'. Without looking at him, she stood to clear the bowls, wondering if she might have some pudding to offer him, as despite what he said, soup and toast didn't seem like much of a meal.

She needed to say something to end the awkward silence. 'Cheese?'

'No thanks.'

She kept her head down, thinking about how to take her words back, and bumped into him at the sink. He was so silent in his bare feet.

'Sorry.' Maddie moved aside.

'I'll do the washing up,' he said.

'Thanks but you sit down. The floor must be cold on your feet.'

'I can take it.' He spoke quietly and Maddie stood still. He was just too near. His scent surrounded her. She began to move away but drew closer to him instead.

'You don't think I can take it?' he asked.

'No.' She was inches from him and filled with so many conflicting emotions. She couldn't look at his face, so stared at the hair on his chest instead. Her fingers hovered but stopped short of touching him.

'Is there something you want, Maddie?' His words seemed to come from his chest. She could see its rise and fall.

'Yes.' Maddie swallowed and decided. She looked into his eyes. 'You.'

'In this? You must be joking.' He pointed to the flowers.

'If I must, but I would prefer you without it.' She pulled him close.

With care, Hannah removed the will from her bag. OT was sitting across the kitchen table, his hands neatly folded. She removed the pink tissue paper. It was all she could find to protect it from the school junk in her bag and thankfully it seemed to have made it through the day unscathed. She held it out. His hands shook a little and this was something worrying; she'd noticed it earlier with the tea cups.

He stroked the outside and carefully unfolded it. The word reverence leapt to Hannah's mind. OT was treating the document with reverence. Wow. Maybe she shouldn't have carried it in her backpack.

'This is one of the artefacts you found in the chest we repaired?'

Hannah nodded. OT's fingers hovered over the text as if he were almost reading braille.

'I've tried to decode it but got nowhere.' Hannah looked at the top of OT's head.

'Understandable. Had this already been opened when you found it?' He looked up.

Hannah swallowed. If anyone else but OT had asked that question, she would have lied but she couldn't with him. 'No.'

'Interesting.' He bent over it again. 'You are correct that it is a will of sorts.'

'Whose?' she asked.

'A Catherine Penventon.'

Hannah tapped her fingers. She was filled with questions but she knew there was no point in trying to rush OT, it just didn't work. She stood up and went to peer over his shoulder, hoping that suddenly she'd be able to read it, but it all just merged together. Turning, she looked out the window at the non-stop rain.

'Very interesting,' OT said as he sat back in his chair.

'What is?' Hannah remained standing.

'Tell me what else you know about the Penventon family.'

'Not much.'

'I see.' He put the fingers of both hands together. To Hannah, it looked like he was praying.

'Well, on the surface, this is a simple will made by Catherine Penventon, leaving Trevenen to her son Thomas, who was to be in the guardianship of her brother James Penventon. Her sister Mary was to have the right to live in the house as long as she remained unmarried.'

'You said on the surface.'

'Yes, I did. I just feel there is something more to this. Did you find any other papers from this time?'

'No. What's going on?'

'It could be nothing, but unless she was a widow and had married a cousin called Penventon, then something is not as it would appear.'

'Illegitimate child?'

'I can't say for certain but it is interesting that this will had never been opened.'

She nodded.

'Have you seen a family Bible or any other family documents in the house?'

'Yes, I think so.' Hannah vaguely remembered seeing something big and thick and dusty but couldn't remember where. 'What's the big deal about an illegitimate child?'

'What do they teach you of social history or culture?' he asked.

'Not a lot or I wasn't listening because it wasn't a test question.' Hannah paced the kitchen floor.

OT shook his head. 'Now, when you find the Bible, could you look on the inside opening and closing pages?'

'Sure, why?' Hannah perched on the edge of a chair.

'Often, families recorded their lineage on them, noting births, deaths, marriages and so forth.'

'Oh. I'll have a good look then. Do you think there'd be one that old lurking about?'

'Well, probably not, but a later one might have included what information they had from the past.'

'Cool.' Hannah paused. 'I do know that Maddie has been doing a bit of poking around the Penventon family history because I saw her notes on the kitchen table.'

'Excellent. Ask her what she has discovered. Now, have you heard from young Will?' He sat back in the chair.

'Yeah. I had an email from him. He's off skiing in a few weeks, the rat.'

'Why is he a rat for skiing?' OT asked.

'He won't be here for half term.' Hannah rolled her eyes.

'Ah, I see.' He carefully covered the will in the pink tissue. 'Are you doing anything special for half term?'

'No.' She looked at her fingernails. 'I don't think so since I haven't spoken more than five words to Maddie since last week.'

'Is that wise?' he asked.

'Probably not, but it's how I feel.'

'Has she tried to speak to you?' he asked.

'Yeah.' She played with her necklace while looking at the floor.

'And you rebuffed her.'

'What?' She looked up at OT and saw the knowing smile on his face.

'You sent her packing?'

'Well, yes. Look, she's a cow.' She put up a hand to stop

OT's automatic correction. 'I have to live with her, but that's all.'

'Is that all you want?' he asked.

'Yeah.' She nodded but felt tears prick at the back of her eyes. 'She's nothing but a meal ticket, really. I didn't choose her, but I'm stuck with her for a few more years.'

'How do you think she feels about it?'

'Well, she chose to go ahead with it.' She turned away.

'Does that tell you something?' he asked.

'Yeah, Dad guilted her into it.' Hannah spoke through gritted teeth.

'She still could have said no. She hadn't adopted you before.'

'No, but she wouldn't have said no because she's too stupid.'

'Is stupid the right word? I think that may be selling both of you short.'

'Yeah, whatever. Do you want some tea?' Hannah hopped up and went to the sink. Her hands gripped its white ceramic sides.

'No, thank you, but do help yourself.'

'Thanks. I may take a walk.' She looked out the window.

'In this weather? In fact, I think unless Maddie can collect you, you may have to stay the night. Unfortunately I'm not up to driving yet.'

Hannah looked out into the darkness of the garden. She couldn't see anything but she could hear the rain hitting the window in blasts. OT was right; she couldn't go out in this weather.

'Hannah, do you wish to talk about it?' he asked.

'I thought you were a history teacher not a psychology one?' she said.

'One needs a bit of psychology to teach, don't you think?' He smiled.

'No, all teachers do is regurgitate necessary information for bloody exams.'

'Then you have been very unlucky in your teachers and if all you ask is that from them, you have short-changed yourself. Hannah, you are a very bright child.'

'I'm not a child.' She swung round from the sink. The tears were streaming down her cheeks and she didn't care that OT could see them. Everything was simple for him.

'Then what you need to do, young woman, is ask for more from yourself, your teachers and from Maddie.'

'What has she got to do with my education?' she asked.

'Everything. She is at home with you and education of how to live life begins and ends there.'

'I'm living and I don't need to learn anything else. Maddie's taught me nothing in the past and can teach me nothing in the future.'

'No? What about the lesson of sticking with something because it is the right thing to do, even when it repeatedly kicks you in the teeth?' he asked.

'Oh, so that's how you see it. You're taking Maddie's side at last.'

'I am not taking anyone's side, I was simply pointing out there is another one. How about altering your own life for those that you love?'

'What's she given up? She took me from London and brought me here.' Hannah wiped her nose on the back of her hand.

OT handed her his handkerchief. 'Before that, what about caring for your father while he was dying?'

'She was his wife.'

'He could have spent his last years in a hospital or hospice, but instead she put her work on hold and nursed him.'

'Yeah ... but how do you know all this?' she asked.

'I have ears. I am interested in other people and I ask questions. I don't just accept what information is regurgitated to me.'

'Thanks.' Hannah walked into the sitting room and considered throwing the cushions on the sofa, but this was not her room. Everything had a place in OT's house. The books were ordered on the shelves just as the cushions were on the sofa. She wanted to hit something. The lights flickered, reminding her that there was a storm raging outside. Shit, she needed to lash out.

'Would you care for a glass of wine or sherry?' OT called.

Hannah's legs collapsed and she fell on the sofa laughing. Now she'd heard everything: OT offering her a drink. What should she do?

'Wine, please.' She whipped one of the cushions off its neat pile and hugged it. She was trapped in OT's house and trapped in Cornwall. She was being handed red wine in a cut crystal glass. She was going crazy.

'Feel better yet?' he asked.

'No. What do you bloody well think?'

'Language.'

'Sod language.' She took a sip. 'Thank you. It tastes really nice.'

'Yes, it's one of my favourites, but I am unable to drink it any more. I'm pleased you like it.'

Hannah looked at what must be whisky in his glass. That too was in cut crystal. She hadn't recalled seeing these before, but then she'd never had a drink here except at Christmas when they had champagne and of course the beers she and Will knocked back. That seemed a long time ago now.

'Do you miss wine?' She swirled the liquid.

'Yes but that's life. I think I shall serve that wine tomorrow night.'

'What's happening tomorrow night?'

'I'm having a few people over for dinner to say thank you. Are you free?' he asked.

'I suppose so. Can I help?'

'Yes, that would be very kind. I'm afraid we will have to eat in the kitchen as the dining room is still a bedroom.'

'The kitchen's nice.' She smiled.

'Yes.'

'But it's not very you, is it?'

'No, quite.'

Hannah smiled. She looked at the glass in her hand. She could imagine the gleaming polished surface of the dining table covered in crystal and silver. The kitchen didn't have that sort of style.

✦ Twenty-One ✦

Maddie's heel caught on the gusset of her knickers and she toppled on to the bed before hitting the floor with a thump. She was winded and couldn't move straight away.

Mark came running into the room. 'Are you all right?'

Maddie picked the black lace off her shoe so she could resume a more ladylike pose. She hoped that nothing but her suspenders and stockings had been visible. Why the hell didn't she have any tights?

'Do I look OK?' She laughed.

'To me, yes, but some might say it was quite a compromising position.'

She slipped off a shoe and threw it at him.

'I take that as an invitation to leave.'

'Exactly.'

Once Mark was out of sight downstairs, Maddie rolled over onto her knees and then stood up. Had he really just walked in here to find her sprawled on the floor with her knickers hanging off her heel? Maddie realised it didn't bear thinking about as she scrambled to finish dressing. She'd never know why she'd put her shoes on first. She'd been in a fluff all day today, but then she remembered why and smiled.

With haste, she adjusted her dress and took one last glance in the mirror. She looked good, even if she said so herself. She was glowing. She bolted downstairs before she thought about that any more.

'Has Hannah gone on ahead?' Maddie noted Mark was alone in the kitchen. Her heart skipped a beat. She'd never pictured him in a suit and he looked edible. Then again she'd never imagined him in a purple and pink dressing gown, either.

'No, she'll be right down,' he said.

'You look wonderful.' Maddie moved closer and ran a hand over his lapel before she straightened his tie.

'So do you. I like what's underneath, too.' He grinned.

She tapped his arm and pulled away when she heard Hannah on the stairs. Maddie picked up the flan she'd made.

'Ready?' Hannah popped her head through the door and Maddie nearly fainted. Hannah was wearing a red sheath dress. It showed her cute little figure, which was normally hidden under layers of jumpers. She looked almost elegant. Only the heavy black eye make-up spoiled the sweet appearance. Maddie wondered if it was the same child. Had the wrong one come home from Old Tom's this afternoon?

'You look lovely.' Maddie stood quietly, bracing herself.

'Thanks. You do too.'

Maddie's eyes opened wide and she almost stuttered. 'Thank you.'

'Shall we be off?' Mark held open the front door. The ground was still very wet but the rain had finally stopped, Maddie noted with relief.

'How many people are coming to Tom's tonight?' Maddie turned to Hannah in the back seat.

'Nine, if you count OT.'

'That's quite a number. It's great that you've been able to help him.'

'Yeah.'

Old Tom's house was ablaze with light as they drove up. Three other cars were there already.

'Looks like we're the last to arrive.' Mark turned the engine off.

'I've got to run.' Hannah slipped out of the door and dashed as fast as her heels would carry her. Maddie watched the flash of blonde hair disappear.

'She cleans up well.' Mark opened Maddie's door and took the flan.

'Yes, a bit of a surprise, really. Except for her father's funeral, I don't think I've ever seen her really try.'

'Old Tom's a good influence on her.'

'Yes.' Maddie picked her way through the puddles to the front of the house. She knew Tom might object to his evening guests traipsing through the kitchen.

'Welcome, Maddie. You look lovely, really lovely.' Tom greeted her with two kisses. She smiled. He appeared dapper in his dinner jacket.

Maddie moved into the room. She hadn't felt this light in years; in fact, not since she was first married to John. Mark seemed happy, too. She watched him shake the old man's hand and saw Hannah take the pudding to the kitchen.

The front door had remained open and in walked Will. He looked so like his uncle that Maddie's heart twisted. She wondered if Hannah knew that Will would be here. Maybe that was why she was all dressed up.

'Hi there.' Tamsin sidled up and handed Maddie a glass of champagne. 'I must say, you're looking amazing. Was this because Hannah had to spend last night here?'

'No. I'm just feeling good.' Maddie gave Tamsin a questioning look.

'Then the glow must be due to the fact that there was no answer at Mark's last night or this morning. He's wearing a huge grin.'

'Tamsin.' Maddie gagged on her drink.

'Don't "Tamsin" me. I now know the truth. Was it good?' Tamsin's eyes twinkled. Maddie could feel colour rushing to her face. She should've known that Tamsin would have guessed.

'Hello, Maddie.' Anthony gave her a kiss. 'You're looking very well.'

'Thank you.' Maddie threw a look at Tamsin, who giggled.

There was a sudden shriek from the kitchen and the sound of a pan hitting the floor. Maddie ran to help but stopped dead in her tracks when she saw Hannah's arms flung around Will's neck. Well, that answered her earlier question. Hannah had made the effort for Old Tom or maybe for herself, which was something indeed.

Maddie stood by the fire and looked around. She recognised Mrs Bates but wasn't too sure who the others were. Mark was chatting to one. He looked up and gave her a wink. She must hang on to her sanity, but it was slipping away.

'Tom, what a lovely idea this is. Are you sure you haven't overdone it?' Maddie held her glass out as Tom refilled it with champagne.

'Hannah has done most of it. I wanted to have a word with you about her.'

Maddie nodded, preparing herself.

'Not tonight,' he said.

'Fine.' Maddie tried to smile. 'She looks lovely.'

'She does indeed. Glowing, now that Will is here. A bit like you with Mark.'

'Tom.' Maddie tried to look shocked.

'It's a small place. Remember, nothing is secret.' He smiled despite his words of warning and went to refill more glasses. Maddie collapsed against the mantelpiece. Could she handle this, now it was out in the open? Hell, it wasn't anything at this stage.

The object of her thoughts was smiling at her over the top of Mrs Bates' head. She didn't want to be here; she wanted to be at Trevenen, alone with him.

Hannah beamed as she walked around with a silver tray in her hands. Maddie wondered how Tom had kept the surprise of Will's visit from Hannah. In the distance, Maddie saw Hannah politely discussing the food with a woman. She couldn't detect any trace of Hannah's usual insolence. Was there hope after all?

Mark came and stood beside her. 'Quite the transformation.' His eyes followed Hannah as she moved about the room.

'Yes.' Just looking at him filled her with desire. Did Mark feel the same way? Was she in this alone? Was he just glowing because of a fantastic night of sex?

'Have I told you how delicious you look tonight?' He smiled.

'Mark, please stop. Everyone seems to know,' she protested, but his finger on her lips stopped her.

'Do they? Why would that be?'

'The satisfied smile on your face, I think.' As she spoke, it became wider.

'I could just pull you into my arms and kiss you here.' His voice dropped to a whisper. 'Which is only the beginning of what I want to do.'

'Mrs Bates, how lovely to see you.' Maddie stood tall and stuck out her hand, desperately hoping that because of Mrs Bates' age, her hearing wasn't what it might have been.

'Yes, dear, good to see you looking so well.'

'Thanks.' Maddie watched Mark smother his laugh in a sip of champagne. 'I've been meaning to ask you about Daphne. I understand you knew her well?'

'I did. Fine woman,' Mrs Bates said.

'Who was Arthur Tripconey?' Maddie asked.

'He was Daphne's fiancé. He never made it home from the war.' Mrs Bates shook her head. 'Bless her, she never looked at another man.'

'What a shame.'

Mrs Bates put her hand on Maddie's arm and smiled. 'I hear congratulations are in order: you've received planning permission for the old barn. Does this mean that you will be staying?'

Maddie's eyes opened wide. She hadn't received a letter yet. 'Yes, I'm staying. Trevenen needs me.'

'Yes, it does. Breathe new life into the old house. Now what you need is to have some children.'

Mark coughed and slipped away. Maddie rolled her eyes and tried to think of something to say. 'Yes, well, I have Hannah.'

'True, but unlike you she's not Cornish, is she?' Mrs Bates looked at Hannah.

'No, she's not, but she's mine.'

'Well, Trevenen's been in the same family for generations. It was what Daphne wanted so much to continue.'

'Did she?' Maddie glanced quickly around the room. 'So you knew I was Nancy's daughter?'

'Yes, dear.'

'By any chance do you know why Daphne didn't try and contact me if she knew I existed?' Maddie asked. This had been bothering her.

'Oh.' Mrs Bates paused and looked at the fire. 'I suppose it's fine to talk of these things now.'

'Yes, please.' Maddie's mouth was dry.

'There was so much pain. Daphne was devastated when Nancy's condition became apparent. Her brother, Diggory, threatened to kill her.' Mrs Bates put a hand to her throat. 'Daphne told me that he tried to convince Nancy to terminate it. That her life would be ruined for ever if she had this child.'

Maddie grabbed the mantel for support.

'Daphne didn't believe in abortion. She knew Nancy had made a mistake but that to kill another life wasn't the answer. Nancy had been silent. Daphne didn't know what to do.' Mrs Bates waved to Tamsin across the room. 'Daphne was consumed with guilt because it had happened when Nancy was with her. She should've seen it coming, but poor Daphne didn't think Nancy knew of such things. Quite frankly, I always put it down to the fancy London school that the girl went to, but Daphne would hear none of it.' Mrs Bates made a tutting sound.

Maddie looked at the back of her hand and swallowed.

'Nancy finally spoke and said she was having the baby. At that point Diggory said she could have the bastard, but Daphne must never make contact again.'

Hannah came and refilled their glasses, giving Maddie a strange look. Maddie knew all the blood had left her face.

'The next thing that Daphne knew was from the small obituary in the *Telegraph*. Then she discovered that Nancy had run away to have you. You see, Diggory had insisted that she give the child up for adoption. When Nancy died, Daphne died in a way. She always felt it was her beliefs that forced Nancy to have the child and therefore she was responsible for the death.'

'Oh, how terrible.' Maddie closed her eyes. Pain. Daphne's pain, her mother's and her own swamped her.

'Yes, she was a broken woman. You see, Nancy was the

child she never had herself. She knew that you'd survived, but that's all. She never felt that she'd the right to make contact as Diggory had made his feelings very clear.'

Maddie swallowed.

'I'm so sorry, my dear.' Mrs Bates patted Maddie's hand. 'Daphne would've loved you. You look a great deal like her, but then so did Nancy. These things are such a sadness.'

Maddie looked across the room to see Mark and Will chatting. She tried not to sink into Daphne's and Nancy's pain. Her mother should have aborted her. Daphne had lived with the guilt that Nancy had died because of her. Mrs Bates was wrong; Daphne would have hated Maddie because by being born, she'd killed Nancy. Pain pierced her temples.

'Thank you, Mrs Bates. That answers so many questions. Do you know what happened to my grandparents, by any chance?'

'I believe they emigrated to Australia after Nancy's death.'

Maddie wondered if her grandmother were still alive, but thought probably not as Daphne had been in her nineties when she'd died. Why hadn't they wanted her?

'Oh, I remember something now. I think Nancy's mother suffered a nervous breakdown.' Mrs Bates sipped her champagne. 'Yes, that was it. She was always a queer thing, if you ask me.'

Maddie yawned and picked up the phone. 'Hello?'

'Hi, Maddie, it's Geoff here.'

'Long time no hear.' Maddie perched on the table, wondering why she was hearing from John's friend.

'Not surprising now that you're six hours away.'

'True.' Maddie laughed. 'When are you coming to visit?'

'Soon, I promise.' He paused. 'Maddie, are you sure you want to reach Susan?'

Her heart sank. 'Yes, well no, but Hannah really wants it.'

'But John never wanted her to.'

Maddie bit her lip. 'I know, but he's gone and she's looking for her mother.'

'She has you,' he said.

'I don't need to tell you that right now I'm not enough.' Maddie thought of the slanging matches he'd witnessed in the days following the funeral.

'Things haven't improved then?'

Maddie paused. 'Well, somewhat.'

'Good.'

'Have you got a number?'

'No, but an old friend had an address in New Zealand.'

'New Zealand?' Susan couldn't have moved further away.

'Yes.'

'OK, you'd better give it to me.' Maddie looked at the address and knew that there was no time like the present to sit down and get this done.

Looking at the balled up pieces of papers, she saw this letter was almost worse than the one she'd written to Peter Johnson. Maddie reread her final draft.

Dear Susan,

I don't know whether news reached you that John Hollis died a year ago on the 31st December. I'm his widow and stepmother to your daughter Hannah.

I know that John wanted to make sure that you never heard or saw Hannah again. It is therefore with mixed feelings that I'm writing. Hannah is nearly sixteen and is grieving for her father and feeling lost in the world. She has asked me to help her find her mother.

I don't know what happened all those years ago nor how you feel now, but your daughter would like to make contact. I would be grateful if you could reply to me and let me know how you feel about this.

Yours truly,
Maddie Hollis

It wasn't any good but it would have to do. She put it in an envelope and sealed it shut.

❧ Twenty-Two ❧

Maddie looked out on Falmouth harbour from the shelter of an archway. The clouds were gathering over St Mawes and the water stirred, licking at the boats. March was a moody month and today it seemed threatening. However, it wasn't going to dampen her mood. Her head was buzzing with all sorts of exciting ideas. After all Tamsin's pestering a few weeks ago, she had had a very productive morning with a visit to the university and a few galleries. She did need to reach out and build a community here. It seemed it wouldn't be too difficult, either.

Leaving the view, she turned into the street and walked straight into someone. Startled, she blurted out her apologies, only to realise the hands steadying her were familiar. Gunnar was smiling.

'Hello, Maddie.'

'Gunnar.' He was the last person she could have imagined bumping into in Falmouth.

'What perfect timing. I am just on my way to lunch. Will you join me?'

Just then Maddie's stomach grumbled loudly, so there was no way she could say no if she had wanted to.

She smiled. 'I'd love to.'

'Wonderful. I know just the place.'

She walked with him through several alleyways until they appeared on the quayside. It didn't look like much on the outside but she had a feeling that when it came to food, Gunnar would be the man to follow.

They were quickly seated at a table by a window overlooking

a small courtyard and Gunnar excused himself. Maddie clasped her hands on top of the menu and wondered how she was going to handle this. She examined her fingernails. A trace of crimson paint lingered under one. She wasn't sure how she had missed it but perhaps in her haze of happiness it had slipped past her. Just the thought of Mark eased her tension. This didn't have to be awful. She hadn't led Gunnar on, but she probably should have told him before now that she was dating Mark. She looked up to see his sunny expression.

'This restaurant has become my favourite while I have been doing a little more research.'

'I didn't think Falmouth was much of a fishing port,' she said.

'Not compared to, say, Newlyn, but it is a great maritime location. You can feel the history around each corner.'

She nodded while looking at the menu. She liked the way Gunnar viewed things. Before long he had her talking about her morning while she tucked into a divine salad of shellfish.

'So have any of the galleries agreed to sell your work?' he asked.

Maddie laughed. 'It's not quite that simple, but let's say there was one which might work out. Time will tell. To be truthful, what I found most exciting this morning was the whole programme at the university.'

'Do you not have your degree?' He frowned.

She smiled at his wording. 'Yes, I do; in fact, my masters. The exciting part was the possibility of working with students.'

'Teaching?'

'Not exactly.' Maddie paused and looked at the inky colour on the mussel shell in her fingers. 'Mentoring.'

'Ah, yes, different. They would come to you with some knowledge.'

She nodded.

'This would make you more permanent here,' he said.

'Yes, but I don't think that that was ever in doubt.'

He gave her a lopsided grin.

She took a deep breath. 'It was a good thing I bumped into

you because I wanted to tell you that Mark and I are dating.' She sat back. It was out. It sounded blunt but she wasn't sure she could have said it better.

'This does not surprise me. I could feel the chemistry between you. But I cannot help but be sad.' He reached out for her hand.

She took it. 'I'm sorry.'

'Yes, it could have been good.' He gave her hand a little squeeze. 'Can we still be friends?'

'Absolutely.' Maddie smiled and turned as a glimmer of warm yellow light softened the grey cobblestones in the courtyard.

The rain beat down on Hannah as she walked along the lane, counting signs of spring. Then there was bloody Maddie singing around the house the whole time. Hannah didn't know what was up, but she didn't like the idea of what she thought it was. Every night this week, Mark had been at Trevenen. He was grinning like an idiot too, but as they'd been bent over plans and estate agents' details the whole time, she could be wrong.

OT had been wrecked for days after his dinner party. She and Will had disappeared early but Maddie and Mark had stayed until his place was spotless. She'd hoped he'd feel well this week because she'd nothing better to do then spend time with him. It was him or Maddie and she knew who she'd choose hands down any day.

Puddles lined the path to Trevenen. She hopped over them. The old house didn't seem to notice the rain. How many years had it sat there in all weather? Even the lock on the door spoke of a different time. The large planks that made up the door looked like they might have come off a boat. Now that was an interesting idea. Thinking about history, she remembered she hadn't found the Bible yet. Maybe she needed to ask Maddie because she might have moved it.

Hannah walked in and put her backpack on the table.

'Wet out there?' Maddie looked up from her sketch pad.

'Duh. What's for dinner?' Hannah asked.

'Don't know. Haven't even thought about it yet.'

Hannah pulled the fridge open. Nothing except a mouldy yoghurt pot and some limp celery. Not a promising start.

'When did you last shop?' Hannah asked.

'Monday, I think. Why?' Her hands were covered in charcoal.

'There's bloody nothing in the fridge.'

'Oh.' Maddie continued to sketch.

Seeing the plans for Trevenen lying on the table, Hannah asked, 'When are you going to start work here?'

Maddie looked up and smiled. 'I haven't received planning permission for the shed yet. We've submitted the plans for here, though.'

'So you think you'll get it?'

'Well, Mrs Bates seemed to think it was done deal and well …' Maddie stopped.

'Well, what?'

'Although the shed isn't on the market, I've had an offer for it.'

Hannah looked at the plans again. 'Is that legal?'

'It's not illegal as I haven't placed it on the market.'

'Oh.' Hannah didn't see any still lifes or photos on the table that Maddie could be working from. She walked closer and saw the sketch of a naked man, a well-developed one, who had no head. Whoever it was, Maddie was furiously working from memory. Her fingers flew and smudged here and there.

'Who's that? He's got a big willy.' Hannah wrinkled her nose.

'Yes, um, he has, I guess.' Maddie looked a bit red in the cheeks.

'Who is it?' There were several finished drawings on the table.

'No one, really.'

'Just your fantasy bloke.' Hannah looked at the defined thighs.

'Yes, exactly.'

'That's gross.'

Maddie coughed. 'The naked male body isn't gross. It's quite beautiful. In fact, artists in the past felt it was far more beautiful than the female form.'

'That's not what I meant. It's gross that you're drawing men's willies even if they just come from your imagination. I mean, it could be Dad.' Hannah shuddered.

'Your father wasn't built like that.'

'Too much information. Just don't go there. Right. Can you put the willy away and think about food?'

Maddie laughed as she stood. 'Fine.'

While Maddie washed her hands, she left the offending sketch on the table. Hannah's eyes kept returning to it. There was something about the stance that looked familiar. Maybe it was the turn of the shoulders or the spread of the legs. Oh shit, it was Mark. Maddie was drawing naked pictures of Mark. Bloody hell.

'How does pasta with pesto sound?' Maddie pulled her head out of the larder cupboard.

Hannah looked at the glow about Maddie and realised what she'd been missing. Maddie was shagging Mark. They couldn't care less about the plans. Hannah looked at the sketches again and then at Maddie as she put a pot on the stove. Hannah turned, walked out of the kitchen and up to her room, slamming her door. She leaned into the corner to where she had a signal for her phone. She quickly punched in a text to Will.

Maddie is sleeping with Mark now. x

She sat, waiting to find out Will's reaction.

Maddie retuned the dial to Radio One because Hannah was in a reasonable mood and her music might keep it that way. Tonight Maddie was going to Mark's for dinner; she didn't know if Hannah had any plans. It was Saturday night and she was pretty sure that Tamsin's boys would be up to something, so with luck Hannah would be included.

Maddie jumped when the phone rang. 'Hello?'

'I was thinking about you,' Mark said.

She smiled, enjoying the sound of his voice while she looked at her sketches.

'I'm just looking at you.'

'What?' he asked.

'I made a sketch of you after you'd left,' she clarified.

'I hope it's decent.'

'Not at all.' Maddie used her thumb to fix the shading on his thighs.

He chuckled. 'What time are you coming over?'

'About seven, I imagine. Are Tamsin and Anthony coming?'

'Yes.' Mark sighed.

'Don't sound so disappointed.' She put the sketch away.

'I want you alone.'

'You had me alone an hour ago.' She laughed as she stirred the pasta and looked towards the door.

'I can't get enough,' he said.

'Me neither.' She checked the doorway again. 'See you in a bit.'

'Yes. You have me worried about this sketch, though.'

'Don't. No one would know it's you. I haven't put your head on.'

'What about the mole on my thigh? A few people could identify me from that.'

'Enough, wicked man. I'll see you later.' Maddie grinned and put the phone down. She'd been so unsure about how their relationship would be once it had turned from friendship to something more, but it was surpassing all her imaginings. She still didn't know how to tell Hannah, but she wouldn't worry about that tonight.

Leaving the pasta on the table, she called Hannah. Maddie needed to get dressed. She smiled at the thought of the evening with Mark. The grin on her face was beginning to feel permanent. Everything looked better, even the sitting room. She hadn't heard the crying noises in a while. This might be because she was finally sleeping better.

She climbed the stairs, contemplating what to wear. It was just dinner at Mark's but she wanted to look good. She flipped through the clothes in her wardrobe but nothing jumped out. Her hands found a soft green silk skirt that fell to her ankles. That would do with a black jumper, boots and a big belt. Finally, she pulled her hair up and dashed down the stairs. Hannah still wasn't in the kitchen. Maddie walked up to her room. 'Are you OK, Hannah? Your supper's on the table.' Maddie stood next to the closed door. She did wonder what Hannah did in there, but after the last incident she'd respected her privacy. 'Are you there?' Maddie knocked and the door slid open, showing her Hannah curled up on the bed.

'Hannah?' Maddie pushed it open a bit more. 'What's wrong?'

'Get out, bitch.' Hannah looked up from the ball she was curled in. Black streaks lined her face.

'Hannah?' Maddie walked in.

'I said get out. Get out! What don't you understand?'

Maddie stood her ground and was able to duck before a book hit her.

'When were you going to tell me? Huh?' Hannah stared at Maddie.

Maddie swallowed.

'Lost for words? Well, you're shagging Mark and I'm the last to know. Even Will, who's at school, knew; but me, who lives in the same house, didn't know.'

'Hannah—' Maddie began.

'Don't try and fix it now. It proves what I've always known. You're just a slut, drawing your pictures of naked men. Just get out. Get out.' Hannah turned away.

'That's not fair. How was I supposed to tell you that Mark and I were going out when you barely speak to me?' As she said the words, Maddie knew they were a cop-out. She could have found a way but she just wanted to keep the happiness to herself. She wanted something she didn't have to share.

'You could have, but you didn't want to. You just don't care. You make that all too obvious.' Hannah's voice was barely audible.

'That's untrue.'

'Yeah, right. Well, let me tell you this, then: I won't be here when he dumps you. As he will; he always does.'

Maddie held herself tall. Hannah's words told her nothing new. 'Thanks for the warning. It's kind of you to care.'

'But I don't care. I'm looking forward to him dumping you.' Hannah paused and wiped her nose on her sleeve. 'He'd never marry you, anyway. He's been married before.'

'So have I.'

'Yeah, well, you didn't leave your husband to die while you swanned off to the States, did you?'

'No.' Snippets of conversations with Tamsin came back to Maddie. Tamsin had repeatedly said that Mark had been young and foolish. Maddie knew this.

'So you don't know.' Hannah smiled.

'Don't know what?'

'Hah, that dear old lover boy left for some architectural course while his new wife slowly died here in Cornwall.'

'I did know.' Maddie glanced about the room. Of course, Hannah had heard her talking to Mark on the phone. How stupid she was to have said those things while Hannah was in the house. Hannah was just angry and hitting out where it would hurt the most.

'I'm sorry you found out this way. That was wrong.' Hannah rolled away from her. Maddie turned and left.

❖ Twenty-Three ❖

Once in the car, she drove to the sailing club, parked and walked down to the pontoon. Too many things were crashing in her head and she hoped being near the water would provide some clarity. Hannah's words were not new but she was right about one thing, Mark had a track record. It was no more than what she deserved. She'd made her own bed and now she was lying in it. Before she had crossed that physical barrier with Mark, she could have kept it all in check, but not now. She'd committed not only her body but her heart. She was such a bloody fool.

The anguish of the last few years hadn't taught her anything. She still stupidly rushed in and gave her whole when she knew she should hold back. She'd done the same with John and Hannah, and look where that had taken her.

A brisk wind blew downriver and penetrated her coat. She wrapped her arms about her body. What was she going to do now? The water didn't hold any answers and she was getting cold. She was late for her dinner at Mark's. In order to warm up, she ran up the hill to her car. Her phone rang as she reached it. She glanced at the screen and saw an international number. 'Hello, Maddie Hollis speaking.'

'Hello, Maddie. This is Peter Johnson. You wrote to me.'

She froze with her key in the lock. 'Yes, yes I did. Thank you for ringing me.' With all that had been happening, she'd forgotten about Peter. What the hell had she said?

'From your email, it sounds as though we may have something to talk about.' He sounded calm, not angry.

'Yes, we may.' Maddie leaned against the car for support.

'You wrote that you're Nancy Penventon's daughter. I Googled you and saw that you were born in 1971.'

'Yes.'

'So I'm your father,' he said.

Maddie swallowed. He wasn't denying it. What now?

'Maddie, are you there?' Concern seemed to come through the phone loud and clear.

'Sorry, I just didn't expect you to come out with it.'

'How could I not? Your date of birth says it all.'

'How do you feel about it?' Maddie tried to picture Peter. She'd seen a few photos of him online, but it hadn't really shown her enough.

'Well, I have to confess your email threw me. That was a lifetime ago. I thought long and hard before I picked up the phone. I do appreciate that you left any further contact my choice.'

'I know you have a family and I wouldn't want to …' She looked down at her freezing feet, hoping to find the words.

'Yes, I realise that. I've told my wife and my sons. It was a long time ago. When did your mother tell you about me?'

Oh, God, the email left too much unsaid. Maddie licked her lips. 'She didn't tell me anything. Well not, directly. She died in childbirth.'

'I'm so very sorry. That explains a great deal,' he said.

'What does it explain?' She looked at the sky but no stars were visible.

'The letters I sent to Trevenen came back to me.'

Maddie could imagine that Daphne wouldn't have wanted Peter to have been in contact with Nancy.

'Look, Maddie, I think there's a lot we need to say to each other, but maybe not today.'

'Yes.' Maddie took a deep breath. 'Yes, I think you're right. Thank you for calling.' They were inadequate words but she wondered if any could be.

'I'll call again. This is my number. Please feel free to use it.'

Maddie slipped the phone into her pocket. She was shaking. The lights shone brightly across the river and Maddie longed for the simplicity of life past. What had she done by contacting her father? God, the choices she'd made. She'd married John, knowing that his first thoughts were always for Hannah. Did she regret marrying him? No, they'd a wonderful year before it all fell apart. Would she have not married him if she'd known it would end the way it did? Maddie paced around her car. She knew she couldn't say. She might have found someone else and realised her dreams of a family of her own, but then again she might never have known the love they shared. And now what about Mark?

Maddie forced a smile and rang the bell. Why had Mark never settled down? Why had he never moved on? If he couldn't, then she might as well end it now and save herself more pain. She'd had enough of that recently.

'I was wondering when you were going to arrive.' Mark pulled her into his arms and Maddie tried to let the fire between them flare, but it flickered and then went out.

'Sorry I'm late.' She pulled away.

'All OK?' he asked.

She tugged at her coat and looked at the floor. Mark nuzzled her neck. Earlier, this same action had her squirming with delight, but right now, although her nerves tingled, she stood still.

'The usual with Hannah.'

'It must've been a bad one.' He took her coat. 'The others are in the kitchen.' He paused. 'Maddie, is there something you're not telling me?'

She looked at him briefly. Now was not the time because everything inside her head was too confused. 'Maybe later.' She squared her shoulders and walked through. Tamsin and Anthony were close together. Maddie smiled. That was what she wanted and she'd been silly enough to let the dream of it happening with Mark seep into her mind. What a fool she was.

'Hi there. What's kept you?' Anthony grinned.

'Fight with Hannah. Nothing new.'

Anthony slid from his stool and poured some wine. 'You look like you need this.'

'Yes, I think I do.' Maddie smiled. 'Cheers. Something smells good.'

'Yes, the boy does make a good curry.' Tamsin leaned forward for Maddie to kiss her cheeks.

'The boy?' Mark walked in.

'That's what all men are.' Tamsin kissed her husband.

'She knows us too well, being surrounded by all that testosterone.' Anthony beamed at Tamsin.

'Ah, but she loves it.' Mark stirred the rice.

'Maddie, would you put the naan bread in the oven for me?' Mark smiled and Maddie tried to return it, but without much success. This was useless, as all she wanted was to go home and cry.

'Sure.' Fiddling with the packaging, she tried to put some perspective on things.

'What has Hannah planned for tonight?' Tamsin asked.

'Nothing. She's sulking.'

'So she picks a fight. Fair enough.' Tamsin said.

'Yes, I suppose I should be used to it. She can't strike out at anyone else except me, I suppose.'

'True, and you are a big girl. You can take it.' Tamsin laughed.

Maddie doubted if she could take much more of it. 'She has been so much better lately, which I put down to Tom's good influence.'

'Yes, I still think of how lovely she looked a few weeks ago and so over the moon at seeing Will. Do you remember what it was like at that age?' Tamsin pulled some plates out of a cupboard. 'Of course you do, as you're in the first flush right now.' Tamsin winked at Maddie.

Maddie fought tears. She was on a crash and burn course. She grabbed the cutlery and went to lay the table with Tamsin. The men had become engrossed with some project they were both working on.

'You're looking a little peaky. Feeling all right?' Tamsin laid the plates.

'Hannah shook me, that's all. When she wants to hit a target, sometimes she's quite accurate.'

'I can see that, but as you said, she can only strike out at you, which is tough. I'm so grateful I've just had boys. Of course, I won't say that when they come home and announce they got some poor girl pregnant. Then I'll kill them.'

Maddie laughed. Tamsin was so balanced. Nothing seemed to ruffle her. Even if her worst case scenario happened, she would deal with it.

Setting the cutlery down, Maddie debated what she'd say to Mark later when Tamsin and Anthony left. Would she ask what had happened with his wife? And then it would be out in the open. No matter what he said, she'd already decided what she was going to do.

'Are you sure there's nothing else going on in your head?' Tamsin sat on the arm of one of the chairs.

Maddie stopped and looked at the magenta of the anemones on the table. She reached out and touched a petal. She would paint some tomorrow. The subtle changes of colour were exquisite. 'Oh, there's plenty.' She shrugged.

'Then spill.'

'I don't know where to begin.' She looked to Tamsin for help but Tamsin just sat there. Maddie was beginning to wonder if the woman had missed her calling in life as a shrink. 'My father rang a short time ago.'

Tamsin jumped to her feet. 'Your what? Did you say your father called?'

Maddie nodded.

'How did you find him? When did you make contact? Why didn't you say anything?'

'I think, maybe, there's been too much going on lately.' Maddie looked at the flowers again. Painting would be good. She'd be able to shut out everything else.

'How do you feel? Did he own up?'

'Yes, and to be truthful I haven't a clue how I feel; it's all too new.'

Tamsin nodded and stared at Maddie. 'There's something else. You're strong enough to take hearing from your father. What's up?'

'I …' Maddie paused. 'I'm not sure about me and Mark.' Maddie stopped as the voices of the men came closer. 'Tamsin, why has Mark never remarried?'

'Can't answer that. You need to ask him.'

'I did a while ago and he said he's not good at commitment.' Everything turned inside her and she felt ill.

Mark carried a large pot in his hands and Maddie hated to think she wouldn't feel them on her skin another time. She'd had happiness with Mark, which she'd never thought she'd experience again.

'Can you grab the bread and the chutney?' Mark asked.

She fled to the kitchen. He was wonderful and she was being foolish. There was nothing sinister in his eyes. They were filled with desire for her and she was spinning the words of an angry fifteen year old into something more. She was a fool. He was a good man and their relationship had just started. Hell, the farthest ahead they'd planned was to Easter and the beginning of the works on Trevenen. Maddie slapped the bread onto a plate and picked up the chutney. She wouldn't let Hannah's words ruin an evening with friends.

The text message still said the same thing when Hannah re-read it.

Yeah, I nu they were an item when I was home weeks ago. Thought u nu. Everyone did. Talk when back. Luv W

Was she wrong to tell Maddie about Mark's past? Had Will betrayed his uncle by telling her? He'd made it sound like it was common knowledge, just like Mark and Maddie's relationship. Oh, what the fuck did she care? Hannah went to the kitchen looking for something, but she wasn't sure what she wanted. The pasta that Maddie left was a congealed mess. Hannah didn't have a clue where Maddie had gone.

She tipped the pasta into the bin because it was making her sick looking at it. She opened a tin of beans and put on toast. It would be better than nothing. Food was required yet she wasn't hungry. She stirred the beans, watching the bubbles break through the surface and splatter the wall. The orange against the pale yellow wall looked odd, or maybe it was just her feeling that way.

Hell, she should be pleased. She knew she'd killed the relationship for Maddie. That unfaithful cow would confront Mark. Maddie wouldn't just let it lie. She didn't work that way.

Hannah rubbed her back. It ached, but that made sense when she looked at her watch and realised she'd been curled in a ball for three hours. Sometimes she was so stupid. Stretching, she grabbed the toast and then poured the beans onto it. It looked like shit. She sat down and began to spoon the beans into her mouth. They tasted like mashed cardboard. Great. She looked around the kitchen to find something to wash it down with. In the corner she spied her half-finished bottle of Coke from a few days ago. Thank God Maddie had missed it in one of her 'everything has a place' modes. Of course, she'd been too busy shagging Mark to notice anything out of place. Just the thought of it made Hannah feel sick. She wondered if baked beans could go off.

The Coke was flat but tasted better than the beans. She knocked it back and picked up the uncontaminated toast. That was better. She turned on the TV. Nothing; Saturday night TV sucked. Life sucked. It was the weekend and she was sitting at home on her own.

She switched the set off, headed back to her room and cursed that they had no internet connection. Hannah kicked the wall. Damn house. She wished she could just leave. She picked up *The Return of the King*. Maybe she could lose herself in that while dreaming of Aragon.

In the kitchen, Maddie scrubbed the curry pot while Mark waved Tamsin and Anthony off. Everything ached and her head hurt. How was she going to do this? Couldn't she just let herself fall into his arms and forget for tonight?

Mark moved behind her and stroked her shoulders. She

held her breath and tried to let go, but she couldn't do it. She couldn't relax; in fact, she couldn't move.

'What's wrong?' he asked.

Turning to him, she saw his concern. 'I—' She paused and twisted her hands. 'I'm really exhausted so I don't think this is the time to talk.'

'Talk about what?' He stepped closer but she backed away.

'Mark, I—' Maddie looked away. She couldn't leave without telling him. Weary as she was, she must do this.

'What's wrong?'

'I don't know.' Why couldn't she just spill it out?

'What's Hannah done?' he asked.

She turned to him and gave a wry smile. 'More than you'll ever know.'

'What?'

'Sorry if I'm being cryptic, but I don't know how to begin. Maybe tomorrow would be better.' He looked hurt. She knew this wasn't right. He'd been honest with her to the best of her knowledge. 'Can we sit?'

He nodded and she led the way to the sitting room, admiring Mark's design as she went. He was an artist as much as she was.

'Do you want a brandy?'

'No, I have to drive home.'

'You could stay.'

'No, Hannah's there.' Maddie thought of her curled on her bed, killing all Maddie's dreams with her quietly spoken words.

'She's old enough to stay on her own.'

'That's not it.' She watched him sit beside her with an ache in her heart. It was now or never and she wished it could be never.

'Maddie, there are things you should know about me.' He studied her. 'I have a feeling that's what this is about.'

'I don't know.' She ran her hands down her thighs.

'I think I can guess what's been said.' He paused. 'Some of it is true and I'm not proud of the way I behaved all those years ago.'

Everything inside her went rigid. Stop. She must hear him

out. Her phone rang. She wanted to ignore it but was worried it might be an emergency.

'I'll just see who it is.' Maddie's voice was wobbly. It was her father's number. 'Peter.'

'Sorry to disturb you again. I do hope that it's not too late, but I just needed to know that you were well looked after as a child. It's been troubling me since we spoke.'

Maddie smiled. 'Yes, I had a wonderful childhood with two very loving adoptive parents. In fact, I didn't know I was adopted until I was sixteen.'

'Thank God for that.' Peter paused. 'No, forget it. I'll ring tomorrow or the next day. I realise it's late with you.'

'I look forward to talking to you again.' Maddie closed the phone and then her eyes. Opening them after a moment, she focused on Mark and was about to explain when her phone rang again.

'Hannah?'

'Maddie, where are you?' Hannah asked.

'What's wrong?' Maddie avoided the question.

'Your father called.'

'Yes, he just rang my mobile,' Maddie said.

'When did you find him?'

'Today, in a way. Are you all right?' She could hear tears in Hannah's voice and then the click as Hannah hung up.

'Mark, I'm sorry.' She stood, knowing she needed to finish what had started here but that Hannah's need felt greater than her own, as always.

'Your father?' Mark stood close, but not touching her. She ached for him to take her into his arms, but all the unsaid words lay between them.

'It's a long story, but yes, my father is alive and living in California.' She sighed. 'I know we need to talk but Hannah's crying. I think hearing that I have a father has set her off.'

He nodded. Maddie picked up her coat and kissed him lightly on the cheek.

Mark walked her to the car. 'Tomorrow?' he asked.

'Yes.' Maddie reversed out the drive.

❧ Twenty-Four ❧

Unable to drink the coffee in front of her, Maddie sat at the kitchen table. Sleep had evaded her last night thanks to the return of the nightmares. They hadn't helped with her tangled thoughts and had given her a stomach upset. In fact, she still had it. It must be psychosomatic with all that was happening. She'd come home to find Hannah curled up and sound asleep. Had Hannah known where she'd been? Could Hannah be so vindictive? What had Maddie done to hurt her? Marry her father? Provide her with a home?

Oh, forget the wretch, Maddie told herself, but she knew she couldn't any more than she could forget Mark. Hannah was a fifteen-year-old girl with no father and a stepmother she hated. Maddie couldn't blame her for all her own troubles; she could only blame herself.

Maddie paced the hallway. Thoughts spun in her head and tangled. She ran to her room and was sick. She needed some fresh air to clear her mind. Throwing on the clothes piled on the chair, she rummaged in a drawer for socks. Her hand fell on the rosary beads that her mother had given her for her First Communion. The smooth beads slipped easily through her fingers. She'd thrown out most of the tangible signs of her old faith but hadn't been able to part with these.

The urge to go to church arrived without warning, taking her breath away. *Hail Mary, full of grace, the lord is with thee . . .* echoed in her brain as she placed the beads back in the drawer. Maybe she'd find strength of mind in church. It had given her some peace a few weeks ago, but she needed more than peace right now. However, she'd take anything at this point. She knew she had to speak to Mark today.

A hymn rang out as Maddie approached the door. She'd forgotten it was Sunday. Funny how that had been one of the markers of her week. How had she moved so far away in such a short time?

The heavy oak door stood in front of her. She wanted – no, needed – to go in, but didn't wish to interrupt the service. Pushing it slowly, she hoped she wouldn't be noticed as the voices sang the chorus. The air was heavy with the scent of narcissi. Maddie crept to the back and tried not to look at the faces around her. A hymnal was placed in her hands and, without looking up, she murmured her thanks. She didn't need the book as the words to 'All Things Bright and Beautiful' were imprinted on her soul.

The rest of service was a blur but she must have gone through the motions, so similar to the ones ingrained in her. While she waited for the building to empty, she avoided prying eyes and conversation by staring at the prayer book in her hands. Finally alone, she let her mind go blank and enjoyed the serenity that seemed to seep out of the stone walls. She watched the light from the windows play on the floor. A work of swirling grey began to form in her head but she shoved it away. No thoughts of painting today. She needed to find the strength to talk to Mark. The sooner she did, the sooner she could pick up the pieces and rebuild her life, such as it was.

Tears streamed down her face. What had she done? All her life, her faith had been her strength and with its help she'd accepted all that she'd been given, the good and the bad. Through John's illness she'd prayed, prayed for the right thing to happen and for the strength to survive. Then John had asked her to do the one thing she couldn't do, but she did it. She'd promised. Maddie closed her eyes.

Each day after John's burial had become a battleground in her head. She'd promised him that she would have the abortion. One of the final things they'd done together was to book the appointment. They hadn't known he wouldn't be alive to help her through. So she'd faced it alone. She'd confronted her beliefs and had to cast them aside to set foot in the door. Life was sacred and she'd thrown one away; one that had been given to her to cherish. Now, more than a year later, she wished she'd followed her heart and broken her promise. It would have been so easy and John never would have known.

But she had. It couldn't be erased now.

Maddie wiped her face. Her sins were far greater than Mark's could ever have been. The crucifix above the pulpit challenged her. She didn't deserve forgiveness, but Mark did. She turned to go.

'Hello.'

Maddie died inside. It was the vicar.

'You never rang.' He placed a hand on her shoulder.

'Sorry.'

'No need to apologise. Can I help in anyway? Ghosts or something else?' he asked.

'I'm fine.' She tried a smile but knew it didn't work.

'Grief can take many forms.' He looked to the stained glass and then to the altar. 'Just as love does.'

Maddie laughed and looked at her hands. The cross on the altar held no answers. 'You understand more than me, then.'

'No, not at all, but I'm open.' He smiled.

Maddie longed to open up. The need to confess was so strong, but the poor vicar wouldn't know what to do with a failed Catholic pouring out her sins, knowing that forgiveness was impossible. The man didn't need to carry her troubles on his shoulders.

'Since our last chat in the churchyard, I dug around a bit of local history but I found nothing of ghosts in Trevenen.'

'Thank you for being interested,' she said.

'I did mention it to a colleague in passing, no real details; I hope you don't mind.'

She shook her head. *Nothing is a secret except that which you never tell.* Once she'd believed that God knew all.

'I told him that you were mourning and he mentioned that

he'd encountered something early in his ministry.' He paused. 'A child had projected their grief outside her own body.'

Maddie stood. 'That's interesting. So a child's grief?' Maddie paused and thought of all the pain in Hannah's life. There was certainly enough to project and Hannah had done some of that last night. Her actions had stated clearly that she was not ready for Maddie to have a relationship. Maddie stood. 'Thank you for your kindness.'

She fled into the graveyard and tried to remind herself of all that was good in her life. She had a house and soon it would be beautiful, with a perfect studio. She had her health; well, sort of, although right now she felt a bit feverish and sick.

She'd been foolish to let the fling with Mark become something bigger in her mind; with or without Hannah's intervention, it would have ended. Hannah hadn't morphed into a charming teenager. The change had been just a brief and delightful aberration. Her stepdaughter hated her and that wasn't going to change. Maddie needed to build up a skin of steel and deal with it.

These things hurt like hell, but it wasn't the end of the world. So what had happened in Mark's past wasn't important except that it held him back from love. He needed to break those barriers down. Maddie closed her eyes. She wouldn't be the woman to help him do it. Having a man in her life didn't provide Hannah with the stable environment that she clearly needed. Hannah was nearly sixteen and would leave home at eighteen. Maddie was sure of that. She could grab what was left of her life then. Maybe Mark would still be around, but she would never ask it of him. She squared her shoulders and walked on.

The dull sunlight filtered through the evergreen trees. She played with her mobile phone and walked towards the gate. As she dialled Mark's number, she was nearly hit by a passing car. The person waved an apology. Shaken, Maddie put the phone into her pocket and went into the village shop.

Before she faced Mark, she might as well save some steps and pick up milk and the paper. Walking in, she found Mark coming out. His scent of fresh soap and a spicy aftershave surrounded her. She nearly fell over.

'Good morning.'

'Yes.' She paused and steeled herself to look into his eyes. 'I was about to call you.'

'Were you?' Mark raised an eyebrow and moved aside to let a woman pass them. 'Shall we step outside?'

She nodded and he led her out into the fresh air.

'Mark?' Maddie saw a flash of pain in his eyes. 'Can we go somewhere and talk?'

'My house,' he suggested.

'No, I don't think so. Not Trevenen, either.'

'The beach at St Anthony?' he asked.

'Yes, I'll meet you there.' She turned away and didn't look at him. Just the glimpse into the depths of his eyes a few moments ago had told her that he knew what she was about to do.

Mark stood by the water's edge kicking a stone into the water. In time, no doubt, she'd be able to look at him without desire, but right now that wasn't possible. A fresh wind blew in from the mouth of the creek and past the boats lining the shore. Aside from a heron at the water's edge, they had the beach to themselves.

'Hi,' she said.

He turned and slowly smiled. 'There's a bench a bit further along. Shall we walk to it?'

She nodded and fell into step beside him, supressing the desire to stroke away his frown and kiss the sadness from his eyes.

'Maddie, there are things I need to tell you.' He spoke so quietly that his words were almost carried away on the breeze.

'Yes, I know there are.' She watched the emotion on his face. He wasn't finding this easy, but then she hadn't expected him to begin this.

'I don't know what you've heard.' He glanced at her briefly before sitting on the bench.

'Well,' she said.

'Never mind what they've told you.' He paused. 'I went to the States on the internship.'

'Yes.' She could see how difficult it was for him to talk about this, which he didn't need to for her sake, but she had the feeling he needed to for his own.

'Look, I'm not proud of my actions back then. In fact, if I could go back in time, I would change a lot, but I can't. Claire and I never should've married. We were too young.'

'You didn't love her?' Maddie leaned forward to watch a heron on the shore.

'No, I loved her with every breath that I took, but I was twenty-two and very foolish. My mum had died and my world was upside down. Claire was a haven.' He threw a piece of bark and watched it fall to the creek below. 'We married just two months after Mum died. Then the offer of the internship in Chicago came. It was the chance of a lifetime. I knew that and so did she.' He took a breath. 'I was full of ambition. The world was going to be mine and this was the first step.'

'How did Claire feel?' Maddie almost whispered.

'She was over the moon too. She wanted my dreams to be fulfilled. She told me to go. It was only for eighteen months. We could survive the separation. I'd come home at Christmas and that would break up the time.'

'Yes, but why didn't she go with you?' Maddie frowned.

'She was in the middle of her training to be a physiotherapist.'

'Oh.'

'I left for the States two months after we were married. With hindsight, a foolish thing to do, but I was so in love and I thought it would be fine.' He paused and stood up. 'I didn't know she was already ill, but this year I found out that she knew.'

'What?' Maddie couldn't keep the surprise out of her voice.

'Yes, she knew even then that she was ill. In fact, she knew before we married.' He looked down at the ground.

'How could she not tell you something so vital?'

'I don't know.' He stood up and paced. 'I've been plagued by it and could only think she was too young, only eighteen.

'I've learned the hard way that you know nothing about life at that age.' He sat down again.

'Still, how could she not share that with you?' She put her hand on his.

'I probably need to ask Tamsin. Claire was her best friend, but all this time I haven't wanted to talk about it.'

'You just wanted to forget.' Maddie released his hand and traced her fingers lightly over the back of it, wanting to take some of his pain away yet understanding that was impossible.

'Yes, in a way, but it was more like I wanted or needed to be the villain.' Mark stared into the distance. 'That was easy, being the bad guy, until I discovered she kept her illness from me. The sense of betrayal is stronger, at the moment, than the anger I felt against myself.'

Maddie nodded.

'I was six months into the internship when she told me she was ill, but she made light of it. I was due home in two months for Christmas. She said she'd be fine until then. She said it was nothing serious, but she lied.' He swallowed. 'I foolishly took her word. She didn't want anyone to know she was ill. She hid it from everyone. But she was dying and I didn't know. I was her husband.' He looked down.

'How awful. Why didn't she say?' Maddie watched the water flow out of the creek.

'I don't know. I keep asking myself, if she knew she was terminally ill before we were married, why did she say yes when I proposed?' Mark pulled his hand away from Maddie and ran it through his hair.

Maddie thought of her own youthful dreams. What girl didn't want a white wedding with a handsome man?

'She knew how I struggled with Mum's deterioration. I didn't cope well.' He gave a dry laugh. 'I honestly don't know what to think. At this point, I can only guess.'

He was looking at her but not focusing. She closed the space between them and placed her arm around him.

'By Christmas, she was dead. I didn't come back. I was too angry with her and with everyone here. I was stupid.'

'Oh God, Mark, how terrible.' She felt a teardrop hit her shoulder.

'I was her husband and I didn't come home for her funeral. I'd left her alone through her illness. The community quite rightly hated me. I didn't want to come back, so Chicago turned to LA and then to London before I could even think about coming home.' He paused. 'I missed so much. I missed my sisters' weddings, the christenings, the lot. I only returned to take my punishment five years ago.'

'Why should you be punished?' she asked.

'Because I was wrong. I let a beautiful woman die on her own, unsupported by her husband. The man who had sworn to love, honour and protect her. And I didn't.'

'How could you if you didn't know?' She pulled him closer.

'That's no excuse. Any man worth his salt would've been on the first plane home once he'd heard his wife was ill.' He wiped his eyes.

'Mark, hindsight is easy. You didn't know.'

'Didn't I, or didn't I want to know? Did I just listen to what I wanted to hear? Did I just want it all? The most beautiful girl around and the best career possible?' His voice cracked.

'You were young.' She looked at his downturned head, wanting to do something to help.

'I've looked back and wished we'd never married. I've hated her for what she did to me. I was so angry that she married me knowing she was ill and didn't share it. She didn't give me a choice. She made me an object of revulsion. Oh, how I hated her, and that makes me even worse.'

'No, it makes you human.' Maddie took his face between her hands and kissed him. Then she lifted her head as she heard someone shout.

'Mark! Maddie!'

Mark stood. 'Here.'

Maddie could see Fred racing towards them.

'It's Tom.'

They both broke into a run.

272

❖ Twenty-Five ❖

Fear grabbed at her insides as Hannah looked at his yellowed skin. She'd seen this before. OT lay on the sofa barely breathing. He was still alive but he wouldn't wake. He felt very cold so she'd covered him with a blanket.

The door hadn't been locked when she arrived this morning. She'd come to talk things through with him. All last night she'd been plagued by terrible dreams and the terrible crying sound filled the night again. She needed to sort her head out. OT could help. He always looked at things straight, not twisted like she did.

Last night she had dreamt of her mother. Weird images morphed into a monster that swallowed her. The image still gave her the shivers and she couldn't lose it. Now she was in OT's sitting room looking at a man only just alive. She knew it although she didn't want to say it. He must have cancer. That would explain his colour. One didn't go yellow for any old reason. Why was this happening to her again? She'd watched her father slip away and now it was happening to OT.

At the thud of the kitchen door, she was on her feet. Hannah flung herself into Maddie's arms and tears she'd been holding back started flowing. Through their haze, Hannah noted that Mark was with Maddie, but she didn't care.

'I'll go and check him.' Mark's voice sounded odd but Hannah could barely hear because she was crying so hard. The sobs just wouldn't stop. Maddie's hands were stroking her head and her back.

'Shhhhhhh.' Maddie held her close in her arms and gently rocked her.

'I've called an ambulance.' Hannah managed to say between sobs.

She could feel Maddie nodding. OT was still with them but for how long? She needed him. He believed in her. He trusted her; or, to use his word, he respected her. She couldn't lose him. She just couldn't.

'How long did the ambulance say they'd be and should we be doing anything?' Maddie spoke quietly, still cradling Hannah.

'They said they'd be here in about twenty minutes and to try and keep him warm.'

Hannah looked at the magnolia-coloured walls and wanted to puke. She hated hospitals and here she was again. Déjà vu. Although this time, there was a distance between Mark and Maddie that hadn't been there before. Both their faces looked bleak and Hannah didn't think this was just down to OT. Maddie had believed her, as well she should. It was the truth. Will had told her and why would he lie about his uncle? He wouldn't. Yet, looking at the concern on Mark's face, she knew he was a good guy.

Tamsin walked into the waiting room. 'Hi all. Came as quickly as I could. The nurse says they have him stable but we should know more shortly.' She sank into the seat beside Maddie.

Hannah watched Tamsin look from Maddie to Mark and then back again. She wondered if there'd been a blow up last night at his house. Now that would have been entertaining to watch.

'Hello, are you with Thomas Martin?' a man asked.

'Yes.' Mark walked to the doctor.

'Mr Martin has regained consciousness and is now sleeping. Later we will complete more tests but it seems that his cancer has spread from his prostate into other areas.'

Mark nodded. 'When will we have a prognosis?'

'Probably tomorrow when some of the results come back. He'll have to stay in here for a few days at least.'

'Are you sure?' Maddie jumped up.

You go, girl, thought Hannah.

'Wouldn't he be more comfortable at home?' Maddie asked.

'I'm sure he would but until we know what we are dealing with, it's essential he stays. I suggest you go home and call later to see how he's doing.'

Hannah watched Maddie collapse into the chair. Tamsin looked bleak while Mark took charge.

'Thank you. Can we stay?' Mark asked.

'If that's what you want.' The doctor nodded and left.

'Look, why don't you all head home and I'll call you later with a report?' Mark said.

'I'm not going anywhere.' Hannah threw a challenging look at Maddie.

'That's fine with me. Mark, do you mind?' Maddie stood still. Hannah thought she looked tired and pale. She certainly didn't look like the woman humming around the kitchen yesterday.

'That's fine,' Mark said without looking at Hannah.

'OK, I'll take Maddie home and you can bring Hannah back later.' Tamsin pushed Maddie through the door.

'What the hell's going on with you and Mark?' Tamsin marched through the car park. Rain had begun to fall and Maddie dashed behind Tamsin.

'What do you mean?' Maddie asked.

'The atmosphere in the waiting room was thick with emotions. Something's up. What's going on?'

'Nothing.' Maddie climbed into Tamsin's car but then opened the door again and threw up.

'What's wrong with you?' Tamsin's voice softened.

'Dodgy tummy. Have you had any problems today?' Maddie asked.

'No.'

'It had to be something yesterday since I haven't eaten today.'

'Why?' Tamsin asked, putting her seat belt on.

'Couldn't face any food after a sleepless night and so the day has rolled on.' Maddie closed the door and Tamsin set off.

'Sleepless night leads me right back to what's going on with you and Mark.' Tamsin glanced at her.

'Look, Tamsin, I told you there's nothing to tell.'

'Bullshit. I'm not stupid. One day you're floating on cloud nine and now you're lurking in hell. Out with it.' Tamsin tapped the steering wheel.

Maddie frowned; she didn't want to talk. She looked at the rain drops beginning to hit the passenger window. Studying them and not thinking was much more satisfying. 'There's nothing to say at this point.'

'What?'

'Nothing.'

'The man's head over heels in love with you and has been for a long time now.'

Maddie swallowed the words she was about to speak.

'Don't tell me I've surprised you.' Tamsin turned out into the traffic. 'Come on, you're no fool.'

'Oh, but I am a fool. How could I ignore all the signs that this was a stupid thing to get into?' Maddie asked more to herself than to Tamsin.

'Falling in love is always stupid, but you do love him.' Tamsin glanced at the mirrors. 'Don't try and deny it. You're in love with Mark.' She paused. 'You liked Gunnar. See, there's a difference.' She cast a look at Maddie. 'OK, are you going to tell me what happened?'

'Nothing.'

'Right!' Tamsin took the roundabout at speed.

'No, seriously. We haven't had a fight or anything.'

'Then what the hell's going on?' Tamsin asked.

Maddie took a deep breath. 'Nothing, Tamsin. Just leave it.'

'Hannah?' Maddie called as loudly as she could while clutching the banister. Maddie had vomited as soon as she stood up and then she'd been stuck on the loo with the runs, which had become bloody. The small sips of water she'd taken wouldn't stay down. She wasn't sure why but all she could think of was the beautiful mussel shell from her lunch with Gunnar. With that thought, she fled to the sink. She couldn't have anything left but her stomach had other ideas.

With small steps Maddie made it to the kitchen and saw there was a note on the table. Hannah was out with Tamsin's boys. The room swayed. Maddie knew she needed help. She tried Mark's numbers but there was no answer on either.

Her head was throbbing as she took her temperature. It was climbing and she was shivering so hard that her teeth rattled. She dialled the surgery and was told to hold after she explained that she was incapable of making it there.

'Dr Grades here.'

'It's Maddie Hollis.'

'How can I help?' he asked.

'I think I have food poisoning. I have a temperature of one hundred and four, can't keep anything down and I have diarrhoea, and there's blood.'

'Any idea what could've caused it?' he asked.

'I'm guessing it was something I ate yesterday.' Maddie's stomach rolled over.

'Explain.'

'Last night I had a curry at a friend's but everyone else is fine. So it must be the lunch I had in Falmouth.'

'Did you say Falmouth?'

'Yes.'

'The Courtyard Café?'

'Yes.' Maddie clutched the table as spasms hit.

'I was wondering if any of ours would be caught by this. You probably have dysentery. There's been an outbreak. A member of their kitchen staff just back from holiday in the Far East is a carrier. The poor sod didn't know.'

Maddie didn't feel any sympathy towards whomever it was who had passed this on. The doctor continued and Maddie managed to answer all the questions, or at least she thought she did. Everything else was fuzzy but she heard that the doctor would come to her. While waiting, she called Gunnar. He too was ill.

*

After a day in bed, Maddie was beginning to feel human again. The antibiotics had stopped the diarrhoea and she was left with just a sore tummy, but it was nothing that live yoghurt wouldn't sort out. She still felt wobbly but she needed to move. A day spent in bed had given her mind time to work through the painting idea she'd had in the Manaccan church. For the first time in a long while, it didn't feel as though it would fade away before she could capture it.

She was in the stables mixing various shades of grey when she heard the postman arrive. Popping her head out of the door, she waved as he drove off. He was her favourite person at the moment. A few days ago, planning permission had come through and yesterday she'd received the paperwork for the sale of the barn. As predicted, it hadn't been on the market long and in the end went to sealed bids. She would have enough money coming her way to fix Trevenen, the piggery and set some aside. So, despite being drained by the damn bug, she felt a new sense of optimism.

A shriek of ear-shattering decibels reached the stables, quickly followed by Hannah shouting, 'In the sitting room!'

'What's in the sitting room?' Maddie dropped the brush and ran to her. Hannah was as white as a sheet.

Hannah shook violently. 'A bird!'

'What?' Maddie frowned. She looked at Trevenen and from the outside all was as it should be. Hannah pushed Maddie towards the house and then Maddie heard a thud as something hit the glass. She ran, wondering how the hell a bird got into her sitting room. She'd heard new noises lately, but not birds.

Maddie opened the sitting room door carefully. A blur of black raced across her view and flew in circles. Maddie slid along the wall to try to open a window. The lock was jammed. Maddie cursed. It hadn't been open since she painted the room in September. The smell of smoke filled the air. Frantically she scanned until she saw the tell-tale puffs coming from the fireplace. What the hell was Hannah trying to do? They'd never lit a fire in here.

Closing the door, she went in search of a broom and WD40.

If she couldn't open the window, then possibly she could force the bird out the front door. Visions of the Hitchcock film filled her mind as she returned. The big jackdaw bashed repeatedly against the far window.

Through the growing haze of smoke, Maddie took the bellows to try and get the flame going again hoping it would move the smoke up the chimney and not into the room. Just as she saw the embers glow and catch, she realised there must be something blocking the flue. Another big bird swooped down the chimney into her face. Maddie screamed and fell back.

Her heart was beating faster than their wings. She wondered if she might die of a heart attack while she set to work on the lock. After using all her strength, she managed to release the window catch. Her heart raced faster with each crash, always anticipating the sound of breaking glass, but it didn't come.

She would have thought they could smell the fresh air but they persisted in their attack on the closed windows. At least the smoke was finding its way out. Wielding the broom, she attempted to persuade the bigger one out. Instead they both took flight around the room, circling wildly above her. Maddie leapt behind the sofa as Mark walked in.

The smaller bird made its bid for freedom but the big jackdaw was hell-bent on the closed window. Mark took the broom and booted the bird in the right direction. He then went to the fire and stoked it a bit more. 'No need to burn the house down for an insurance pay-out now that you have money to restore it.'

'Tell that to Hannah.' Maddie stood up.

'Will do.' He smiled.

'I don't know what prompted her to light a fire.'

'I thought it'd make the noisy animals move,' Hannah said as she entered the room.

Maddie stood still. Hannah hadn't mentioned that she'd heard anything. Maddie had convinced herself it was all in her own head.

'What animals?' Mark asked.

'The crying ones.' Hannah looked at Maddie and Maddie

pushed her hair back, feeling shaky now that the excitement had passed.

'Well, it might work, but more likely by burning the house down.' Mark smiled.

Maddie shrugged her shoulders. She didn't have the energy to discuss the perils of lighting a fire in an unswept chimney or things that cry in the night.

'Because of the recent warm weather, the jackdaws are nesting early and took advantage of your chimney,' Mark explained.

'Did I kill their babies?' Hannah went pale.

'I doubt they would've gotten that far.' Mark poked the fire again.

'Why are you here, anyway?' Hannah looked at Mark.

'That's gratitude for you.' He laughed. 'I came by to tell you that Tom will be coming home tomorrow. I have a nurse lined up.'

'That's brilliant. What did the doctor say?' Hannah asked.

'They did a CAT scan and the cancer has spread, but with a new cocktail of drugs they may be able to knock it back into check. Tom will need the nurse for a week or so and then he should be fine on his own as long as we all keep up the visits. He's still with us thanks to you, Hannah.'

'Yeah.' Hannah shrugged and walked away.

Maddie shook her head. She couldn't make Hannah out. For the last few days she had been beside herself with worry about Tom and now she was behaving oddly.

'Hannah, I'm going in to visit him. Do you want to come?' Mark asked.

'Yeah,' Hannah yelled from down the hallway.

'You're obviously feeling better. See what happens when you spend time with other men?' Mark kept a straight face.

'Clearly after such a punishment, I'll mend my ways,' Maddie said in a mock serious tone. 'Twenty people were infected all because of one member of staff.' Maddie stopped. She really didn't want to think about it.

'Are you sure you should be on your feet? You still look washed out.'

'Thanks.' Maddie pushed her hair back and felt tatty. 'I think the damsel in distress look is my finest and, thanks to the birds, I've achieved a new level.'

Mark laughed but he wasn't looking at her. 'You do seem to need rescuing frequently.'

'I was doing well on my own but you arrived to steal my glory.' She tapped his arm.

'I did indeed.' He grinned. 'Do you need anything in Truro?'

You, her heart called out at the same time she felt the nausea overtake her. The excitement must have shaken everything up again. She picked up the broom from the floor, hoping the feeling would pass. 'No, thanks.'

'See you later.' He smiled.

She placed a hand on his arm. 'We need to talk.'

'Yes.'

Hannah yelled for Mark to hurry up. Maddie twisted her hands together while she watched him walk away.

'Mark, do you love Maddie?' Hannah glanced at him. He looked so like Will in profile.

'That's quite a question from you.'

'Yeah, so?' She shrugged.

'Why do you want to know?' Mark glanced at her.

'I want to know what you want from her.' Hannah wondered how long Mark would go on being deliberately thick.

'Why?'

'What's this, twenty questions?' she asked.

'You started,' he said.

'True.' Hannah sighed.

'Tell me why you want to know and then I'll tell you the answer.'

'Are you going to fuck her around like you did your wife?' Hannah stared at him, waiting for him to flinch.

'You don't mess with your words, do you?' A corner of his mouth turned up.

'No, why should I?' she asked.

He laughed and shifted gear as they came to a roundabout. 'No, I'm not. Does that answer your question?'

'Not really. You do love her, don't you?' She wasn't sure why she asked this.

'Yes, but so do you.'

'Crap.' She bit her lower lip.

'Really, then why would you care if I love her or not?'

'She's OK sometimes and besides, what else have I got?' She looked at her hands. 'I guess I really never thought about it.'

'What made you now?' he asked.

'Don't know. Maybe OT being so sick. How long do you think he'll live?'

'They don't know. It depends on how well these drugs work. He's not a young man.'

'I know. Life sucks sometimes.'

'Yes.' He spoke quietly.

'My dad wasn't old.' Hannah thought about that a bit. He was forty-two, which was old but not *old*.

'Nor was Claire.'

'That was your wife.' She fought to loosen the seat belt so she could watch him more closely.

'Yes.'

'Do you love Maddie more?' she asked.

'Differently.'

'Why differently?'

'I was very young when I loved Claire. I'd just lost my mother and she'd been there with me through it all.'

'How does that make it different?' Hannah looked out the window. What was he saying about love? How can love be different? Either you did or you didn't.

'We were too young to marry in many ways, but we thought we knew best. I'm not saying that I didn't love her because I did.' He paused. 'I still do.'

'Really?'

'Does love stop?' he asked.

'No, I guess not. I still love Dad.'

Mark turned into the hospital car park. Hannah looked at

the buildings. Poor OT was stuck in there but at least he'd be out soon.

'Penny for them?' Mark locked the car.

'Not worth it.' She smiled. Mark wasn't so bad.

It was nearly four o'clock when Maddie came out of the stables. She stretched her arms up. She hadn't painted for this number of hours in ages. Her muscles ached. She'd been mixing colours when the jackdaws had caused havoc and somehow the paint had made its way onto the canvas in a bold stroke. She was pleased with her work today. Whether anyone else would want a study in greys and black she didn't know, but she'd find out soon enough.

On her way to the house she noted the signs of spring all around. No wonder the jackdaws thought it was time to nest. The winter hadn't been anywhere near as cold as London. It was mid-March and she and Hannah had lived here seven months. She stopped. She couldn't imagine being anywhere else now. The landscape, which had been so strange to her eyes, was now heartbreakingly familiar, from the trees bent in the direction of the prevailing wind to the gentle slope of the fields to the sea. All of these things and more filled her head and her heart.

Her heart and head may have been full of the joys of spring but not her stomach. It wanted hot buttered toast and it directed her straight to the kitchen. Someone must have picked up the post and piled it on the kitchen table.

Flicking through the bills, she stopped at the envelope with a New Zealand postmark. Her hand stopped. Maddie ran her finger along the edge to open it. The handwriting was almost childlike.

The warm air of the kitchen felt stuffy so Maddie released the catch on the window and then sank into a chair, forgetting about her hunger. Her hand shook as she opened it. Halfway across she stopped. A feeling of trespass crawled across her skin. Closing her eyes, she finished tearing the envelope. Maddie shivered. She unfolded the sheets of paper and tried to hold them steady.

Maddie,

Thank you for letting me know that John had died and that Hannah is OK.

It is nearly thirteen years since I left. Much has happened in my life, which has shown me very clearly what I have done to Hannah. I can now say I'm truly sorry and I finally know what I gave up when I walked away. I can't begin to explain my actions all those years ago nor do I intend to ask for forgiveness. I know that that would be a step too far.

However, nothing has changed. Although I can look at what I've done to her and know I've caused so much damage and pain, I still can't be a part of her life.

Please continue to look after her. I know John will have chosen wisely this time. I do not want to hear from you or her again.

Susan

Maddie's hands trembled as she turned the page over and looked at the return address. Susan Smith, Sacred Heart School, Wellington, NZ. Tears ran down Maddie's face. The pain of Susan's desertion had haunted John until he took his last breath.

Hannah swept past Mark and into the kitchen. She looked at Maddie.

'What the hell is wrong with you?' Hannah slammed the kettle on.

'Are you all right?' Mark asked. He sat beside Maddie and placed a hand on her arm. 'What's happened?'

'Yeah, why are you dripping like a tap? Do you want tea? That tea in the hospital is crap.'

'Hannah, can you leave us alone for a few minutes?' Mark spoke quietly.

She took out three mugs and left them on the counter. 'Tea's down to you, Mark.'

'No problem.' He turned back to Maddie. 'What's happened?'

Maddie handed Mark the letter. He scanned its contents and pulled her into his arms.

'What are you going to do?' he asked.

'I don't know,' she said. 'I keep thinking that Hannah doesn't need to know this, but then I wonder …' She paused. 'I wonder if this might at least close the chapter for her, so to speak.'

'I should imagine she's mourned the loss of her mother for years.'

Maddie nodded. 'She's still grieving over her father and I think also for Tom. Does she need more on her plate right now?' Maddie pulled out of Mark's embrace and stood. 'But she asked me to find her mother and I have. I just don't want her to have to face even more pain.'

'I can understand that,' Mark said.

'What should I do?' Maddie asked.

'Do what your heart tells you to do.'

'I keep asking myself if I were her would I want to know.'

'And?' he asked.

'I would.'

Hannah was tired of waiting so she came back in. 'Are you two finished with whatever? Hey, you haven't made the tea!'

'Sorry. I'll make it now.' Mark stood up.

'Never mind. Look, are you going to tell me what's up or am I going to use my imagination?' Hannah stood in front of them.

'I'll leave you two alone.' Mark stood.

Hannah watched Mark exit the room and then turned to Maddie. 'So it's all about me, is it? What have I done this time?' She walked around the table.

'You haven't done anything.' Maddie stood and hunted down some kitchen roll.

'If I haven't done anything, why the hell are you crying?' asked Hannah.

'A letter arrived.'

'And that made you cry?' Hannah frowned.

'Yes, it did.' Maddie stopped and picked up some papers. 'The letter's from your mother.'

Hannah stood still. *A letter from her mother?*

'I don't have a mother.' Hannah placed her arms across her chest and sat on the table.

'You do and she lives in New Zealand.'

'New Zealand?' Hannah stood still. What the hell was going on? Fuck, this wasn't supposed to happen. Hannah looked at the letter in Maddie's hand. 'Did you go and find her because you want to get rid of me? Because I'm an inconvenience?'

'No! When you asked me for help a while ago, I looked. I was finally given an address and I wrote to her.'

'You what?'

'I wrote her a letter and told her of your father's death and your desire to know her.'

'Why were you crying, Maddie?' Hannah asked.

'I was crying because your father wasn't here.' Maddie sat down and left the letter on the table. 'I was crying for you and for your mother.' Maddie paused, taking a deep breath. 'I was crying for me and the decisions I had to make.'

'What decisions?' Hannah didn't get that bit, but she could understand the others.

'Whether to tell you about the letter and other decisions I've made in the past.'

'Why wouldn't you? She's my mother.' Hannah frowned.

'I know that. I was trying to decide what your father would want me to do.'

'Oh, he hated her.' Hannah shuddered.

'Yes, he did, but he loved you.' The corners of Maddie's mouth turned up.

Hannah felt the sting of tears forming. So Maddie wasn't alone in the letter equal tears equation. 'OK, so what did she say?'

'That's the hard part. I think it's best if you read it.' Maddie moved away but Hannah still felt her gaze.

'Fine.' Hannah pulled the letter across the table, feeling the bumps of the oilcloth beneath the heavy paper. Hannah glanced up and saw Maddie starting to leave.

'Do you want me to stay or to go?' Maddie asked.

'Stay.' Hannah paused. 'Please.'

❖ Twenty-Six ❖

Maddie watched Hannah disintegrate before her eyes. She shouldn't have given her the letter. She should have kept it to herself. She went to Hannah and pulled her into her arms.

'She doesn't say why.' Hannah spoke into Maddie's shoulder.

'She doesn't say much.' Maddie stroked Hannah's back.

'It's not fair. She has to tell me why. Why did she leave me?'

'I wish I could answer that but I can't.' Maddie hugged her closer. 'She did say she was sorry.'

'What good do fucking words do? Sorry doesn't tell me anything!' Hannah sobbed. 'Was I so terrible that she had to leave, had to leave Dad?'

'You're not terrible.'

Hannah pulled back and looked at Maddie.

'Well, not all the time, and you weren't a teenager then.' Maddie smiled. 'I'd be willing to bet that it has nothing to do with you. Nothing at all.'

'Yeah, right. It must do because she's now working with other kids but she couldn't stand me.'

'She hasn't told us and guessing isn't going to help.'

'No. I want to talk to her.'

'She specifically says she doesn't want to hear from you.'

'It would take seconds to find out the number of the Sacred Heart School in Wellington if we had internet.' Hannah glared at Maddie. 'I'm calling Abi and she can Google it.'

'Are you sure you want to do this?' Maddie asked. She'd hoped that Hannah would let it go. Hannah nodded and picked up the phone. Maddie walked outside and took a few deep breaths. Her stomach felt hollow. She walked back to the kitchen a few minutes later.

'Could you put me through to Susan Smith, please.' Hannah held the phone in her hands.

Maddie swallowed. 'What are you doing?'

'She owes me this.'

Hannah blew her nose. 'She hates me, I know she does. You hate me.'

'I don't hate you.'

'Yeah, right.' Hannah looked at her stepmother eating a piece of toast. She didn't look good, but Hannah doubted she did either. It was one in the morning.

'Hannah, what have I ever done to make you believe that I hate you?'

Hannah opened her mouth and then shut it. She had a point but Hannah didn't want to think about it right now.

'What did she say?' Maddie asked.

Hannah got up and paced the kitchen. What had her mother said? Not a lot. Hannah fought back a wave of tears. 'Maddie, do you want kids?'

Maddie blinked. 'What?'

'You heard me.'

'I'd always wanted kids, yes, but then your father died and so did that dream. But I have you.' Maddie smiled.

'Susan never wanted kids.'

'Is that what she said?'

Hannah nodded. 'She said she was so depressed and trapped that she couldn't breathe.' She bit her lip.

Maddie reached out and grabbed her hand. 'I wanted you.'

'Really?'

'Yes.'

'But what if you'd had your own? I wouldn't have mattered.'

'Of course you would have. Just because there was another child wouldn't have changed how your father or I felt about you.'

Hannah jumped up. 'Nice words but that wouldn't have

289

been the case. You, Dad and the baby would have been the family and I'd have been the outsider.'

'It's not true but it never happened anyway.'

'Yeah, I know, but it always bothered me.'

'Did you tell your father?'

Hannah shook her head and leaned against the range. 'Wait, maybe I did years ago when you two first started dating.'

'Oh.'

'Yeah, I used to think about it a lot, but yet in a funny way I also wanted a sister.' Hannah looked at Maddie. 'You OK? You've gone all white.'

'Just tired, I think.'

'Yeah, me too.' Hannah stood up and looked at the odd reflection of her and Maddie in the big mullioned window. They were broken up into distorted pieces. She turned to Maddie. 'Thanks. You know, you're not so bad.'

The paint hit the canvas with force. Maddie hadn't done this since she was in art school. The vivid gashes of colour intersected the peaceful grey beneath. She stood back and took a breath. The large canvas exploded with life. Maddie shivered.

The sun had begun to brighten the sky as Maddie walked back to the house. Had the bluebells been there yesterday, Maddie wondered, or was it just the angle of the sun that brought the tight violet heads to her attention? Her vision felt clearer, which was crazy.

The kitchen was warm and she put the kettle on. The phone rang.

'Hello, Mrs Hollis, this is Jack from the estate agents.'

Maddie swallowed. 'Is there a problem with the buyer?'

'No, that's all on course.'

'Good.' Maddie could breathe properly again.

'I know you aren't looking to sell Trevenen but I have this buyer who passed the house yesterday and, well, put a staggering offer on the table.'

'I'm not selling Trevenen.'

'I know that but I felt I had to tell you.'

'OK, fine, tell me and then you can tell the person that Trevenen is not for sale.'

'Thanks. Are you sitting down?'

'No, go ahead.' Maddie rolled her eyes. The guy was over-playing this.

'Fine. He's offered a million.'

Maddie laughed. 'A million what? Rupees, dirhams, Monopoly notes?'

'I told you you'd need to sit. A million pounds.'

'Bloody hell.'

'So are you selling now?' he asked.

Maddie looked around her kitchen. 'No, but thanks for letting me know.'

'You've just turned down the lottery.'

'Yes, it's mad I know, but Trevenen and I belong together.' Maddie put the phone down. She touched the lintel. 'So Trevenen, someone wants to pay a million pounds for you. What do you think?'

Silence filled the room and the click of the kettle switching off made her jump. 'Don't worry. You're safe.'

Without warning, pain ripped through her gut and she doubled over. Her stomach had settled a bit but she'd never had such lingering effects from antibiotics before. But then she'd never had dysentery. The pain lessened and the heaving began but there was nothing left in her stomach.

'Maddie, what in the hell are you doing?' Mark asked as he came into the room.

'Nothing important.' Maddie bit her lip. The convulsions stopped and she quickly wiped her mouth with a tea towel. 'What brings you to Trevenen?' She forced a smile.

'Trouble at the mill, I'm afraid.'

'Really?' She rubbed the back of her neck, knowing she was paying the price for painting for so long.

''Fraid so. I had a call from the planning board late last night.'

'How bad?' she asked.

'They've pulled permission.'

'What?' She ran her hands through her hair. She had a buyer.

She was just beginning to breathe easier and now ... now what?

'All's not lost.' Mark reached out and touched her hand. 'Just delayed.'

'How can they grant permission and then pull it?' This didn't make any sense. Maddie shook.

'Someone messed up.'

'How?' she asked.

'One of the clerks lost an objection that had been filed on time so permission's suspended until they've considered it.'

'Bugger. I didn't need this. What do I do about the buyer for the barn?' She twisted her hands, wondering if she could take much more.

'He's keen so I'm sure he'll wait a few more weeks.' He took her hand in his. Tears appeared in her eyes; she seemed to feel emotional all the time at the moment. Her glance darted about the room. Maybe she would have to sell Trevenen after all. She began to walk out of the house without releasing Mark's hand, dragging him with her. She needed to think.

Before long they were on the old footpath down to Frenchman's Creek. Dappled sunlight created a carpet of browns and greens underfoot as the breeze shook the new leaves above. Maddie didn't want to talk. The strength of Mark's hand in hers was all she wanted to focus on.

The old whitewashed cottage appeared just before Maddie could see the creek. The soft green light filled her with peace and she smiled at Mark.

'That's better.' Mark stopped walking and studied her. 'You'll get the permission, I'm sure.'

'I hope you're right.' She tipped her head to one side and looked at him.

'Trust me.'

She turned from his intense gaze. 'I want to.'

'Then do.'

She nodded.

Maddie watched Hannah walk into the stables, with sunlight falling behind her.

'Maddie, the doctor called. He wanted to know if the runs and stomach upset have stopped.' Hannah stood glancing at the canvas.

'That was kind.' Maddie put her paintbrush down.

'Yeah, he said to give him a ring at the surgery after six to-night.'

'Will do.'

'How are you feeling?' Hannah asked.

'Well, totally wiped out from the medication, but that's nothing new. I still have nausea, but it's not as bad.' Maddie mixed cadmium yellow with a hint of crimson.

'Maddie?'

'Yes?' She looked up.

'I heard about the planning stuff.'

Maddie laughed. 'No secrets.'

Hannah smiled. 'No. Will we be OK?'

'Yes, I promise.'

'Thanks.' Hannah turned to go but then stopped. 'What's up with you and Mark?' Hannah continued to look at the painting and not at her.

Maddie opened her mouth and shut it again. Did she really know? They were two broken people who needed time to heal.

'Is it over? Was it because of me?'

'Hannah, where's this coming from?' Maddie spoke softly. Things had improved so much yet she was still cautious with the child.

'Well, I was talking with OT and, well, he thinks I'm wrong to not want you and Mark together.' Hannah moved her toe in circles on the dirt floor.

'Oh.' Maddie didn't know what to say.

'Yeah. He may be right, but I think I'm just not ready yet. I'm not ready for someone to replace Dad.'

Maddie put her palette knife down and walked to Hannah. She held open her arms and waited to see what would happen. Hannah moved forward and gave her a swift embrace.

'No one will ever replace your father.' Maddie stood back and saw the pain on Hannah's face.

'But you need to find love too.' Hannah looked at her feet.

'Yes, I do, but that's not what I meant. Your father was unique in your life and mine. No one can replace him.'

'Yeah, I get it.' Hannah looked up.

'Good, and thanks for realising I need love too. Happily, I'm willing to wait a bit. I think you and I have been a bit shaken up and any emotional involvements at this stage would be too soon.' Maddie smiled.

'Is that a long way of telling me that you and Mark have split?' Hannah asked.

Maddie laughed. 'I wouldn't say split, but more put on hold.'

'Hold? You guys are too weird.' Hannah laughed as she left the stables. 'By the way, I emailed Susan from school yesterday.'

'Yes?' Maddie knew it shouldn't hurt that Hannah was still trying to get Susan back into her life but it did.

'Nothing really. I just wanted you to know.'

'Thanks.' There was nothing else Maddie could say.

Tamsin was busy making OT dinner when Hannah arrived. Tamsin had made it plain that he needed building up and she'd take over all the cooking. No one, especially OT, was complaining about this.

'Tamsin, what's Maddie going to do if they don't give planning permission again?' Hannah took a brownie from the tea tray.

'Be cold for another winter.'

'Yeah, that's obvious, but can she make it all work, you know, keeping up the old house and stuff without the extra money?' Hannah asked.

'Good question, but I think she can. She's resourceful and strong.' Tamsin popped the casserole in the oven.

Hannah nodded. She hadn't thought of Maddie as being strong, but she guessed she was.

'What's happening between her and Mark?' Hannah asked.

'Why do you ask?' Tamsin turned to her.

'Well, one minute they're all over each other, then the next nothing, yet even I can tell they're in love.' Hannah took another brownie and waited to see if Tamsin was going to complain. 'Does Mark want children?'

Tamsin put the oven glove down and gave Hannah her full attention. 'Yes, but I think it's a dream he gave up a long time ago.'

'Do you know why?'

'Yes and no. When Claire died, I think he abandoned all hope of leading a conventional life and embraced one as a loner.' Tamsin turned to the sink and began filling it.

'So where does that leave Mark and Maddie?' Hannah asked.

'Nowhere at the moment, I think.'

'Not a good place.' Hannah picked up the crumbs off the table.

'No, but I think it might be where they need to be for the time being.' Tamsin cleared the empty brownie plate.

'Did you know that Maddie is going out with Gunnar tonight?'

'Is she?' Tamsin asked.

'Yeah and I don't get it.' Hannah shook her head and went to sit with OT in the other room.

❧ Twenty-Seven ❧

Holding her diary, Maddie sat on the edge of the bath. She was weeks late. It could be the dysentery, the antibiotics or the stress, but Maddie knew it wasn't. She didn't know whether to laugh or cry. She was carrying Mark's child.

They didn't use any protection the first time they were together and, to be honest, she hadn't given it any thought as it had taken her years to fall pregnant with John. Now, after one night of unprotected sex, she was pregnant. Maddie tried to let the words sink in.

Hannah was sitting at the kitchen table when Maddie came downstairs and she looked up from her cereal. 'Are you sick again?'

'Look that good, do I?'

Hannah nodded.

'I'm fine.' Maddie watched Hannah shrug as she returned to the history book she'd been studying. Maddie was still adjusting to the change in her attitude. Hannah had her spiky moments but for the most part she was calm and spent much of her time with Old Tom, who was hanging in there but not doing well. Hannah was cherishing every moment with him.

'I'm off into Helston. Do you need anything?' Maddie asked.

'No.'

'OK, see you later.' Maddie turned away from the smell of coffee as she thought she might throw up again. She was pregnant. She was going to have a baby. The happy thought went round in her head as she drove.

The air was buzzing with activity. A new green covered the trees and she pondered the right mix to create the exact colour.

If she kept working at this pace, she might have enough for the exhibition in three months. Painting had filled the place in her life where Mark had been. They had, without words, moved to give each other space. She loved him so much. The void was huge but she knew that Mark needed to come to grips with his past in his own time.

Pulling into a parking space, she wondered how Mark would react to the news. Should she tell him? Not yet. It was very early days. She'd keep it to herself until she was past the risky stage.

The chemist shop was busy and her attempts to find the tests proved futile so she had to ask. She didn't know why this made her feel embarrassed because she was thrilled. Maddie still couldn't believe after having had so much difficulty conceiving before that it had happened so easily. Just as she picked up a test to take it to the counter, Mrs Bates walked up to her. Damn.

'Maddie, how lovely to see you. You and Hannah have been so helpful to Tom.' Mrs Bates glanced at the blue package in her hand. Maddie willed her not to mention it.

'He means the world to us.' Maddie shifted from one foot to the other.

'I've been meaning to ask you.' Mrs Bates paused. 'If you've tried to locate your grandmother?'

Maddie nodded. 'I found an obituary for her.'

'Shame.' Mrs Bates looked at Maddie's hand again. 'You obviously have other things to think of now.'

Maddie's heart sank. Mrs Bates must have drawn one of two conclusions and they would be that either Maddie or Hannah were pregnant. 'Is that Miss Jenks over there? Are you giving her a lift?'

'Oh, she must be finished.' Mrs Bates dashed away.

Maddie wondered if Mrs Bates was a gossip but then she remembered that nothing here remained secret. After she paid, she headed to the nearest public loo. She couldn't wait and needed to know for sure. Pulling the cubicle door closed, she ripped the package open. In a few minutes all would be clear, but as much as she wanted this child, doubts circled her joy.

Watching the second hand on her watch, she listened to

women coming in and out. She wouldn't look for the blue line before the time was up. What did she want it to say? Did she deserve a child of her own?

The modern building didn't look welcoming or even open as Maddie stood at the door of the Catholic church. She wasn't sure why she was here. She was pregnant. The line was blue and suddenly nothing made sense.

From her mobile she'd called the surgery to make an appointment with the midwife. Hannah's reaction to the news could be volcanic so Maddie didn't want her to know just yet. Maddie needed a bit more time before she could share the news with Hannah or anyone. She had to be prepared for the fallout.

The door gave way and once inside, her hand automatically dipped into the holy water. She made the sign of the cross, genuflected and slid to her knees in the last pew. She stared at the crucifix above the altar. Her mind went blank.

'I hate to disturb you but it's six o'clock and I need to lock the church.'

Maddie's eyes focused on the priest who stood beside the pew. 'I'm sorry, Father, did you say it was six?' Her knees complained as she stood.

'Yes.' He smiled.

Maddie took a breath. 'I don't suppose you have time to hear my confession?'

'Where have you been?' Hannah stood by the door.

'In Helston,' Maddie said.

'That was hours ago and I couldn't reach you on your phone.' Hannah wanted to scream but the happy smile on Maddie's face stopped her. Had the woman spent the afternoon shagging Mark or something?

'The battery died.' Maddie looked at the shopping bags in her hands.

'What were you doing there?' Hannah paused. 'Oh, forget that. Dr Grades has rung five times. He says it's urgent.'

Maddie frowned.

'He said to tell you that you're to be at the surgery at eight tomorrow morning without fail.' Hannah put as much emphasis on the words as she could. The woman was on another planet.

'OK.'

'Maddie, is there something wrong with you that you're not telling me?' Hannah placed her hands on her hips. She wasn't going to let Maddie into the house until she knew. She didn't need another person dying on her. Dad and OT were enough. Hannah knew that OT wouldn't be with her for much longer. He didn't seem to be improving at all. Why wouldn't the drugs work? Why hadn't they for Dad?

'Don't worry. I'm fit and healthy. I've no idea what Dr Grades wants to talk to me about, but everything is fine.'

'Are you sure?'

'Yes. Now I'm starved so could you let me in?' Maddie asked.

Hannah stepped aside and tried to shake the feeling that things were about to go decidedly pear-shaped.

Rain pelted at the windscreen which, after yesterday's sunshine, was awful. Maddie felt queasy. She ran her hand over her stomach and it growled at her. It would have been better if her breakfast had stayed down.

Entering the car park, she wondered what it was that Dr Grades found so urgent that he needed to see her before the surgery opened. She pulled her coat tight around her and dashed in.

'Mrs Hollis, I'm so pleased you got my message.' He stood back and indicated she should head to his office.

'Please, sit down.'

She didn't like the sound of his voice. It was far too serious.

'It's been a week since you came off the antibiotics, yes?' he asked.

Maddie nodded.

'You called the surgery yesterday to make an appointment with the midwife?'

'Yes, I'm seeing her next week.' She frowned.

'Why didn't you tell me you were pregnant two weeks ago?' he asked.

'I had no idea I was.' She didn't like this line of questioning.

'I see.'

'I'm sorry but what do you see?' Maddie kept her hands neatly clasped on her lap.

'There's a problem.' He paused. 'The antibiotic you were on is the most effective one around for dysentery, but it is not recommended in any way for pregnant women.'

Maddie swallowed, not wanting to think what this meant.

'You're in a relationship?'

'No, not really.' Maddie thought of Mark and where they stood at the moment.

'You know the father?' He looked intently at her.

'Yes.' She loved the father of her child.

'Have you told him?' he asked.

'Not yet. I'm not sure where you are going with this.'

'Mrs Hollis, I would never have prescribed the drug if I'd known you were pregnant.' He paused. 'It carries huge risks of congenital anomalies, childhood cancers and spontaneous abortions.'

'Just what are you saying?' Maddie swallowed.

'I'm saying that I recommend that you have a termination immediately.'

'No.' Pain stabbed Maddie everywhere.

'I can understand that you may not want to do this, but it is very early in the pregnancy and—'

She interrupted him. 'No, you don't understand.' She took a breath. She hadn't told anyone about the abortion before yesterday and now she was about to tell the second person in less than twenty-four hours.

'Are you Catholic? Is that what the problem is?' he asked.

'I am but I've had to give up a child before and I will never do it again.' Maddie said each word slowly.

'This is not your first pregnancy?'

'No.'

'When was the last?' he asked.

'Last year.'

'You gave the child up for adoption?' he continued.

Maddie considered not answering. It was all so private. 'No, I had an abortion and I won't do that again, no matter what you tell me the risks are.'

'Mrs Hollis, I'm aware that this is an emotional issue for you. Abortion is never an easy answer. You clearly have suffered from post-abortion syndrome. Have you spoken to anyone about it?' His expression softened.

'I haven't spoken to anyone about it until yesterday. Counselling is not going to change my mind.'

Dr Grades shook his head and made a note on her file. 'Well, if you insist on going ahead with the pregnancy when you've been made aware of the risks, then there is one other thing.'

'Yes?'

'You say you had an abortion last year. Were you and your husband the same blood group?'

'No.'

'Then you need to find out immediately the blood group of this child's father as you are rhesus negative. If he is rhesus positive there's a risk to the foetus.'

Maddie nodded.

'Mrs Hollis, go away and think about what I've said. Don't be too rash in your decision. Talk to the father of the child. See how he feels about the risks.'

Rain lashed the mullioned panes of the big kitchen window. Maddie listened to the tap of the drops, totally disconnected from the turmoil within. What had happened to her since she'd arrived at Trevenen in August? What had the house done to her? It had revealed secrets. It was the key to the information she'd never hoped to know about her mother and father. It was the reason she was in Cornwall and by being here she'd met and fallen in love with Mark.

The child within her was small but it must know it was safe. She would protect it and Trevenen would protect it as it had done for past generations of Penventons. No one was going to threaten this baby. No one was going to make her act against her child. No one. Especially not the man she loved.

Maddie stood, feeling stronger. She picked up the letter sitting on the table. She recognised the council office's address. It was probably just the letter confirming what Mark had already told her. If they didn't grant permission for the shed then she'd have no choice now but to sell Trevenen. Maddie held her breath and opened the envelope.

Steam rose off the surface of the road as sunlight baked the remains of the morning rain. Hannah walked down the lane past Trevenen to OT's. She began to sing. Will was coming home tonight for the beginning of his Easter break. He had a month off, the sod. Not that she was complaining, really. She couldn't wait to see him. It had been way too long.

She nipped a white camellia flower off the bush by the gate. It had no scent but it was so beautiful. She'd put it in a vase for OT. She stopped outside the kitchen door and took a deep breath. The house now had the smell of illness about it. She couldn't describe it but she knew it all too well from the time with her father. However, unlike on Dad, the drugs finally seemed to be having a positive effect on OT.

'Hello, young lady.' The kindly woman who helped with OT greeted her.

'How is he?' Hannah grabbed a vase.

'In fine form and waiting for you,' she said.

Hannah smiled and walked through. He definitely looked better. The yellowness seemed to have faded. Hannah hoped that this was a good sign.

'You have brought me a Victory White. So beautiful, aren't they?'

'Yes. How do you remember all the names?' she asked.

'Because I chose them and planted them with care.' He smiled.

'As you do everything.' Hannah laughed.

'Exactly. Why do things any other way?' He smiled at her.

'We won't go there at the moment.' Hannah eased the bag from her shoulder.

'What have you brought me?' OT asked.

'I finally found the Bible.' She pulled it out of the bag and placed it on the sofa beside him. She knew he wouldn't be able to lift it and it might crush his legs if she put it on his lap.

'Let's see if this can shed any light on Catherine's life.' He carefully opened the Bible. 'Here we are. This traces the family back to Philip Penventon who died in 1601.'

'Any mention of Mary or Catherine?' She looked to where his finger pointed. 'Who came next? Philip's son?'

'This is a bit odd as the line is not direct. It would appear Philip didn't marry; it was a Thomas Penventon who really founded the dynasty.'

'Thomas was Catherine's son.' Hannah's mind raced ahead. 'Could Philip have adopted Catherine's child?'

'You may be right but unless this Bible has information on the distaff side, we may never know.' OT studied a back page closely. 'Ah, here's Catherine mentioned with her death date 1570. Now let's go back to the front to see if it matches Thomas's dates.' He handled the book so gently. Hannah knew it was old. She'd flipped through the pages and discovered it had been printed in the early 1700s.

'Thomas was born in 1570.'

'Excellent.' Hannah didn't know whether to be excited or sad.

'Mary died in 1590; let me see if there are some notes at the bottom.' OT bent closer to the book. 'The person who wrote these facts in the bible refers to letters he found.' OT looked up.

'Letters?'

'Ah, it goes on to say that they think there was another baby, a girl called Thomasina. It was noted in correspondence.' OT squinted. 'But the baby died almost immediately.'

Hannah sank back against the sofa. 'Where would Catherine and Thomasina be buried?'

'Most probably Catherine would have been buried in the

local church but her child would be another story.'

Hannah frowned.

'First, as far as we are aware, Catherine was not married.' OT put his hand up to stop Hannah from interrupting. 'So it would be unlikely that Mary or her brother Philip would want to bring this to anyone's attention.' He took a deep breath. 'At that time, children who were not baptised were not accorded a proper burial in any way, therefore Thomasina could be buried anywhere.'

'OK, I get it, I think.' Hannah stood and paced the room. She decided that when OT took his nap shortly, she had a date with the local graveyard.

'I'll have sparkling water, please.' Maddie stood beside Tamsin at the bar and tried to avoid her questioning look. 'Dodgy tummy still, so trying not to give it anything to complain about.'

'Have you told the doctor that you are still having problems?' Tamsin asked.

Maddie remembered the conversation of a week ago and she didn't like his prescription at all. 'Yes. He's says it happens sometimes.'

Tamsin took her wine and moved to a table in the corner. The pub was quiet and Maddie was grateful because she didn't have the energy to socialise. Trying to hide the symptoms of the pregnancy was adding to her exhaustion. Hannah kept giving her funny glances when she slipped off to bed at eight with the excuse that she had a good book to finish.

'Any word yet on the planning permission?' Tamsin sat down.

'No.' Maddie took a sip of the water. 'Mark says this isn't unusual.' She glanced at her bag. In it was an offer of one million pounds for Trevenen from the estate agents.

'Hmmm.' Tamsin paused and looked closely at Maddie. 'How and where are things with you and Mark?'

'Nothing like being direct.' Maddie laughed.

'Yes, I just wondered as Hannah mentioned that you've been out with Gunnar a couple of times.'

'No secrets from you, then.' Maddie grimaced. She had a big secret to keep from Tamsin yet she needed to get information from her. She just didn't know how to ask without making her friend suspicious. 'Mark and I are not an item, as you say, at the moment. We seem to have stepped back.'

'Whatever for? And are you leading Gunnar astray?'

'Certainly not. I finished all romantic links with him ages ago, but he's tremendous company and uncomplicated.'

'The man's happy to have you on those terms?' Tamsin leaned back and took a look at Maddie.

'Absolutely.'

'Is he gay?'

'Definitely not. We've become good friends.' Maddie realised how nice it was to have a simple relationship.

'Friends, huh. So where does this leave Mark, or is he relegated to the "just friends" league?'

Maddie attempted a laugh, knowing he was more than just a friend. What could she tell Tamsin that would make her drop the inquisition? 'I don't need to tell you that Mark had things he needed to face.'

'True.' Tamsin nodded. 'You didn't dump him because of that?'

'Good God, no. If anything, it made me love him more.' Maddie stopped. Shit. She'd just said that she loved Mark. Big mistake.

'So then tell me, why are you two not together?' asked Tamsin.

'He needs time to come to his own peace and I realised that I needed time too. The events of the past year and a bit have left me, well ... emotionally tired, at best.'

'That all sounds bloody wonderful but to me it sounds like you are both hiding.'

'To you it would.' Maddie laughed.

'Life's short. You of all people should know that. You're in love. Don't let it slip away.' Tamsin sipped her wine.

'I won't.' Maddie nodded, wondering how on earth she could stop it slipping away.

'You don't sound totally convinced.'

'I am but I may not move on your time schedule.' Maddie shrugged.

'Don't be a bloody fool.'

Maddie ran a finger around the rim of her glass and wondered how she could get around to why she'd wanted to meet Tamsin today. She needed to know Mark's blood type and she couldn't ask him.

'I was reading an interesting article the other day about blood types and diets,' Maddie plunged in, crossing her fingers under the table.

'Where the hell did that come from? Are you trying to tell me I'm fat?' Tamsin looked down at her ample cleavage.

'No, I just found it interesting. What blood type are you?'

'O.'

'Positive or negative?' Maddie continued.

'Does that affect how I eat? I'd heard of the blood group diet thing before, but never the bit about positive or negative.'

'Really?' Maddie knew she was in dangerous waters here.

'I'm O positive. So what does that say?' Tamsin asked.

'Solid meat eater.'

'No surprise there then. So had I been negative what would that mean?' Tamsin asked.

Maddie wracked her brain for something plausible. 'Fish, I think.'

'Interesting.'

'Yes, I thought so.' Maddie plunged on. 'Do you know Mark's blood group, by any chance?'

'Haven't a clue. You'll have to ask yourself. I wonder if it's the ancestry thing they are trying to tie into. In which case, my family have always been farmers, so meat it is. Both Anthony and Mark come from the fishing lot. I can't remember Anthony's type, but I think it's positive too, in which case it is a load of bull, or some farmer stole into the bloodline somewhere before me.'

Maddie laughed. She found it interesting that Mark's family

306

belonged to the sea, but it didn't give her the answer she needed. 'I'm just off to the loo.'

'Are you sure you're all right? You went just as we arrived!'

'Seriously, I'm fine.' And Maddie knew that she would be. But she still needed that information.

❧ Twenty-Eight ❧

'Hey, Maddie, are you in the dining room?' Hannah stuck her head around the door. There was no answer so she continued looking. Eventually she came up the stairs to Maddie's bedroom. She must be home because her car was here, unless of course she was out with Tamsin or someone.

Hannah hesitated at the door. She heard noises but thankfully not ones of passion. Someone was being sick. Hannah strode through the bedroom to Maddie's en suite and found her on her knees with her head in the loo. She was heaving but nothing was coming out.

'Maddie, I thought you said you were OK?' Hannah rushed to her.

The convulsions stopped and Maddie leaned back on her heels. 'Don't look so worried.'

'How can you say that? You've been ill for so long now; surely there's something seriously wrong with you? Don't lie to me.' Hannah wrapped her arms around herself.

'I will not lie to you. There's nothing wrong with me.' Maddie stood up.

'Then what the hell's causing you to puke all the time?' Hannah paused. 'Oh God, you're pregnant, aren't you?'

Maddie nodded as she washed her face.

'Whose child is it?' asked Hannah.

Maddie swung around. 'Hannah, how can you ask that question?'

'You've been dating two guys, unless this was an immaculate conception.'

Maddie gave a short laugh and perched on the loo seat. 'I never slept with Gunnar.'

'So that leaves the Holy Ghost or Mark. Well, I know which of the two I would prefer.'

Maddie laughed.

'I'm glad you find it funny. Does Mark know?' Hannah asked

'No.'

'Why not? I thought letting the father know was one of the first things you did, or have I got that wrong too?' Hannah crossed her arms against her chest.

'I'm not ready.' Maddie looked at her feet.

'Not ready? Not ready to what? Do the huff and puff stuff? Paint the nursery? Give me a clue here.'

'Hannah, things aren't that simple.' Maddie glanced at her and then looked away.

'Yes, they are, but never with you. Tell Mark. He has a right to know. Hell, I think he'll be thrilled, personally. He'll make a great dad.'

'You think so?' Maddie half-smiled.

'Yes and you must too or you wouldn't have played Russian roulette with the old birth control thing. You're not a stupid woman, although I'm beginning to wonder.'

'Just when have you become an expert on me?' Maddie sighed.

Hannah heard how tired Maddie sounded. She decided to let it drop.

'Hello? Where is everyone?' Tamsin came through the bedroom door. 'I expected non-alcoholic champagne at the very least.'

'What?' Maddie asked.

'Well, I just heard from Mrs Bates that you're expecting, and I was just wondering when you were going to tell your best friend. Not, of course, that sharing the news with one of the biggest talkers in town isn't one way of doing it.' Tamsin leaned against the bathroom door frame without her usual smile.

'Damn. I was hoping she'd forget what was in my hand

when we met in the chemist.' Maddie ran her fingers through her hair.

'Does Mark know yet that he's a papa-to-be?' Tamsin asked.

Hannah watched as Maddie shook her head.

'I think you'd better do it quick before Mrs Bates spreads the word and the village begins to put two and two together and come up with two possible candidates on the paternity front.' Tamsin pursed her lips.

'See, I wasn't the only one.' Hannah sat on the edge of the bath.

'No, let them wonder.' Maddie's voice was barely audible. She put her head in her hands.

'What are you saying?' Tamsin came up to Maddie and lifted her head. Hannah could see tears rolling down Maddie's cheeks. She just didn't get it.

'I'm not saying anything.' Maddie stood, towering over Tamsin in the tight space of the bathroom. Hannah moved out into the bedroom. She might be in some danger from flying blows in a minute from the look of them.

'Are you trying to tell me that Mark isn't the father and that Gunnar, who only yesterday you said you'd never slept with, is?' Tamsin asked.

'All I said was that I'm not saying.' Maddie uttered the words carefully.

'But you just told me,' Hannah said.

'Did I?' Maddie pushed past Tamsin into the bedroom.

'No matter what you're saying now, and I haven't a clue why you are saying it –' Tamsin took a deep breath – 'it doesn't make any sense when you say you love Mark. He's the father and he has a right to know.'

Hannah was riveted as Tamsin almost spat out the words. Now she knew why the boys never stepped out of line. Tamsin was shit scary.

'No.' Maddie said the word and walked downstairs.

'I think she's lost her mind with the pregnancy,' Hannah said.

'Maybe.' Tamsin marched off after her.

Hannah wasn't going to miss this. She knew who she would back in a fight any day and it wasn't her stepmother. No one was a match for Tamsin.

Maddie walked to the stables and slammed the big doors behind her. Great sobs shook her body. She could barely breathe. This wasn't right. She couldn't deal with this now. Mark mustn't know it was his child. If he knew that the child was possibly damaged, he would ask her to do what John had done. She couldn't do that again.

Maddie swung around as Tamsin pushed into the stables with anger written on her face.

'You've no right not to tell him. It's his baby. So what's this nonsense?' Tamsin asked in clipped tones.

'Tamsin, back off.' Maddie didn't know what else to say.

'No, I won't. Mark was desperately hurt before and I won't stand by and let you do that to him.'

Maddie saw Hannah standing in the doorway. She had no idea what was going through her mind. Maddie did know one thing for sure: she wasn't setting a very good example by having unprotected sex and having a child out of wedlock. Suddenly, the fact that Hannah hadn't blown up at the news struck Maddie. If anything, she had reacted calmly.

'Currently, I'm not doing anything to him.'

'Yes, you are. The word will spread like wildfire and he'll find out whether it comes from you or someone else. How would you feel?' Tamsin asked.

Maddie stared at Tamsin. She just wasn't getting it. Maddie needed to protect this child.

'The baby is mine.' She turned from Tamsin and looked at the painting on the easel. Its smooth strokes of blue, which hinted at the depths of the sea, became an angry squall in her head.

'I know this is your first pregnancy and it's all overwhelming.'

'Oh, shut up. You don't know anything.' Maddie swung back to see her friend's small body in fighting stance.

'Look, I do know. I've been through it three times the whole way and have lost two. I know.' Tamsin wasn't backing down.

'No, you don't.' Maddie sucked in air. Tamsin had lost two. She hadn't killed them.

'You'll be fine. The first one is always the toughest.' Tamsin came nearer.

'It's not my bloody first,' Maddie said between clenched teeth.

'What?' Tamsin stopped moving.

'You have a child somewhere?' Hannah came closer to them.

'No.'

'But you just said this wasn't your first,' said Hannah.

'You've had miscarriages; they're awful, aren't they?' Tamsin spoke softly.

'No.'

'If it wasn't miscarriages and you don't have a child stashed somewhere, you've had an abortion.' Hannah's voice became louder. 'You can't have. You're too Catholic to do that. Even I know that.'

Tamsin's hand reached out and touched Maddie's arm. Maddie felt a shiver of cold go through her. They knew what she had done.

'It's OK, Maddie.' Tamsin wrapped Maddie in her arms.

'What, did you get pregnant like your mum in your teens?' Hannah walked to within inches of Maddie. 'That must've been weird to realise the same thing happened to you.'

Maddie's head shot up and she pulled away from Tamsin. 'No, I didn't fall pregnant in my teens, and, unlike my mother, I didn't have the child.'

'So what's the big deal then?' Hannah stood with her hands on her hips.

'Hannah, an abortion's always a tough decision.' Tamsin turned to her.

'Yeah, I get that, but even so, it must have been a while ago, before Maddie met Dad, so you'd think she should be over it by now.'

'I don't think one ever gets over losing a child, no matter how it happens,' said Tamsin.

Maddie looked at Hannah and she knew the girl didn't have a clue.

'So when did it happen?' Hannah pressed on.

'You don't want to know.' Maddie turned away from her.

'Yes, I do. I know it couldn't have been with Dad because you guys were always at it, trying to make me a brother or sister. So when did it happen? Just before you met Dad? Was that why you didn't have any children? Did the abortion mess your insides up?'

Maddie swung back to her. 'Hannah, you've asked me never to lie to you so please do not keep asking these questions.'

'What are you trying to say? That you had an abortion with Dad?' Hannah paused and stared at Maddie. 'I don't believe that. Dad would never let you do that. You must've done it without him knowing. How could you?' she screamed.

Maddie wanted to shout back, but instead spoke as calmly as she could. 'I did it because he asked me to.'

'No, he'd never do that. You killed my brother or sister.' Hannah shoved her, pushing her to the floor.

Pain ripped into Maddie's back as the wind was totally knocked out of her.

'You bitch!' Hannah yelled as she fled from the stables.

Maddie watched her run away.

'Oh my God, are you all right?' Tamsin helped Maddie to sit up.

As Maddie got her breath back, she felt suddenly empty. She'd told the priest everything in confession and hoped that would be the end of it. She wanted to leave the pain in the sanctity of the confessional, but now it was truly out in the open.

'I'm a bit winded but should be fine in a minute.' Maddie tried to collect her thoughts. Now Hannah knew the truth, whether she accepted it or not.

'John asked you to abort?' Tamsin asked.

Maddie nodded. It seemed strange hearing the words from someone else.

'When?'

'A week before he died.' Maddie couldn't look at her friend.

'I don't know what to say.'

'There's nothing to say. I fell pregnant. It was a gift. It was part of him to bring forward, but he felt that I couldn't do it all. I couldn't work and raise Hannah. There wouldn't be enough of me to look after her.' Maddie shook her head. 'He was right.'

'No, he was wrong; terribly wrong to you and to her.' Tamsin paused. 'Can you stand?'

Maddie winced as she rose. There was a sharp pain in her lower back.

'OK?'

Maddie nodded.

'So when did it happen?' Tamsin asked.

'A week after the funeral.'

'Who went with you?' asked Tamsin.

'No one.' Maddie laughed bitterly.

'Alone?' Tamsin held open the door to the house.

'Yes, no one knew and I was too ashamed and desperate about what I was doing. I hadn't even been to the doctor.' Maddie sighed. 'I'd been so happy, even though I knew that John would never see his child. It made me hopeful when all other hope was gone. John, however, saw a different side.'

'Sit down. You look far too pale.' Tamsin led her to a chair.

'Is that a surprise?'

'No.' Tamsin gave a small laugh. 'OK, I now get why you are so protective of the baby. It makes sense in a way.'

'Oh, I'm glad I've sorted that for you,' Maddie said sarcastically.

'But what I still don't understand is why you won't tell Mark. He'll be over the moon. I know he will.'

'No.'

'So, you're going to keep the knowledge that he's the father from him? I just can't see that working and I can't see why you would want to. Am I missing something here?' Tamsin tilted her head to one side.

'No.'

'OK. Where's the sugar? I know you normally have tea

314

without, but I think you need some.' Tamsin scanned the countertop.

'In the left-hand cupboard.' Maddie watched Tamsin stand on tiptoe to reach the canister.

'Got it.' Tamsin paused. 'What were you taking this antibiotic for and when?' She held out the prescription box. 'This stuff is terribly strong. Anthony had to take it after our trip to Egypt. Vile. Medicine was worse than the illness.' Tamsin looked at her. Maddie's throat tightened. She'd forgotten she'd stored the old box there. There were three tablets left and she'd meant to take them to the health centre to dispose of them.

Tamsin turned the box oven in her hands. 'Maddie, you're afraid that there may be something wrong with the baby. That's why you won't tell him.' Tamsin looked intently at her friend. 'Mark isn't John. I know in my heart he'd never ask of you what John did. Does the doctor know?'

Through her tears Maddie could only nod.

'What did he say?' Tamsin asked.

'Terminate.' Maddie wondered how one word could hurt so much.

'No.'

Maddie sobbed.

'You can't do that. I understand.' Tamsin came and fell to her knees in front of Maddie. She took Maddie's hands in hers. 'You must tell Mark. You don't have to live with this fear alone.'

'No, I can't do that to him and I can't risk it.' She glanced at the table where the sales agreement for Trevenen awaited her signature. She was leaving. That was the answer.

❖ Twenty-Nine ❖

It was midnight when Hannah walked into the kitchen and turned on the light. It illuminated a pool of blood; Maddie lay near it on the floor. Hannah screamed but Maddie didn't move. Hannah picked up the phone and called for an ambulance. She prayed like she hadn't prayed in a long time as she sat on the floor beside the unconscious, but breathing, Maddie.

The ride to hospital was a blur. She hadn't been able to reach either Tamsin or Mark, but Fred had come to the rescue. She tried to shake the images of all the blood on the floor out of her head as she paced the waiting room. Maddie's skin had been so white and cold. Hannah had caused this. She knew it in her heart. She pushed Maddie to the floor. The baby had miscarried. That's what the paramedics had said.

Fred walked into the room. 'I found a parking space and I reached Mum. She's on her way.'

Hannah sank into a chair. Maddie would hate her for ever. Dad had asked Maddie to abort her last child and now Hannah had pushed Maddie and she'd lost this one.

The medics had asked Hannah so many questions about Maddie and the pregnancy and she just didn't know the answers. She'd failed Maddie and herself. She should have come back earlier. OT had been sleeping for hours but Hannah had just stayed by his side, not really sure she was ready to come back and apologise. OT had yet again made her see the other side of the story. She couldn't have fucked things up more if she had tried.

Fred put his hand on her shoulder. 'She'll be OK.'

'She's lost a lot of blood. It was everywhere.' She blinked but the image didn't go away.

'Don't think about it. You got help and she'll be fine,' he said.

Maddie wouldn't be fine. She'd lost her baby and Hannah had caused it.

Tamsin came running into the waiting room. 'How is she?'

'Don't know.' Fred stood.

'Tamsin, I'm so sorry.' Hannah put her head in her hands.

'It's not your fault,' Tamsin said.

'But it is. I pushed her. She fell. I caused the miscarriage.'

Tamsin held open her arms. 'We don't know that.'

Hannah didn't move. Tamsin walked to her as Mark arrived. Hannah had never seen him look so worried. Did he know what had happened? Did he even know Maddie was pregnant? What had Tamsin told him?

'Where is she?' Mark's voice wavered.

'Still in surgery, I guess,' Fred said.

Tamsin put her arm around Hannah's shoulders and pulled her close. Hannah held back the tears. She needed to be strong.

A doctor appeared at the door and spoke to Mark before Hannah could speak.

'Are you the father?' he asked.

Hannah watched Mark's face. If she'd thought he looked bad before, she hadn't a clue. Tamsin hadn't told him.

'He is,' Hannah said. Mark looked at her.

'How is she?' Hannah asked the doctor, unable to meet Mark's eyes.

'We've completed the D&C. She's lost a tremendous amount of blood but she is stable.'

'Can we see her?' Tamsin asked.

'No, she's still in recovery,' he said.

'For how long?'

'It will be a few hours yet. She may need another transfusion. Time will tell.' The doctor gave them a smile.

Hannah watched Mark sit down.

'I've contacted her GP and he'll be here shortly if you wish

317

to speak to him.' Hannah watched the green-clad figure disappear down the hallway.

'Tamsin?' Mark's voice broke.

'I only found out today, Mark. I don't even know how far along she was.' Tamsin went to sit beside him.

'She didn't tell me.' Mark put his head in his hands. 'Are you sure it's mine?' Mark looked at Hannah.

'Yes, positive.' Hannah wanted to help Mark but she didn't know what to say or where to begin. 'Mark, I'm sorry.' Hannah took a deep breath. She needed to try and make it right. 'It's my fault.'

Tamsin stood up. 'No, don't be an idiot, Hannah, it's not your fault. Things are never that simple. What we need to do right now is focus on the fact that Maddie's still with us, thanks to your quick action.'

'But—' Hannah tried to go on.

'No buts. Now, Fred, take Hannah and get us all some tea.' Tamsin pushed Hannah out the door.

Hannah turned to see Tamsin talking to Mark. She wanted to know what Tamsin was saying.

'Leave them to it. Mum will know how to handle it. She's good like that. What a hell of a shock to find out you're a father and then that you're not.'

'That has to be the fucking understatement of the year.' Hannah couldn't hold back the tears any more.

Fred laughed and threw his arm around her shoulders. 'Yeah.'

Maddie sat up and looked at the flowers on the small table beside her. She tried to study the colours but couldn't. She hadn't been able to stop crying since she'd come to and they'd told her she'd lost her child. The only person she'd seen was Dr Grades. He told her the test of the foetal tissue had indicated that the miscarriage had been caused because the foetus hadn't been viable. The antibiotics had done their job, killing everything in her.

Shaking her head, she knew had to stop thinking about it

and must pick herself up and face life again. Maddie heard a discreet cough.

'Excuse me.'

A grey-haired man stood by the curtain opening at the bottom of her bed. She'd said that she wouldn't receive visitors. She wasn't ready to face everyone's pity. Maddie blew her nose and dried her eyes. When she looked up, he was still there. Something about him felt familiar but she couldn't place it.

'Maddie?' the man asked.

'Peter?' Maddie swallowed. She was hallucinating; her father couldn't be standing there.

'Yes. May I come in?' he asked.

She nodded.

'I know you didn't want to see anyone but Hannah thought that you might see me,' he said.

'You've spoken to Hannah?' Maddie blinked.

'Yes, I've been staying with her at Trevenen since yesterday.' He came through the curtain.

Maddie opened her mouth and then shut it.

'I'm on my way to France to give a course. I chose to fly through London and was going to suggest we try and meet.' He laughed.

'Please sit down.' Maddie pointed to the edge of the bed.

'When I called the house, I discovered a very upset girl and she eventually explained why. I came immediately.' Peter sat.

'Thank you.' Maddie swallowed.

'You look so like your mother.' He smiled.

'I didn't know that until I found the photos.'

Peter nodded. 'She was so beautiful and full of life. Coming back to Trevenen made it seem like yesterday.'

'Did you love her?' she asked.

'I think I did. It was so long ago now.' He paused. 'I was certainly devastated when my letters came back. I assumed she didn't feel the same. I wish now that I'd returned there myself.'

Maddie gave him a small smile.

'I see that you've inherited my artistic genes.'

Maddie laughed.

319

'Your style's not that dissimilar to my own,' he said.

'I noticed that too.' Maddie paused. 'Peter, I have so many questions.'

'Yes.' He nodded.

Maddie looked at her father. 'How long are you here for?'

'Unfortunately, I must leave today. In fact, I take the train to London in an hour.' He stood up.

'Oh.' Maddie swallowed a lump in her throat.

'I'll change my return flight, if you want, so that we can meet properly?'

'Yes, please, I'd like that,' she said, fighting back yet more tears.

Peter stood and then bent down and kissed Maddie's cheek.

'Before you leave, can you tell me something?' she asked.

'I'll try.'

'Reading my mother's diary, it seemed that it was one-sided; that she went after you.'

Peter laughed. 'Funny, that. I was doing my best not to give into my feelings for her. She was so young. Believe me, it was very mutual.'

'Thanks.'

He squeezed her hand. 'We've a lot of catching up to do and I look forward to it.'

'Hannah is beside herself with guilt and worry.' Tamsin turned into the village. 'Why wouldn't you see her?'

'I'm sorry, but I needed to sort things through in my head. I'll make sure that Hannah knows that she is not to blame in any way and that I love her.'

Tamsin pulled into the drive and Maddie's heart lifted at the sight of Trevenen bathed in the April sunshine. The cherry trees were in blossom. Maddie knew that she could do this.

In those few days alone in the hospital, she'd allowed herself to come to terms with what had happened. It didn't make the loss any easier to bear, but she accepted that it was meant to be. The consultant, who had come to check her, had spent some time reinforcing that the foetus would not have survived and the fall had nothing to do with the miscarriage. He also re-assured her that there was no reason that she couldn't conceive again. She accepted that this wouldn't be happening with Mark, though. She could only begin to imagine his pain and anger at being told he was the father of the baby she'd just lost. She had been so blind.

Tamsin put a hand on her arm. 'Go and be with Hannah. She needs you.'

'Thanks.'

'Oh, and you might want to explain to her why people were around measuring the house.'

'Shit.' Maddie's hand flew to her mouth. She'd walked to the post box with the sales agreement after Tamsin had left. She'd thought the walk would help with the stiffness and cramping. 'I guess I've some explaining and apologising to do.' Maddie left the car slowly. She still had severe bruising.

'I think I should come in with you,' Tamsin added.

'No, Hannah and I need to do this on our own. Just call later to check that there are no dead bodies lying around.' Maddie gave her friend a smile.

'Will do. In fact, better than that, I will pop round with a casserole so you don't have to think about food.'

'Thanks.' Maddie took a deep breath and left the car. Reaching the house, she noticed the flaking paint on the door. Why hadn't she painted that yet? She laughed. It wasn't im-portant; other things were. Maddie swallowed and pushed the door open.

'Hannah, I'm home,' Maddie called.

Hannah flew out of the kitchen but stopped short of flinging herself into Maddie's arms. 'Oh, Maddie, I'm so sorry! I know you can never forgive me.' Hannah's face was wet with tears.

Maddie opened her arms. 'There's nothing to forgive.'

'Tamsin told me it was the medication, but the fall started it, I'm sure.'

'No, that's not what the doctors told me. Please don't think that.' Maddie continued to wait with open arms.

'But I didn't believe you about Dad. I'm so sorry.' Hannah went into Maddie's embrace.

'Hannah, we all have things to learn. Your father was thinking of both of us. He was thinking of the strain it would've put on me, knowing me as he did. The key thing is that it's in the past.' Maddie stroked Hannah's hair, which was so like John's.

'I thought I was going to lose you too. It was awful.' Hannah spoke through her tears.

Maddie flinched as Hannah squeezed her tight, putting pressure on her bruises.

'Oh, shit, sorry. I forgot about that.' Hannah pulled back. 'I've made some cake. Would you like some?'

'You made cake?' Maddie opened her eyes wide.

'Yeah, it was a recipe that Abi gave me.' Hannah looked away.

'Abi cooks?' Maddie leaned against the table.

'Yeah, and I needed to talk to someone about all that was raging in my head and OT wasn't up to it, so I hope you don't mind that I called her.'

'No, of course not.' Maddie tried not to think of the phone bill.

'Maddie, why are you selling Trevenen? I thought you loved it.'

'I do and I'm not. Long story. Hand me the phone. I have some calls to make.'

It was sunlight that woke Maddie and not the sound of a child crying. This made a welcome change, especially after the hospital and the maternity ward. She rolled over and grimaced. These bruises wouldn't give her any peace, and nor would her conscience about Mark. She hadn't spoken to him. She didn't want to but she knew she must. She owed him that, at the very least.

Once downstairs, Maddie found the table laid for her with a note from Hannah saying she hoped she'd slept well and would see her after school. Maddie brushed away the tears caused by Hannah's thoughtfulness. She wasn't sure how long this new model Hannah would be around but she was enjoying it.

The post was in a neat pile: a letter from the estate agent and one from the council. She didn't know which to open first. The agent hadn't been pleased. He'd booked a holiday on the basis of the commission he'd receive. However, he did calm down when she explained.

She picked up the council letter. Reading the contents, she could tell that Mark had been hard at work for her as the consent had gone through with revised plans. Over her bowl of cereal, Maddie thought about Mark and his pain. She tried to think of the words she needed to say to him. She debated if it was best to drive over and apologise face to face, or to phone, or even write a letter. The last was her first choice but she knew it was the most cowardly way.

'Damn, just go and get dressed, get in the car and do it. If you think about it any longer, you never will,' she told herself in her best imitation of Tamsin.

Maddie placed her dishes in the sink and walked down the hall. She stopped in front of the photo of Daphne and Daphne's mother and aunt.

'Well, ladies, this has been one hell of a ride so far. Care to tell me if Trevenen has any other secrets that are going to turn my life upside down?' Maddie shook her head. 'No, the secrets of Trevenen didn't do that. I was more than capable of doing it myself.'

Dressed and decided, Maddie closed the door behind her. Her key was in the lock when she heard the phone ring. She dashed back in.

'Mrs Hollis, this is the secretary at Mullion School. I'm ringing to ask if Mark Triggs has permission to take Hannah into Treliske Hospital.'

'Is something wrong with Hannah?' Maddie's heart raced. 'No.'

Maddie heard Mark's voice asking for the phone. Her mouth went dry.

'Old Tom has been rushed to hospital in a coma. It doesn't look good,' he said.

'Right. I'll meet you there.'

Maddie went onto auto-pilot as she whizzed through the lanes. Her brain registered how Hannah must be feeling, and Mark too. He cared deeply for the old man and her presence wasn't going to make things any easier. However, she must go and face the music with Mark and be a support for Hannah.

The tears marking her T-shirt didn't really register as Hannah held OT's cold hand. The lights on the monitors had gone flat about ten minutes before. Maddie and Mark were speaking with the nurse, leaving her alone with OT. He hadn't been dead when they had arrived. All the lights were flashing, but now nothing. How could life be there one minute and gone the next? They didn't have lights to tell them when Dad had died. It was just the silence. No more raspy breathing.

Maddie had held her when they realised OT had gone. She hadn't let Maddie hold her when Dad had died. She had shut Maddie out. This time her support felt right.

Only minutes ago, OT had opened his eyes and looked directly at Hannah and smiled. Mark had seen it. She hadn't imagined it. He was with her for a moment or two, then the bright blue eyes closed. At first, she didn't realise she was crying. They were silent tears. Not like the sobs that marked the end of her father's life.

OT's hand was yellow, cold and almost felt like wax. Was he now just a waxwork? After Dad had died, Hannah had fled the room and never looked at the body again. Now, sitting here peacefully with OT, she wished she had spent more time with her dad's body. She said a silent 'I'm sorry' in the direction of the ceiling, noting the yellow stain on it that matched the colour of OT's skin.

Maddie's soft footsteps interrupted her thoughts. Hannah looked at her stepmother. Mark wasn't with her. Hannah knew that Maddie must not have been ready to see Mark yet. She seemed so empty and alone.

'Are you ready to go or would like to stay a bit longer?' Maddie whispered as if she didn't want to wake OT.

'Whatever.' Hannah looked at the still face.

'You can take all the time you need.'

'I'm OK. He wouldn't want me to go all maudlin, as he would say, so I won't.'

'Doesn't stop it hurting.' Maddie's mouth turned up into a smile.

'No. Did Dad look like wax at the end?' Hannah asked.

Maddie laughed. 'I guess he did but I never thought of it that way.'

'I want to go and see my mother.' Hannah stood up.

'O ... K.' Maddie cocked her head. 'Do you mind if I ask what made you come out with that now? She's a long way away.'

'Well, people are dropping around me like flies. I would like to see what she's like while she's still alive.'

'Right. Well, maybe during the summer.' Maddie held out her hand.

'Yeah, I know.' She took one last look at OT and she was sure he was smiling.

❖ Thirty ❖

Hannah watched Maddie open the bottle of wine.

'I don't know about you but I need a drink.' Maddie's hand shook.

Mark nodded.

'To Tom.' Maddie raised her glass.

'Yes. To Old Tom.' Mark took a sip of his wine.

The front door burst open and Tamsin came in.

'That wine looks good. Do you think you could spare me a glass?' She pulled up a chair.

'You bet.' Maddie grabbed one.

'Bloody shame about Old Tom. I'll miss him, but at least it was quick in the end.'

'Yeah.' Hannah thought about the body lying in the hospital bed. It wasn't OT any more and she wanted to think about him in his workshop and not looking yellow and cold. 'When will the funeral be? Mark, do you know yet?'

'I spoke to the undertakers a little while ago, so probably at the end of this week, I think.'

'Fine. That gives us a bit of time to organise things.' Tamsin tapped her fingers on the table.

'That's a good point. Hannah, did he have an address book that you know of?' Maddie topped up Mark's glass.

Hannah noticed how Maddie was looking at him. Had they spoken yet about the baby? Maybe Maddie should tell Mark about what had happened when she was pregnant before. 'Yeah, I think in the study.'

'Great. Shall we divide the list and contact everyone?' Tamsin took a piece of paper and started writing things down. 'What about the newspapers?'

'In hand.' Mark looked up.

Hannah thought he looked shattered. She hadn't realised that he would be that upset by OT's death. He'd taken control of everything, just like he'd done when he rescued her. He was a bit of a rock, really.

'Look, guys, I'm off to bed.' Hannah tried to give Tamsin the eye to tell her to leave now but Tamsin looked glued to the chair.

'Really? Have you spoken to Will yet?' Tamsin asked.

'No. I'm sure he's heard by now but I'll ring him in the morning.'

In her room, Hannah cried as she ran her hands over the repair on the old chest. Why did everyone she love have to die or disappear?

Hannah had had no joy in the churchyard. If Catherine had been buried here or in the church, the evidence was lost. She wondered if the church records went back that far. But even if they had, as OT had told her, only Catherine's death would be recorded, not Thomasina's.

She went to put the Bible back where she'd found it in the sitting room. Thankfully, she'd found it before OT had died. He'd helped her to pull it all together, but she'd have to do the rest by herself.

Sunlight fell on the fireplace as she came into the sitting room. Although she knew it was just a smugglers' hidey hole, she couldn't shake the feeling there was something more to it. She walked to the door. With the bright light, she could actually see the join in the wood panelling.

With a quick click, the door popped open. Hannah hesitated on the threshold. Why had Maddie always been so spooked? The crying, yeah. It was spooky and just plain weird. But it must be the wind or an animal. There was a wind today but Hannah didn't hear that sound.

Propping the door open so that all the light could come in,

Hannah fell to her knees and ran her hands over the slates. They were mostly smooth but there were some indentations.

'What on earth are you doing?' Maddie asked.

Hannah shot to her feet with her heart racing.

'Maddie, I know I thought you were insane when you said it, but I sometimes heard the crying too.' Hannah stepped back into the sitting room. Maddie came closer but Hannah could see her hesitation. 'It was the cry of a baby, wasn't it, and not the wind or a cat?'

Maddie nodded.

'Do you hear it now?'

Maddie swallowed then moved through the door and stopped.

Hannah's mouth was dry. There was a connection here, she just knew it. Maddie was a Penventon and something had been calling out to her. Thomasina had been.

'No, I don't hear it any more, nor have I since I fell pregnant.' Maddie's voice trailed off over the last words.

Hannah took Maddie's hand. 'Sorry.'

Maddie squeezed her hand.

'I know you mentioned that the sitting room was added in the 1700s, but do you know when the dining room bit of the house was tacked on?' Hannah let go of Maddie's hand and went onto her knees again.

'No. It's old but not as old as the kitchen part. What on earth are you doing?' Maddie asked.

'I think there is something written on the slate.'

Maddie frowned. 'That's funny. You know when you found me on the floor and I got that black eye?'

Hannah nodded.

'I was thinking that the slate looked like old headstones, which of course they could have been. Probably rejects, as nothing was wasted.'

'That's it!' Hannah said.

'What are you talking about?'

'I think Catherine's daughter Thomasina is buried here.'

'One of us is clearly insane. Who are Catherine and Thomasina?' Maddie asked.

'Oh, yeah, I forgot to tell you about the other stuff I found.' Maddie raised an eyebrow.

'Sorry.' Hannah paused. It was all fitting together. God, she wished she had OT here.

'I'm still in the dark.' Maddie sat on the arm of a chair.

'Do you have any large bits of paper?'

'Of course.' Maddie frowned again.

'Remember when you took me to that place where we did that brass rubbing?'

Maddie smiled and dashed off. Hannah sat back on her heels. She knew she was right. Thomasina was buried here at Trevenen.

Maddie was back in a flash and Hannah whipped the paper out of her hands, along with the soft charcoal. Hannah went to work rubbing the stone. Letters appeared. At first it just looked like the charcoal was only picking up the natural markings on the slate but when Hannah came out of the door and placed the paper on the floor, it was clear.

THOMASINA PENVENTON
Born 15 January 1570
Died 16 January 1570

Hannah clutched Maddie's hand. Maddie gave it a squeeze and then went to the stone. Her fingers traced the rough carving. Hannah wondered if she was thinking of her own babies.

The bier carrying the coffin moved slowly through the village towards the church. Maddie couldn't stop the smile spreading across her face as she looked at the scene in front of her. The solemnity of the occasion should have been with her, but all she could see was the timelessness of the top-hatted master of ceremonies as he appeared, directing the old horse carrying the coffin.

The whole village had turned out for Tom. Mark and Hannah

were leading the procession behind the coffin. Maddie was still amazed that Tom had left the bulk of his estate to Hannah, with Mark as executor. It would provide nicely for Hannah's education and then some. She was a very lucky girl. Thankfully, she wouldn't come into control of the money until she was twenty-five. Maddie shuddered to think what would happen if she was let loose with her fortune now, but she guessed that Tom knew that.

'Don't start,' Maddie whispered to Tamsin, who had begun to giggle.

'Can't help it. It's like something out of a comedy film.' Tamsin put a hand to her mouth.

'I know but ...'

'Well, Old Tom had a great sense of humour and would've loved this pomp and circumstance. He would've seen the lighter side.'

'True.' Maddie smiled at Anthony, who had just caught up with them. He looked ill at ease in the dark suit.

'Sorry to be late. Crisis at the new site.' He walked in step beside them.

'Haven't missed anything yet.' Tamsin took his hand.

Maddie refused to let the twist of jealousy overtake her. Their love was so special. She looked to the man she loved, walking in front holding Hannah's hand. Despite every hour spent planning the funeral, they'd avoided speaking of personal issues.

Regretfully she acknowledged that she was far too experienced with funerals. John's had been simple in comparison, but then she'd sorted everything beforehand. This week had been crazy with all that had to be done.

Tom Martin had lived a fascinating life. Teaching was only part of it. The more they had pored through his house, his papers and finally his will, the more the complexities of the man had emerged. The strangers who walked behind were from his academic and publishing life.

Mark looked back and smiled. Her heart flipped. He'd been kind but distant as they each worked through the arrangements separately. Maddie knew she must try to explain if she could. She wanted to.

'Don't the daffodils look gorgeous in the sunlight? Strange that there are so many left this late,' commented Tamsin.

Maddie looked at the field filled with bright yellow. The breeze bowed their heads as the coffin passed by. Their bold colour stood out in contrast to the dark clothes of the mourners against the blue sky. Maddie knew that on a normal spring day this warm everyone would be shedding layers and exposing all the white flesh of winter to the sun. But today everyone was hidden in black. Hannah's small form looked almost tragic. It was the same dress she'd worn for John's funeral. Maddie hadn't thought she'd still have it. Today it was a bit shorter and sorrow didn't seep out of her in quite the same way as it had before. Hannah had changed beyond recognition in many ways. This week she had been almost sensible, even when she found out she no longer had to rely on Maddie for everything thanks to her sudden inheritance.

The vicar led the procession into the church and Maddie gazed appreciatively at all the flowers covering the altar. The women of the village had done a wonderful job, creating such a dramatic and joyful arrangement.

Maddie slid into the pew beside Hannah. Mark remained outside. He and Anthony were two of the four pallbearers. As she watched the coffin make its way to the front of the church, she studied him. Her love for him hadn't gone; it had grown. How could she have not trusted him? Sadness swept over her.

'All right, you two?' Mark whispered as he sat down beside her.

Maddie nodded but couldn't speak. She tried to focus on the vicar but gave up and looked at the colours playing across the top of the coffin as sunlight poured through the stained glass windows.

The words of the first hymn sprang from her lips by memory but Maddie couldn't tell what they were. The organ's last notes faded and the vicar welcomed them to celebrate Tom's life. Maddie tried to be attentive but her thoughts kept returning to the man at her side. He looked serious as he listened to the readings they'd chosen together. Her heart filled when he stood and walked to the altar to read. She didn't hear the words, only the sound of his voice.

Hannah's beautiful singing sounded out. Through the love of this man that they celebrated today, Hannah had begun growing into a thoughtful young woman. Maddie could hardly believe it.

Mark's rich baritone made it hard for her to think of anything but being in his arms. When would the longing for him disappear? She closed her eyes and forced herself to listen to the service as it finished.

The coffin, hoisted high, emerged into the brilliant sunshine. Maddie blinked. Hannah's hand sought hers and they picked their way through the disturbed rain-heavy ground to the graveside.

As she watched the casket being lowered into the earth, tears ran down Maddie's face. She couldn't stop them. Just over a year ago, she'd watched a similar scene with unbelieving eyes. Hannah's clasp tightened.

'It's Dad, isn't it?' Hannah whispered in her ear.

Maddie nodded and listened to the words of the vicar. It was all so final. She wondered if Tom had ever known love and loss. Maddie turned to Mark, who was watching her, his eyes filled with sadness. Why had she caused him such pain?

Hannah took the first fistful of earth. Maddie dragged her thoughts back to Tom. 'May you rest in peace.'

Maddie turned away and walked towards the road. A new headstone caught her eye. She paused and read it. It was Daphne's. Why had she never come to pay her respects before? Silently, she apologised to her great aunt. There were no flowers on the grave, unlike most. She would remedy that tomorrow. The grave next to Daphne's was much older. Maddie's heart stopped. It was Arthur's. Daphne was finally resting beside the one she loved. Maddie swallowed, brushing aside her tears.

*

'Thank you for a beautiful service,' Maddie said to the vicar as they stood outside the village hall.

'Tom was a good man,' he said. 'How's Hannah coping?'

'You can see for yourself that she's sad but OK.' Maddie smiled.

'And you? You've had a great deal to come to grips with lately.' He bowed his head a bit.

Maddie sighed. She wouldn't ask how he knew. 'I'm fine. However, I do have a question for you. Hannah was exploring the house in what appears to have been a secret room for smuggling and she seems to have found a gravestone for a new-born child.'

'Interesting. A gravestone, you say?'

Maddie nodded.

'Dates?' he asked.

'Fifteenth January 1570 appears with the name Thomasina. She died shortly after her birth and her mother Catherine did not survive her long.'

'Thomasina, meaning twin,' the vicar said.

'See, I told you, Maddie: Thomasina was Thomas' twin.' Hannah beamed.

'Aren't you supposed to say "excuse me" when you interrupt?' Maddie smiled.

'Oh, sorry, yes. Are you asking what we should do?' Hannah asked.

'I was about to get to that, but right now I should go and make sure everything is organised.' Maddie began to move away.

'Tamsin has it sorted,' said Hannah.

'Do you mind if I ask if this is where you thought you had a ghost?' the vicar asked.

Maddie blushed. 'Yes, in fact it is.'

'Do you still hear the crying?'

'No,' she said.

'That fits with what my colleague had experienced before.'

'What was that?' asked Hannah.

'Extreme emotion causing unexplained effects.'

'Are you talking about poltergeists?' asked Hannah.

He nodded.

'How cool. But don't they need to be exorcised or something?' Hannah wobbled a bit on her high heels.

'I don't understand,' Maddie said.

'In this other situation, the extreme grief and other emotions caused things to happen.'

'Things?'

'In this case, it was objects moving and strange cries coming from nowhere.'

'Cool. So Maddie's grief at losing my dad and …' Hannah stopped and looked at Maddie. 'And mine could have caused this? Or it could be the ghost of Thomasina, unhappy at being laid to rest in the foundations?'

'I wouldn't know for certain, but all things are possible.' The vicar smiled. 'As the crying has stopped, I think we can leave Thomasina in peace until after Easter and then we can investigate.' He bowed slightly and disappeared.

✦ Thirty-One ✦

The champagne tickled her nose and Hannah sneezed, almost spilling it. Will slid behind her. She hadn't seen him for days.

'So you're an heiress now?' He nuzzled her neck and Hannah turned to him.

'That's why you're here, then? You want me for my money?' She eyed him over the rim of her glass.

'Might be, but you were already irresistible.' He smiled.

Hannah gagged. 'Idiot.'

'Totally,' he agreed.

'How come you haven't called?' she asked.

'Thought you might need some space, and Maddie too, with all that has happened recently.'

'Oh.' Hannah tried to find Maddie in the crowd but couldn't. Looking at Will made her think about how Maddie and Mark were more like polite strangers at the moment.

'Have you missed me?' he asked.

'Maybe.'

'Just maybe?' He put on a hurt look.

'What do you think?' Hannah leaned against the window frame and smiled. The hall had filled up with so many people. She'd need to circulate and meet all these old friends of OT. Old was the key word.

Will leaned over and kissed her cheek. She loved the smell of soap that surrounded him and lingered with her when he pulled away.

'I hear that your mother has been in touch,' he said.

'God, nothing's a secret.' She rolled her eyes.

'Since when's that news?' he asked.

'True. Hope to be able to visit her soon.'

'Why after all these years?' Will studied her closely.

'She said sorry.' Hannah still hadn't figured it all out but she guessed some things didn't have answers. 'Yeah, I know. A bit late, really, but I am glad she did it.' She smiled.

'So you now have the money to fly away, oh rich friend of mine.' He winked.

Hannah laughed and thought about the money. Maddie didn't need to worry about her any more. Hannah took Will's hand to her mouth and kissed it.

'That was nice but why?' he asked.

'No reason. Right, I'd better be social.' She let his hand go.

'Well, if you must.' Will bowed and backed away.

Hannah faced the room with a smile. She was a free woman and she could control her own destiny now, thanks to OT. She raised her glass in silent toast and then she looked to the sea of wrinkled faces. Where did she start? There was a crusty bloke in the corner who looked approachable. Out of the corner of her eye she caught sight of Maddie and Mark leaving the hall. She wondered what was up and her glance followed them out to the playground.

'Thanks for stepping outside with me.' Maddie sat on one of the swings.

'No problem. How are you feeling? I know going to funerals must not be high on your list of things to do.' Mark sat in the other swing.

'No, it's definitely not, but that's not the reason I dragged you out.' Maddie looked up to the sky and hoped she could do this.

'No?' Mark raised an eyebrow. 'You've got my full attention.'

'Good. I like that.' She just wished she could keep it for ever and not just for these few minutes.

'Do you?' he asked.

Maddie was quiet for a moment. 'Yes.' She turned to look at him. 'I need to apologise, but I don't know where to begin.'

'OK.' His face gave nothing away and that made it harder; but then she didn't deserve to have it easy.

'First, to put the record straight, the baby I lost was yours, well, ours. There was no one else. Gunnar's a friend, nothing more, and it was never really any more than that.' Maddie looked at her hands in her lap as she pushed herself back and forth without taking her feet off the ground. The seat twisted around, just like her thoughts.

When he didn't say anything, she continued. 'I hadn't realised I was pregnant or I would have told Dr Grades about it when I was so sick. Not that I was wholly in my right mind at the time. You see, I hadn't thought it was possible.'

'Really?' Mark sounded surprised.

She looked at him and every single nerve on her body remembered that first time they made love. 'Yes. John and I had tried for a baby from the moment we married. Nothing happened. Because of that, I really didn't think that one unprotected night would bring me a much wanted child.'

'So you wanted my child?' He sounded so surprised that Maddie knew more than ever how much she had hurt him.

'Yes.' She nodded.

'Not just any child?' he asked.

Maddie winced. 'No, but to be honest, I would have accepted any child.'

'Then I don't understand, Maddie, if you wanted my baby, why you didn't tell me?'

Maddie licked her lips. She'd known this wouldn't be easy. She would have to lay herself bare and let him think what he would. 'Mark, I love you. I dreamt of us having a future together. Before everything happened, I'd hoped that you and I could ...' Maddie paused, desperate for the right words. 'Could get married when Hannah had had time to become used to the idea that I could love someone other than her father.'

She sighed. 'That's what I wanted with my whole heart and soul.' A breeze lifted a curl from her neat swept-up hairdo. She wished Mark would say something but he was totally silent. She couldn't bring herself to look at him, so she stared at her feet instead. 'Then I realised that I was late. I took a test and I knew I had been given a gift. I never thought I'd have another one.'

'*Another* child?' he asked.

'Yes.' Maddie bit her lip. This should be easier now. She'd spoken of it three times. 'I fell pregnant shortly before John died.'

'What happened?'

'I was thrilled, yet that was tempered with the fact that John wouldn't be around to share his child's life.' A burst of laughter escaped the hall as someone walked out to have a smoke.

'John made me promise to have the pregnancy terminated. He knew how hard this would be for me, but he also knew that Hannah's and my future wouldn't be easy either. He chose to focus on those he knew, not the child he didn't.' Maddie dragged a breath in. She'd forgiven John for what he asked of her and she'd forgiven herself. She wasn't going to cry, she told herself. She'd been doing far too much of that lately. The smell of crushed grass alerted her to the fact that Mark was no longer on the other swing but right next to her. His shoes were facing hers.

'So, when Dr Grades called me in and told me that because I'd been on the strong antibiotic I should terminate immediately, something inside me snapped.' Wringing her hands, she continued. 'I didn't want to put you in the situation where you'd want me to end the pregnancy.'

Maddie dug her heel into the ground. As much as she'd accepted Tamsin's wise words and that sometimes things were meant to happen, it still hurt. It hurt like hell. 'I guess I wasn't able to trust the man I loved not to ask me to have an abortion. Because John ... ' Maddie swallowed, willing herself to push on and say it all. 'I couldn't take the risk of you asking me to do that, even if it meant losing your love.'

Maddie finally looked up. He was inches from her. 'I'm so sorry I didn't trust you. I should have. You're not John.'

Mark was so close but still silent as he looked over her head to the church tower.

'Thank you,' he finally said.

'I owed you the truth. You deserve love. You're a wonderful man. I do hope that you can put this behind you and find a woman that's worthy of you.' Maddie knew she should be relieved. She'd told him everything now.

Rising from the swing, she moved sideways so that she didn't touch him. It would be too much. There was nothing else she could do but head back inside with a forced smile on her face and make sure that all was going as planned for Old Tom's send-off. She'd known that apologising to Mark wouldn't remove the pain but hopefully she'd cleared things up for him. This time, when a woman let him down, he at least knew why. With head held high, she set off.

'Where are you going?' he asked.

'Inside to check things,' she said, looking towards the hall.

'They're fine. Tamsin's there,' he said.

Maddie smiled. 'True.'

'What are your plans?' he asked.

'Plans?'

'Do you want more children?' Mark placed his hand on her arm, preventing her from moving away.

A tear trailed down her cheek. 'Oh, I think I may have blown my chances for that, but I hope with my whole heart that you do have children. You'll be the most wonderful father.'

'What if I told you that I don't want any unless you're their mother?'

Her head shot up and she looked at him. He was smiling.

'I'm afraid I'm not up for teasing at the moment,' she croaked.

'I've never been more serious in my life.' Mark lifted her head. 'I love you.' His eyes said more than his words. 'Marry me?'

'You're serious?' Maddie kept blinking, thinking he would disappear before her eyes.

'Yes.'

'After what I've put you through?' she asked.

'I can say with hand on heart that I've certainly been in hell.

To find out the most important person in my world nearly died because she didn't trust me, damn near killed me. But at the same time, I knew beyond all reason that life wouldn't be worth living without you.' His thumb brushed the tears from her cheeks. 'You haven't answered me.'

'Is this some ancient Celtic funeral ritual? Am I about to see the two of you go at it here in the playground to stick your finger up at death?' Hannah stood a few feet away.

'I suppose we could give it a try. Maybe the other mourners might join in the fun. What do you think, Hannah?' Mark asked.

'Sick.' Hannah stood with one hip jutting out and her arms crossed.

'Not really.' Maddie stood tall and straightened her suit. 'There's a lot to be said for ancient rituals.' She laughed at the disgust on Hannah's face. 'Was there something you needed?'

'No, I thought you might need something from me.'

'And what would that be?' Mark pulled Maddie closer to his side.

'Well, you see, the wind is blowing in the direction of the hall and I happened to hear a proposal and a lack of an answer.' Hannah grinned. 'I thought you might just need my permission first before you get married and have lots of brats?'

'Do we have it?' he asked.

'Yes, you do, so long as I don't have to babysit. No, wait a minute. Not sure this can go forward after all.' Hannah tapped her head with her palm.

'Why?' Maddie snuggled in closer to Mark and enjoyed the smile appearing on Hannah's face.

'Well, if you marry him, then he becomes my stepfather. That totally fucks up my relationship with Will.'

Mark burst out laughing. 'I suppose it does. However, you've given your permission and you can't change your mind. Now my heart is waiting for Maddie's answer.'

'Yeah, Maddie.' Hannah stood with hands on hips.

'On one condition,' Maddie said.

'You have some cheek,' Hannah pointed out.

'Yes, I do.' Maddie smiled.

'What's your condition, then?' Mark asked.

'That you come and live at Trevenen,' she said.

Mark smiled. 'I think I can manage that; but only when it has proper heating.'

'Excellent. That means he'll get it sorted extra quick.' Hannah laughed. 'So give the man your answer.'

'Yes.' Maddie was breathless.

'Right, I'm outta here. Off to celebrate your engagement with some of OT's lovely champagne. He'd so approve.' Hannah dashed back to the hall.

'You're crying.' Mark wrapped her in his arms.

'Am I?' She smiled.

'Yes. Why?' he asked.

'I've missed you and the feel of you so much it hurts to be in your arms again,' she said.

'How will it feel when I kiss you?' He lowered his head, stopping just above her mouth.

'Exquisitely painful but I'm sure with repeated application, other feelings may take over.'

He laughed. 'Shall we try?'

'Yes.' Her lips met his. Pain had nothing to do with what she felt.

The sound of a cork popping pulled them apart. Tamsin stood with a bottle and glasses in her hand.

'Tamsin,' Mark almost growled.

'I've no intention of being at the end of the queue waiting to congratulate you on your forthcoming marriage!'

Maddie looked to the hall and saw everyone standing outside with a glass in hand. She laughed and took a glass from her friend.

'Here's to the worst kept secret in town.' Maddie looked at Mark. 'I love you.'

Liz Fenwick on the origins of

The
Cornish
House

Have you ever seen a house and fallen in love? I have many times. Call me fickle and I can be when it comes to beautiful houses. But one house has held my heart above all others and I have never even set foot through the door. On one of my first visits to Cornwall in 1989, we ventured down a back road and went past a house, a house set in a fold in the land. It instantly stole my heart.

I wrote the first draft of *The Cornish House* in 2006. So I had obviously been thinking about this house for a fair bit of time. At any opportunity I would detour past it, for it is truly off the beaten track. I would wonder who lived there now. And more importantly who had lived there in the past because it was clear this house had been standing a very long time.

In 1996 we bought our own Cornish home and it came with a fascinating history and its own mysteries that can't be solved. The previous owners found a cannon ball while renovating the sitting room. You begin to wonder how a civil war cannon ball arrived in the foundation of the house. Battles were fought nearby but none were recorded in the village. The mind boggles with possibilities but no definite answers.

When I began thinking about the story that became *The Cornish House* there was only one place I could set it. Not in my own home, but the one I had lost my heart to first. It just had an aura about it.

From my mother-in-law I inherited a fabulous collection of books on Cornwall and most importantly the one that was vital to my research on this book. This was *The Cornishman's House* by V.M. and F.J. Chester. It describes how Cornish domestic architecture developed.

From the knowledge I gained in this book, I began building Trevenen from its earliest roots with the Penventon family. The two were completely intertwined. Like all manor houses of the time, it was a simple hall house. Originally it had one large room open to the ceiling. The next addition was the creation of a solar at the far end making a first floor. As the family grew in prosperity the first floor was extended and stairs were added on the outside of the building.

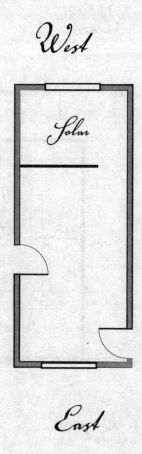

West

Solar

East

During the 1500s, the Penventon's influence had grown, as had their land ownership. To show the world their increasing wealth, they enhanced the house with a whole new wing. This tripled the size of Trevenen by adding a dining room and hall as well as bedrooms. This was the form that Trevenen was in when Catherine Penventon lived there.

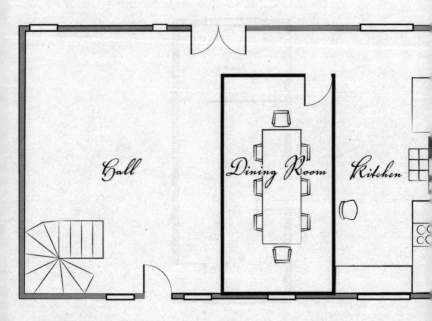

West

Hall *Dining Room* *Kitchen*

East

Catherine escaped to Trevenen when her husband died. She had inherited the manor from her paternal grandmother. Catherine was the eldest of four children. Her marriage had been a failure because she hadn't produced an heir. Her mother-in-law was a bitter and spiteful woman. She spread a rumour that Catherine was at fault for her husband's death. She said he had died of a broken heart because of Catherine's inability to bear an heir.

So Catherine came to live at Trevenen with her youngest sibling Mary. The community did not embrace them but shunned them. Even those that worked the land for them did not help more than they were required to. Catherine and Mary did all they could to become part of the community but to no avail. A fisherman who passed by the house regularly was the only one to become friendly. Eventually Catherine and the fisherman fell in love. Catherine thought she was barren, but found to her dismay and delight that she was not. Their relationship broke all the rules.

Mary, in fear and concern, contacted her younger brother, Philip, and his wife for help. They arrived and saw Catherine through her pregnancy. They managed to keep the pregnancy hidden.

The only one outside the family who knew was the fisherman. Catherine died giving birth to the twins, Thomas and Tomasina. The baby girl died a few days later and was buried outside the house where Mary could look upon the grave and pray for the soul of the child and that of her sister. The fisherman would come and visit the grave regularly until he died, but never spoke to his son because Philip took Thomas as his own son. Philip and his wife had lost their child through illness at the age of two.

As an adult, Thomas had the grave covered with a large slate bearing a simple inscription. Time passed and the family grew and prospered farming the land. In the 1780s the front of the house was remodeled to make it uniform and fit with the Georgian ideal, but the back remained unchanged.

Three hundred years after Catherine's death, the house was extended again, and they built over the grave as the inscription had faded to almost unreadable. It became part of the floor in the storage space surrounding the new fireplace. By then no one knew of the lost child or even remembered Catherine's connection to Thomas.

When Maddie inherits Trevenen, the house has been well loved, but funds have dried up

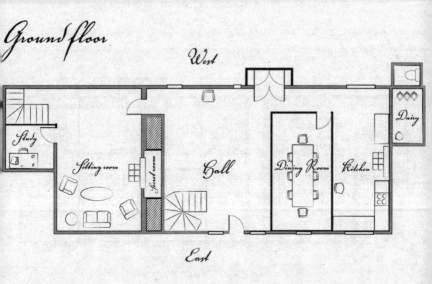

Ground floor

West

Study · Sitting room · Secret room · Hall · Dining Room · Kitchen · Dairy

East

and farmlands have been sold off over the years to pay for its upkeep. Nell, Maddie's great aunt, had inherited the house jointly with her brother Diggory. When he died he left his share to her. Nell lived in Trevenen on her own and farmed the land until the day she died.

During the writing of this book I drew inspiration from many houses. I spent happy hours on the Internet looking at floor plans of old manor houses. Like the story itself the house evolved taking on a unique shape and, if you will, almost a life of its own. The last two pictures were drawn by

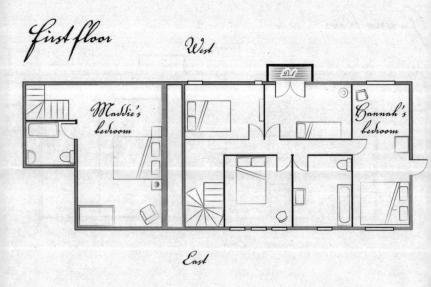

East

an artist from my own sketches of what I thought Trevenen would look like. Like all fiction it is drawn from imagination and in my case I would love to find Trevenen and live in it as I have pictured it. But everyone's Trevenen will be unique…

Drawings by obroberts

352